THE SUMMER OF CHRISTMAS

JULIET GIGLIO
& KEITH GIGLIO

sourcebooks
casablanca

Published by Sourcebooks Casablanca, an imprint of Sourcebooks
P.O. Box 4410, Naperville, Illinois 60567-4410
(630) 961-3900
sourcebooks.com

Library of Congress Cataloging-in-Publication Data

Names: Giglio, Juliet, author. | Giglio, Keith, author.
Title: The summer of Christmas / Juliet Giglio & Keith Giglio.
Description: Naperville, Illinois: Sourcebooks Casablanca, [2022]
Identifiers: LCCN 2022004366 (print) | LCCN 2022004367
(ebook) | (trade paperback) | (pdf) | (epub)
Subjects: LCGFT: Romance fiction. | Novels.
Classification: LCC PS3607.I357 S86 2022 (print) | LCC PS3607.I357
    (ebook) | DDC 813/.6--dc23/en/20220207
LC record available at https://lccn.loc.gov/2022004366
LC ebook record available at https://lccn.loc.gov/2022004367

Printed and bound in Canada.
MBP 10 9 8 7 6 5 4 3 2 1

For Riki, Randy, Ginny, Sabrina, Ava, and Eric.
In memory of Joe.

CHAPTER 1

IVY GREEN KNEW IT WASN'T real. She knew everything she was looking at was fake. The snow that floated down from the sky on a winter night. Fake. The aroma of hot chocolate that filled her senses. Fake. The perfect voices from the unseen Christmas carolers singing "God Rest Ye Merry Gentlemen" that was piped in from the trolley whose tracks began at the Nordstrom's, ran past the Apple Store, and reached its destination at the old Farmers' Market. Fake. There was nary a caroler in sight, but the music was grand.

Of course it was fake, it was Los Angeles. Christmas at the Grove. So perfect for Hollywood. They didn't call it the dream factory for nothing. It didn't bother Ivy in the least. She loved everything about the make-believe fantasy of the outdoor mall. It was Los Angeles and Hollywood at their best, playing with emotions. Making people believe their dreams could come true.

Yet Ivy's dreams were coming true. Ever since she was a little girl, she had loved the movies. Her third-grade teacher once called her parents in for a conference when Ivy brought a DVD of *Pulp Fiction* to school and played it for her classmates. Her dad taking her to see *Kill Bill: Volume 1* that year might not have been the best idea. Her mom countered Tarantino with the movies of Nora Ephron. Ivy remembered loving *When Harry Met Sally* the first time that she saw it. Although she had no idea why Meg Ryan was moaning in the Katz Deli scene until years later. With her movie-loving parents exposing her to the world of film, there was no other dream that Ivy was ever going to follow. She convinced her high school librarian to obtain a subscription to *Variety*, the Hollywood "newspaper." She fantasized about moving to Hollywood and breaking into the business. Not as an actor. Not as a director. But as a writer. Now, approaching her final semester at USC Film School, armed with a well-received (by her faculty advisors) screenplay, she was starting to feel like she had a chance.

Ivy's other dream, also since she was a little girl, was to marry Nick Shepherd. Nick and Ivy met when they were eight years old and had been together, in one way or another, ever since. Now, at the age of twenty-two, Ivy was confident that her dreams were becoming a reality. She had no idea how real things were going to get.

"Look at the snow, Nick," Ivy enthused as she squeezed his arm.

Nick looked up at the snow being propelled from machines on the top of the movie marquee. He was mildly amused and unimpressed. "It's fifty-five degrees and people are wearing Canada Goose coats." Nick was in his leather jacket and blue jeans. He was visiting Ivy for the holidays from their hometown. He was six-one, naturally fit from working year-round at his parents' vineyard.

They had been together for a long time, growing up together in Geneva, New York, meeting when they played Mary and

Joseph for a church nativity pageant. Geneva was a small town on the shores of Seneca Lake, in Upstate New York in the heart of the Finger Lakes. Ivy and Nick had gone to elementary school together (where their mutual crush started), middle school (where they were always passing notes to each other in class), and high school (where they had their first kiss) and won "best couple" in the yearbook. They were always together until college.

When Ivy went west to California, Nick stayed local: learning to be a vintner at Cornell University in the neighboring town of Ithaca. He loved making wine and working at the family winery. And he loved Ivy. They had been together forever and always. During college, they perfected the long-distance relationship. They were both so focused on their craft and doing well at school that they had never even considered dating other people. They saw each other in the summer. The first summer, at least. After that, Ivy started getting summer internships at Hollywood production companies and Nick went off to Napa to study at a vineyard. Their schedules didn't line up, and they didn't see each other. But they always had Christmas. Every year from December fifteenth to January fifteenth, they were inseparable in their hometown.

Nick was visiting Los Angeles for the first time. Ivy had planned a great tourist-filled week that included Disneyland, a hike up to the Hollywood sign, a ride on the roller coaster at the Santa Monica Pier, and sunset at the Malibu Winery. Ivy also wanted to take Nick down to Olvera Street, the birthplace of LA, for an authentic Mexican Christmas. She had a goal: to have Nick fall in love with LA and join her on the West Coast. Her plan all started at the Grove. They both loved Christmas, and there was nothing more Christmassy in LA than the giant decorated tree at the outdoor shopping mall.

"Nick, have you ever seen a Christmas tree this big? It's taller than the one at Rockefeller Center."

"Is it real?" he asked.

"Does it matter? It brings joy. Like Santa..." Ivy alluded to the decorative giant Santa overhead in his sleigh being pulled by his reindeer over the tree.

"You like all this?" Nick wondered.

"I love it."

Ivy took his hand and led him closer to the crowded fountain. The water "danced" to every Christmas song that played on the speakers. Green-and-red lights bounced off the dancing fountain, which gave it all a magical, seasonal effect. Ivy had fallen in love with the movie business and Los Angeles during the last four years at USC Film School. She loved everything about the city of dreams and was hoping Nick would too. Especially with the big news she had to tell him. And ask him. She looked up at the Christmas star high on the tree, closed her eyes, and made a silent wish that his answer would be yes.

"Nick, I have to ask you..."

"I'm not Nick," the oversized dad said, trying to get closer to the fountains with his family. "Can you take our picture?" Ivy was glad to help out.

Ivy took their phone. The family posed. Smiled. Ivy stopped and said, "The framing is a little off. How about Mom on that side? Two kids in front." She checked the shot. "Still not working for me. Waiting for the fountain...and the lights to change. Don't move. One, two, three. Got it!"

The family looked at the shot. It was perfect. "That's an amazing picture. Thank you," the mom said.

"Are you, like, a film director or something?" the dad asked.

"A screenwriter," Ivy told them.

"Anything we've seen?" the daughter wondered.

"Not yet, but soon, I hope." Ivy smiled. It was time to tell Nick her good news and her plans. Their plans. Ivy always thought of her life as a movie. So, what would happen next—to use a screenwriting term—was a real turning point in her life. Also known as a *whammo!*

Ivy said goodbye to the nice family and turned to where Nick last stood. But Nick wasn't there. He was gone. The Grove wasn't just crowded, it was packed. It was a private-public outdoor mall filled with decorated Christmas stores, a Santa booth, and oversized hanging ornaments. It ran about three blocks, built on a place that used to be Gilmore Park, which was once a theme park for the preschool crowd. But where was Nick? He was always one to run off and explore. She saw him outside of the Apple Store, on his phone. "There you are," Ivy said. Nick quickly put away the phone.

"Sorry," he said, "I needed some Wi-Fi. I just checked the weather. It's sixty degrees here, but it's twelve degrees back home."

"It still feels cold to me. I think your blood thins when you live out here."

Nick took his leather jacket and wrapped it around her. Ivy noticed his tight-fitting Shepherd Winery T-shirt. His family winery. The one Nick's parents had started. The logo was a shepherd tending a flock of wine.

"That's a new logo," Ivy said.

"Do you like it?" he asked.

"It's great. I miss hanging out there."

"I miss you hanging out there too."

"We belong together, Nick."

"Always," he said.

"I can't believe I finally got you to come visit me."

Then at the same time, they both announced: "I have something to tell you…" They stopped, laughed, and said "Jinx," having said something at the same time. Something they had done since they were kids.

"You first," Nick insisted. Ivy started talking a mile a minute. She let Nick know her great news. The script she wrote for her senior thesis won a screenwriting award. Former winners of that award had gone on to have long careers working in the film business. Ivy spoke rapidly about what this might lead to. She never would have been talking about herself so much, but this was Nick. Her Nick. Her *always Nick*. She could tell him anything.

Ivy's phone was suddenly buzzing. She looked at the caller ID and was immediately excited. "Oh my God, it's Charlotte Adams. I have to take this."

"Who's Charlotte Adams?" Nick asked.

Charlotte Adams was the hottest agent in town. She had a knack for discovering new writers and harnessing their skills to boffo success. Charlotte was Hollywood royalty, having grown up in the business. Her father was an Academy-nominated producer, and if Charlotte had a new script to sell, every studio would stop to read it and want to meet the hot new writer. Ivy answered her phone and listened excitedly.

"You do!" Ivy exclaimed. "Yes. Yes. I can meet you tomorrow. Thank you!" She gave Nick a thumbs-up. He listened as Ivy joyfully nodded and yes-yes-yes'ed to everything this Charlotte Adams was saying.

Nick waited patiently, always a good guy. Ivy finished the call. "That was Charlotte Adams. The biggest agent in town. She used to be married to my film school professor. He recommended she read my script. She loved it and wants me to get my career going as soon as possible," she blurted out. "I'm meeting her tomorrow morning." Ivy quickly posted an Instagram with a selfie of her at the Grove: *Just signed with a great agent! #goals #screenwriting #charlotteadams*

"That's great," Nick said quietly. He was very happy for Ivy. He really was. But still, he didn't seem that happy. He suddenly seemed different. For a moment Ivy thought, *Why is he acting this way? Is he jealous?* He seemed fine five minutes ago. She decided to keep it to herself and not ruin their first night together in LA.

"So, what does this all mean? The script? The agent?" Nick wondered.

"It means I have to find a place to live after graduation."

"So you're going to stay in LA?"

"I thought maybe we could find a place to live. Together. I have some apartments we could look at tomorrow," Ivy added. There—it was out—she wanted Nick to move to LA so they could be together.

Nick smiled. Keeping his feelings inside.

"Why are you acting this way?" *So much for keeping it to yourself,* she thought.

"What way?" he said defensively.

"That you're not excited for me."

"I am excited for you. I'm just tired. I landed two hours ago..." And in truth, he had just arrived. Nick was exhausted. But Ivy had insisted on going out and experiencing "fake Christmas."

Ivy had noticed something earlier at the airport. When she'd arrived to pick Nick up, he wasn't even looking for her. He was on his phone. They had not seen each other in months, and yet Nick didn't seem that excited to see her. In fact, he'd seemed subdued.

Ivy dismissed her negative thoughts. She realized Nick might've been tired because he had taken two flights, and one had been delayed. She also knew that last week Nick had worked nonstop at the wine tour in the Finger Lakes where the wineries gave out Christmas ornaments. Shepherd Winery would always draw over five hundred people each day for that popular yearly event. It was no wonder that Nick seemed a little off, she rationalized.

"I really am happy for you," he said. "I'm proud of you. I love you."

Ivy kissed Nick for the last time, but she didn't know that. "I love you too," she told him.

Her phone started vibrating. It was from classmates all calling to congratulate her, and Ivy was eager to fill them in. She held up one finger to Nick, indicating to give her a moment. He wandered off again.

Ivy found Nick on a bench, looking up at the stars, which were not to be seen.

"Let's go get a picture with Santa," she suggested. "The last time we did that was senior year of high school."

The line for Santa was long but moved quickly. As they waited in line, Ivy was getting more and more calls and more and more texts. She could see Nick was getting a little frustrated. She put her phone away.

"You don't have to do that," he said.

They waited in line. Both quiet. Ivy decided it was time: "I found this Spanish-style townhouse apartment on Orange Grove," she said as she scrolled through the pictures on her phone and showed Nick a picture. He didn't respond. They were now being brought in to see Santa.

"What does a USC Film student want for Christmas?" Santa bellowed and laughed. Ivy was curious. Who was this?

Nick was stunned. "You know Santa?"

Ivy went to sit on Santa's lap. She instantly recognized him as Rob, a struggling actor who she knew from a student film. Ivy waved Nick over. They sat on Santa's lap, and she introduced Nick to Santa Claus.

"What does Ivy Green want for Christmas?" Santa asked.

"I want Nick to move to LA so we can be together." Ivy smiled, looking at Nick. Santa turned to Nick, asking him the same question. As the woman playing Santa's elf aligned the camera, Nick said the words Ivy never thought she would ever hear from him—and especially not while they were sitting on Santa's lap.

"I want to break up," Nick blurted out.

The photo was taken at exactly that moment. Sadness, shock, and bewilderment showed on the faces of Ivy, Nick, and Santa.

Ivy hustled away. Nick followed her. The Grove was emptying. Dinner patrons were leaving. Movies had let out. Tired children were being carried home by their parents, who were also carrying packages.

Nick found Ivy sitting by the fountain. He sat down next to her. Neither of them said anything as "I'll Be Home for Christmas," the Muzak version, played.

"I'm sorry," he said, not for saying it but for having to say it.

Ivy was more confused than angry. She just didn't understand.

"I met someone else."

"Who?"

"It doesn't matter."

"I bet it was Courtney Clark," Ivy said. Courtney Clark was a girl who had a crush on Nick in sixth grade and had spread bad rumors about Ivy.

"Courtney Clark? That was sixth grade!" Nick protested.

"You kissed her!" Ivy countered.

"Why are you talking about what happened in sixth grade?"

"Why are you breaking up with me on the happiest day of my life?" she snapped. At least, she'd thought it was going to be the happiest day of her life as she'd won an award and she was now going to be represented by one of the best agents in town. But Nick, the literal love of her life, the only man she had ever been with, the one person who understood her more than anyone else, the man who knew Christmas was extra special for her—Nick Shepherd had broken her heart.

Ivy demanded to know more as she went from confusion to anger as Nick told her about a graduate student from Cornell who was interning at the winery. They had spent a lot of time in the vineyard, and they just clicked.

"So that's why you've been on your phone all day." And he had been. Nick explained that he'd wanted to be a man and tell Ivy in person.

"If you were a man, you wouldn't have cheated on me."

Nick's phone rang. It buzzed between them. "I have to take this," he said.

"Go away. Get out of here," Ivy said. She was determined that Nick was never going to see her cry. Because when she did, the fountains at the Grove would be the second-most spectacular water feature for tourists.

"I only want the best for you, Ivy."

"The best for me is for you to leave. Take the rental car and go back to your Cornell cutie." Ivy turned around to watch the dancing water fountain. She could hear Nick answer the phone and say, "I can't talk right now." Ivy watched as Nick walked away. Out of her life forever.

She was not sure how long she stayed there, staring at the fountains. The lighting went from green to red. The song "Have Yourself a Merry Little Christmas" started to play, and the fake snow fell as it did every hour on the hour.

One hour. That was all it took for Ivy to go from the best day of her life to the worst day of her life. She had given her heart to Nick in second grade. And now he'd returned it. The fountains of tears began to flow. Spectacularly. She was a really great crier. The few remaining natives and tourists looked over at her. Ivy hugged Nick's jacket as she sobbed to the song.

Everyone around her was happy. Everyone except her. She couldn't believe that everything she'd planned to do with Nick would never happen. Her phone rang again. She answered it, unable to hide the sniffles and sadness.

"Hi, Mom... I have some great news. I won the contest for best screenplay. An agent loved my script, and she wants to represent me."

Ivy looked out at the empty street. "Why am I crying... because I'm so happy," she lied to her mom. Ivy wasn't going to spoil her mother's Christmas the way Nick had ruined hers. And at that moment she decided that she would give herself forty-eight hours to get over Nick. That was two bottles of chardonnay, four sappy movies, and a box of See's Candies. Then she would sweat it out at Body By Simone and get back to work. She told her mother she loved her. Called an Uber to get home and stuffed Nick's leather jacket into a trash can. Ivy walked the wrong way, turned, didn't look where she was going, and walked right into the moving trolley.

On the ground, suffering more from embarrassment, Ivy thought how this Christmas was already the best/worst Christmas ever.

CHAPTER 2

IVY NO LONGER BELIEVED IN happy endings. She was devastated. She poured her hurt feelings into a new script about her and Nick. She called it *When Joseph Met Mary*. It was all about their romance. But when she got to the third act, she wasn't sure how to end it. She knew she needed to kill Nick in the script. She spent a few weeks thinking of the best way to terminate him. In the end, his demise came about in a snowmobile accident. The ice of Cayuga Lake cracked, and Nick and his snowmobile sank to their death. She was pleased with the script. And so was her agent. Charlotte loved that Ivy had the guts to turn a happy romantic comedy into a romantic drama. Ivy realized she had Nick to thank for that. Too bad he was dead under the lake.

Tarantino had beat out Ephron.

The script went out for sale to the studios. Ivy waited for her phone to ring, for her email to ding with good news. But there was none. All the studios passed. Some of the coverage comments were *it's too indie* and *too cast dependent*. All that meant was that it didn't fit the high concept, four-quadrant, preexisting proof of concept tentpole mandate that dominated Hollywood at that time.

But film executives liked the writing. The script became a calling card. It showed that Ivy had a great voice. Charlotte sent her out to meetings.

Ivy set off on the "bottled water tour". Going from studio to studio, meeting to meeting, hearing how much people loved her script and her writing. Most of the time, all she got out of it was a bottle of water. The bottle water tour ended quickly. Ivy was dying from encouragement. Her agent wanted her to write another script. She did. That script didn't sell either. She went out on another bottled water tour. She started to keep the bottles and redeem them at the local Vons supermarket. Money was tight, and every deposit helped. Ivy had been invited to the ball, but no one wanted to dance with her.

Her friends would try to fix her up. But Ivy didn't date. Not since "the Departure." That's how she referred to the breakup with Nick. She masked her calls with her parents. She didn't want them worrying about her. She made excuses to stay away from Geneva, even though it was her hometown.

"I'm not going to come home for Christmas because a classmate needs me to A.D. her low-budget film. She lost her first location, and the new church location is only available on December twenty-sixth," Ivy fibbed to her parents.

"Oh, dear. That's too bad. But what does 'A.D.' mean?" her mom asked, completely buying Ivy's excuse.

"It means *assistant director*. It also means I don't have time to fly home to Geneva for Christmas."

Even now, Ivy winced a bit when she remembered that conversation. She didn't feel good about being dishonest to her parents but rationalized it as only a small white lie as, after all, it was partly true. In all honesty, Ivy didn't want to go home to Geneva and risk running into Nick. She had spent every Christmas with him since they were eight years old. Christmas and Nick were interchangeable, and she teared up as she realized that life was never going to be the same. Her parents were oblivious to Ivy's pain and didn't seem upset that she wasn't coming home because they had a solution.

"Why don't we fly out to LA and spend Christmas with you out there?" her mom suggested.

"You don't have to twist my arm. I'd love an excuse to leave this subzero tundra," her dad added.

And so it was that Ivy's parents and her younger sister flew out to LA for Christmas that year.

Linda, Ivy's mom, adored the old-style restaurants on Olvera Street, where they participated in a Mexican dinner party complete with mariachis, a puppet show, and an upbeat line dance around the festive locale. Her sister, Carol, loved jogging in shorts on the beach in December where her legs lost their pasty white sheen and took on a bronze tan. And Mitch, her dad, was a big kid at heart as he fully embraced the Christmas-decorated Disneyland and didn't seem to mind waiting three hours to get onto the new *Star Wars* ride. Ivy's family had such a great Christmas in LA during that first year that they ended up making it a tradition. For the next five years, they flew to California for Christmas. In truth, Ivy was surprised by how quickly her family acclimated to the lighted palm trees in Los Angeles because growing up, they'd always favored a white Christmas.

Ivy would never admit it, but she was nostalgic for the white Christmases of her childhood. She missed sledding down her backyard hill, driving through the neighborhood where all the Christmas lights reflected off the glimmering snow, and gazing at the pine trees when they were covered with white. In LA she tried flocking her Christmas tree with white to make it look like snow, but it never took on the magical effect of real snow.

Then five years AD (After the Departure), right after Christmas, she received a text from Cleo, a film school friend. Cleo was going to intern at the esteemed Sundance Film Festival in Park City, Utah. She wanted to know if Ivy also wanted to intern. They could room together. Meet celebs. And see movies. For Ivy, getting to the Sundance festival was another one of her dreams. But in her dreams, she went as a screenwriter whose movie was premiering. She never thought she would go as a volunteer intern.

An intern at Sundance would have to stand in the freezing cold or in a crowded waiting room, organizing the lines and the guests. Ivy was directing the crowd—red tickets here, ticket holders in the tent, waitlists over there—when she ran into Andy, another friend from film school. Andy was an assistant at Brilliant Pictures, a new indie company. They caught up, and Andy invited Ivy to his company's party on Main Street at 350 Spur.

Ivy arrived at the crowded party around midnight. The rustic bar was packed with festival attendees. She envied those who wore badges that said FILMMAKER. Hers said VOLUNTEER. She hoped her scarf would hide it.

Ivy found Andy. They reminisced and had a few cocktails and fancy finger food.

She started to get the sense that Andy liked her. She realized that when, filled with liquid courage, he blurted out: "I really like you." Before Ivy had to address the awkwardness, *he* appeared. Parting the crowd—or did the crowd part for him? He was coming toward Andy, but he was definitely smiling at Ivy.

"Who is that?" she gasped.

"That's my boss," Andy revealed.

"Hi, I'm Drew Fox," said the very tan and handsome producer. His bleach-blond hair was tousled, and Ivy resisted the temptation to smooth it down. He was dressed in that hip, effortless way that showed he understood fashion. He dressed high-low. An expensive black cashmere sweater with Levi's jeans. She couldn't help herself and glanced at his left hand for any sign of a wedding band. She noticed he wore no ring.

"I'm Ivy Green," she said and smiled.

"She's with me," Andy blurted.

Drew grinned as Ivy quickly explained, "Andy and I are old friends. We went to film school together."

"Andy works for me. And if he goes back to the condo and sleeps it off, he might still work for me tomorrow," Drew said. He wasn't mean. Andy nodded and told Ivy and Drew good night.

"I didn't want him to embarrass himself," Drew said with the most dazzling perfect white smile she'd ever seen. She wondered if his mom or dad was a dentist or an orthodontist or maybe they worked at a drug store where they got great discounts on Whitestrips and gave them to Drew for every Christmas and birthday. Maybe that was why he called his company Brilliant Pictures. But Ivy realized that she needed to stop daydreaming and join in the conversation.

"I like the name of your company," Ivy told him.

"Oh, Brilliant Pictures. My friends think that calling it brilliant makes me sound arrogant." Drew laughed.

"No, it just sounds like you have high expectations for your projects."

"And who is the real Ivy Green? Tell me about yourself."

Ivy wondered what version of herself she should tell him and decided to use her tried and true story that she always told when she took a general meeting. "I'm from a little town in Upstate New York where it snows one hundred inches a year. When I got into USC, I bought a one-way ticket and just never went back. What about you?"

"My story isn't as interesting. I grew up in Malibu."

"So, you're a surfer."

"Why does everyone assume that?" Drew laughed.

"You just look like you belong on a surfboard. Be honest, where do you go surfing?" Ivy said and realized she was flirting with him.

"If I did surf, it would be the Wedge in Newport."

"Oh, not Zuma?" Ivy said playfully. Zuma Beach was the quintessential Malibu beach and the first beach that Ivy visited when she first arrived at USC. Ivy grew up watching old *Gidget* surf movies with her mom. *Point Break* with her dad. Ivy loved the water—especially Seneca Lake, where she'd grown up. Ivy's brain went fuzzy, and she remembered how Nick had wanted to buy a boat. Ivy quickly snapped out of it as Drew asked her if she'd seen anything good so far at the festival.

"No, but I saw something horrible," Ivy said.

"What was that?"

"The movie about the dead cowboy. I mean, I get the metaphor about the dying old white man, but to have a dead cowboy as the protagonist? Sorry, I like to be entertained."

"That was my movie. I produced that," he divulged. Ivy smiled. *Well, it was nice meeting you,* she thought. "How would you have changed it?" Drew wondered.

"I would have *Sixth Sense*-ed it. We shouldn't know the

cowboy is dead until the end. And I would have had some gender balance. I think you had ten cowboys and the woman who did all their cooking."

"I wish I'd met you when we were developing it." Drew looked at her. Then a smile of recognition washed over him. Pleased with himself. "Wait, you're Ivy Green, the screenwriter. Charlotte Adams told me about you. You wrote that biblical screenplay that got some buzz. *When Joseph Met Mary*," Drew said.

I really have to change that title, Ivy thought. "No," she insisted.

"You didn't write it?"

"I did. But it's not a religious movie. It's like *Boyhood* or *The Notebook*. It's about a romance between two kids that begins when they are playing Joseph and Mary in a Christmas pageant. We follow their love story."

"Like *Two for the Road*," Drew added.

"Audrey Hepburn was great in that movie," Ivy agreed.

"Audrey Hepburn was great in everything."

They smiled at each other. Each sensing something was happening between them, but they didn't know what.

"Have you read it? My script?" she asked.

"No," he admitted. "The title threw me off. But it's in my Dropbox."

Ivy looked at him, wondering if he would ever read her script. She doubted it. "Well, it was nice to meet you." Ivy smiled, reaching out to shake his hand.

"Yeah, I've got to make the rounds." Drew nodded.

They shook hands, and that was it. Too bad because Ivy was hoping to spend more time with him. But she realized it just wasn't meant to be. They exchanged emails. The next two days she looked for him on the streets in Park City and on the shuttle. But she never saw him again. Ivy returned home from Sundance and found her roommate had left her. The roommate had moved out, cleaned out the fridge, and abandoned Ivy with two months of back rent that was still owed. There was no way Ivy could pay the double rent, and she wasn't going to ask her parents for money.

So Ivy moved to a studio apartment, got a second job at Trader Joe's, and started doubting herself. She had loved hanging out in Park City. It was cold. There was snow. And she always felt she looked great in sweaters. Maybe the dream wasn't going to come true for her in LA. Maybe it was time to head back home to Geneva. For the first time in years, she wondered how Nick's life had turned out. She opened her computer and searched for him. But Nick was a ghost. He had never been one to be on any social media. She was feeling truly down in the dumps, when her phone miraculously rang. It was Drew. The producer from Brilliant Pictures. He had finally read the script. He hated the title, but he liked the story. A lot.

"Is this *Joseph Met Mary* romance autobiographical?" he asked.

Ivy hesitated. And for the first time, she wasn't honest with Drew. "No. It's not. It's an amalgam of lots of things I witnessed as I grew up. But that's okay, right?"

"Of course. You're a writer. You're supposed to make stuff up," Drew said, and then he revealed that he'd sent it to his financial partners. If that was okay. Ivy told him it was. She thanked him. They said goodbye. Her phone rang again a few minutes later. It was Drew again.

"I never do this. And I don't want you to think this is creepy, but would you want to go to a premiere with me tonight? I have an extra ticket."

Ivy said sure. Unclear if it was business or a date. She had to figure out what to wear to a premiere. There wasn't time to go out and buy something new, and there wasn't any extra money in her bank account anyway. Ivy decided to wear her go-to meeting outfit: black jeans, a nice blouse, and her black ankle-length lace-up boots. She sucked in her stomach, wishing she hadn't eaten an entire bag of popcorn last night. The salt was definitely adding five pounds, or at least it felt that way. Her hair looked thrashed and she wished there had been time to get a blowout, but she reminded herself that she had no money in her budget for hair that month. She told herself that writers didn't need to look good, but she only half believed that. She had no idea she was about to be hit with another *whammo*, a huge turning point in her life.

Drew picked her up in his Audi convertible with the top down. They talked shop. Ivy relaxed as she realized it wasn't a date after all. They drove to Hollywood, and they pulled up to the valet. The premiere was at the famous TCL Chinese Theatre. Lights were shining. The press were everywhere. Photographers snapped photos of everyone who walked the red carpet. Drew touched her back to guide her, and Ivy was suddenly awestruck. He led her around the crowd (the crowds always seemed to part for Drew), and Ivy realized she was about to walk the red carpet. The cameras flashed. Ivy was caught up in the moment. The crowd screamed. Ivy, always the fangirl, turned to see who it was and did not look where she was going. She tripped over her own two feet and fell on the red carpet. The photographers did not miss it. That photo was still on the internet. Ivy looked up and, backlit by the spotlights in front of the Chinese Theatre, Drew smiled warmly, extended his hand, and helped her up.

They sat in their seats. Drew waved to some friends. The friends were wondering who Ivy was. "A great new writer," he announced to everyone. Ivy was liking this Drew guy. A lot. But then he said, "I'll be right back. Do you want popcorn?"

"Always." Ivy smiled.

The movie started. People cheered at their own names in the credits. Drew had not come back. About ten minutes into the movie, Ivy knew she hated it. She was resentful. How did something like this get made? She suffered alone through the two hours and twenty minutes. Drew never came back. And she never got her popcorn. The movie ended, and Ivy followed the crowd to the after-party. Her name was on the list. She found Drew at the bar, talking to some friends. Some very pretty blond-haired, long-legged friends. Actresses! Drew grinned and waved her over. Ivy waved goodbye and walked out of the party. He chased after her, catching up with her in front of the theater on the now-quiet street. She was looking at Lucille Ball's handprints.

"Ivy, where are you going?"

"Home," she sighed.

"I'll drive you."

"To Upstate New York? I'm done with this. I'm done watching bad scripts get made. I'm done being stood up, even if this isn't a date! I am done with you. And I am done with this town! It's given me nothing but a broken heart." Ivy walked away.

She had taken two steps when she heard Drew say: "That's too bad because I just sold your script, *When Joseph Met Mary*."

Ivy stopped and looked at Drew, her face a question mark.

"That's what I've been doing for the last two hours. I've been on the phone. My finance people loved your script. It matches our brand. It's set up. I already called your agent."

Ivy found herself flying into Drew's arms. Crying. Happy. Drew was laughing and teasing her. Then somehow at that moment—their lips found each other as she stood on top of Lucille Ball's footprints.

Ivy didn't remember much after that. They went back to the party and celebrated. She woke up the next morning in Drew's Downtown Los Angeles loft. He was already hard at work on his laptop. The first thing he said was, "What do you think about Amari Rivers for the lead?"

CHAPTER 3

AN ANXIOUS IVY WALKED INTO the Ivy, a hip restaurant in the heart of Los Angeles, to meet the actress who might be playing her alter ego in *When Joseph Met Mary*. Ivy had never been to the Ivy but knew it was a place where stars liked to hang out and get noticed.

She had spent that morning searching Google for stories and images about Amari. She wanted to dig deeper than the celebrity magazines that littered the newsstands. She had seen Amari's face many times on television, Instagram, and the covers of *People* and *Us Weekly* magazines. Amari had become very popular on a reality television show. She was a walking, talking exclamation point. She'd won all of America's hearts, which led to a one-song "fail" at a singing career. Next, Amari tried movies. Sexy, outspoken, and street-smart, she was not afraid to go after what she wanted and show vulnerability when she didn't get it. From the reality show, she was cast as one of the bridesmaids in a wedding comedy called *Beer Boy*. She stole the movie in a now-famous scene where she crashed the bachelor party. The buzz around town was *Amari was rising.* She had many movie offers, but Amari was drawn to Ivy's script.

Ivy had stared at Amari's flawless complexion on her computer screen. She had noticed that Amari Rivers was truly stunning, and she had immediately felt intimidated. Ivy had added another coat of mascara and looked at her face in the mirror and sighed. She had realized she could never be as pretty as Amari and she had suddenly felt unnerved and had wondered why she needed to meet the beautiful actress at the Ivy restaurant. But Drew had insisted that she go because Amari really wanted to get to know her, and they needed Amari to formally agree to be in the movie.

That was two hours ago, and now there was no turning back. As she looked around the restaurant, she realized that she recognized lots of people seated around the tables. But these weren't friends of hers. They were studio executives she'd met on her many bottled water tours. There were also movie and television stars that she'd watched over the years. Someone was waving at her, someone who actually seemed to know her. Ivy instantly realized that it was Amari Rivers and that she was even more gorgeous in person. Amari got up and hugged her, which felt awkward to Ivy, but she did her best to hug Amari back.

"I should have warned you that I'm a hugger." Amari laughed.

"Hi, I'm Ivy. It's so nice to meet you."

"You too. I had to meet the girl who wrote *When Joseph Met Mary*. It's such an incredibly sweet story. My agent wants me to do this thriller. But I told him I like your script better. It speaks to me. Plus, this will be a movie my nana can watch. I had too much T&A in the *Beer Boy* movie. It's frightening to think how many men and women fantasize about me."

Ivy wasn't sure how to respond. Was Amari Rivers saying

that she wanted to do her movie? *Her movie?* "You were so good in *Beer Boy.*"

"Thanks. I am very career conscious. Reese was *Legally Blonde,* Jennifer fought for her life in *Hunger Games,* and Emma was *Easy A*—all smart career moves. People know me from the reality show, they liked me naked in suds of beer, but now I need to show that I can act. And not just with my boobs. You have written a great script and a great character. That is why we are having this lunch. I want to know a little more about you before I say yes."

"Of course, whatever you need to know," Ivy managed to say. But inside she was freaking out, and a raucous party in her head interrupted her rational thoughts. Amari was seriously considering signing on. Ivy wanted to run to the bathroom and call Drew with the good news. Then she thought, *I should wait until there is good news.*

"So, have you really known the Rick character since second grade?" Amari asked.

"Yup. We met in elementary school. His real name is Nick," Ivy confirmed. And like everyone else from Geneva and the Finger Lakes, she pronounced the word *elementary* with five syllables and put the emphasis on *men* so that it sounded like "el-uh-men-ter-ry" as opposed to the more common pronunciation with four syllables: "el-uh-men-tree."

"El-uh-men-ter-ry," Amari said, trying to say it with Ivy's pronunciation. Ivy wasn't sure why Amari was repeating what she'd just said. "Oh, sorry, I was just trying to get into character. Which is why I really wanted to meet you. To see and sound like you. I mean like Ilsa. My agent said this script was autobiographical, which I absolutely love." Ivy was about to tell Amari what she'd told Drew, which was that *When Joseph Met Mary* wasn't autobiographical, but then Amari continued: "Honesty and integrity are so important in movies. I think that's what really attracted me to your story." Ivy realized that for the first time in a while she was going to have to be honest. "So, what happened to Nick?" Amari inquired.

"We broke up."

"But then he died in a terrible snowmobile accident," Amari said.

"Well, he didn't actually die in real life," Ivy admitted.

"Oh, what's happened to him?"

"I kind of fell out of touch with him," Ivy said, which was true. But it hadn't stopped her from regularly stalking him on social media. Actually, Nick had no social media accounts of his own, so she searched his sister's socials for snippets of his face or mentions of his whereabouts. She didn't learn much about Nick during those recon moments, but she saw that he was still as handsome as ever. She also knew that he still had the same cell phone number because one drunken night she called him but when she heard his voice, she quickly hung up. "He's still living in Geneva. Running his family's winery," Ivy told Amari. This was something that she only knew from Nick's sister's Facebook post.

"Did you really meet at the church pageant?"

"Yup. I didn't want to go, but my mom was busy at her Christmas boutique and needed a place for my sister and me to hang out for a few hours. So, we went to the pageant rehearsal, and I was cast as Mary," Ivy said.

"Wow. I bet every girl wanted that part." Amari winked. "You were the lead. There's no Christmas without Mary."

"Probably, but since we were at church, everyone had to pretend to be happy for me. Nick was the cutest boy there, and when he was assigned the Joseph part, I couldn't believe my luck."

"Then all the girls really hated you." Amari laughed.

Ivy smiled at the memory. It had been a long time since she'd thought about her "meet-cute" with Nick. But that's what it was in rom-com terms—a "meet-cute" where the boy and girl met in an incredibly cute way.

"I hope you didn't start dating in second grade."

"Oh no. We waited until fifth grade." Ivy laughed.

Amari took out a notepad and wrote that down. "I like to take notes when I'm researching my character. Part of the actor's work. So, where did you first say I love you to Nick?"

Ivy furrowed her brow. She knew exactly where they first said I love you, but she didn't want to reveal this too quickly to Amari. She wanted her to think that maybe she'd forgotten about it and had to dig deep into her memory. She paused for a few moments. But no, it was right there on the surface. "Hmm… I think it was at his family's winery. It was Christmastime, and we were sitting on the deck, staring out at the lake," Ivy finally admitted.

"You were sitting outside in the snow?"

"We were wearing giant parkas. It was the only private space we could find. We were both in high school, and my parents wouldn't let me have boys in my bedroom, especially Nick. Not that they were able to stop us though." Ivy smiled at a memory and blurted out without intending to: "On the night of my eighteenth birthday, he snuck into my bedroom."

"That's why it felt so real in the script. Because it was real," said a very thrilled Amari. She was scribbling down everything that Ivy said. "So, who was louder?"

Ivy had not meant to tell Amari such personal memories, and she was relieved when a good-looking waiter stopped by their table.

"Good afternoon, ladies. Are you ready to order?"

Ivy suddenly looked panic-stricken. She'd completely forgotten to study the menu ahead of time, something that she normally did due to her menu phobia. It wasn't a clinically proven phobia, but Ivy knew it was real. Ever since she'd moved to Los Angeles, she'd struggled with what to order when she went out. Especially at business lunches. There were too many choices on this menu. She didn't know if she wanted a very expensive salad or overpriced fried chicken or a wallet-busting pizza. She also knew she was trying to lose five pounds before the filming started—if it started at all.

"How is the burrata salad?" Ivy asked the waiter, stalling for time.

"Delicious. It's served with roasted baby beets, arugula, and pine nuts."

"How old are the baby beets?" Amari wondered.

"I don't know," the waiter admitted.

"Please go check," she demanded.

The waiter looked at Amari's serious face and blanched. He quickly left.

"I hate when the baby beets are uprooted too early," Amari said.

Ivy wasn't sure what to say. "I've never been here."

"It's an outdated place. Not hot anymore. This menu is so 1999. But I thought it would be fun to meet Ivy at the Ivy. Let's take a selfie," Amari said. She held up her phone and leaned over to Ivy, snapping their photo. Amari checked the photo and groaned. "Oh, this picture is hideous. Not you. Me."

Ivy looked at the photo and saw immediately that Amari was stunning, per usual. "You look great."

"You really think so?"

"Yes."

Amari posted the photo to her Instagram account, typing in the words *Meeting Ivy at the Ivy*.

Then the waiter reappeared, looking red in the face. "The baby beets were just harvested a few days ago," he blurted out.

"Hmmm..." Amari hesitated.

Ivy jumped in. "That's fine. I'll have that beet salad with the burrata cheese."

"I'll have what she's having." Amari proceeded to order exactly what Ivy ordered, including her water with lemon. "I am just trying to get into character." She smiled. She wanted to really immerse herself in the part. She wanted to study Ivy.

The waiter left as fast as he could. Amari looked into her purse and pulled out two matching silver bracelets. "I thought that since I might play you in the movie that we could be soul sisters, and I got us matching bracelets." She handed Ivy a slim silver bracelet with the words *Soul Sister* engraved on it. Amari put the matching one onto her own wrist.

"Thank you so much. This is so nice," Ivy purred as she slipped on the bracelet. Ivy was quickly realizing that Amari Rivers was actually the nicest person in the world. While they ate lunch at the Ivy, tourists snapped photos of Amari. She never protested or said no. High-powered studio execs stopped by to say hello to the star. Amari introduced Ivy as "the talented writer of *When Joseph Met Mary*."

Amari whispered to Ivy, "We really need to change that title."

Ivy agreed. She had always meant it to be just a working title, but then it got some heat and her agent said she couldn't change the title. At least not yet.

Of course Ivy stained her white blouse with beet juice. Amari made her feel better by doing the same.

"Now we have to go shopping." Amari laughed.

Fueled by their love of *Pretty Woman*, both the song and the movie, Amari took Ivy on a shopping spree. While in a dressing room, trying on a $488 T-shirt, Ivy was able to text Drew.

STILL WITH AMARI.

DID SHE SAY YES?

WE'RE SHOPPING NOW.

YOU AND AMARI? WHY? WE NEED HER TO SAY YES!

Ivy couldn't help it. She snapped a photo and sent it to Drew. When she emerged from the dressing room, Amari was in the same exact outfit.

Ivy had no idea that the day was just getting started. Amari and Ivy rode down to Malibu in Amari's Mini Cooper convertible. Amari had little regard for the curves of Sunset Boulevard as they raced toward the Pacific Coast Highway. Ivy was exhausted. She wanted to go home. But she couldn't. Amari was talking about the movie as if she was going to do the movie but still hadn't said yes.

Ivy wound up at the Malibu beach house of an aging wannabe producer. People were hanging out in the middle of a Thursday, drinking wine and watching the dolphins frolic. She thought about calling an Uber. But Amari promised she would drive her home. She didn't say when. After the party, they hopped back into Amari's car and stopped at the New Beverly

Cinema. It was the movie theater that Quentin Tarantino had purchased, and he personally programmed all of the movies. Amari and Ivy sat in the back and watched Madonna in *Desperately Seeking Susan*, a fun comedy about amnesia and mistaken identity. It was about a bored suburban housewife obsessed with the ultracool Susan. Amari also watched Ivy. Studied her, more like it. She started eating her popcorn one kernel at a time—just like Ivy.

They went to the restroom together. In her own stall, Ivy was able to text Drew.

> AT THE NEW BEVERLY. WATCHING
> DESPERATELY SEEKING SUSAN.
> **WTF?**
> WITH AMARI. IT'S REALLY GOOD.
> **SHE SAID YES?????**
> WORKING ON IT
> **SO WHAT'S REALLY GOOD?**
> THE MOVIE.

After the movie, Amari asked Ivy if she was tired. Ivy lied. She was up for anything. She kept bringing up her script, and Amari kept deflecting. Ivy hoped the next destination on the Amari Express was a coffee shop or an all-night diner so they could talk. It wasn't. It was a *loud* dance club in Downtown LA. Near Drew's apartment. Ivy and Amari danced the night away. At least until two in the morning, as that was when things closed in Los Angeles.

"I'm in. I'll do your movie," Amari finally said. "I have the sense we can work together. We can be soul sisters."

"Oh my God, thank you, Amari," Ivy gushed as they hugged. Someone asked if they were twins. Ivy was beaming.

She walked back to Drew's place from the club. Her phone had died hours ago. She arrived at Drew's condo.

"What happened? You disappeared!" Drew exclaimed.

"I was with Amari. Lunch, shopping, movies. You know, *Desperately Seeking Susan* is very underrated. After the movie, we hit that new dance club across from the Crypto.com Arena." Drew just stared at her, wanting to know the only thing he wanted to know. "Oh, and she said yes. She's doing the movie!" Ivy shrieked.

Drew was ecstatic. He had a bottle of champagne on ice. He popped the cork and yelled, "Let's celebrate!"

But Ivy was already asleep on the couch. In a deep, deep, well-deserved sleep.

The next day, Amari made her deal. The movie was a go. It would take a few months for the contracts to be drawn up, but the movie was officially a green light. Ivy was ecstatic at how her professional life was finally moving forward. And her personal life had suddenly gotten a big green light too.

When Drew's family invited her to their ski house in Mammoth Mountain for a week of spring skiing, Ivy jumped at the opportunity. Drew worked a lot during the day, while Ivy went out skiing with his brother and sister. Each night they gathered for dinner, and it was a lovefest. Ivy was starting to feel really connected to Drew's family.

That night in their shared bedroom, Drew held her tight as he told her, "I really like spending time with you."

"Me too."

"Oh, you like spending time with yourself," Drew joked.

"Ha-ha. You know what I mean."

"You spend a lot of time at my apartment," he whispered.

"Maybe I should pay rent." Ivy laughed.

"Actually, I was thinking maybe we should move in together. We could find a bigger place in DTLA."

Ivy nodded. She knew that DTLA meant Downtown LA. And she was open to the idea. "Let's look at a few places before the movie starts," Ivy said.

CHAPTER 4

IVY WAS ASLEEP WHEN HER phone freaked out, waking her up. She had been dreaming of being lost in a vineyard. Naked. No one was around. And then she heard a voice, calling her home. Not any voice. His voice. He was saying "If you film it, I will come" in a *Field of Dreams* homage. Those were the words Ivy thought she heard in the dream. She rarely had dreams she remembered, but when she did, she gave them deep thought. Now she did not have time for deep thought. Her phone was blowing up. Texts and Instagram posts.

YOU'RE IN DEADLINE!!!! the text screamed. Deadline was the go-to site for breaking Hollywood news. The text was from a friend from film school. The friend had screen-grabbed the headline. AMARI TO STAR IN CHRISTMAS MOVIE! Another text popped up. Another friend. Another website. Ivy read the articles. Her eyes found what she was looking for—her name. *Written by Ivy Green*. There it was. Someone reporting that her dreams were coming true. Ivy texted the links to her sister's and her parents' cell phones, and then she grabbed some leggings and flew out the door.

Since her car was on the fritz again, she did the most unheard of thing in LA and walked the mile to the "rock and roll" Ralphs (it had earned the nickname as so many musicians aka wannabe rock stars worked there during the day)—and bought five copies of *Hollywood Reporter* and *Variety*. The movie announcement was on the cover of each one.

"What did you do?" the Bon Jovi look-alike working the register asked.

Ivy pointed to the article on the front page. "That's me...I mean, my movie. I wrote it."

Bon Jovi high-fived her, announcing on the PA, "Customer at register five sold her script. Front page of *Variety*," and then handed her his demo CD. "Just in case your movie needs a kick-ass song over the closing credits."

Ivy hit the gym. She resumed her barre classes. It was nice to be back in the gym. She had tried working out in her apartment, but her HIT classes did not do the job and had annoyed the neighbors below her.

Ivy showered. She had missed a text from her agent, Charlotte. GREAT PRESS. COME TO OFFICE @ 10 A.M. TODAY.

Ivy rarely visited the agency office, which was located on Wilshire in the heart of Beverly Hills. Seven floors of modernism holding two hundred and fifty agents. She had gone there once before when she first met and signed with Charlotte. Her correspondence with Charlotte over the years had been via emails. And they'd been few and far between. Ivy wasn't even sure Charlotte liked her. At one point, Charlotte had loved her—and her potential—but Ivy still had not been able to generate enough money to quit her many day jobs. She had done some tutoring. The one thing she was never going back to doing was working at a coffee shop. She couldn't imagine working in a coffee shop in Los Angeles, where every table was filled with screenwriting squatters working on their script for the price of one coffee and five refills. But unlike ninety percent of those squatters, Ivy had just sold a script that was green-lit.

Ivy quickly changed into something professional/presentable and exhausted herself getting from Los Feliz to Beverly Hills. If only she had checked her text before her barre class. She was drained because the thirty-minute ride took an hour. *(Thank you, 101)*. She decided to cut over on Coldwater Canyon, hoping to avoid the 405, but it seemed like all the drivers were using the same GPS. It was an ungodly hot day in Southern California. Everyone around her in traffic was doing the same thing. Rolling calls. Listening to music. And blasting the AC. Ivy's air conditioning in her car had broken, and she didn't have the money to fix it. Hence the second reason she was exhausted. Her car was hotter than it was outside. At every stoplight, Ivy would hang her head out the window.

Whenever she would go to the agency, she would never valet park. She had a fear that her car would break down in the valet and Peter Sherman, the CEO of the agency, would not be able to get out, find out it was Ivy's car blocking his exit, and have her dropped as a client.

But she was late. And she had no choice. She handed the car keys to the valet and sprinted for the elevator, not waiting to hear if her car would start or not. She went up to the lobby, gave her name to the receptionist, and was prepared to wait.

"Follow me, Ms. Green."

"You can call me Ivy."

The assistant smiled and escorted her to Charlotte's office.

Ivy remembered it. But this time it seemed like the office had gotten bigger. Charlotte was waiting for her.

"You are *en fuego*. I've been fielding calls about you all day," Charlotte said.

It was still the morning, but Ivy wasn't going to correct her. She wondered who was calling, and why? Charlotte was up and hugging Ivy. Then she was out the door with a "Walk with me. Your team's in the conference room."

A team, Ivy thought. *I have a team?* Ivy was confused but smiled and kept pace. Assistants walking her way parted as Charlotte marched down the hall.

"You're like a caveman," Charlotte told her.

"A cavewoman?"

"Caveman. Cavewoman. Who cares? You created fire with your script. And just like the caveman, you're who everyone wants to hang around with. The caveman who can make fire is the hottest person in town and gets paid lots of money because now the rest of the town can eat."

Ivy had never learned about cavemen in film school. Charlotte continued: "Your script is the fire. Two of the hottest stars have signed up to be in your script. We have to get your next job lined up while you're hot."

"Like the caveman fire."

"Now you're getting it. Yes, it's important to set up something now just in case…"

"In case of what?"

"In case the movie sucks," Charlotte said as the doors to the glass conference room opened. Ivy followed inside to a room of twenty eager waiting agents. They were all excited to meet her. She was still reeling from the "in case the movie sucks" line as the agents introduced themselves. There were three from TV Lit. Ten from Motion Picture Lit. Two book agents. One podcast agent. Somebody from Audio Books. Someone from New Media. And two from Talent.

They all had ideas about what Ivy should do next. Almost as a collective hive they told her: *We can't wait. We have to set up your next job right away. I had one client who had a major movie star walk off the set twenty days into production. Killed the writer's career. And he had bought a house. What about interactive fiction? Game show? It's not what you can do for me today—what you can do for me tomorrow. You fail upward.*

It gave Ivy a lot to think about. She was still worried about Charlotte's clarion call of "in case the movie sucks" as she and Charlotte sat down to lunch at the Grill on the Alley. Ivy had heard about this place. It was where studio heads and high-powered producers had their reserved tables. She looked around. People were wondering, whispering, and learning who she was. Ivy remembered some of their faces from earlier meetings.

"There's Carl Angelo. Great exec at Universal."

"I met him. He passed on my script."

"Film has no memory, Ivy. Remember that."

That lunch went well. Ivy still had no idea what she was supposed to do next. But she wasn't going to worry about it. She had spent the last five years worrying about her career (and her love life); she was going to enjoy this time. Except when they got back to the agency, after Ivy said goodbye and thank you to Charlotte, Ivy went to get her car and discovered it was dead on arrival. She turned the ignition, but nothing happened. She would have to get a new car.

The deal was made with Brilliant Pictures. Charlotte had

found a very shrewd lawyer who got Ivy more money than she'd imagined. A $50,000 upfront option on the script. Writers Guild minimum plus ten percent for the rewrite. Against a $300,000 full purchase price, which would be paid on the first day of production, and $50,000 solo writing credit bonus. And if the movie didn't suck, she would get residuals each time the movie aired.

Ivy was suddenly the one everyone wanted to meet. All the execs were now reading with prejudice as Charlotte said they would. They loved Ivy and wanted her to rewrite some of their scripts that were stuck in development hell. Most of them were very bad.

Later that night, she Ubered over to El Coyote to celebrate with her film school friends. They ordered many street tacos—and many more margaritas. They asked Ivy to tell the story of how she did it. She was the first one to really break through as a screenwriter. Her classmates were mostly all working but none of them as a writer. They had become assistant editors, assistant directors, assistants for managers. One just got a job at a casting agency and brought a client's headshot to dinner hoping Ivy could get him a part so she could get a promotion. Other friends were not there. They had given Hollywood five years and gone back home to very nice lives and having very nice babies. When the check came, it was brought to Ivy. She was still waiting to be paid from Drew's company, but she did not feel right telling her friends that. So she picked up the bill.

Ivy went into the bathroom. Like a movie moment, she was in the stall when she heard two of her friends at the sink talking about the check. "She's rich now," she heard one of her friends say. "I heard she got a million dollars for the script."

Her celebratory dinner had not been the party she had hoped

it would be. A week later, after buying a modest Prius, Charlotte's assistant had called and told her to be at the Pacific Park amusement center on the Santa Monica Pier at 7:00 p.m.

Drew was out of town in New York meeting with the financial team that owned Brilliant Pictures. Ivy went solo. Charlotte greeted her at the entrance. The Santa Monica Pier and Pacific Park were closed for a private event. Food and rides were all free. Ivy hung out with Dana, Charlotte's new assistant. They became fast friends.

It was a great night. Until it was not. Charlotte summoned Dana with some ridiculous task, leaving Ivy with two cups of ice cream. There was an older man sitting on a bench, watching the roller coaster. Ivy thought she recognized him. It was the famous director Ray Arthur. Ivy introduced herself and told him that he had once spoken at her film school and that she really enjoyed what he had to say about visual storytelling in a screenplay. She jokingly offered him the extra cup of ice cream as a thank-you.

He accepted, and they spent the next thirty minutes talking, Arthur asking her about her script and how she was handling it. "People treat you differently when you have success. Everyone wants to be your new friend. And your old friends—if they are writers—treat you differently." Arthur calmed Ivy down about her anxiety that the movie would suck and thanked her for the ice cream. "You're at the Gates of Oz, Ivy," he said thoughtfully.

Ivy was thrilled. "That's how I feel. How did you know?"

"We're movie people," Arthur said. "We've all been there. Just remember it was just as hard once Dorothy got through the gates. She had to go back out and kill the wicked witch, she learned that Oz was a liar, and in the end she just wanted to go home."

Ivy smiled at him, nodding. But deep down, she felt he was wrong. She was never going home again.

Preproduction began. Ivy drove her new Prius over to Brilliant Pictures to surprise Drew. She was the one who was about to be surprised. Another whammo.

Drew was meeting with his location manager.

"Ivy, I want you to meet Lane, our location guy. He's found some perfect spots for us to film," Drew said.

"Nice to meet you." Ivy shook hands with Lane, who was in his early thirties and seemed very eager to please.

"I've got some great interiors and exteriors to show you," Lane said. They all sat down as Lane opened up a notebook of photos.

"Here's where we could film the church. There's a large parking lot for our equipment, and the inside has gorgeous stained glass," he told Ivy enthusiastically.

She looked closely at the church. "It's great. It looks familiar."

"This is the main street. Most of the stores are willing to let us film outside on the sidewalk," Lane said as he revealed a quintessential downtown.

"Oh, wow. This looks a lot like Geneva," Ivy marveled. And that's when she realized that it had been over five years since she'd returned home, which was why she wasn't completely sure that it was her town as there were some stores and eateries that looked new.

"And here's where we think the Ilsa character lives with her family," Lane pointed out.

Ivy looked at the Victorian-style home with the wraparound porch. She might not have been home in a while but one thing she knew for sure and that was that the house they were thinking about filming in was none other than... "That's my house!" Ivy exclaimed.

Drew grinned. "I thought you'd love this extra touch."

"Your parents were terrific. They're thrilled to have us film in their house. Especially your dad," Lane said.

"I wanted to surprise you." Drew beamed. "We got a forty percent below-the-line credit from New York state. We're going to film the movie in your hometown! Isn't that great?"

In my hometown. Where I grew up. Where Nick still lives, Ivy thought.

WHAMMO!

CHAPTER 5

NICK STROLLED THROUGH THE SUN-FLECKED Shepherd vineyard that overlooked Seneca Lake. He stopped and took a deep breath. The long cold winter was over. Summer in Central New York was stunning. Eighty degrees and no humidity. Lush green hills reflected in shimmering blue waters. The vineyard never looked better. *We did it, Dad,* Nick thought as he inspected the grapes carefully, looking for signs of ripening. But his dad wasn't around anymore. He had died almost three years ago. Nick had only inherited half of the winery, but he had also inherited his dad's gift for sarcasm. He remembered how after the breakup with Ivy, he had returned home to work full-time. Nick had graduated from Cornell with a degree in viticulture and enology. Basically, he went to college to learn what he had been doing his whole life.

His dad had joked that it was "time for that Ivy League education to pay off." Nick's dad had always had a cutting wit, and you never knew if he was serious or joking. "Sorry, didn't mean to say *Ivy*. Where is she, anyway?" There was his dad with his wit again. Nick didn't want to tell him that he was no longer talking to Ivy.

Shepherd Winery had always been a mom-and-pop business. Now it was a mom-and-son business. Their wines had been good but never great. But Nick used what he'd learned in college, and it was starting to pay off. Big time. Like the other person he no longer spoke of, he also had dreams. Only his were in the Finger Lakes.

After Nick's dad's sudden death, Nick became the general manager, and he quickly made the decision to expand, something his father was always a little nervous about. He began by doubling the size of the winery and making it a place people could visit and tell their friends about. Forget social media. Word of mouth was the original and best Twitter ever. It was a beautiful Craftsman with high arching ceilings in the style of the twentieth century American Arts and Crafts movement and modeled after the turn of the century U.S. national park lodges, particularly Yosemite's Ahwahnee Hotel, where Nick's mom and dad had honeymooned. Nick was proud of his family winery, and sometimes he wished that Ivy could see all that he had achieved. But he knew that would never happen, as Ivy no longer visited their hometown. He figured that she was too busy being fabulous or maybe still angry.

Adding a new wooden deck that overlooked Seneca Lake brought in more customers, making it a must-stop on the Seneca Lake Wine Trail. Nick had minored in marketing and made sure that the winery was a year-round business. Shepherd Winery had a great view of the leaves when they changed in autumn. So Nick started a fall foliage wine tasting. It sold out every night. For Halloween, he had created a costume tasting/social mixer. Everyone came in a Halloween costume. There were a lot of drunken mistakes that first night, which led to some long and short courtships. But not for Nick—the only thing he was dating was his winery.

Nick made sure that Shepherd Winery continued to be the most popular winery on the Seneca Lake Wine Trail's twenty-eighth annual Deck the Halls! weekend. Hundreds of cars and tour buses would traverse the Finger Lakes Wine Trail and stop at various wineries all decorated for Christmas. And no one decorated for Christmas better than Nick. Everyone got a special ornament for their Christmas tree, branded *Shepherd Winery*. Along with their tasting, everyone could sample some food. And there was no better chef than Nick's mom, Frannie Shepherd. Her food samples were so popular that people paid for extra tastings to try her cuisine. Nick's parents had met when they were students at Cornell. They had "met cute" at the dining hall where they both had work-study jobs. Frannie was the supervisor and Nick's dad was the dishwasher. Frannie would always tease Nick's dad about not getting the dishes clean enough. Their first date had been at a wine tasting. They'd dreamed about opening their own winery. It had started small with just the two of them. It had grown from a small business to a bustling winery where Nick now had twenty employees and sold thousands of bottles each year.

Nick's dad's ashes were scattered in the vineyard, closest to the lake. The place Nick would go "talk" with him when he needed to. At first business was slow during the pandemic because they had to close the tasting room, but then they opened up an outside area and wine enthusiasts quickly converged. Covid was terrible for many aspects of the economy but not wine. People needed to relax, and Nick wanted to help them do that with the Shepherd wines. As everything opened back up, even more customers arrived, and Nick doubled the size of the winery. And then it happened—the best news of all. A wine that Nick created had won a major prize at the New York Wine Classic. It was a big deal. To celebrate, the Shepherd Winery had even closed its doors for an invitation-only event to be held that night. The whole family was coming to celebrate. His mom was proud of him. His dad would have been proud of him too. And he was sure Ivy would have been proud of him.

Ivy? he thought. *How the hell did she show up in my head?* Luckily more thoughts of Ivy were interrupted by his mother, Frannie, who called to him from across the vineyard.

Francine Shepherd was turning sixty that year, but you'd never know it from the way she looked. She still had her youthful figure and easy-going smile. She started running marathons after her husband died and had discovered it was both meditative and rejuvenating.

"You were right about that deck," she told Nick.

"And you were right about the new sorrel appetizers," he said, returning the compliment to his mom. Nick knew that he and his mom were a good team. Technically they were co-owners of Shepherd Winery even though Nick had the more important job as wine vintner.

"We doubled our numbers from last year's Fourth of July, and that's all because of you," Frannie told her son.

"That's probably why I'm so exhausted. I need a vacation." He laughed. "More important—I need to get on my boat." Nick smiled. "I can't believe that it's already July sixth and I still haven't been on the water."

"Maybe you're just waiting for the right person to take out on the lake." Frannie winked. Nick shut down. He did that whenever she wanted to talk about his dating life, or lack of it, squashing any kind of conversation with his mother about his love life. She was the last person he was going to talk to about girls, and besides, ever since the breakup with Ivy, he never liked to talk about his feelings. Preferring to keep things all corked up, just like a good bottle of wine, he thought. But Nick also knew that if something stayed corked for too long, it might turn rancid. And he realized that if he didn't get over Ivy, he was destined to become like a bad wine that had developed a paint thinner taste.

"Come on," Frannie said. "The banners are here!"

Nick was excited. His mom sprinted out in front. He tried to keep up. But she was fast. Nick saw his family, friends, and workers gathered in front of the winery. His sister, Denise, the local high school drama teacher, was there with her husband, Kenny, the editor-in-chief of their small-town paper. There was a young photographer with Kenny. Her name was Rory. She was a gorgeous blond with an unstoppable smile.

"There he is! The man of the hour. Ladies and gentlemen, Nick Shepherd!" Kenny called out. Everyone cheered. Nick pumped his fists in the air. He was willing to share credit, but if people wanted to cheer him—so be it.

"Great job, baby bro," Denise said as she hugged her brother. Kenny came over, hugged him, and before Nick could ask, he was introduced to Rory.

"Nick, this is Rory. She just got a job here as a staff photographer."

"I hope it's all right for me to take some pictures of you," Rory said as she nodded to Nick. She didn't shake his hand, as that had gone out with Covid. Nick thought to himself: *I wouldn't mind anything you do.* He was smiling at Rory. Maybe it was time to put the past behind and look toward the future.

A countdown had begun. Two of Nick's best workers, Jorge

and Max, were positioned on ladders on each side of the wine entrance that stretched to the roof. Five! Four! Three! Two! One!

The banner unfolded. At least one did at first. The one that announced WINNER! GOVERNOR'S CUP WINE OF THE YEAR 2021. Jorge had forgotten to untie one part. He did, and the second banner unfolded. This one said WINE OF THE YEAR 2021 on top with the picture of the wine label. And that label had a name. The wine of the year was called Poison Ivy. A cabernet franc. And the picture of a woman's face on the label, hidden in ivy, may or may not have been Ivy Green herself. At least it was a very close facsimile.

"This is amazing!" Denise said.

"Wine of the year! Governor's Cup!"

Rory snapped pictures of the family celebrating and of Nick holding up the Governor's Cup like a championship trophy. Later, she also snapped one of Nick looking up at the banner. She wondered what he was thinking.

Nick reflected on Poison Ivy. His wine of the year. He remembered how it all came to be. It was a few years after the breakup. As he was rebuilding the winery, adding the decks, opening the restaurant, he also remembered being solely focused on making the perfect cab franc, hoping it would release Ivy from his thoughts. He stayed up for hours on end, mixing grapes, striving to find the perfect blend of the deep aromas of blackberry and currants, tasting over and over until he was finally satisfied. Either that or he was too exhausted to continue. And when he decided to name the wine, Poison Ivy seemed like a perfect fit.

He remembered sampling the first bottle of Poison Ivy with Denise and Kenny, the night of their wedding.

"It's got an angry bite to it. Passionate. Nice," Denise had said.

"What are you calling it?" Kenny had asked.

"Poison Ivy," Nick had said. He had not known if he was doing it for memory or malice. He had only known it felt like the perfect name.

"Will you be shipping to LA?" Denise had asked.

"Maybe someday. Not now," Nick had replied. So, he was safe. Nick had a high school friend, Tugg, a tattoo artist, design the label. Tugg had also known Ivy in high school. The first presentable batch came a year later. Nick remembered pasting decorative labels onto a case of Poison Ivy wine bottles. The image on the labels was of a young woman's face who just happened to look a lot like his ex-girlfriend, Ivy. Green vines twisted over the pretty face. It was the same image that was on the banner.

Poison Ivy was an instant classic. Nick had no choice but to put the award-winning cab franc into the yearly production. The Shepherd Winery gift store was quickly filled with T-shirts and hats with the words *Pick Your Poison*, and no one was more chagrined than Nick when Poison Ivy became their best-selling wine. Even though Nick had been the one to break up, he had initially felt that Ivy had driven him to that moment. He recalled thinking that she had changed and was no longer the girl he had fallen in love with. He had always believed they wanted the same things, until she encouraged him to move away from his family. That was not the Ivy he remembered. Nick had always imagined their life together here. Not there. In LA where the old joke was there was no *there* there. He had meant the wine to be a limited production, but his mother entered it into the New York Wine Classic, which was known as the Oscars of New York wine competitions. Poison Ivy surprised everyone, most of all Nick, when it was recognized as the Best of Show and won the most prestigious award of the competition, the Governor's Cup, which was a large silver chalice.

Upon winning the top prize in the New York Wine Classic, the Shepherd Winery became an overnight sensation. They were suddenly thrust onto the map of the best wineries to visit in the Finger Lakes. Everyone wanted to stop by and taste Poison Ivy. "Give me some poison" was what Nick heard at least once a day. And over the Fourth of July, it was especially popular. Everyone loved to joke about drinking the poison. Nick was probably the only one who didn't want to drink the cabernet franc. He'd tasted the real Poison Ivy. He didn't want to be reminded of what he'd lost. He wanted to dump the wine out and never make another bottle.

Now here they were in the winery, getting ready for the party to be held that night. The party to celebrate Nick's success.

"If Ivy ever finds out you made a wine called Poison Ivy, she will buy a bottle and smash it over your head," his sister said. Nick wanted to pick up the phone and confide in Ivy, but after what he'd done to her, he just couldn't make the call. He hadn't heard from Ivy since that awful day of their breakup when he did what he felt he had to do. He did stalk her a little bit online and learned that she was doing well, which made him feel good. But then Covid hit, and she seemed to disappear off social media. He hoped she was okay.

"She's never going to find out. She's off in La-La Land, la-la-ing away." She was living her life, and Nick was going to start living his. And that was what he intended to do that night at the party. Before he left Nick invited the photographer, Rory, to swing by the party, under the pretense that she could take some pictures.

Nick cold-showered away the past, slipped on a tight T-shirt and jeans, and returned to the winery. The nighttime celebration party was in full swing. His mom had insisted on cooking the food, and it was out of this world. But where was Kenny? His best friend brother-in-law was nowhere in sight. Denise said something was happening back at the newspaper office and he would be there soon. Nick made the rounds thanking everyone, handing out bonuses. Not a big bonus, but a bonus. They weren't just his workers. They were his family.

Nick saw Rory sitting alone at the bar in front of the Governor's Cup. "Having a good time?" he asked.

"I am. But it just got better. Hey, can I get a picture of you standing in front of the Governor's Cup?" Nick went behind the bar. Smiled and posed with the shiny silver cup.

"How's this?" he asked. He leaned across the bar to talk more closely with Rory.

"Not bad, Nick Shepherd. Not bad at all." She was admiring the picture she took. "So, what's the real story of Poison Ivy? Who is the wine named after? Kenny talks a little loudly, and I couldn't help but overhear some things. Who was she?"

"Kid crush. Middle school romance. High school sweethearts. Long-distance lovers which never worked. We were geographically incompatible."

"I'm liking it here more and more," Rory said.

Nick leaned closer to her. Smiling. And who knew what might have happened between them if...if Kenny hadn't rushed in with copies of tomorrow's edition of the *Geneva Gazette*. He passed around a few newspapers on his way in, and suddenly everyone at the party was buzzing about something other than the award-winning wine. Kenny and Denise rushed up to Nick. Kenny went to hand him the paper. Denise pulled it back.

"Nick, don't freak out," she said.

"Freak out? Why would I freak out?"

Nick grabbed the paper. On the cover was the headline: HOLLYWOOD COMING TO GENEVA! The article had something to do with a movie coming to film in town.

"Oh, they're going to film a movie here. That will be great for business," he said.

"Oh yeah," Kenny said. "It's great for the town. Hotels. Coffee shops. Wineries."

"So what's the problem?" Nick asked.

"It's a movie called *When Joseph Met Mary*. Does that sound familiar?" Kenny asked.

"Is it a religious movie?" Rory wondered.

"No," Nick said. "It's not." He read the article—or rather scanned it. There she was in the press: the project, written by former Geneva resident Ivy Green, was to begin production in a week.

"I'm really not interested," he lied.

"That makes you an anomaly. The whole town is already going crazy," Kenny enthused.

But Nick wasn't listening because he was realizing that for the first time in five years, he might actually see Ivy again. His plan to try to forget her was clearly failing. Once again, the universe had other plans for him. Nick was flooded with thoughts—the way it was when he would pour wine flights to a winery full of customers. He needed all the voices in his head to drink and be quiet. "I wonder if the script is about us. Ivy and I did meet at a Christmas pageant," Nick said.

"Wow. That would suck." Kenny grinned. "I wonder what the sex scenes would be like."

Nick gave a small smile at the memory.

"Oh, is that a smile?"

"Shut up," he said. But he was laughing too. "I wonder who is going to play me?"

"Griffin James," Kenny told him.

"Griffin James? I'd do him," Rory said.

"Who the hell is Griffin James?" Nick exclaimed.

CHAPTER 6

WHERE AM I? GRIFFIN THOUGHT as he woke up from an exhausted sleep triggered by one airplane cocktail and an Ambien chaser. He was in the back of a limo looking out at a lot of cow butts. He remembered catching the red eye from LAX and landing in, what was it, Chicago? Philadelphia? Mexico?

"Where are we?" Griffin asked his driver.

"We just got off 90 and are now on 14 South. Should be there in twenty-five minutes."

Griffin had no idea what those numbers meant. He didn't even drive a car. Well, he could drive a car. Just not legally, since his license was taken away for too many speeding tickets. The last one was not his fault though. He was driving through Ohio. That was his excuse. He wanted to get out of Ohio as quickly as he could. He had some crazy relatives there.

"I'm going to need more to go on than that, my friend."

"I'm sorry, Mr. James. I picked you up at the Buffalo airport, if that helps."

"That explains the red and blue hat with a Buffalo on it." It came back to him. Drew suggested landing in Buffalo to avoid the paparazzi. There was a direct flight from Los Angeles to Buffalo. And Buffalo was a few hours' drive to the set. Griffin was coming right off another movie. He was worn out. It wasn't the paparazzi that worried Griffin. It was his fans. *The Griffineers.* That unruly, *let's rip off his shirt* mob who followed him wherever he went. Such was the price of fame. It hadn't always been that way.

It started when Griffin had been a TV tween star. He had played a warlock in a sitcom who accidentally got enrolled in an all-girl witch school. It was called *Broommates.* Hijinks ensued. So did his Q rating.

"Your Q score is forty," his manager-mother said. "This is great. Tom Hanks is forty-six." At the time, Griffin was fourteen years old and not even aware of what a Q score was. "It measures your popularity and our brand. The higher the Q score, the more highly regarded the person is," his manager-mother explained.

"I have a brand?" Griffin wondered.

"Yes, you're the guy who every girl wants to lose her virginity to," his mom said matter-of-factly. Griffin did not like talking to his mom about that. He was fourteen and was not going to use his celebrity to achieve his manhood. But the girls he knew personally distanced themselves, and he didn't know why. "Your father's been doing a great job on social media."

His father, Greg, had a beer on his stomach as he was typing away. "I love flirting with your classmates on Instagram!"

Griffin was aghast. "I don't have an Instagram! Let me see that!" He took the phone and looked at it. "'The real Griffin James'? I'm the real Griffin James!"

"There are a lot of people who might pretend to be you," his dad said.

"Like you?" Griffin said, raising his voice. His dad chuckled, caught his beer as it fell off his belly and gulped.

Griffin started scrolling. He was shocked by what he read. Not just from the fact that his father was capable of this but what he had written. It was creepy. Griffin stammered while reading one entry. "'You must be from Iraq because I want to Baghdad that ass!' What the hell! You sent this to Lena Goenka! She's the class president. This is racist."

"No, it's multiculturalism," his mom said. "You're being diverse!"

"Lena is from India. Not Iraq."

"Same difference," his mom said.

"Iraq and India are not the same!" Griffin exclaimed. He told his parents to stop his social media immediately. But the damage was done. Lena, his first crush, broke his heart when she called him a creep as he tried to explain his dad controlled his Instagram.

How did this even happen? Griffin's dad and mom had met in Ohio. In high school, his dad was the star quarterback and his mom was the cheerleader. Great looking couple. His mom still held it together. His dad did not. His body was now shaped like a beer keg. Short. Round from neck to toes. And like the keg, filled with beer. They came to LA to pursue their dreams of acting. As with so many others, they didn't make it. They stayed in LA, found other jobs, and had Griffin. "That's why there are so many good-looking people in LA. All the good-looking people come here and reproduce," his dad had once told him with a mixture of bourbon and bitterness.

Griffin remembered playing basketball at the YMCA in Burbank. He was a good defender, but he could not shoot straight. Turned out his vision was bad, but his parents didn't like the way he looked in glasses. No wonder Griffin's grades got worse and worse the harder the classes got. During one of Griffin's basketball games, his mom flirted with one of the dads and got invited to the end-of-season party for the kids at a very nice house in Mandeville Canyon on the toney West Side of LA. Griffin remembered his mom didn't bring his dad, but she brought her skimpy red bikini. As she teased the director, Griffin played in the pool looking out over the mountains. A woman was watching him. Taking his picture. Griffin was confused. Who was she? She was talking to his mom. His mom stopped flirting and started chatting it up with this woman. Griffin remembered hearing his mother say, "I'm not just his mom. I'm his manager." He had no idea what any of that meant. The woman turned out to be a casting director. Griffin was soon auditioning for a national television commercial. He got it. It was fun, but he was bummed he was missing school and the trip to the zoo. He loved the zoo. His mother loved being on the set, the ex-cheerleader/failed actress that she was.

Everyone at school thought the TV commercial was cool. They asked Griffin if he was now rich because he was famous. Griffin had no idea about money. He remembered something about his parents setting up a Coogan Account. It was a bank account that protected the money child actors had earned. It was named after a child actor, Jackie Coogan, who had earned millions of dollars as a successful child actor only to discover, upon reaching adulthood, that his mother and stepfather had ripped him off. *Oh, the irony,* Griffin thought. From the commercial, he got the TV show *Broommates*, and that ran for five years.

Griffin dropped out of middle school and had a series of on-set studio teachers from fifth grade through twelfth. After the success of *Broommates*, he was offered a family, four-quadrant movie. This was a movie that would appeal to men, women, children, under twenty-five and over twenty-five. It was called *A Boy's Best Friend*. Griffin played second fiddle to a CGI dog who had the ability to talk in a *Chicken Soup for the Soul* kind of way. Griffin hated it. America loved it. He had to do the sequel. Griffin became a very bankable piece of talent. Offers came in.

At fifteen, he bought himself a car, even though he didn't have his license, and a new house for him and his parents. It wasn't until he walked in on his mother riding reverse cowgirl on his business manager that Griffin found out what was really going on. His mother had been cheating on his dad with the manager. His dad had been cheating on his mom with the second assistant director of *A Boy's Best Friend*. Griffin had to fire them all. Agents. Managers. Lawyers. His parents! *How do you fire your parents?* It wasn't as hard as it sounded. But during the litigation, Griffin expressed he didn't want his parents to go to jail. He was emancipated at sixteen, and his parents were ordered to pay him back the two million dollars they had stolen. To do so, his dad sold Griffin's childhood memorabilia on eBay and his mom wrote a tell-all book which should have been a *tell all lies* book about what went down on the set of the TV shows.

Griffin was feeling all alone in the world. He refused to do the third dog movie. He started rejecting everything that was sent to him, looking for a smart script. His agents got mad at him and dumped him. He had one more commitment—a really bad sci-fi movie—after that, he would figure out what to do next. His dream was always to own a movie theater. It was the only place he was ever truly happy. He was definitely not happy doing *MoonGlow*, where he played the grandson of an *Apollo* astronaut who had walked on the moon and claimed he'd seen aliens. When Griffin first read the script, it was charming. Now it was an over-bloated, CGI mess. Just like the overbearing Euro-trash director he had to listen to yelling, "Cut! Do it again!" Griffin was suspended thirty feet in the air in front of a green screen as the director was screaming at his director of photography. She was screaming back adding lots of F-bombs. The film was already behind schedule.

Griffin's cell phone rang. It was Drew Fox, FaceTiming him. Drew's father had produced the *Broommates* television show. Drew was always very nice to Griffin, almost like an older brother.

"Griffin, it's Drew." Griffin was genuinely excited to hear from Drew. He was one of the good ones in Hollywood. He had recently produced an independent film about a dead cowboy that Griffin adored. "How are you?"

"Hanging in there. See." He flipped the phone to show Drew where he was, hanging above the set with the crew and the cameras far below him.

"How long have you been up there?"

"Feels like forever. Waiting to fight the Trikillion or some shit."

"Why?" Drew wondered.

"Long story. I meant to call you. I loved *Dead of Winter*. It had meat on the bones. Great movie," Griffin said with genuine enthusiasm. That was the name of Drew's breakout Sundance hit about the dead cowboy. The lead actor was rumored to be up for an Oscar.

Drew cut to the chase: "I'm about to go into production on something I think you would love. It's a little more grounded."

"Grounded would be nice," Griffin said, his feet dangled in the air.

"It's a small indie. I'm paying favored nations. Scale plus ten. Amari Rivers just signed on. Love for you to play opposite her." Griffin knew that Amari was rising, as the agents would say. She was a singer, actress, YouTube celebrity. And damn talented. And the tub scene in *Beer Boy* had everyone talking. "It's a small indie. Shooting in the middle of nowhere. Finger Lakes. Upstate New York."

"What's the story?" Griffin asked, waving to the director that he was not ready. It didn't matter. A crane started moving him around in front of the green screen.

"It's about a couple that meets in second grade, and they go from friends to boyfriend and girlfriend. Always finding their way home to each other. It's like *Boyhood* meets *When Harry Met Sally* with one of those you didn't see coming endings."

"I'll do it," he blurted out.

"Don't you want to read the script?"

"Of course," Griffin said, a little embarrassed by his eagerness. "Send it over."

Over the course of the day, as he battled Robotrons and acted across from a tennis ball that took the place of a space creature to be CGI'd in later, Griffin read the script and loved it. He hated the title. But inside the script was a tender story about a couple that destiny wanted to bring together but fate had other plans. And the ending—he loved the ending. It was shooting in a small town where the screenwriter grew up. Griffin had grown up on the backlot of a movie studio. He wanted something real. This movie would get him out of LA to Upstate New York. And there was nothing more real than a Christmas movie shooting in July.

It was a great part, and it would lift his spirits. He found himself humming, "We need a little Christmas, right this very minute…" Yes, this was going to be great.

The moment the director yelled "It's a wrap," Griffin ran from the overproduced sci-fi pic into a waiting limo and got on the plane to Buffalo. He felt great escaping Hollywood until—

"They found me!" Griffin shouted out to his driver.

"I'm not sure I know what you're talking about, sir." The driver looked out and saw that the magnificent Belhurst Castle built in 1885 was surrounded by a mob of young people, mostly teenage girls. Griffin's fans—the Griffineers—had found him. Someone had leaked his travel info.

"Fuck me," he said out loud.

"I think everyone out there would love that chance, sir."

Griffin ordered the driver to stop the car. They were far enough away to not be noticed. Yet. The limo straddled the street and the entrance to the Belhurst castle. Griffin noticed a young college couple walking around the limo. He rolled down the window.

"Hey, you want to make fifty bucks?" Griffin realized that didn't sound too good, so he added something worse: "Take off your shirt."

"I'm not into that, man," the guy in the Hobart and William Smith (HWS) shirt said. Luckily, the young woman recognized Griffin.

"You're that actor, Griffin James."

"I am. And I could use some help."

"The Griffineers," the co-ed said. "We saw them. Read about the movie. Cool."

"You know what else is cool? Twenty-four-hour limo service. Give me your shirt, hat, and sunglasses, and I'll give you fifty bucks and the limo for the day," Griffin said. "You okay with that?" he added to the driver.

"It's all overtime to me."

Griffin and the guy did a quick exchange of shirts. They were about the same size. Griffin got out of the limo, grabbed his luggage, and put on the shades, blending in like a local college kid with the HWS shirt and baseball hat. He had instructed the limo and the students on what to do. The limo would approach (it did), the Griffineers would notice it (they did), the guy in the back would then roll down his window just enough to extend his hand out the window and give the fans a thumbs-up. He did. And they went nuts. Screaming. Cheering. The limo would then start pulling away slowly so the fans could follow it. As the pied piper limo and fans cleared the front of the building, Griffin walked up to the beautiful castle entrance.

Drew was waiting outside the entrance, distracted by his phone.

"Drew! How are you?"

"There you are," Drew said, quickly putting away his phone. Something which Griffin took note of. After his parents and agents and lawyers, he had come to not trust anyone. *But this is Drew,* he thought. *Always a stand-up guy.* "I'm so sorry. The rest of the crew is at the Hilton down the road. I figured your fan base would camp out there. Instead, they stormed the castle. I don't know who tipped them off, but when I find out, someone is getting fired. Let's get you checked in. I have to run to a meeting."

"Welcome to the Belhurst Castle," the white-haired receptionist greeted them. Griffin took a moment to admire the design of this classical castle that was a hotel. He took in a long deep breath, something his therapist or Apple Watch had told him to do—remember to breathe, to take it all in. Drew watched Griffin in his zone and grew a little impatient.

"I have Griffin James checking in—"

"No," Griffin said, snapping out of it. "It should be under the name Archibald Leach."

"Who's Archibald Leach?" Drew wondered.

"Cary Grant's real name," the receptionist answered as she tapped away on her keyboard.

"Oh, yeah, right. Got a lot of balls in the air. I just wanted to tell you, Griffin, how happy I am to be working with you on this. We're going to make a great movie." Drew made Griffin feel better and then hustled out.

Griffin went to his room and looked out the window overlooking Seneca Lake. He loved the water. Calming. He showered and went to get changed when he noticed his luggage was not in the room. He called downstairs, and the receptionist was baffled. She had no idea where his suitcase was. It was supposed to have been brought up to his room. *The Griffineers,* Griffin thought. One of them must have gone rogue and gotten into the hotel.

Griffin put back on his travel clothes and the newly acquired HWS outfit. He walked to town, keeping his head down. He passed the entrance to Hobart and William Smith college and realized what the HWS stood for. Students there for summer classes wandered the downtown streets. Griffin blended right in. He found a secondhand thrift store and bought some clothes that were trendy enough for Melrose but at a much lower price.

For the first time in his life, Griffin had to watch his money. He had sold the house he bought for his mom and dad to pay off the credit card debt his parents had accumulated plus the cars they had bought. So here he was, one of the most popular celebrities of his age, financially endangered, without a permanent address, and doing an indie. But he was happy. And intended to stay that way. He looked around the college town that was going to be his home for the next four weeks and smiled. There were mom-and-pop stores. Hip coffee shops. But what got his attention was the ornate movie theater. Closed down. The marquee read: SAVE OUR CINEMA. It made Griffin sad. The movies were his church, his religion. While his mom and dad would go off on their failed auditions, their neighbor whom Griffin came to call his aunt Laura was his babysitter. Aunt Laura didn't have any children, was all alone in the world, but loved movies. She would take Griffin to see everything everywhere—from the Rialto in Pasadena to the Bruin and the Fox in Westwood to the TCL Chinese Theatre in Hollywood. Griffin loved the movie palaces. Now he was looking at the gorgeous movie theater that was closed and dying. He was drawn to it, the movie magic pulling at his heart. He stepped into the street, not hearing Ivy Green honking the car horn...the car driven by the screenwriter about to hit the star of her movie!

CHAPTER 7

IVY'S RENTAL CAR JERKED TO a stop. She was shaking as she realized that she'd almost hit a college kid on Main Street. She tried to tell herself that it wouldn't have been her fault as the stupid guy was walking backward into the street as he stared up at the soon to be closed movie theater. He jumped when he realized that her car was about to collide with his body. Ivy stepped out of her car, frantic about what she might have just done.

"I am so sorry," Ivy blurted out.

"It's okay," the college guy said.

"You sure?" she queried.

"Still got all my body parts. Think I'll live."

And when the college guy laughed, Ivy thought that his chuckle seemed familiar. Perhaps too familiar. She recognized his voice. Ivy took a closer look at the guy and realized that this wasn't a Hobart and William Smith student—even though he was wearing a HWS T-shirt and covering his eyes with sunglasses. He was only trying to look like a student, but actually he was someone else... Could it be...Griffin?

She was about to blurt out his name when she stopped

herself. Was this really how she wanted to meet the actor who was starring in her movie? She wanted him to like her, not hate her. She wanted him to think of her as the esteemed screenwriter of his movie, not the lady who almost mowed him down and took his life away. Now Griffin was giving her a discerning look too. He noticed her out of state license plates on the rental car. Ivy wondered if he might be recognizing her too. But that would be impossible as there were no photos of her on the web. She was just a crazy lady who needed to pay more attention when she was driving. She smiled to herself. Relieved.

But then she remembered when Drew insisted that they upload a photo of her from Sundance onto her IMDb page, which she knew was shorthand for Internet Movie Database. Ivy had been so excited when Drew first revealed that she had her own IMDb page and that it listed *When Joseph Met Mary* in production. Her smiling face was at the top of the web page, beaming out in happiness to all who wondered who she was. She'd been so proud. Too proud. Now she cursed that photo as she wondered if Griffin had gone to the IMDb page about the movie and seen the face of the screenwriter.

Ivy's mind could go a mile a minute, like a runaway train. A honking horn pulled her out of her reverie. Traffic was building up behind Ivy's car. She looked nervously at Griffin.

"If you're okay, then I think I'd better move along."

"Yeah, before the angry driver has road rage." He laughed.

"Huh? Oh yeah, ha-ha," Ivy said. And if she'd had any doubt before about whether or not this guy was Griffin, it disappeared. Nobody talked about road rage except for Angelenos. It just wasn't something that happened in Upstate New York. This guy was definitely Griffin James.

Ivy rushed to get back in her car. She gave Griffin one last look. "As long as you're okay…" Her words lingered in the air. He was already rushing up the street, trying to avoid the small crowd that had formed around him.

Ivy closed her car door and as she drove slowly away, she was flooded with memories because they had been stopped directly in front of the old movie theater, the site of her first date with Nick back in ninth grade. It was a revival house. They'd gone to see *Notorious*, an old Hitchcock movie. Ivy's dad had raved about the movie and he'd wanted to join them, but Ivy's mom had gently put her foot down against that three-some. And so it was that Ivy had her first date with Nick. It had been a magical night. Just as Ingrid Bergman was falling in love with Cary Grant, teenage Ivy was falling for teenage Nick. Ivy's eyes welled up at the memory, and for perhaps the thousandth time in the past five years, she'd been reminded that she wasn't completely over Nick. She knew that the best way to push those thoughts aside was to call Drew, her new boyfriend. She tapped her phone.

"Call Boyfriend," she said. A robotic phone announced, "Calling Boyfriend." Ivy chuckled as she heard the phone say that, remembering how she and Drew had each changed the name in their phones to reflect their newfound relationship status. She wondered if Drew smiled when her number came up as *Girlfriend*. Drew picked up.

"Hey, girlfriend." Drew's voice emanated happiness. All at once the bad moments of the morning washed away for Ivy. She felt happy again.

"Hey, boyfriend," Ivy responded. "How's the Belhurst? You know you're staying at the swankiest place in town."

"I know. It's a castle! I got Griffin settled in. Amari is going to love it."

"Is she there yet?" Ivy asked.

"Not yet. She just texted. She made her driver pull over when she saw a farm stand. Insisted on getting some fresh corn."

"I hope she realizes that she's not going to be cooking at the Belhurst." They both laughed.

"It's good to hear your voice. I can't wait to see you. Naked. You know we haven't fooled around in a few weeks." Ivy blushed as he said these words.

"Me too, but we've got to keep it on the QT."

"You sure?" Drew countered.

"Yeah. You're the big producer. I don't want people to think that the only reason that you bought my screenplay is because I'm sleeping with you."

"Wait...that isn't the reason?" Drew laughed.

"Ha-ha. Listen, I've got to pull in this coffee shop now to get some scones for my dad. Can't go home empty-handed."

"You're such a good daughter."

"You know me so well. See you later," Ivy said as she ended the phone call.

Driving through her hometown of Geneva, waves of nostalgia flooded over Ivy. It had been five years since she'd last been home. The town looked sweeter than she'd remembered. She passed a new brewery and a new cafe. It felt good to be home again. Maybe it wasn't such a bad idea to have the movie filmed in her hometown.

Ivy parked outside Monaco Coffee, where she'd worked the summer before grad school. The place was brand new then, and she'd been their first employee. Now she stood in line along with everyone else. She could see that it had become a popular place as there were at least ten people in front of her. She took out her phone to check her emails.

Two college students were talking in front of Ivy. The co-ed leaned over to her boyfriend. "Did you hear there's a movie coming to town?" the co-ed asked.

"In the theater?" the boyfriend wondered.

"No. We're not going to watch it. They still have to film it. And they're going to do it here."

"Here? In Geneva?" The boyfriend seemed incredulous.

"Yes, it's something called *Mary Loves Joseph*." Ivy mouthed the correct title, *When Joseph Met Mary*. She pretended to text while she eavesdropped. She smiled to herself.

"I wonder why they're filming in Geneva?" the boyfriend persisted.

"It's supposed to take place in Geneva. I think the writer grew up here," the co-ed said.

Ivy smiled some more. Coming home was starting to feel better now.

"Who's in it?" the boyfriend asked.

"Griffin James. And Amari Rivers."

"Oh, she's hot."

The girlfriend did not like that response.

"Ivy? Is that really you?" a man standing next to a barista called out. Ivy looked up. One of the Monaco Coffee shop owners walked over and gave her a big bear hug.

"Josh, so good to see you!"

"Come on, you don't need to wait in line. What do you want?" Josh asked.

"A latte, and how about some scones? Are you still making those blueberry–lemon zest ones?"

"Of course. How many do you want?"

"How many you got? Four would be great," Ivy said.

"Come back here and grab them," Josh said. She walked behind the counter with him as she filled a white bakery bag with scones.

"You know you were my best employee. No one has ever matched your work ethic," Josh said loudly. The other employees laughed. "Laugh all you want—this girl could show you all a thing or two." But Josh was laughing with them.

"I was motivated. I needed to raise money for my tuition at USC," Ivy told the employees. Trying hard not to sound like she was a total geek.

"And I see that's paid off. I just read that your script is being turned into a movie. Right here in our little hometown of Geneva," Josh said.

Then the co-ed and her boyfriend looked at Ivy. Impressed. "Oh-em-gee, it's her. Can we get your autograph? And maybe a selfie?" Ivy blushed and obliged. For one millisecond she understood what it was like to be Griffin and Amari. And it didn't suck.

"Thank you, Josh. My dad will love these." Ivy beamed.

She left Monaco Coffee and got back in her rental car. She turned the corner and stopped at Don's Own Flower Shop. She could have easily walked, but LA had taught her to drive everywhere. Even one hundred yards. Ivy wanted to get her mom a nice bouquet.

Stepping into the florist triggered more memories, and she wished that she'd chosen another flower shop. As she looked at the flowers in the glass case, she remembered getting Nick's prom boutonniere there. She had been all pins and needles that day of her prom, and not just because she was excited about the dance. Up until that night, she and Nick had done everything but have sex because they'd been holding out for their prom night. And on that special night, she and Nick were going to lose their virginity together. But that wasn't the way it had happened because just a few hours before prom, she had suddenly gotten her period. At the time she was devastated. All her plans were for naught. There was no way she was going to have sex with Nick while she was menstruating. That was too gross. Of course Nick had been disappointed too. Now the memory made her smile. How young she'd been.

Ivy looked into the cooler and took out a summer bouquet. Perfect for her mom. She paid for the flowers and left the store.

Back in her car, Ivy turned the corner onto Main Street where her parents lived. She'd always loved having a Main Street address. As a kid it made her feel like she was Becky Thatcher living in a Tom Sawyer world. She pulled into the driveway of a two-story white clapboard house. It looked even better than she remembered it. After living in the brown desert of Los Angeles, the lush green foliage overwhelmed her senses. The green was so green. The gardens were even more beautiful than she remembered. The lilies, dahlias, and the hydrangeas all were blooming.

On the porch were her parents, Linda and Mitch. Ivy couldn't believe it, but they were actually hanging Christmas lights! They practically jumped off the porch to embrace her before she was barely out of the car. Ivy's parents made sixty look young. Mitch was an English professor at Hobart and William Smith, and he always said that teaching college students kept him perennially youthful. Linda owned a Christmas boutique in town—the kind that was open year-round. It was no wonder Ivy loved Christmas so much—it was baked into her DNA.

"Ivy! You're here," Mitch exclaimed.

"So good to see you!" Linda smiled. Ivy handed her mother the beautiful bouquet. Linda's face lit up. "My favorite. You remembered."

"Of course. And this is for you, Dad." Ivy handed him the bag of scones.

Mitch opened the bag of scones and immediately began eating. "These are great. Your mother has me on a low-carb diet, and I haven't had one of these in months."

"Don't get used to them," Linda joked.

Ivy loved the fact that her parents were still so in love. They were the couple to which she had always aspired. Too bad she hadn't found that special someone. *What about Drew?* she thought. *That became complicated fast. Was it work? Love?* But if she were honest with herself, she had already found that other half, her soulmate, in Nick, and she had thrown it all away.

"Hey, big sister," Carol greeted her. She was Ivy's baby sister, four years younger. Carol looked like the graduate student that she was in old jeans and a T-shirt. Ivy was dressing more upscale. She hugged Carol.

"So good to see everyone." Ivy smiled.

Linda looked at her. "I can't believe you're actually home. It's been, like, what…"

"Five years," Ivy confirmed.

"All it took was having a movie filmed in her hometown to bring her back," Carol cracked.

"It's not like I haven't seen you over the past five years," Ivy said defensively.

"Honey, it's okay. We're just happy you're home. Wait until you see all the changes we've made to the house," Mitch said.

"Great. I should get unpacked. I want to check out the production office," she said excitedly.

"Of course. Let me help you with your stuff," Mitch said as he finished the scone and licked his fingers. He opened the bag to take another one, but Linda pulled it away from him. He laughed.

Ivy walked into the house. She noticed that the old wallpaper had been removed from the dining room and the walls were now a light-blue color. The kitchen cabinets had been painted white and the kitchen looked much brighter. In fact, all the rooms looked like they'd been updated—at least slightly. But when she got to her bedroom, it was as if time had stood still. She dropped her suitcase and sat on her bed. It was the same pink bedspread from her childhood. Dance trophies on her dresser. The walls were covered with photos from high school. Ivy singing in a high school musical. She looked closer. There were too many photos of Nick taped to the walls. She grimaced. She began taking down the photos and tossing them in the trash can. Carol entered the room and made herself comfortable on the bed.

"I told Mom she should take down those old photos of Nick, but she wanted to respect your space," Carol said.

"Classic Mom. But you're right. They should have been taken down and burned up." Ivy smiled. "I hear that's the way to get rid of bad karma."

"Karma's a bitch," Carol said.

Ivy unpacked her script and laptop and put it on her childhood desk. She set up a workspace in case she needed to rewrite some scenes. Carol picked up the script. Flipped through the pages. She paused to read the ending. "Very interesting. I see you kill Nick at the end of the movie."

"It's not Nick. The character of Rick is an amalgam of everyone I dated," Ivy protested.

"Give me a break. You changed one letter. Who are we kidding, Ivy? Of course this movie is about you and Nick. Classic Freudian slip."

"Just because you're getting a master's in psych doesn't mean you can assume everything is psychological."

"Isn't it?"

The two sisters laughed, albeit a bit awkwardly. Ivy and Carol had never been as close as they should have. Ivy blamed the four-year gap in their ages. But to be honest it was probably because she'd always spent so much time with Nick. He'd been her best friend since they were eight years old. All the time she'd spent with him crowded out the bonding time she should have had with her sister. Now she felt bad about it, wishing they were better friends but thinking it was too late.

"Where's your new boyfriend? Dad said you were dating the producer," Carol probed.

"We thought it would be better if he stayed at the Belhurst Castle with the actors—in case they need anything."

"And…"

"And nothing," Ivy insisted.

"So, you're not a couple that is out in the open, because you still have some doubts," Carol psychoanalyzed.

"Darn your psych classes," Ivy said. But she was laughing. "Yeah, we decided that we would keep our relationship on the down low until the film wrapped. Don't need to confuse the crew."

"I guess this means you're finally over Nick."

"Yes, Nick broke up with me. And yes, I am over him. And yes,

I'm now dating Drew who…" Ivy stopped. She was looking out her window, and there on the sidewalk in front of her house was none other than Drew. She couldn't have been happier to see him.

She stuck her head out the window and called out, "Drew!" He looked up at her and waved. Ivy noticed that her parents were outside with him. They were all looking up at something on the roof.

Ivy twisted her head farther out the window to see what they were looking at, and she saw her. It was Vera, the indie film director, standing up on the roof over the garage. Vera was a tiny dynamo.

"I love it! So authentic!" Vera called out to Drew. She lifted the director's eyepiece that was around her neck and peered through it with a Dutch angle—which was really just a fancy word for tilted angle. "If we're going to fake Christmas in July, it might as well look real!"

Ivy called out to everyone below, "What are you all doing here?"

Drew looked up at Ivy and motioned for her to come down. She loved how his eyes twinkled with happiness when he saw her. "Vera and I were at the production office and we were going over the location photos, and I realized that I should just bring her over to see the actual house that we're filming in."

"What?" Ivy was shocked.

"Your dad said we could film inside your house," Drew said.

"I thought you were just going to film the exteriors and cheat the interiors in a studio."

"That wouldn't be authentic," Vera called out.

Ivy was starting to hate how Vera threw around the word *authentic* all the time. "I don't think my parents would like that."

"It's cool, honey. I told Drew that we wouldn't mind." Mitch smiled.

Even Linda gave Ivy a thumbs-up. "It'll be fun!" Linda grinned. Ivy couldn't remember the last time her mother had used the word *fun*. What was happening to her family? Who were these people, because she didn't recognize them! Was it really the excitement of having a movie filmed in their hometown?

"And Vera's thinking about putting me in the movie!" Mitch called out.

"What?" Ivy almost fell out of her window in shock.

CHAPTER 8

IT SEEMED LIKE ALL ANYONE in Geneva wanted to talk about was the movie. The one person who did not want to talk about the movie was Nick. The customers who were at Shepherd Winery for lunch chatted away about the coming production. Nick had to pour, smile, nod, and listen to the movie talk.

"I hear they get a forty percent tax break for filming in Upstate New York," someone said.

Nick didn't like that. Why should his taxes help pay for a movie? *Especially hers,* he thought.

"Yeah, but they're going to spend a lot of money when they're in town. We're all still coming back from Covid. This Hollywood money goes a long way," Nick heard another local at the bar chime in. Nick realized that Shepherd's was more crowded than usual for a Tuesday. There were a few locals like Yes Indeed Ed, the local car salesman. *Can you get a good price from Ed? Yes indeed.* Ed was a local celebrity. He had car dealerships all around the Finger Lakes and spoke in an over-the-top voice.

"Ed, they should put you in that movie," someone yelled.

"Yes indeed!" Everyone laughed. Ed turned to Nick. "This

is going to put Geneva on the map, Nick." Nick remembered that the customer was always right and didn't want to tell Yes Indeed Ed that Geneva was already on the map. "Isn't it great, Nick?"

"It's just a movie, Ed. Don't want these slick film people to come in and put one over on us. Breaking things, ruining people's lives, then running and hiding in LA." Was he talking about the film or Ivy? Nick said that a little too loudly. The patrons at the bar all stopped to look at him. "Enjoying the Poison Ivy?" he offered to the bar and got a lot of nods. Yes, Nick was acting weird and even he knew it. *Why?* he thought. *Why am I angry? Jealous?* This was all Ivy's fault, he wanted to scream to the crowded tasting room with packed lunch tables. He didn't have a moment to enjoy his day—this was supposed to be his time to shine. He had won wine of the year! There were banners in front. But all he could hear was the movie talk.

"I heard they might be filming at the Presbyterian church up on Main," someone else said. Of course they would. It was Nick and Ivy's church...where their story began. Ivy did this. She wrote that story. He had a suspicion it was their story. Now she came back to town to throw it in his face. Why couldn't she have filmed the movie somewhere else in Upstate New York? It's a big state. *She did this on purpose,* thought Nick, not knowing much about the movies. *Just like her to upstage me,* he thought. *I had a plan for us, but she had a different one for herself.* Nick glanced at the Governor's Cup. He was in need of a good mood boost.

"You're the owner?" a thirty-ish man asked Nick. The guy was dressed casually, but expensive casual. He seemed like he was from out of town.

"I am. Is there a problem?" Nick asked.

"Not at all. Just want to say this is one of the best-looking wineries I have ever been in. And I've been to a lot lately."

"Thank you."

"See you soon," the guy said as he and his group headed out the door. *Oh, good, they're coming back,* Nick thought. He went to clear the table when Claire, one of his regular waitresses, beat him to the table and snatched the fifty dollars.

"No, that's mine."

"Isn't that for the bill?" Nick asked.

"They paid with a card. This tip is mine."

"A fifty-dollar tip? How much did they spend?" He was incredulous.

"One hundred bucks tops. I love these film people," Claire said as she tucked away her tip.

So that explained the extra people. *Fine,* Nick thought. *Maybe it won't be that bad after all.* Like everyone else, his business had taken a hit during the pandemic. If this movie brought income, fine, so be it. He would stay in the bar, pour wine, and not once go near the movie production. That was his plan, which quickly ended as a lot of things do—with the *beep* of a text message. It was from Kenny. LOOK WHO'S BACK IN TOWN.

Nick waited for the pic to follow. The first picture came... It was someone's arm wearing a white blouse. From far away. Out of focus. Kenny was never going to be a spy. Another picture: this one of Kenny unaware he was taking a camera shot of himself. Then there was a third photo. A familiar woman with long blond hair getting into a car. Ivy never had long blond hair. Maybe she'd grown it out. *Is that Ivy?* There was another shot of the blond driving away in a rented convertible. And he saw that it was her. More texts flooded in from other friends. IVY'S AT THE BOOKSTORE. IVY'S AT THE FLOWER SHOP. IVY'S AT THE BELHURST. IVY AND SOME GUY—this was the one that got to Nick. It was the first time he saw Drew—tall and out of focus. Were they a couple? They looked like a couple.

Joe Buff, Nick's high school rival, now a local cop, chimed in with the clearest pic of Ivy and texted to Nick: IS SHE SINGLE? Joe Buff had always had a crush on Ivy. There was one time, and one time only, that Nick and Ivy had broken up in high school. Nick couldn't remember what had happened to cause the breakup, but he remembered Ivy had gone on one date with Joe Buff. To their favorite ice cream place. Nick had worked there during the off-season so he could save some money to buy his dream Silverado truck. What wasn't a dream was when Joe Buff had walked into the ice cream store with Ivy. Nick then had to scoop and serve them both. There were cordial hellos and goodbyes and the gross image of Joe Buff licking away at the cone in some weird attempt to make Nick jealous. He had quit that job the next day. It would take him a week to win Ivy back, who admitted she had only gone out with Joe Buff to make Nick jealous.

Now, Nick was way past all those high school mind games. But then—he saw the last photo, through the window of the ice cream shop, where Ivy was licking Drew's cone. Nick turned off his phone. He took a deep breath.

"Hey, Nick," Claire called out, "your sister's on the phone."

He took the phone from her and without even listening said, "Yeah, yeah, Denise. I know. Ivy's back in town. The whole world is letting me know that she is licking some dude's cone."

"As usual, baby bro, I have no idea what you are talking

about. But I think you should come over to the high school. I have to show you something."

"I'll be right there." Anything Denise asked him to do, Nick would do. No questions asked. He hopped in his truck and headed to the high school.

Denise had returned to Geneva to teach high school a few years ago. She was an arts education major and taught English and drama and worked on the school play each year. Kenny, who was Nick's age, had always had a crush on Denise. And they always got along and fit well together. Nick, Kenny, and Denise would often hang out together. One night, when Nick had been ill, Kenny and Denise went off to Canandaigua to see the rock band Journey. They had gone as friends and had returned home as a couple, hand in hand, singing "Faithfully." They had married at the winery last year.

Now Denise was turning thirty. *Maybe she's pregnant,* Nick thought. He knew they had been trying but no luck so far. Maybe that was why she was calling. That would be so great. It would be the good news he needed to hear today.

Nick parked in the principal's spot. He used to do that in high school and always got in trouble. He walked in the main entrance and toward the auditorium. Wow, school tax rates must've been higher. The school looked great. The expansive lobby had dozens of lockers next to large glass cabinets filled with memorabilia from Geneva High. He saw Joe Buff's high school jersey. Buff had led the school to the regionals and had blown out his knee. There were other faces he remembered. His eyes came upon a photo from his senior prom. Nick and Ivy were of course the king and queen. The couple everyone admired. Nick smiled as he remembered that night. The after-party was at Morrison's lake house, the lake house where everyone hung out. The one with the pier, the boats, and the extra bedrooms upstairs where he and Ivy did absolutely nothing because she'd gotten her period.

"Nick!" Denise yelled. She was walking back into the auditorium. Nick snapped out of it and followed his sister inside. She was on stage setting up a table, putting down copies of papers. Stapled script pages.

"What are you doing?"

"Setting out the sides," Denise said.

"What are sides?"

"The lines for the actors. For auditioning. I got a job." She smiled.

"You already have a job. You teach here."

"I got a job casting background extras for Ivy's movie. Isn't that great?"

Nick had no idea what a side was or a background extra—he didn't care about that. "Good luck to you. Good luck to her. I don't want to know anything about it."

"I think you should read the script."

"Why? I'm not interested."

"You will be. Sit. Read it. You can't take the pages anywhere. Pretend to be an actor. So I don't get into any trouble."

Nick sat down and started reading the script. "Fade In," Nick read out. "*EXT...*"

"That means *exterior*. That scene is going to be filmed outside. *INT* means *interior*," Denise said.

"I always thought actors made up the lines," Nick confessed, feeling a little silly at his sister's look.

"Just read!"

So Nick read. It was a page-turner. And two pages in, he knew he was right. It was about his and Ivy's life being played out from second grade on. Except this was about a guy named Rick. And Ivy was named Ilsa. As he read, he forgot he was reading and felt like he was seeing a movie—their movie—his and Ivy's love story. At one point he sniffled. They had broken up. Denise handed him a tissue. Another sniffle. Denise handed him the whole box. Nick read some more and then stopped cold.

Denise watched him go back a few pages...reread them. He finished the last page and looked up, his face a mix of shock and bewilderment.

"She killed me," Nick said.

"Yep," Denise agreed.

"In this movie, she kills me."

"Well, it's not like she murdered you. You died tragically."

"I can't believe she killed me." Nick got up with the script in hand. "Where is she?"

"I don't know, Nick. I need the script back," Denise chastised.

"After," Nick said.

"After what?"

"After I find her."

Denise reached for the script. He held on. Denise ripped it from his hand, the cover page coming off in Nick's hand. There on the cover was the address for the production office at the high school.

"She's here. In this building," he realized.

"Nick, don't go there."

"Oh, I'm going." Nick stormed out, walking through the hallways of the high school. He could see the film crew setting up offices and editing bays. Nick got to where he thought Ivy might be. The principal's office. There was a sign on the door: *Brilliant Pictures. Employees Only.*

I'm an employee, Nick thought. *I'm the guy who dies at the end of the movie.*

He burst into the principal's office. No one was there. It was empty. He heard the sound of someone using a Keurig, making coffee. He saw her from behind. Her long blond hair. Her tight-fitting leggings. Her yoga-type top. Nick had to admit Ivy still looked hot. Maybe even better than before. Was she taller? Did she grow an inch in LA? *Get out of your own way,* Nick said to his brain. He felt his anger building.

He blurted out, "How could you do this? Write about our love life? Put all of our pain and emotions on the screen for the whole world to see! And that ending? How could you do that to me!"

Then Ivy turned—but it wasn't Ivy. It was Amari. She faced Nick with a Cheshire cat smile, loving that she had the upper hand. She was checking him out, up and down. Loving all the body parts Nick showed in his tight-fitting T-shirt. "There are a lot of things I might want to do to you," Amari said, "but maybe we should get to know each other first."

"You're not Ivy."

"I'm Amari. I'm playing Ivy in the movie." Nick looked around, confused. Amari was never one to seem confused. She laser-targeted him, coming closer with her plunging neckline. "You're Nick—the guy Rick is based on."

"I guess so," he said. He felt off-balance. It was the way she was looking at him. Like she was about to unwrap the Christmas present she'd always wanted. "I'm very sorry I bothered you," Nick offered.

"I'm not. I'm an immersive actor. I want to inhabit the character I play. Ivy wrote you. I want to get to know you better, a lot better."

He was slow to answer. She was throwing him off his game. "Sure, I guess I can answer a few questions."

"Talk is cheap. I want the experience. The deep character research that gets inside of you. Show me where you two would sneak off to. Tell me when you knew it was love. You took her virginity—what was that like?"

He gulped. "Uh, sure, but right now, I'd really like to talk with Ivy."

"Nick, look at me. And not at my boobs, in my eyes."

"I wasn't."

"Look at me, and I'll tell you where she is. Don't say a word. Just look." Amari stepped closer to him. Gazing into his eyes. Nick did the same. Part of him didn't know what was going on. He was in an emotional free fall—he had gone from anger to confusion to attraction.

Attraction? He felt something in his lower region. He was awakened. Amari leaned in closer and closer. Nick forgot about emotions. His thoughts went primal. Were they about to kiss? Amari was hot. This couldn't be happening. He leaned in just a notch when—

"I have no idea where Ivy is," Amari said. Switching off the heat and going into AC mode, cooling off. Flipping it back on. "But if I see her, I'll tell her how cute you are." She winked. "See you soon, Rick—I mean Nick."

CHAPTER 9

THE NEXT MORNING, IVY RAN down the stairs of her family home like she was late for the school bus, which in some ways she was. She was heading out to scout locations. A rented minivan was idling out front, waiting for her. Ivy had overslept. She'd pulled on some shorts, grabbed a baseball hat, and yogurt from the fridge, saying a quick goodbye to her parents as she ran out. They barely looked up.

"You're late," Bruce Danton, the assistant director in charge of moving things along, said to her. Ivy apologized, but Drew and Vera and Lane, the location manager, didn't even acknowledge her, all deep in thought. Maybe Drew was upset that Ivy decided to stay with her parents and not at the Belhurst Castle. Ivy had wanted to keep their relationship professional. But she wasn't starting off very professionally. She was late for the location scout. The movie's first day of filming was the next day, and Vera wanted to review the locations.

There was another reason why Ivy hadn't wanted to stay at the Belhurst Castle, something she hadn't revealed to Drew. It was where she and Nick had thought they would spend their wedding night—if they had gotten married. Nick had suggested that when they had begun high school. Nick was always the more romantic of the two of them.

Nick! I have to get Nick out of my head. But she knew this was next to impossible.

As they drove around Geneva to give Vera the lay of the land, Ivy would gaze at the town. Every street corner had a memory of Nick. They circled back to Main Street to the scene of the crime: the Presbyterian church where she and Nick had met during the Christmas pageant. She'd never realized just how close the church was to her house. It had always felt like a mile away. Ivy wondered why the great Bruce Danton, who acted like he knew everything, didn't just have them all trek to the church on foot. It was only four blocks away from her house, an easy walking distance. *LA people,* she thought, *they will always drive the four blocks.* She paused for a moment as she realized: I'm an LA person.

The church was still beautiful but much smaller than she'd remembered. Vera loved the gothic architecture and called it "breathtaking." Drew and Lane went to talk with the minister and the church secretary to finalize the contract. Ivy soaked it all in. This was the church where she was raised. She'd loved the children's sermons with Miss Kim. She'd loved singing in the choir. She'd loved the Christmas pageant. It was where she had met Nick when they were eight years old. They had been thrown together by Miss Kim who directed the Christmas pageant. Ivy had been thrilled. Nick had grunted okay but he was nice. He had to hold her hand as they walked down the aisle. They had been adorable in the play. Ivy had been so excited she dropped the baby Jesus. Nick, the Pop Warner football star, had caught it before it hit the ground. He had held it up like Jesus was the lion king!

The damn circle of life had now brought Ivy back here. She shrugged it off. She thought of the improbability of meeting one's soulmate at that early of an age. But it had happened. She'd loved going to church, but she had stopped going—why? What was the break? Oh yeah, the break*up*. Her childhood church was where she always had her faith restored. She took a breath, smiled. Drew and Vera were walking out, saying goodbye to the minister.

"Don't worry, we're going to take real good care of this place," Drew said.

"We're not going to change a thing..." Vera added, then whispered to Bruce, "See if you can move that statue over there."

"The Jesus one?" he asked.

"Yeah, it will dominate the frame, ruin the shot. What's next?"

They got back into the van. Bruce announced, "The train station."

"Train station?" Ivy asked. "We don't have a train station in the script. What scene?"

"The reunion when Ilsa comes home from college," Drew said.

"That was at the bus stop," Ivy said.

"Trains are more cinematic," said Vera.

"I thought we wanted real," she said.

Vera took a breath. "I also want it to look really good. A bus stop in front of a smoke shop doesn't read 'Christmas.'" Drew glared at Ivy. She knew what he was saying: *Don't argue with the director.*

Ten minutes later, Ivy was outside the historic Geneva train depot with Vera, Drew, Bruce, and Lane. Vera was pacing around the station in excitement.

"But it isn't even a working train station," Ivy was still protesting.

"Seems like it's working to me. I hear a train coming," Vera said.

"I mean it's not for passenger travel. Just freight," she insisted.

"We're not making a documentary," Vera reminded her. "Even though—maybe we are…"

What did she mean by that? Ivy thought as a freight train chugged toward them. A mass of steel that was determined not to stop. Lights shone out like eyes. Vera got very excited.

"Love it!" She held up her cell phone and began filming the train. Testing out different angles. Her enthusiasm was contagious. Even Ivy started to feel it.

"You're right. It is perfect," she admitted.

"And authentic!" Drew said. He was standing next to a historical placard on the wall of the station. He read: "When the Lehigh Valley Railroad expanded its line to Buffalo in the 1890s, Geneva was chosen as the place for the railroad's largest, most ornate station between New York City and Buffalo."

"I love the Romanesque Revival red brick. Look at the leaded glass windows, fanciful roof with several peaks, valleys, and miniature towers and dormers," Vera enthused. Ivy and Drew looked impressed. Vera just shrugged. "Art history major at Bard. If I didn't make it as a director, I was going to work at a museum."

"I'll see if there's someone I can talk to about getting permission to film here," Lane said.

"Great! And get me the train schedule so we know what times the trains pass during the day. I want to make sure we're filming when the train roars past!" Vera yelled over the train whistle blowing in the distance. They all got back in the van and went on the winery scout.

Ivy smiled. As the writer, she knew it was a privilege to be on the set. She wanted to be in Vera's good graces and not cause trouble. She also wanted her movie to be a hit. But after Bruce announced, "I have a list of thirteen wineries to look at," Ivy couldn't help interrupting again.

"Can I see the list?" Ivy asked. She had a pit in her stomach, hoping Nick's winery wouldn't be on it. Drew handed over the list of possible winery locations. And there it was, number thirteen— Shepherd Winery. Ivy blanched. She needed to convince them to use a different winery before they arrived at number thirteen.

Ivy read the list out loud. "Peters Winery. That might work. They're a small place that would probably let us use it because my sister used to babysit the owner's kids when she was in high school." Ivy continued to look down the list. "Curtis Winery is really nice too. Owned by a Syracuse couple. They have some great ice wines." But as they visited each winery on the list, nothing was pleasing to Vera or Drew. They didn't even stop in at numbers six through eight. When they got to number ten, Ivy was getting more and more anxious. They were getting closer to the unlucky number thirteen: Shepherd Winery. Nick's winery. Ivy started pushing back, irritating Vera. She even started suggesting the staging of a shot. The director's job. Not the writer's.

Drew pulled her aside. "What are you doing, Ivy?"

"We passed so many good wineries. Curtis was great. SabAva had outdoor seating," Ivy told him.

"You want to keep things professional, keep it professional. You are the writer. Vera is the director. It is not your job to choose a location. Do you want to get kicked off the set of your own movie a day before it begins filming?"

Ivy didn't like what Drew was saying, but she didn't disagree with him.

They all got back into the van. Lane took out his list and punched in the address for Shepherd Winery in the GPS. Drew noticed that Ivy was tense. "Don't worry, Ivy. We'll find a location." Drew had no idea what was really bothering Ivy, and she certainly wasn't going to tell him.

They drove in silence for a few minutes. Up ahead they saw...a large sign for Shepherd Winery that pointed toward the lake. It was like a beacon guiding them in the right direction. It was also the best-looking winery sign they'd seen. Beautifully painted. Great logo. Ivy felt her stomach doing somersaults. She wanted to throw up. They turned onto the long drive-way toward the water. As they got closer to the winery Vera squealed, "I love it!"

Ivy was stunned. This wasn't the Shepherd Winery that she remembered. It was so much grander. And yet in spite of its size, it had retained its mom-and-pop charm.

"This is it! It's so authentic! I've got to film here!" Vera yelled excitedly.

"We haven't even been inside," Ivy said.

"I like how it's set back from the road. Not going to have any sound issues," Drew said.

"And there's plenty of parking for our trucks," Bruce added.

"And it's on the lake. It's perfect!" Lane said.

Ivy didn't say a word.

"Have you ever been here before?" Drew wondered.

"A few times," Ivy said, which was such a lie. She'd gone to the old Shepherd Winery almost every day after school during her senior year.

"Because the girl on that banner looks a lot like you and she has your name," Drew said as he looked at her oddly.

Ivy looked up. How did she miss it? Maybe she was too busy looking for Nick. Hanging from the eaves of the winery was a giant banner for "Poison Ivy—winner of the Governor's Cup."

The group pushed the heavy oak door and walked inside. There was a table filled with Poison Ivy cab franc wine bottles. Ivy recoiled when she looked closely at the label as she recognized the woman's face that was covered by ivy vines. It looked like her! Since when had she given permission to be the face of a wine that was derogatory to her name? Around the wine bottles were Poison Ivy T-shirts, coasters, and bar towels. Ivy was horrified. Her face was on all of them. She was furious.

Vera looked at Ivy, curious. "What's going on here? Is this you?"

Things got worse when *he* walked in. Nick was wearing jeans and a tight black T-shirt. Ivy wondered when he'd gotten so buff. His arm muscles were sculpted, and his chest was expanded. She couldn't see his stomach, but she had a feeling that he had one of those "six-packs" as it looked concave and his shirt tucked easily into his slim-cut pants. She hated to admit it, but he still looked good. Too good. A bit older and more weathered but still sexy. She pushed those feelings down deep and focused on her anger. She was determined that this was not going to be a happy reunion. She called out to Nick. Everyone in the bar was suddenly watching them. Except for Drew and Vera, who had wandered into another room.

"Poison Ivy? Really? What did I ever do to you?" Ivy asked Nick.

He looked startled to see her. Even though he knew that Ivy was in town, he still wasn't ready for this moment. He searched for the right thing to say and stumbled with: "It's a cab franc. Just won wine of the year at the New York Wine Classic." What an idiot he sounded like, and he knew it.

"So it says on the banner. I do know how to read," Ivy said in an icy voice.

"Good for you," Nick returned. And before he knew it, things got ugly. He had meant to be all zen, and this certainly wasn't the calm demeanor he'd wanted to project when he first saw Ivy again.

"Last that I remember, I never gave you permission to use my face on your wine bottle."

"It's a facsimile. And last that I remember, I didn't allow you to kill me off in a snowmobile accident in your movie. How long did you spend thinking about that one?"

"It's called art," Ivy said.

"I'd call it my life." Nick glared at her.

"It's not autobiographical."

He laughed out loud. A crowd was gathering around them. Everyone wanted to see what would happen next. Ivy glared at them, about to say something when she noticed that Vera and Drew had returned from the other room. They were oblivious to what had just transpired between her and Nick.

"Are you the owner? This is an amazing winery," Vera said.

"Thanks." Nick smiled.

"That's Vera. Our director," Ivy told him.

Vera gave Nick a *namaste* greeting. Ever since Covid, she had stopped shaking hands with people. "Nice to meet you."

"Likewise," Nick said. "Are you here for a tasting?"

"That's a great idea. I bet you have amazing wine. But we're also location scouting. And I'm really hoping that you'll consider letting us film here. This is perfect for our movie," Vera told him.

Nick didn't even have to think about it. There was no way in hell he was going to let them film in his winery. Especially since Ivy killed him off in their movie. "Sorry, but we don't allow filming here. This is a working winery."

"Hi, I'm Drew. The producer. And before you say no again, please know that of course you'll be compensated."

"Sorry. The answer's still no. Your money's no good here." Nick laughed.

Drew pulled Ivy aside. "What's the deal with this Nick guy? Why's he being such a dick?" He saw it all over her face. "Oh... so this is Rick. Why didn't you say so?"

"There's nothing to say. Everything with Nick is in the past," Ivy said, trying to convince him. She knew that guys could hate being around a girlfriend's ex-boyfriend. "He means nothing to me," she insisted.

"No worries," Drew said. "I just really want this winery for filming. Vera's set on it. Let me see what I can do." He swaggered back to Nick. "Nick, let's talk business. What can I do to make this happen? We'll pay you well for the location. And I might even be able to put you in the movie."

"Yeah," Nick said, poker-faced, "that's not going to happen. Besides, I'm already in the movie. I'm the guy who dies at the end." He walked away. He was good at walking away, Ivy thought. And this time he did it with a pretty good exit line.

Drew and Vera stared at her.

"What?" Ivy said.

"Fix this!"

She walked outside, hoping to find Nick in the vineyard, but he was nowhere in sight. She was upset. Why was Nick being so mean to her? After all, *he* was the one who dumped her. Yes, she killed him in the script, but in real life, he murdered her heart. And now he was refusing to let them use his winery as a location? She felt horrible. If she couldn't get the winery, Vera would be furious with her. Ivy wondered if she could emotionally survive the filming of her story. She walked to the edge of the property and looked out at the shimmering lake. It was stunning that day. She found herself tearing up as happy memories of her childhood flooded back. Kayaking, paddle-boarding, and going out on the occasional motorboat. She'd forgotten how beautiful it was on the lake. Lost in thought. A voice called out to her. A familiar voice.

"Ivy? Ivy? Is that you?" a woman's voice called out.

Ivy turned to see Nick's mom, Frannie, walking toward her. She quickly wiped the tears off her face and put on a forced smile. "Mrs. Shepherd!" Ivy wondered if Nick had told his mom the true story of their breakup.

"Oh, you don't need to call me Mrs. Shepherd anymore. Call me Frannie. It's so good to see you, Ivy." Frannie stopped in front of Ivy and lifted her arms in greeting. Ivy wasn't sure if Frannie wanted her to lean in for a hug or not. For an awkward moment, she hesitated. She decided that she'd waited too long. A hug wasn't going to happen.

"You too, Frannie." She smiled.

"We've missed seeing you around here," Frannie said.

"I've missed this place too."

"Congratulations on the movie. Everyone in Geneva is really excited. Thanks to you, business will boom this summer," Frannie told Ivy.

"Thank you. And that's kind of why we're here. At Shepherd's. We were really hoping that we could use the winery as a location for filming," Ivy explained. She wasn't optimistic and assumed Frannie would agree with Nick and say no. Which was why she was so surprised when Frannie said—

"That's wonderful!" Frannie was beaming. She actually looked thrilled by the idea.

"I'm glad you think so, but Nick said he won't let us use it."

"Oh, that's ridiculous. There's no downside for us. A great free advertisement that we can use for years. I can see the busloads of people stopping by—just to see the location where *Mary and Joseph* was filmed."

"*When Joseph Met...*" Ivy started to correct Frannie but then stopped. "I'm glad you love the idea, but what about Nick?"

"Well, I am the co-owner. And I think it's a terrific idea. I'll talk to Nick." Frannie smiled.

"Oh, Mrs. Shep—I mean Frannie, that would be so great," Ivy gushed as she finally leaned in for that hug. She had forgotten how wonderful Nick's mom was. Back in college, when she used to think that she'd get married to Nick, her friends would tell her how lucky she was going to be to have a mother-in-law like Frannie.

As the hug ended, Frannie said, "I am really sorry about what happened. You know that Nick can be an idiot at times." Ivy suddenly knew that Nick had told his mother the truth. At least he'd done that.

Back at the van, Ivy climbed in with Drew, Vera, Lane, and Bruce. Everyone looked at her expectantly.

"So, did you get it?" Vera asked.

"I'm working on it," Ivy said.

"Did you talk to Nick?" Vera wondered.

"I talked with his mother. She's the co-owner."

Vera smiled and high-fived Ivy. "Great idea! We won't shoot the winery location for a few days. See what you can do."

Drew smiled broadly. Pleased. And Ivy realized that he wasn't jealous of Nick. In fact, he didn't care about Nick at all. All he really cared about was getting the right location. But at that moment, it didn't really matter to Ivy because tomorrow her movie was going to start filming, and she was ecstatic!

CHAPTER 10

IT WASN'T CLOSE TO CHRISTMAS morning, but it sure felt like it to Ivy. When she was five years old, she woke up before anyone else in the house and ran down the stairs looking to see if Santa had brought her presents. She looked at all the gifts under the Christmas tree and opened every one of them believing they were all for her. She didn't understand why Santa would bring her a cordless drill, but she didn't care. Santa had come to her house, and that was all that mattered. Now, today, she had that same joyous feeling. This wasn't Santa, this wasn't even Christmas—but it was the first day of production of her Christmas movie.

She had spent last night with her family talking about the movie. They had always been supportive and were incredibly proud. Her dad was already trying to figure out how to fly her back to Geneva for a weekend seminar teaching screenwriting. As they were getting ready for bed, the doorbell rang at midnight. It was a delivery man with a basket for Ivy. It was from her agent. The basket was Christmas themed, filled with Christmas earrings, candy canes, and designer chocolates. Even her mom was impressed with the goodies inside.

Ivy read the note from Charlotte. *Congratulations, Merry Christmas. Check your bank account.* Ivy did that just before she went to bed. There was a new deposit. From Brilliant Pictures, LLC for the purchase price of the script. Ivy knew that scripts were optioned until the first day of production, at which point they were officially purchased. That was when the writers got a big payday. It was more money than she had ever seen in her account. She thought it might be an error. She called Charlotte. It was only 9:00 p.m. in LA.

Charlotte told her, "That money is all yours, darling. I built an escalator clause into your back end. The bigger the movie gets, the more money you get. And there's more coming. A hundred-thousand-dollar production bonus when shooting wraps. My phone has been blowing up. A lot of people back here want to meet you. Come home soon!"

Home? Ivy was home... *Wait,* Ivy thought. *Home is LA.* This was a visit. It was a coincidence that the movie was shooting here. She could easily have been in Canada. This visit to Geneva was going as well as it could considering the Nick factor, or dick factor as she'd told her sister. "Nick is being a dick. He won't let us shoot in the winery."

Get out of my head, Nick Shepherd, she said to herself. *Let it go. Either Frannie will convince Nick to let them film at Shepherd Winery or Drew will figure things out. He'll find another location to film. He's the producer. That's his job.* Technically writers rarely went to the set of their movies. Something which Ivy felt was odd and pushed for in her contract. Total access. Her agent stated she liked this about Ivy...liked how Ivy talked about maybe directing someday. She slept very well the night before the filming began.

The next morning, a production assistant (P.A.) drove Ivy to the set. As they approached the train station, Ivy saw the signs: *WJMM* with arrows. *When Joseph Met Mary.* (*Yes,* she said to herself, *change the title.*) The signs were posted for the cast and crew, to help them find the day's location. But in this case, Ivy wondered how anyone could miss it. Behind the hustle and bustle of the film trucks was the historic train station. The art department had spent all night dressing it up. The station had been transformed to look like a working station for the Amtrak Empire Service Line from New York City. Gaffers and best boys were securing lights and laying cable. Sheets of snow were on the roof of the terminal. And Christmas trees (fake) lined the platform, where extras came dressed in their winter clothes. Hats, scarves, and earmuffs were all around. Decorations abounded. The lampposts were wrapped up to look like candy canes. Fake snow covered the ground and the trees. The train station which hadn't been used for passengers in decades was ready for its Christmas close-up.

"It's beginning to look a lot like Christmas," Ivy said out loud to the production assistant. It was Christmas in July. But it felt and looked like the real thing. Ivy jumped from the car and practically skipped onto the set. Produced screenwriters had told her that the greatest feeling a screenwriter could have was walking onto the set of your own movie. There was Vera, talking with her director of photography, who was responsible for what the camera would capture. She and Vera wanted this to feel like an old-time movie. Vera had argued with Drew to shoot in black and white with an aspect ratio of 1.33 to make it look like an old classic, pre-1950. Drew quickly rejected that idea. But Ivy had been intrigued.

Ivy saw Denise, Nick's sister. She had not seen her since just before the breakup. Ivy had anticipated seeing her. She knew Drew had hired the local high school drama teacher to help with the background casting. That is, the extras who would fill the frame, the shot, and make it look like the town was bustling and filled with Christmas shoppers. When Ivy used to come over to Nick's house to watch a movie, he would always fall asleep. She and Denise would stay up watching old movies. Ivy approached Denise, a little nervous. Suddenly, the movie went to the back of her mind, and front and center was the thought *Denise was almost my sister-in-law*. In fact, during one summer, they called each other "Sis." They were that close. Denise had been rooting for Nick and Ivy to make it as a couple.

"Hello, Ivy."

"Hi, Denise."

"Congratulations on the movie," Denise said. It was like a poker game. No one was showing their cards.

"Thanks. You too. The extras all look great. I wanted to explain—"

"Nothing to explain. My brother was a jerk to you. I was so angry about what he did. I missed you, Ivy," Denise said.

"I missed you too," Ivy said as they hugged. And that was it. Denise was on her side.

"Welcome home. Gotta run. It looks like some of the actors are getting too into their parts," Denise said as she ran over to a couple carrying their luggage. They were dressed in Hawaiian shirts. They tried to explain to Denise that their characters had just returned from an island honeymoon. Denise sent them to the wardrobe department to change.

Ivy walked over to Vera to say hello, but Vera was busy, deep in directing mode. "Ivy, stand to the side. We're working here." Ivy knew that all of her work was done. She was staying on the set with her producer credit, and in case she needed to fix any lines in the script or was needed for script changes. She also hoped that she could watch the completed footage at the end of the day. The smell of food wafted in the air. Ivy followed it. A very good-looking chef manned the craft services table. He had salt-and-pepper hair. He smiled at Ivy and with a very thick French accent said, "*Bonjour.*"

Her movie mind flashed to Disney's *Ratatouille*. "Are you making cappuccinos?" Ivy asked.

"Cappuccino, no. *Café crème*, yes," the French chef said as he handed her a drink that looked just like a cappuccino. *Oh, the French,* Ivy thought.

"You're craft services?"

"I am. I am J. B. Nadal. I prefer on-set chef."

The *café crème* was so good. And the pastries looked divine. She felt herself gaining a pound just by looking at them.

"There you are!" Amari called out. Ivy turned and immediately recognized the blouse Amari was wearing. It was exactly like one she used to wear. It was last seen way in the back of her closet. *She looks just like me,* Ivy thought.

"Oh my God, that shirt. I had one just like that," she said.

"You still do. This is it. I stopped by your house yesterday, and your mother showed me your closet. I borrowed a few things. I hope that's okay. Vera wanted to keep it real," Amari said as she twirled. It was Ivy who was twirling—inside her head, at least. Amari had gone to her house and went through her clothes with her mother. What was that about? Ivy worried: *What else did she find?*

The answer came quickly: "Oh, and I met Nick the other

day," Amari offered. "Girl, he owns a winery. The dude's got arms like tree trunks. He is hot. I can see why you dated him. How could you ever break up with a guy that hot?"

Ivy was getting agitated. Was it embarrassment? Anger? Jealousy? "I didn't break up with him. He dumped me," she said coolly.

"Oh, that makes a lot more sense." Amari smiled. Ivy's mind was racing to find the perfect comeback line. But like any writer, she knew that line would not come to her until later that night. She just stared at Amari, until Bruce called everyone together. Vera wanted to talk to the cast and crew. She had them huddle up. The huddle formed, and Ivy was late to the arm lock. Denise noticed and had her squeeze in.

"I want this to be real," Vera said. "Really real. Slice of life. We're going to be on sticks, off sticks. We'll shoot rehearsals. We'll do what it takes for as long as it takes to get the shots we need. Film is life. Now, let's make a movie." Everyone cheered. Ivy smiled. She settled in at the video village with Drew. It was where key personnel would sit on director's chairs and watch the scene on video as it played out. Ivy had learned in film school that video playback while filming had been created by none other than Jerry Lewis.

"Pretty exciting," Drew said. "I got a good feeling about this one. Great director. Great actors. And great production designer." Drew didn't mention the script. He was going over things with his assistant and was in work mode. Ivy knew not to bother him.

"Cue the smoke!" Bruce called. Ivy sat back and put on her headphones and watched the movie she had written come to life. The scene about to be filmed was near the midpoint of the movie. The midpoint was the middle of the story. It usually hinted at the ending. It was like an intermission in a Broadway musical. A big emotional moment. Ivy remembered coming back from college after her first year and how it was so emotional for her to reunite with Nick. Bruce screamed, "Quiet on the set. Places. Roll sound. Roll camera!"

"Action!" Vera said as she pointed at the actors like it was a *go* signal. The background extras milled out, all dressed for winter. Amari, playing Ilsa, was looking for Rick. He wasn't to be seen. There was a burst of steam from the train which obscured the end of the station. Through the steam Rick was to emerge and see Ilsa. Ivy watched intently as emerging from the fog/steam was—the real Nick. Not Rick. Not Griffin playing Rick. Nick Shepherd walking into the shot, very confused. It took a while to recognize him in the fog, but Ivy knew it was him. What the hell was he doing ruining the first shot of her movie?

Ivy yelled out, "*Cut!*"

Everyone stopped. Looked over at her. Vera glared at her. "I don't know what they teach you at USC, but at NYU the only person who yells cut is the director, and that's me!"

"That's not Rick, I mean Griffin," Ivy said. By now, all eyes were on the real Nick standing confused, admiring the train.

Amari ran over and hugged him. "Nick! You made it! Great to see you again," she gushed. Ivy watched as Amari gave Nick a very long hug. Amari was proving that she was indeed a hugger. *But why is she hugging Nick? He doesn't seem to mind. Where did they meet?* Ivy wondered.

Drew saw Griffin approaching the set with a ham-and-cheese croissant in his hand.

"Griffin, where were you?" Vera asked.

"Oh damn, did we start? So sorry. J. B. was getting me a ham-and-Brie croissant. The caterer is off the rails!"

Drew escorted Griffin to the set as Bruce brought Nick to Ivy. There was a small exchange of recognition between the fake Nick and the real Nick. The real Nick was dropped off right next to Ivy in video village. He smiled. She glared.

"What are you doing here?" Ivy asked.

Nick was in a good mood. He joked, "Is this the part where you kill me?"

"I would have invited you to that scene. How do you know Amari?"

"We met yesterday. She's super friendly."

Ivy put on her headphones to hear the scene as it played out. Nick did the same.

Bruce screamed, "Quiet on the set! Places! Everyone back to one!" Everyone moved back into position. It was like watching time go in reverse. The actors and extras returned to their marks—small pieces of tape unseen on the ground. "Roll sound. Roll camera!" Bruce yelled out.

"Action," Vera said with her signature pointing at the actors. Griffin emerged from the steam. He rushed toward Amari, and they embraced. There was suddenly a giant scream of delight from thirty or so Griffineers. They must have had Griffin radar. They had found him. Vera called, "Cut!" and told Drew to do something.

Drew had made sure the town's sheriff would be on set the first day. "Sheriff Peters, can you tell them to vacate?"

"I can't do that. They're allowed to be here," Sheriff Peters explained. He was also eating a ham-and-cheese croissant. Drew wondered how much over budget they might go on the food.

"You have to get them to leave," he said.

"They have cameras on their phones. I'm up for reelection. Sorry."

Drew wanted to rip the croissant out of the sheriff's mouth. The Griffineers were now chanting "We want Griffin." Griffin nodded to Vera and walked over to his fans.

"Hi, thanks for coming out," he said. They cheered. "We would love to have you stay and watch, but it's not helping us with the filming if you scream." They screamed again. "So how about this, you stay quiet, very quiet. And I will take a picture with each of you during my break." The Griffineers nodded with silent smiles.

Griffin walked back to the set and pulled Drew aside. Griffin was still "miked up," which meant he was wearing a microphone. Anyone with headphones could hear what he had to say, including Ivy and Nick. Drew offered a thank-you to Griffin, but the young actor would have none of it. He cared about his career and took his job seriously. "Drew, you're the producer, take care of this. This can't happen every day. Find the person who leaked the production schedule and fire them!" Griffin walked away. Drew looked around, all eyes on him. Slightly embarrassed. Ivy had been on enough student films to know how important good chemistry was on a film shoot. So far day one of filming was highly combustible.

"Did you hear that?" Nick said excitedly. "The guy playing me just bitch-slapped that dude. Who is that?"

"That's my boyfriend," Ivy blurted out. She meant to say that Drew was the producer. But she hoped *boyfriend* had carried more weight. Nick laughed again.

"Why are you even here, Nick?" she demanded. "You already ruined the first shot of the movie."

"I came to tell you that you can film in the winery," Nick said, without even looking at her. His eyes had found something else. Amari.

"Really?" Ivy said.

"What's past is past. Oh, and you can have it at no charge," he said, still distracted. Ivy was too happy to notice what had caught his attention. "Thank my mom. She always liked you better than she liked me."

"She did." Ivy smiled.

"Quiet on set! Scene sixty. Take three!" Bruce called out. They were going to try to film the scene again. The reunion. They watched as Griffin went to kiss Amari, who were playing Rick and Ilsa, who were really Nick and Ivy. The snow machine that was secured to scaffolding high above the set did not work. "Cut!"

"Wasn't this at the bus stop?" Nick asked Ivy.

"We changed it. Trains look better."

Someone shushed them. "Take four!" was heard. This time Ivy and Nick watched Amari and Griffin kiss. Ivy remembered how important that kiss was. They both had been so nervous being apart for close to a year. They had agreed not to see other people. That had been easy. They had both been busy with their studies. And, as in the script, Ivy and Nick had been a little nervous about their reunion. The kiss was going to be their test. Ivy had told Nick, "When we kiss, if all our memories and magic swirl around us—past, present, and future—and we feel like we're the only people in the world, without a care, then we'll know that we are meant to be together."

That real kiss had been extraordinary. The one Ivy watched on the video assist looked pretty good too. She wondered if she kissed Nick now, would all those feelings flood back into her? *No, no, no. Get out of your own way,* she yelled at herself, internally of course. That was then. This was now, and there was no going back...was there?

"What did you think?" Ivy asked.

"Pretty good. I liked it better at the bus station. That felt more real." Nick hopped off the chair. "Gotta get to work. Have your boyfriend call me about the winery." He walked away.

Vera yelled, "Cut!"

Bruce yelled out, "Moving on!"

Ivy wondered: Was she moving on? Or was she still stuck emotionally in Geneva, New York?

CHAPTER 11

IVY WAS EXHAUSTED. THE FIRST day of filming was over. They were in the auditorium of the high school, which now served as the screening room for the production. They were looking at the day's footage, also known as the "dailies." Vera and Ivy watched intently while Drew texted on his phone. What Ivy really wanted was to go home and collapse in her childhood bed and sleep for about ten hours. But she also needed to prove to Drew and Vera that it was valuable to have her around.

The first day of shooting had dragged on, no thanks to those crazy Griffineers. Ivy hadn't realized that Griffin was such a teen heartthrob. During college, she didn't own a TV for a while and completely missed all the new shows, including the one that Griffin was on. And she also never watched *Entertainment Tonight* or those other gossip shows like *TMZ*. She preferred to read her news. Deadline and *Variety* were her go-to sites.

"Can I see that scene again?" Vera called out. They rewatched the master shot of Amari waiting for Griffin at the train station. Amari, playing Ilsa, paced back and forth. Griffin, playing Rick, walked through the fog to meet her. Ivy had rewritten the scene to reflect Rick's lateness since they couldn't actually show Ilsa stepping off the train. Ivy watched as Amari jumped into Griffin's arms. She winced as she remembered watching Amari hugging Nick hello in a similar manner. The scene ended.

Vera turned to Drew. "What do you think?"

"I think it's good," he said. But he was more focused on his phone.

"Ivy? What do you think?" she asked.

Ivy suddenly felt insecure. Not sure if she should echo Drew's practically monosyllabic comment. Should she tell Vera what she really thought, or what she thought Vera wanted to hear? "Ilsa is not into PDA. She's more private. But Amari was all over Griffin. She was really too big in this scene," she said quickly before she lost her nerve to reveal her true feelings.

Vera looked at Ivy. For a moment, Ivy was sure that she was getting kicked out of the auditorium. But then Vera smiled. "I agree. Too flirty. We're not making a soap opera." She glared at Drew.

"Uh, yeah, I agree. Of course," he added absentmindedly.

"Really insightful note, Ivy. I knew it was going to be a good idea to have the writer on set." Vera glared at Drew again. And what Ivy didn't know was that Drew had a secret. He hadn't really wanted to have her on the set for the entire film. It cost him more money. Vera was the one who'd convinced him.

Ivy smiled at Vera. "Thank you. I appreciate that." But Ivy also had her own secret. She was starting to not like Amari—and not because of her acting. She didn't like the way that Amari seemed to be all over Nick. Flirting all the time. And maybe she wasn't objecting so much to the acting on screen but what was happening off-screen.

"Okay, kids. That's it for me. I've got to run." Vera opened up her backpack and took out her running shoes. She laced them up. She was literally going to go running. Drew and Ivy looked at her in surprise. They'd already put in a twelve-hour day, filming and watching the dailies. "Don't look so surprised." Vera laughed. "One of the best things I learned in film school was to always stay in shape during production. Gives you energy throughout the day." She grabbed her keys and ran out the door.

Drew and Ivy were suddenly alone together for the first time in days. Ever since they'd arrived in Geneva, there'd been a whirlwind of activity. Ivy had almost forgotten that she and Drew were dating. They hadn't had sex together in two weeks, which was quite a stretch for them. She suddenly wanted to spend some time with him.

"Any plans for tonight?" she asked.

"Uh, yeah."

"Oh." Ivy was disappointed.

"And I'm actually kinda late. So I'd better get going. Come on, I've got to lock up," Drew said impatiently.

"I was hoping that you could come over," she said sadly.

"Maybe another night," he said.

Drew held open the door, and they both walked out of the high school. "See you tomorrow," she said. But Drew had already rushed off and didn't seem to hear her. Ivy wondered why he was acting so mysteriously. Was she going to lose *another* boyfriend?

Ivy's phone rang. It was her mom. "Hi, sweetie. Can you pick up some blueberries for me at the market? I want to add them to the salad."

"Sure," Ivy said, when in truth all she wanted was to go home and relax. And figure out why Drew was blowing her off.

Fifteen minutes later, Ivy was pulling into her driveway. She was still marveling at how easy it was to get around town. Unlike LA, there was no traffic! If she'd gone to the market in LA, it would have taken her at least forty-five minutes. Ivy stepped out of her car and noticed an unfamiliar car in the driveway. Her parents must have invited someone else over, or maybe Carol had a new boyfriend.

She walked into a dark house, and suddenly the lights flashed on and there was a loud "SURPRISE!" Ivy was stunned! She looked around to see her living room filled with her family and neighbors. The room was in the midst of getting decorated for Christmas! The fake tree was in its usual spot, loaded with white lights and homemade ornaments. Christmas-themed pillows were thrown on the couch. A giant wooden nutcracker welcomed everyone at the entrance.

"Wow! I didn't expect this!" Ivy exclaimed.

Mitch stepped over and hugged her. "All the neighbors wanted to come over to say hi and to see the house decorated for Christmas in July."

Ivy looked around the room. There were Jim and Candy, the next-door neighbors. She used to babysit for their kids. And there were Collin and Sue, who lived down the block. Ivy used to ski with their kids. Her childhood friends, Kathy and Lauren, were talking and drinking at the punch bowl. She hadn't seen them much since high school. It was amazing how none of them had moved away.

Ivy saw Wyck, the production designer, waving his staple gun with one hand and a cup of red holiday punch in another hand. He was stapling garlands around the windows and adding colorful red balls. There were white Christmas lights everywhere. "Hi, Wyck. This all looks amazing." She beamed.

"Thanks. Your parents are so cool," Wyck said as he gulped the rest of his punch. Linda rushed over with a pitcher and refilled his drink. "Thanks, Linda."

"We wanted to celebrate your first day of filming on your movie!" Linda told Ivy happily. Ivy also knew that her mother would use any excuse to throw a party. She could still remember the Groundhog Day party her mother threw for her back in fourth grade.

"Mom, I love it, but you know we have an eight a.m. call tomorrow. I'm working," Ivy said.

"Well, I guess I should go home then!" said a familiar voice. Ivy turned to see Drew. He'd never looked so good to her. She was thrilled to see him. She ran over and hugged him.

"Other plans, huh? So this is what you were actually doing. Coming to my house! You jerk!" Ivy joked.

"I wanted to surprise you."

"I do love a surprise," she said.

"He's the producer of the movie," Mitch told Jim, the next-door neighbor.

"Oh, the guy with the money," Jim said.

"I wish I had the money!" Drew said, and everyone laughed. "I am just the one who found the people with the money to make this movie." Ivy looked lovingly at him. He really was great in these party situations. "What's a guy gotta do to get a drink around here?"

"We'll get it for you. Come with me, Ivy," Linda said and winked at Drew. Ivy followed her mother into the kitchen and the swinging doors closed behind them. "So, what's going on with the producer? He is hot!" Linda said as she started to make a mistletoe martini.

"Mom!"

"Just sayin' you could do a lot worse," she said.

And I have, his name was Nick, Ivy thought. "Well, if you must know, we are kind of seeing each other," she revealed.

"I knew it! I told your father that I thought something was going on between you two when Drew was over here for the location scout."

"Oh no. Was it obvious?"

"Yes. I mean, maybe not. I'm just observant. I noticed that he couldn't take his eyes off you. And that's always a sign," Linda said.

"That's actually kind of nice to know, it's just that..."

"Look, Ivy, it's okay to move on from Nick."

"Mom, I am definitely over Nick. But for now, Drew and I are trying to keep our relationship kinda under wraps—especially from the crew." Linda looked at Ivy, surprised. "So please don't say anything to the production designer."

"I have no idea who you're talking about," Linda said, playing along.

"You know—Wyck—the guy who is staple-gunning everything in your living room."

"Oh, honey, I know who you're talking about. I was just trying to show you how I'm going to keep your relationship with Drew a secret," her mom explained. "Speaking of Drew, you'd better get this mistletoe martini out to him before he dies from thirst."

"Thanks, Mom."

"Maybe you could accidentally give him that drink under the mistletoe."

"Mom!"

Ivy returned to the living room and found Drew surrounded by the neighbors, charming everyone with his great stories about Hollywood. She handed Drew his drink, and he sipped.

"Wow! This is fantastic. I love Christmas in July," he exclaimed.

"Ivy, you missed some great stories. Drew was telling us about the time he went to Sundance and ended up on the chairlift with Kristen Stewart," Mitch said enthusiastically.

Ivy just smiled because she'd heard this story at least four times before.

"Did you meet Robert Redford?" asked Sue, their neighbor from down the street.

"Yeah, I worked with him on a movie," Drew said.

"Was he nice?"

"Actually, he was."

"I bet he was cute, too!"

"I've got a question for you..." Everyone turned to look at Ivy's sister, Carol, as she asked, "How come so many assholes go into the film business?"

Drew looked at Carol, completely caught off guard. "Ha-ha," was all that the usually loquacious man could muster.

"Don't mind her. That's my sister, Carol. She's getting her master's in psych. Probably just asking that question for a paper she's writing." Ivy grinned.

Now it was Carol's turn to say *ha-ha* and walk away.

"Your sister's tough," Drew said to Ivy.

"Bacon-wrapped date?" Linda asked him.

"Oh, no thanks, Linda."

"What about some baked Brie? It's delicious with this cranberry topping."

"Oh, thank you, but no," Drew said.

"We also have some mini turkey sandwiches."

"Drew's a vegan, Mom."

"Oh, I'm sorry. I guess that's why you haven't eaten anything."

"No worries. I'm all good. We have a great caterer on the set. I'm trying not to gain any weight." Drew pinched his stomach, but there was absolutely no fat there. "And without my Peloton, it's not going to be easy." Drew actually looked worried, which Ivy thought was ridiculous. He didn't have a fat cell in his entire body.

Kathy and Lauren, her childhood friends, had been hovering behind Ivy, hoping to talk with her. She turned and hugged them hello. "I guess you're a celebrity now," Lauren joked. But it had a ring of truth, as everyone at the party was waiting to talk with Ivy.

"Ha-ha. No. I'm just the writer." Ivy smiled.

"This is all so cool. You have a movie!" Kathy gushed. "And LA—what's that like? Living there? I bet it's amazing."

"It is. I see celebrities every week," Ivy said jokingly. But Kathy and Lauren took her seriously.

"Really? That's so cool!" Kathy said, wide-eyed.

"It's just like any other place except sometimes I run into Jennifer Garner at the CVS when shopping for nail polish."

"Wow. That's so cool," Kathy said again. Ivy realized that "cool" must still be Kathy's word of choice. She'd been using it since they were in sixth grade. They'd been best friends all through middle and high school. Ivy had moved across the country to go to college while Kathy stayed home for college.

Lauren and Kathy looked at each other for an awkward moment. Lauren blurted out, "We were really sorry to hear about you and Nick."

"It's okay. That was five years ago."

"We just never thought you guys would break up. We figured you were going all the way to the altar," Lauren said.

"Well, it didn't work out that way," Ivy said a little sadly.

"Have you seen him yet?" Kathy wondered.

"Yes. At the winery. And I also saw his Poison Ivy wine bottle."

"Awful. I can't believe he did that to you," Kathy said in support. "I don't care what those judges said, I don't think it tastes that good."

Ivy smiled. She loved how supportive her friends were and regretted drifting apart.

"What have you all been up to?" she asked, trying to be polite and shift the conversation away from herself.

"I'm lifeguarding at Watkins Glen this summer. Then I go back to my second graders in the fall," Kathy replied.

"Still working at the hospital. Working on getting my master's in nursing at night," Lauren said. "But tell us more about LA. It sounds so exciting. I wish I could get out of here."

Ivy looked at their shining faces and wasn't sure what she should reveal. *The heavy traffic? The fall fire season? Earthquakes? Gloomy days of rejection?* No. She couldn't let them down. "The beaches are great. So is hiking in the Hollywood Hills. And the movie theaters are like palaces," she said to her friends, who hung on to her every word.

"What about the guys? Are they hot?" Kathy asked.

"They're not too bad." Ivy smiled as she looked over at Drew.

After the neighbors left, Drew lingered. He moved closer to Ivy on the couch. For some reason, that felt awkward to her. Probably because Mitch and Linda were sitting across from them. Linda noticed the awkwardness and went to a cabinet to take out a photo album.

"Want to see little Ivy, Drew?"

"Mom," she protested.

"I'd love to see little Ivy." Drew smiled.

As they flipped through the pages Ivy noticed that she had been a pretty cute baby. She was an adorable toddler too. But then around age five, she started to look a little goofy with her big hair and glasses. At age eight, Nick started to show up in the background of photos. At the school field trip, the soccer team, and of course the church pageant. As the photo album pages were turned and they got closer to high school homecoming and prom photos, Ivy closed the book. She wasn't sure if it was because she didn't want Drew to see photos of her with Nick or because she didn't want to think about how in love she had been with Nick back in high school.

"Sure are a lot of pictures of Nick."

Ivy didn't know what to say. Mitch noticed the awkwardness. He turned to Linda. "We really should get to bed, honey. Lots to do tomorrow. To get the house ready for filming."

"The production designer is doing a beautiful job without us," Linda said.

"Honey..." Mitch glared at her.

"Oh, right. Yes. Besides, I'm so tired." Linda got up and put away the book. "It was really nice to have you over, Drew. We'll have to do it again. And maybe next time I'll serve something you can eat."

After Ivy's parents went upstairs, she was finally alone with Drew. They started making out. It felt so good to feel his tongue in her mouth. She moaned with pleasure.

"I've got a really nice hotel room at the Belhurst," Drew said between kisses.

"So I've heard."

His blue eyes twinkled invitingly. Ivy was enjoying the flirtation with him.

"Okay, but I'm not going to tell my parents. I'll come back before morning, all right?"

Drew nodded. Ivy took his hand, and they tiptoed toward the door. They opened the door slowly, but it let out a big *creak*.

From upstairs, they heard Linda call downstairs, "Bye, Drew. Bye, Ivy."

Ivy just laughed. There was no way she could ever put something over on her mom.

At the Belhurst Castle, in Drew's darkened hotel room, Ivy discovered that having produced-writer sex was a lot better than having struggling-writer sex. She wrapped her legs around Drew. Moaned with pleasure. "Oh, Nick…"

"What? You said Nick." Drew stopped and looked confused.

"I said *dick*."

"I heard Nick."

"No, no. I said your dick. It's amazing," Ivy said as she quickly recovered.

He smiled. "Thanks."

"Mmmm…this is so good." And at that same moment, Nick was at his mom's house, eating dinner with her. It was their Friday night ritual. It was almost eleven o'clock, but he'd worked late to close up the winery.

"How was the movie set?" Frannie wondered. She was serving

him his favorite, pork tenderloin with her famous seasoned rub. It was a popular dish at the farm-to-table restaurant at the winery.

"It was nice."

"That's all? Nice?"

"Okay. It was weird. There was a guy playing me who didn't really look like me. And he was late to pick up the Ivy character at the train station, which is total BS."

"You've never been late a day in your life," Frannie protested.

"I know. Ivy said it's dramatic license," Nick grumbled. "Besides, I never picked her up at the train station—it was always the smoke shop where the bus dropped her off. Ivy said that wasn't cinematic."

Frannie nodded sympathetically. "Dramatic license."

He laughed. His mom always knew how to cheer him up. "This tenderloin is amazing. But I'm actually not that hungry. I ate too much at lunch."

"Where?"

"Oh, the set had an amazing lunch spread. It's called craft services. Not sure why since there were no arts and crafts involved. But the caterer was incredible. Reminded me of the stuff you like to cook."

"That's nice." Now it was Frannie's turn to be noncommittal. "What was the actress like who is playing Ivy?"

Nick paused for a moment, then smiled. "Hot. Really hot. I think she likes me."

CHAPTER 12

FRANNIE WOKE UP EARLY ON Thursday mornings so she could get the best dibs at the Geneva summer Farmers' Market. She had a short list of produce she needed for the Shepherd's Cafe, the farm-to-table restaurant she ran at the winery. She glanced at her notes: heirloom tomatoes, string beans, purple potatoes, and morel mushrooms. She liked to be there right when it opened. Usually, she was the only one there that early—along with the vendors. This morning was different. Across the grassy field, she saw a Distinguished Gentleman—a term she reserved for good-looking middle-aged men with silver hair—who seemed quite at home in the market. He struggled with several heavy bags of produce. She watched him in amusement until she realized the Distinguished Gentleman was standing directly in front of her favorite mushroom vendor. She suddenly got worried. He was loading mushrooms into his bags. *They'd better not be fresh morels,* she thought. The type of mushroom that was only available in the late spring and early summer. Frannie rushed over to the vendor, who knew her well.

"George, good morning," she said, out of breath. Her hair was tousled from the sprint across the field.

"Ah, good morning, Frannie. You're late today," he said jokingly. He always liked to kid her about arriving at the market before 7:00 a.m.

"I hope you haven't sold all of my morels," Frannie said.

The Distinguished Gentleman turned to her and gave her an apologetic smile. It was a gorgeous smile. Frannie felt the color in her cheeks rising.

"I'm so sorry. I didn't know you were still coming," said George.

"But I need them," she protested, hating how her voice sounded mildly hysterical.

It was then she heard his voice for the first time—the Distinguished Gentleman. "I am sorry, miss, that I seem to have bought up all your morels." English tinged with a bit of a French accent. If Frannie hadn't been so upset about not getting her morel mushrooms, she might have swooned. She was a sucker for French accents. Instead, she found herself returning his smile in a way that she hadn't done in the three years since her husband died.

"I'm sorry too," she said.

"What were you going to use them for?"

"Cooking," she said with a tinge of sarcasm.

"Of course. But how?"

"I gently sauté them in butter with a sprinkle of salt and cracked pepper."

"Really? Keeping it simple. Letting the flavor of the morels come out. I like that," he said.

"Thank you." Frannie discovered it was hard to be angry with this handsome man. She gave him her full wattage smile.

"Isn't the pretty lady curious what I plan to use them for?"

Pretty lady? Is he flirting with me? Frannie wondered. Nobody had flirted with her in a long time. "What are you going to cook with *my* morel mushrooms?"

"I am so glad you asked," he said with that delicious French accent. "I am going to make lasagna with asparagus, leeks, and morels."

"Interesting," she said.

"It's a creamy vegetarian lasagna, and the smoky morel mushrooms add a sophisticated flavor. I have a great idea. Why don't you join me for dinner and try my lasagna?"

Frannie was surprised, unsure about what to say. But before she could respond, he was already scribbling an address on a slip of paper. This man had confidence.

"Here. Please join me for dinner. Six o'clock. Tonight."

Frannie took the paper. She felt like a schoolgirl, and all she could blurt out was, "Okay."

"I look forward to our rendezvous," he said and walked away, smiling.

Did he just invite her on a date? How had that happened so quickly? She knew practically nothing about him. Then she realized...and called out after him, "What did you say your name was again?"

"I didn't. But it's Jean Baptiste. Everyone calls me J. B. See you tonight at six." Then he flashed that fantastic grin again, and he was off.

Frannie opened up the paper and noticed the address. 238 Exchange Street. That seemed about right. She figured he lived in the downtown area. He seemed cool and hip.

Later that afternoon she was trying to decide what to wear that evening for her date with J. B. She liked how his name sounded on her tongue. It had been years since she'd been asked out. Her bed was littered with jeans and casual shirts. A low-cut black dress that she'd only worn once. Frannie looked at the clothes and decided to venture into her closet again. She stepped toward the back where she'd hung her really old clothes from thirty years ago. In the farthest reach of the closet was the white-eyelet dress that she'd purchased on her honeymoon in Greece. She smiled at the sight of the dress and unzipped it.

Stepping into the dress, she noticed it was starting to yellow at the hem, but it still fit her. It was a bittersweet moment as she remembered her honeymoon. They went on a cruise to Greece and island hopped. The food had been amazing. Dolmades. Moussaka. Courgette balls. Octopus. The feta and the baklava were out of this world.

Suddenly Frannie realized that she was thinking more about the Greek cuisine than she was about her deceased husband. She sighed. It had been three years. Everyone kept telling her that she needed to start dating. Especially Nick and Denise. They wanted to see her happy again. She told them that she was happy, which was true. But she wasn't fulfilled. Not romantically. She took off the dress from her honeymoon and tried on the low-cut black dress. It felt right. She was ready for this date.

Frannie was applying her mascara when there was a knock at the front door. She heard the door open.

"Mom? Mom?" Denise called out.

"Up here."

Denise ran up the stairs to find her mother in the black dress. "Wow. Where are you going?"

"On a date."

"Really?" Denise said wide-eyed.

"Don't act so surprised." Frannie laughed.

"That's great, Mom. Who is he?"

That was a good question, Frannie thought. But she wasn't going to reveal that to her daughter. "A nice man who likes to cook."

"Great. Very happy for you. But I was hoping that I could look in your closet. Some of the extras for the movie need to wear some period dress. And you have more clothes from the nineties than anyone else I know."

"Since when did the 1990s become period clothing? Sure, take a look. I'd better run or I'll be late."

"Have a great time. And, Mom, stay out late. As late as you want." Denise smiled knowingly. Frannie just rolled her eyes.

"I'm sure I'll be home by nine o'clock, in time to watch my shows." Frannie grabbed a bottle of Shepherd's award-winning wine, Poison Ivy, and ran out the door.

She drove slowly down Exchange Road, looking for the address. She didn't see any apartment buildings and was confused. She checked the paper again. Finally, she decided to get out of the car and look for the address on foot. She held up the slip of paper and looked at the number: 238. She noticed a storefront with that number, but it didn't look like a place to live. In fact, it looked empty. Then she noticed young men and women walking in and out of the storefront, carrying walkie-talkies and boxes of water and soda. *Could this be where J. B. lives?* She ventured forth, nervous but excited.

Frannie opened the door, and there he was—J. B. She breathed a sigh of relief before she looked around and noticed that they weren't alone. In fact, they were surrounded by about fifty people, all sitting at folding tables and chairs. *This doesn't seem like a date!*

"You made it!" J. B. smiled. He came over to her and kissed her first on one cheek and then on the other cheek. Very French. She relaxed a bit.

"I did. Some place you've got."

"Thanks. You look great."

"I didn't really know what to wear."

"Oh, *mon dieu*." J. B. slapped himself on his forehead. "Did I forget to mention that I'm the caterer for craft services on a movie?"

"Yes," Frannie said, wide-eyed, as she tried to hide her shock.

"So sorry. I hope you can forgive me. They are filming an outdoor Christmas scene tonight, and so this is where they wanted the cast and crew to eat dinner."

"It's okay. Is this the movie written by the local girl, Ivy Green?"

"Yes. It is. Do you know her?"

"Of course. Everyone knows Ivy. It's a small town."

"Yes, yes. She's a lovely girl. Now you must sit, sit."

Frannie waited as J. B. pulled out a chair for her, and she sat down at a round folding table. It was covered with a light-blue tablecloth topped with a mason jar filled with fresh daisies. She had to admit—he had done a nice job of creating ambiance in an industrial setting. She didn't know anyone at the table. They were all busy eating. The lasagna looked delicious. Frannie wasn't sure what to do so she introduced herself. "Hi, I'm Frannie Shepherd." Across from her was Vera, the production designer, the cinematographer, and an empty chair. Vera's eyes darted upward in recognition.

"The co-owner of Shepherd Winery," Vera said. Frannie nodded. "We owe you a debt of gratitude." Vera turned to the cinematographer and the production designer and added, "She made it possible for us to film at the winery we wanted." Everyone applauded and thanked her. For the first time, Frannie felt very at ease.

J. B. rushed over with two plates of lasagna. "Come with me. I have a nice table for us outside." He smiled. Frannie followed him outside to a Christmas set where they sat down at a table for two. They were surrounded by Christmas garlands and poinsettias. A large pine tree was decorated with colorful balls and other ornaments. She smiled at all the Christmas decorations. J. B. put a red cloth napkin and silverware in front of her.

"It feels like Christmas out here. I love it," she gushed.

"*Bon appétit!* Or as you Americans say, dig in!" When Frannie took the first bite, she was overwhelmed. Flavors of morels and asparagus washed over her. She'd never had a lasagna so delicious.

"This white sauce is fantastic. You must give me your recipe."

"Ha-ha. You are such a comedienne. I never give away my recipes," he said, smiling.

"Seriously?"

"Yes. I am very serious about this. My recipes are like my children. I nurture them and watch them grow. The bad ones I burn." Frannie looked worried. "That was a joke." J. B. laughed.

"Consider it professional courtesy," she said. J. B. laughed again. But he was confused. What did she mean? "I'm not just the co-owner of Shepherd Winery. I'm also the chef for the farm-to-table restaurant called—" And before Frannie could say the name of her restaurant, J. B. interrupted her.

"Shepherd's Cafe! I read about it online. I've been meaning to go there."

"Really?" Now it was her turn to sound incredulous.

"Whenever I go on location, I always like to check out the hot local restaurants. It was fortuitous that I met you at the market," J. B. said exuberantly. "So, tell me about your restaurant."

There was nothing Frannie loved more than to talk about Shepherd's Cafe. J. B. only had eyes for her. He didn't notice the art department dismantling the Christmas tree and taking apart the set behind him. Frannie didn't notice either. Both their eyes were filled with excitement.

"It's farm-to-table. We source all our produce and meat locally. And, of course, we pair our wines with the meals."

"Of course." J. B. listened closely.

"I try to rotate the menus, but my favorite thing is to have a chef's surprise each night."

"*Fantastique*," J. B. exclaimed as he clapped his hands together.

"When the guest orders the chef's surprise, they take a leap of faith as they have absolutely no idea what I'm going to make for them."

"That's a brilliant idea. I love it. One day when I own a farm-to-table restaurant I am going to put the chef's surprise on my menu too." J. B.'s eyes were shining.

"How long have you been a caterer for movies?" Frannie wondered.

"Too long. It's really not what I set out to do. After the CIA—"

"The Culinary Institute?"

"Of course."

"Good, because I was worried that you might be a spy or something." Frannie and J. B. laughed. "But please, continue."

"After culinary school, my plan was to open a restaurant where I could be the chef. But I couldn't find any investors, so I heard about a quick way to make some money working as a movie caterer. My plan was to earn and save for two years and then open my own restaurant. That was twenty-five years ago," J. B. admitted with chagrin.

"Life doesn't always turn out the way you plan." Frannie knew that she was also talking about herself. J. B. nodded in agreement.

Frannie never thought it would be possible to go on a date again, much less really enjoy it. She'd heard the term "movie magic" and felt that it now applied to her. Without the movie, she would never be sitting with J. B. Who knew what was going to happen next? She looked forward to finding out.

CHAPTER 13

IVY HAD WOKEN THAT MORNING in her childhood bedroom wishing she had spent the night with Drew. But professional meant professional. It didn't mean sleeping over at the hotel with her producer boyfriend. Now Drew was late. Fifteen minutes late. She was waiting for him in the parking lot of Watkins Glen Park. It was their first day off. It was Saturday and there was no filming. Week one of shooting had ended, and they had plans to spend the day together. They would drive in separate cars.

The weather was beautiful, but where was Drew? She had written down the directions for him in case he lost a GPS signal. But Drew didn't want it. Ivy dialed Drew's phone again, and he didn't answer. *Yep,* she thought, *he got lost.*

Twenty minutes later, Drew finally arrived. "Sorry. I got lost. No GPS, and cell service in this place is nonexistent."

"That's why I wrote down the directions."

They began the hike. It was chock full of stairs and paths cut into rocks. Drew talked fast but walked slow. Ivy had to keep waiting for him. She wondered if he loved the sound of his own voice.

"You and Amari really do look alike. I never noticed that."

Maybe it was because she was spending too much time with her psychoanalytic sister, but what Ivy heard was *I always knew Amari was a bombshell beauty—but I never thought of you that way.*

Drew continued talking (no surprise there). "Maybe we could use you as a stand-in on the set. Amari doesn't like the one she is working with now."

A stand-in! A stand-in was used in place of the actor while the cinematographer would light the scene. She would wait until the shot was ready before they would bring in Amari. There was no way Ivy was going to do that. "Can we not talk about work? Or Amari?"

"What should we talk about?"

"We don't really have to talk about anything. Look around you, Drew. Look at those waterfalls. Isn't it amazing how the rocks created stairs?" They were walking on the bridge underneath rocks that produced a waterfall. "This goes on for miles." And it did. "We're going on the Gorge Trail. My favorite. It's only a two-and-a-half-mile trail, but we'll climb eight hundred steps. Not like the one in Santa Monica. That's, like, one hundred fifty." Drew climbed and sweated as they hiked through and around the gorges. At one vista they could see seven waterfalls. They walked through caves that led to a path behind a waterfall. They got soaked. For Ivy, it was a theme park. She loved it. Drew did not. He was drenched and didn't want to laugh about it. He was more concerned about his phone.

"You told me this was an easy hike," Drew whined. Some people looked his way.

"It is." Ivy started hiking a trail that meandered away, through a small passage behind two opposing rocks. "See if you can keep up."

Drew was having a hard time walking. It was slippery, and he had the wrong footwear.

"I told you to wear sneakers. Not your Cole Haans." Water cascaded over the rocks they were walking on.

"Where are we going, Ivy?" He was getting impatient as they walked through a cave. Drew could hear rushing water. Ivy was awaiting him, arms displaying the waterfall and a swimming hole behind her. They had to dive off the rocks to go swimming.

"Ta-da. The secret swimming hole." Ivy was already taking off her T-shirt to reveal her bikini top underneath. "Don't you love it, Drew? Better than any trail in LA."

"Too bad you can't hike it in December. That's what I love about LA. An endless summer."

"I don't know. I kind of miss the seasons. Maybe because we're filming a Christmas movie, I'm feeling nostalgic. You know what would be fun? If you came back with me this Christmas. Hang with my family."

"Here? No way. Sorry."

She hadn't expected him to shut down the idea so quickly. "My parents really like you, Drew. It's pretty amazing here when the real snow is falling. There's no winter in LA."

"Ah, yes, my college roommate was from *New Yawk*. He also made that argument. That four mediocre seasons are better than a never-ending superior one. Where else but LA can you hit the beach on Christmas morning?"

"Stop with the Beach Boys. Your endless summer never started. You dress like this cool surfer film producer, but you never even go in the water. We go to the beach. You roll calls from the sand."

"I go in the water." He did. To a small degree. Drew didn't like lakes. He didn't like rivers. He despised bays. Hated oceans. He only liked an in-ground pool that was heated to 86 degrees.

"Great, go in now. Jump in. Don't be afraid," Ivy urged him.

"You're really acting different since we got here. Maybe it has something to do with Nick."

"Nick? Leave Nick out of this. I asked you to come home and hang with my family this Christmas, and you said no. Without even thinking about it. We wouldn't even have this conversation if you would just jump in the swimming hole."

"You really are a New Yorker. You're so pushy."

"You think I'm pushy?" Ivy smiled. Drew didn't really have time to answer because she shoved him off the rocks into the swimming hole below.

Drew was furious before he hit the water. He was already screaming back, "I can't believe you did that!" But Ivy didn't hear him. She jumped in with a squeal of joy and her signature cannonball. She swam toward Drew, who was paddling to get out of the water. Which he did.

"Where are you going?"

"I can't believe you did that," Drew said again. He stomped away. Ivy didn't bother telling him he was going in the wrong direction.

———————

"You pushed Drew off the rocks into the swimming hole? Why?" Carol wondered.

"I don't know. I asked Drew to come home for Christmas,

and he said no. Then he was teasing me about Nick. So I pushed him. I used to push Nick all the time when he teased me."

"I think the pushing is a sign of something deeper." Carol was already into analyst mode. Ivy was becoming more and more intrigued by her sister's statements. "You are establishing competitive measure markers using data metrics so you can make an emotionally sound decision." Ivy looked confused. Carol explained: "Nick and Drew. You set up these scenarios where they have to perform a task and you score who does better."

"I can buy that. What I don't get is your saying 'emotional decision'. There is no emotional decision. I am with Drew now. I just wanted him to go swimming with me."

"Like you used to with Nick."

"Nick loves the lake. He always talked about building us a lake house and getting a boat."

"Well," Carol said, "he got the boat."

"Nick bought a boat?"

———————

Not just a boat. A 2018 Bayliner VR5, stern drive motor (not outboard) to be specific. Nick was on it that moment. He did love the water. His boat gave him the freedom to decompress, a chance to escape. It seemed the one thing he could not escape was Amari. And maybe that wasn't a bad thing. Amari was driving his boat, running it at full throttle. She wore a bikini, or what passed for one. She was waving to everyone on the lake. Slowing down to let them take pictures of her. But she didn't slow down in the *Slow Down* zone. The police boat, aka the navigation team staffed by the sheriff's office, pulled up alongside them.

"Damn," Nick said. "I'm going to get ticketed."

"You're not getting anything. Except maybe me," Amari teased. He blushed. "Let me handle the police," she added.

The police boarded his boat. Nick watched as Amari sauntered over in her skimpy bikini, exchanged a few pleasantries and a few laughs with the police.

"Nick, can you take a picture of me with our boys in blue?" The two policemen handed Nick their cell phones. He juggled them as Amari posed and played it up for the police. They were about to leave when she asked the police to take a picture of her and Nick. Amari got Nick to take off his shirt. She put her hand on his chest. Kissed him on the cheek. "Thanks, boys," Amari said. The police motored away.

Nick had never seen anyone get out of a ticket. "That was impressive."

"My boobs did most of the work."

"They're pretty impressive too."

"Oh, Nicky, are you flirting with me?" He didn't answer. Was he? Amari held the phone up in the air. "No cell signal. I'll post these cute pics of us later."

"You're going to post the pictures. Of us. Wouldn't everyone see them?"

"You mean Ivy. Time to tell me the truth. I want the whole story about you and Ivy. For the movie."

"You mean like research?"

"I got you out of a ticket."

"You were the one speeding."

"I like to go fast. So do tell."

And he did. As they drove around the lake, Nick told his side of the story. His memories of falling in love with Ivy. He talked about how their coastal separation had broken them up and how long-distance relationships didn't work. He also opened up about his hopes and dreams. And he told Amari about the lake house he was building. They boated past the house.

"That's it?" Amari reacted to the half-built house on the lake. "That's your dream house?"

"I thought it might be. Ivy and I used to come out here and talk about building this place."

"What else did you do out here?"

"Nothing. Just talked. And sometimes we didn't even do that. We just listened to each other breathe, watching the sunset. This place has great sunsets."

"I don't think I could be with you alone and not do anything," Amari offered. Nick took the bait.

"We're alone now," he said, surprised to hear the words come out of his mouth.

"Exactly," Amari said as she began kissing Nick passionately. Very passionately. Yeah, Nick thought, she looked like Ivy. But she wasn't. He was kissing Amari. "Did Ivy kiss you like this?" she asked, French-kissing him. "Or like this?" Nick grunted a yes to both.

He opened his eyes, seeing the blond hair. Just like Ivy's. But this was Amari, and Ivy never would have made that move with her hand. He was caught up in the moment. The moment was getting bigger by the second. Nick couldn't stop kissing Amari, but he had to. He had no choice. He had a huge erection. He jumped off the boat and into the water to cool off.

Ivy hoped Drew had cooled off. But he was not answering his phone. She got a text from him: KEEPING IT PROFESSIONAL.

Ouch. Well, it was a short shoot. Four weeks. Three weeks to go. She spent Saturday at home with her family. Her mom decided to cook a Christmas dinner. It was amazing. All of her favorites including stuffing. Her dad surprised everyone by bringing out a bag of presents. He gave Ivy a book about William Faulkner's years in Hollywood. Her dad, ever the professor, explained that Faulkner spent a few years in Hollywood and ultimately returned home.

"Is this supposed to inspire me to move back home?"

"Entirely up to you, Ivy. I support you in whatever and whomever you choose." There was that *who* again. Why did this keep coming up? "The truth is," Mitch said, "you inspire me. You did something I was too scared to do. You wrote something, and you put it out there. You had no problem with all the rejection that befalls the creative."

"I have a big problem with rejection. On so many levels. I love the book, Dad." She hugged him. "You know, Dad, there's still time. I'm sure the manuscript in your bottom desk drawer could still be dusted off." She kissed him good night. Mitch stayed awake and started thinking about his unfinished novel.

Sunday morning, growing up, was always church. Ivy's mom and dad were now deacons and had kept the church going during the pandemic. They set up all the video feeds to the service, checked in on all the members, and worked at the food pantry. They volunteered whether they had the time or not. Inside the Presbyterian church, her parents were rock stars and very proud to welcome her back. Ivy had grown up with this tradition. Heck, it was where the idea for *When Joseph Met Mary* came from. This was where she and Nick had done the play.

Ivy had church-shopped in LA. She had gone to a Christmas

Eve service in a church near her then-apartment in Hollywood.
She had recognized an actor whom she had loved when she was
growing up. After two weeks of watching him, alone, she had
worked up the nerve to say hello. But on that Sunday, he wasn't
there. She had learned he had made the choice to leave this earth.
All the sunshine could make people sad. Everyone wanted the
same thing. Chased the same dreams. Tried to stay on the merry-
go-round for as long as they could. The whole entertainment
industry had a severe case of FOMO. So they lied to themselves.
Back home in Geneva, Ivy was adjusting to how normal life was,
how down to earth everyone seemed. They cared about each other.
At the church community time hour, she actually autographed
some church bulletins. The cell phone in her pocket kept buzzing.
She had forgotten to turn it off. She went to do so but stopped.

"Oh, hell!" she said too loudly. How could she not? There on
her phone was a picture of Amari and Nick on a boat. Amari's
boobs falling out. Amari hanging all over the grinning Nick.
The Amari-supplied caption read: *IT'S CALLED RESEARCH,
LADIES!* There were close to twenty thousand comments: *Who's
the boy toy? Go for it! I'd take a ride with that guy.* Ivy was
fuming.

"So, how's Nick?" Reverend Jackson asked.

"I am not Nick's keeper. He is the shepherd. He's the one who
is supposed to be watching his flock, not dumping it. Not slutting
around five years later with the actress who is basically me!" Ivy
blurted out—but only in her mind. In reality, all she said to the
Reverend Jackson was: "I'm not sure."

After church, and needing to get in a better mood, Ivy took
a walk and stopped in to get an oat milk latte from Monaco
Coffee, browsed the books in Stomping Grounds, and wound up

at her mother's Christmas store. Her mother was happy she was there. She was behind on filling orders and needed some help.

"It's July."

"Not to the people who came to town to make your movie. They've been here every day buying stuff. Christmas came early for the store. The whole town feels that way. You are our Christmas financial miracle. And in July." That made Ivy feel so much better. She was all smiles. Her script had done this. Despite what did not turn out to be a stress-free, no-conflict weekend, it was all worth it.

Bells rang on the door as it flew open. Five eager teenagers, all wearing Griffin James T-shirts, started searching around the store. Cell phones out. Griffineers.

"Can I help you?" Ivy asked.

"We're looking for Griffin James." One Griffineer showed her phone filled with pictures of Griffin. "We heard he was here."

"I've never heard of him," Ivy said.

"He's in the movie!"

"What movie?" she asked.

The teens left. Then Linda said out loud: "You can come out now." Griffin emerged from the back room. He had wandered into the Christmas store and taken refuge from his fans. Since then, he had been helping with orders all morning.

"Thank you, Linda," he said. "Sometimes it gets to be too much."

"No problem. I can use the help."

"I love being an elf," Griffin said. He turned his attention to Ivy. "And you, what a performance. 'What movie?' 'I've never heard of him.' You are the big sister I never had who would have always protected me." They spent the next few hours chatting, getting to know each other, wrapping toys. Griffin was the little brother she never had. He called an Uber to take him back to the Castle but not before he bought a Christmas scarf. "I'm going to wear it for the ice-skating scene tomorrow."

"I think Vera will love it."

"See you on the set. Get some rest. Week two is when things get really weird. Strange weather. Cover sets. Tech failures. Hookups. Breakups." And he was gone.

Ivy's mother asked: "There's an ice-skating scene? How are they going to do that in July?"

"It's the movies, Mom. They can do anything. They can make you think rich people are unhappy, hard work always pays off, and love conquers all."

"And don't forget the Christmas miracle," Linda added with a smile.

Ivy laughed. The Christmas miracle was a trope of Christmas movies and books since Charles Dickens had rebranded the holiday with his book *A Christmas Carol*. It was the one trope that Ivy didn't believe in. How could she? It was July.

CHAPTER 14

IVY SAT IN A CANVAS director's chair watching as the art department put up a synthetic ice rink. It was the scene in the movie when Ilsa told Rick that she'd been accepted at USC. Ivy remembered how they were both a little sad as it meant they were going to be separated by three thousand miles. Ivy was lost in thought when...

"Ivy? Cocoa?" She looked up. Drew handed her a steaming cup of cocoa. It was a peace offering. She smiled. "I'm sorry about Saturday," he said.

"Thanks. I love hot cocoa. And I'm sorry I pushed you," Ivy admitted.

"J. B. is making it today to get us in the Christmas spirit."

"It's delicious."

"So what do you think of our rink?" Drew asked proudly.

Ivy considered it. "It's not exactly what I'd imagined when I wrote the scene. It's plastic."

He was aghast. "Do you know how much real ice would cost? At least ten thousand dollars. This synthetic stuff keeps us on budget."

"Is it going to look like ice?" Ivy wanted to know.

"Of course."

"How do the actors skate on it?"

"That's what stunt doubles are for." He sounded exasperated.

"And the extras? They can't be the only ones in the scene. At least not the scene I wrote." Ivy wasn't sure why she was being a little snarky with Drew that morning. Maybe it was the lingering feelings from their hike. She didn't like how he put down her hometown.

"You're really giving me a hard time about this."

"I just want the ice to look, well, real," Ivy said. "Authentic."

"Don't worry—when all the actors have their winter gear on and they're gliding around the ice, it's going to look very real." Then Drew got a phone call and stepped away from Ivy.

The production crew finished laying down the fake ice, and Ivy realized the rink looked tiny. She didn't understand how all the actors would fit on the ice, much less make it look real. Everything about the scene was suddenly looking too fake to her. She had a pit in her stomach. It got even worse as she noticed Nick walked onto the set carrying two coffees. What was *he* doing here? Ivy wondered.

Nick looked around for a moment, unsure. Amari ran over to him. She was dressed in a pretty winter sweater that Ivy thought looked awfully familiar. She wore an adorable pom-pom hat. Everything about her screamed cute winter clothes. Ivy tried to look away, but she couldn't help watching as Nick smiled at Amari and handed her a coffee.

"One non-fat latte with no foam," Nick said.

"You're a doll. Thank you!" Amari took the coffee and reached up to kiss him.

What? Ivy couldn't believe that they were kissing. And in public! She was horrified. What Ivy didn't realize was that Nick quickly pulled away. But Ivy didn't see that moment. She was too busy fuming to herself. She tried to project a happy exterior and put on a big smile. She got up from the director's chair and strode across the set to find Drew inspecting the plastic white picket fence that was being constructed around the entire ice rink in the parking lot of the high school against a patch of pine trees. Ivy checked to see that Nick was watching—he was—and she marched up to Drew, turned him around, went in for a kiss—and sent his cocoa flying in the air! It soaked his shirt. Something he was not happy about.

"What the hell, Ivy?"

"I'm so sorry, I just..."

"Just what?"

"I just don't understand how this is going to look real."

"Bruce," Drew called out. "Can you take Ivy through the shot? She's nervous. And I have to go find a new shirt."

Bruce stepped over to her. "Here, let me show you how the rink is actually bigger than you think." Ivy followed Bruce over to the asphalt portion of the "ice." She noticed that two skaters were lacing up rollerblades. "So, Amari and Griffin will skate on the plastic part of the ice, wearing actual ice skates. And when he twirls her, we'll use a double since Griffin can't really skate." Ivy nodded. This all made sense so far. "Then to give the illusion of a larger ice rink, we'll have extras on rollerblades in the foreground, but we'll never see the rollerblades. We'll only see their upper bodies. We'll do that for the large, establishing shot. Come here, look through the lens, and you'll see what I'm talking about." Ivy followed Bruce over to the camera set up.

Drew returned, wearing a Seneca Lake T-shirt. "How soon

before we can get the first shot off?" he asked. Ivy smiled as she watched Drew kick into producer mode.

"I'd say about thirty minutes. Griffin's still not finished with hair and makeup," Bruce said. She wondered if Griffin was stalling because he was nervous about having to skate.

Ivy moved over behind the camera and looked through the lens at the ice-skating rink. She noticed that from the camera's perspective, in the foreground, she could only see the rollerbladers from the waist up. Two extras were now gliding back and forth on the asphalt, but it looked like they were wearing ice skates with actual blades, not wheels. In the background, she could see the plastic ice that actually did look like ice now that she was farther away.

"That's so cool," Ivy said to no one in particular. Then Drew joined her.

"Now you get it?" he said, perhaps a bit smugly, but Ivy brushed it off.

"You were right. It does look real."

"Just trust me. I'll always take care of your story," he said.

"Thanks. Sorry about the shirt." Ivy walked back across the set to her canvas chair and almost stopped because sitting in the chair next to hers was Nick. She'd figured he'd left after dropping off the coffee. He'd already noticed her so she couldn't turn around and run off. She became resolute and walked to her chair and sat down.

"Hey, Ivy," Nick said.

"What are you doing here?"

"Well, that's not very welcoming. But if you must know, Amari invited me. And I wasn't too busy at the winery this morning, so I thought I'd stop by."

"Great," Ivy said. Sarcasm dripped from her voice.

Nick ignored her unfriendly remark. "I don't see how this can look like a real ice rink."

"Well, you wouldn't understand this because you're not in the film business, but when all the actors have their winter gear on and they're gliding around the ice, it's going to look very real," Ivy said, almost duplicating what Bruce had told her. She hated how snarky she sounded but Nick seemed to bring out the worst in her ever since she'd returned home to Geneva.

"Okay. You're the pro. So, what's up with you and this Drew guy?"

"Well, if you have to know, we're going to be moving in together. In Downtown LA."

At that moment, Bruce came rushing over to them. "Do either of you know how to skate?" They both answered yes at the same time. Bruce laughed. "Of course you do. This story is based on your love story." Ivy noticed that Nick's face got red. Was he blushing, or was that a sunburn that she hadn't noticed?

"Loosely based," Ivy said as she looked away.

"Anyhoos—we're short on extras for the scene, and Vera thought it would be nice to include you two. Ivy, you could have your Hitchcock moment," Bruce said. Ivy knew what he was talking about. In almost every classic Alfred Hitchcock movie, Hitchcock made sure to insert himself in one scene. During film school, it had always been fun to look for that Hitchcock moment. But now, sitting there with Nick, Ivy didn't want her Hitchcock moment. At least not with Nick!

"Sure, happy to help," Nick said nonchalantly. "Just let me go home and get my skates. I can be back in fifteen minutes."

"Great!" Then Bruce turned to her. "Ivy?"

"Sure," she said, knowing that she didn't really have a choice. If Vera wanted her to do something, she was going to do it. "Just let me go home and get my skates. I'm sure my mother kept them."

"Need a ride home?" Nick asked.

"Nope. I've got a rental car," Ivy said. The last thing she wanted to do in that moment was to get in a car with him.

"Okey dokey! See you back in fifteen. We'll start filming then," Bruce said enthusiastically. His walkie-talkie squawked, and he sprinted away.

———————

Back on the set, Ivy and Nick laced up their skates. They watched as stunt doubles for Amari and Griffin twirled around the fake ice. They both finished lacing at the same time. They walked toward the open door of the fake rink. Even just walking, Ivy was wobbly at first, but she noticed that Nick was steady.

"When was the last time you went skating?" Ivy wondered.

"I was just going to ask you the same thing," Nick said.

"So?"

"Probably the last time I was with you."

"Me too. Senior year. Christmas."

"You had just gotten into USC."

"Early decision. I was so happy." Ivy looked away as she said it. It seemed so long ago and it was. Nine long years ago. She was caught up in the memory when—

"Ivy? Ivy?" Vera said. Ivy looked quickly at Vera. "I need you and Nick to fill out the background of the shot. You don't have to skate—you can just hold onto the board if you want. But we need to start the shot now. You ready?"

"Ready," Ivy said. Even though she wasn't. And as the camera rolled, Ivy and Nick scooted onto the ice and skated slowly in the background.

In the foreground, Amari and Griffin held hands while they slowly skated. "I'm going to be three thousand miles away. I hate that. But I really want to go to USC," Amari said.

"Don't worry. It doesn't matter if you're three miles away or three thousand miles. I'll always be there for you," Griffin said to Amari as they acted out the scene.

"*Cut!*" Vera screamed. She turned to Drew and the cinematographer. "I think the zoom needs to be slower. Can we practice the dolly move before we bring Amari and Griffin back in?" The camera crew nodded in agreement as they pushed the camera slowly on the dolly.

At the other end of the tiny rink, Nick was staring at Ivy. "Did I really say that?"

"Yes, you did. You said that you'll always be there for me," Ivy reminded him.

"Oh."

"But that didn't happen."

"I wonder what would have happened if USC had rejected you and you'd gone to NYU instead. We would have been on the same coast," Nick said.

"Hmmm. I guess we'll never know," Ivy said as she almost lost her balance.

"I never liked the way we ended things," he admitted.

"That makes two of us," she said, unable to look him in the eyes.

Nick looked sadly at Ivy. He was about to say something when Vera called out again. "Let's take it from the top!"

The scene played out again.

"I'll always be there for you," Griffin said. Then he grabbed the side of the rink and pulled Amari in for a kiss. A long, beautiful kiss which Ivy remembered only too well. She looked away, saddened by the memory. She couldn't bear to look at Nick during the kiss. But if she had, she would have noticed a small teardrop from one eye. He was clearly caught up in the emotion too.

"And cut!" Vera yelled. "Let's take that again, from the top. And wardrobe! Can we try a different hat on Griffin? That pom-pom hat looks too goofy. Not cool enough for Rick."

Ivy watched as the wardrobe department came scuttling over, holding a black knit cap and a blue knit cap both sans goofy pom-pom. They held them out to Vera. Ivy realized that she had been about to break down and cry. Luckily, the wardrobe department had saved the day for her. Nick was watching her closely.

"I don't think that pom-pom hat was too goofy. I remember you gave me one like that."

"And you never wore it," Ivy teased.

"So maybe it was too goofy." Nick smiled. "I'm glad we can talk like this. You know?"

"I know. You're just happy that I'm not trying to kill you," Ivy said.

"Only in your script." They were both smiling now. It felt almost normal to her.

"What about we both move forward? Try to be friends?" Nick suggested.

"I'd like to move forward," she said, still smiling.

Her good mood lasted for five seconds as Nick "moved forward" by walking toward Amari.

"Hey, Nick," Amari called out. "Look at me, I'm skating."

She flashed a grin as she skated toward Nick and Ivy. Amari pretended to slip on the fake ice and fell into Nick's arms. Ivy rolled her eyes. Just when she'd thought things were getting better. Rory, the reporter, caught it all, snapping photos of Nick holding Amari in his arms.

Ivy left the ice. She knew she was off her game. Nick had confused her. Flirting, then not flirting. Then finally opening up. Ivy decided that if Nick was moving on, she was moving on too.

"That one is fuming," Olivia, the hairstylist, said to Ella, the makeup artist, as they put away the hair and makeup materials. "I think she still loves the real guy."

"I'm thinking she is going to go for Drew," Ella said. The hair-and-makeup crew always knew all the on-set gossip. "Do you want to bet on it?"

"I think everyone would want to bet on it," Olivia said. And that was how the Team Nick/Team Drew betting pool was born. As members of the crew learned about it, it would get bigger and bigger with a sizable amount of money in play for the person who would correctly predict who would end with who and when. Was it going to be Drew? Or Nick?

CHAPTER 15

SHOOTING WAS GOING WELL. THE production was deep into the second week. They had scheduled to shoot Thursday and Friday night on Main Street. Night shoots meant call time was 7:00 p.m. Crew reported to the set so they could prep everything before the sun went down at 9:00 p.m. They would stay up all night filming. Cast arrived an hour later when ready to film. They were all set to go. The street had been decorated with fake snow and lined with Christmas lights. They were about to shoot the Rick and Ilsa shopping on Main Street montages, which would take their characters from ages twelve to twenty. Vera called *action*. The ominous clouds must have heard her. The skies opened up with an unexpected summer thunderstorm. The wind and the rain ruined the set and cut out the power for ten minutes.

The cast and crew who weren't responsible for trying to save the set sought refuge at Eddie O'Brien's Bar and Grill. The production had rented it out as the holding location for the crew to stay cool. It was where the cast and crew would eat lunch at midnight and dinner the next morning. Night shoots were weird. Drew and Vera sat at a table by a window watching as the PAs tried to save the set while the rain continued to fall. A PA carrying an inflated eight-foot Santa had slipped, and the inflatable Santa had gotten loose and was starting to fly in the wind, only to land in the middle of the street and get popped by a passing truck. "There goes Santa," Vera commented. No one was happy. The rain cost them half a day in production. Each moment they were not shooting, they were losing money. "How long is this going to last?" Vera wondered. "Drew, check your weather app."

"I don't have a weather app. I live in LA."

Ivy found Drew and Vera and joined them. She had gotten drenched in the rain. "What a storm," she said, almost marveling at it. It had been a while since she'd experienced a summer storm. The air would change, and one could almost smell it coming.

"You're from around here. How long is this going to last?" Vera asked.

Ivy chuckled. "If you want to talk about the weather in Upstate New York, wait five minutes."

"What the hell does that mean? Why do we have to wait five minutes?"

"It's just an expression."

"I don't need an expression. I need a forecast."

Ivy shuddered a little. She knew she had somehow developed a small habit of annoying Vera, who was her director and who should not be annoyed. Ivy still answered: "I heard rain for the next two days. But it's really good."

Vera tried to keep her cool. "How is it really good?"

"All the farms and the wineries need some rain. And it's better for the lakes around here."

"I don't care about the farms and the wineries and the lakes," Vera said, smoldering. "I care about shooting the movie!"

Ivy looked at Drew as he informed her, "We had the shopping scenes scheduled for later today and all day tomorrow. The town council agreed to shut down Main Street for us. We can't postpone and shoot next week because the arts and crafts fair comes in."

"I love that fair," Ivy reminisced out loud. Drew was glaring at her. "The following weekend is the Taste of Geneva!" Vera stared at her, annoyed. Ivy stood up, flustered. "I'm going to get a coffee. Sorry."

"Good idea," Drew said. "We'll be right here trying to figure out how to save the shooting schedule."

Ivy got her coffee. She knew she had to keep her head in the game. She had spent the last few days watching the film shoot (going very well), watching dailies each night (the footage looked great), but in truth, she was most focused on checking Instagram. Amari was all over it. With Nick at the ice cream shop. Ivy doubted Amari ate ice cream. With Nick at the Del Lago Spa and Resort. With Nick at the Corning Glass Factory. Nick would never go to the glass factory, no matter how many times she'd asked him. Too many people, he would argue. But Ivy guessed he had no problem going with Amari. That was all over Instagram. Ivy had cyber-stalked her way to exhaustion.

She shook her head to clear her thoughts, when Griffin stumbled into the bar. He saw Ivy and leaned into her for a hug. She still felt awkward hugging a big star like Griffin and reached out with one arm, balancing her coffee and phone with the other.

"Griffin, are you all right?"

He told Ivy that he had gone back to the hotel to change. "But there they were," he said, "in front of the entrance. Like Gandalf saying *you shall not pass!*"

"What did you do?" Ivy wondered.

"I had to *Goodfellas* it." She knew exactly what Griffin was talking about. In the movie *Goodfellas*, Henry (played by Ray Liotta) took his date Carmela (played by Lorraine Bracco) to the famous Copacabana nightclub. In one long fluid shot, the camera followed Henry and Carmela as they walked in through the back entrance, greeting and tipping people, tasting the food in the kitchen, and winding up front and center in the club. Griffin had entered through the back door of the hotel, tipping the staff, taking selfies with the chef, and getting into the service elevator to his floor, only to open his hotel room door and find three Griffineers climbing through the window. "My fans. My wonderful fans. They call me, follow me, stalk me. They must have jumped from the tree. They're like freaks. Super freaks. They steal my underwear and sell it on eBay."

"That's really, really sad."

"This is really, really starting to get to me, Ivy. I'm emotionally exhausted. I miss home."

"Where's home?"

Griffin thought about it. "I have no idea. I have gone from production to production for the last year. A part of me just wants out."

"There you are," a voice chimed in. Ivy looked at the young woman. "Hi, I'm Rory. I met you at the winery."

"You work with Kenny on the paper." Ivy was suspicious. Had Rory been listening to Griffin's breakdown? But then he snapped up.

"That's right. We had an interview. Nice to meet the local press." It was amazing how Griffin could turn it on in a second. He was no longer "vulnerable" Griffin. He was confident Hollywood Griffin. "Have you met Ivy, our fabulous screenwriter?"

"And producer," Rory added.

"It's a small credit."

"I heard the movie hit a rough patch. A disaster as your set was destroyed by the storm. Any comments?"

"No. No problem at all. You two have fun. I have to go to work." Ivy walked back toward Drew and Vera. There was something about that reporter that Ivy did not like. Her return to the table was greeted by Vera.

"Nice of you to join us again," Vera sniped. She ran hot and cold with Ivy. More like lukewarm and subzero.

"Griffin was having a meltdown. His fans keep finding him," Ivy explained. Drew muttered that he would deal with it, but Ivy told him she would. She had a plan. When asked how, she declined to share her plan.

"What if we shoot in a mall?" Drew suggested, excited by what he thought was a genius idea. Vera was about to tell him how bad it was.

"A mall isn't real. A mall represents death to small town mom-and-pop stores. This movie is about the authentic true spirit of Christmas, and you want to stick us in a mall?"

"Sorry to ruin your integrity. I forgot I was dealing with a New York artist."

"Give me an extra week."

"We don't have the money. What if we cut the shopping sequence? I'm not even sure we need it."

Vera considered this. Ivy knew about things happening on a film set that led to a movie's story being changed. They had to stick to the script. That was what Vera had said in her kickoff speech. Now she was considering cutting a scene that was so important to the movie. "Do we need it?" Vera paused.

"Yes, we do need it," Ivy said. "It's the last time they see each other. It's not goodbye, but they both sense it is. They muddle through the holidays together, knowing that...knowing their relationship is being tested." She spoke quietly, "But I have a solution. What if we turn a closed mall into Main Street? Not just any mall. A dead mall. The Finger Lakes Mall closed during the pandemic. Never reopened. Used to be the place all us kids would go. Maybe we can take one wing, decorate some storefronts, throw up some lights, and turn it into Main Street."

Drew was not sure. Vera was. "Love it! The dead mall becomes our set." She turned to Drew. "Why didn't you think of that?" He started to defend himself, but all Vera cared about was: "Get me access to that mall." Drew went into producing mode.

Rory moved close to the conversation and offered, "The county owns it. Mall went bankrupt last year. I can make some calls if it helps."

"Who are you?" Vera asked.

"Reporter—Rory Jones. Covering the movie for the paper."

"Thanks, Rory. We can use all the help we can get," Drew said.

For Vera, this day kept getting worse. She snapped at him. "I said no press on the set." Vera climbed up on a chair and called out to the department heads in the dining room. "Okay, lunchtime is over! Where's Wyck?" Wyck was eating next door. "Get him over here!"

Wyck grabbed his grilled cheese sandwich and carried it to the bar table. "What's going on?"

"We need to turn the wing of a dead mall into Main Street by tomorrow morning to stay on schedule. Bruce, let the crew know. Early call. Drew, get me into the mall. Ivy, you know that woman who does the background extras?"

"Denise. She's Nick's sister."

Vera was too frazzled. "Who the hell is Nick?"

"Nick is Rick," Drew said.

"Griffin is Rick! What are you talking about? We need extras. You're from around here. Start calling…and I need you to rewrite the scenes." Ivy was lost in thought. "Are you even listening to me?" Vera practically yelled.

Ivy turned to her with a smile. She had just come up with a genius idea. "What if we did it like the walk through the seasons shot in *Notting Hill*?" Ivy suggested, referring to the classic Richard Curtis comedy. "But instead of the seasons changing we see Rick and Ilsa walk into a store, shoppers wipe the frame, and Rick and Ilsa come out a year older. Carrying different presents. We can shoot two nights in one day and get back on schedule."

Vera hugged Ivy. "I love *Notting Hill*. That's a great idea. Can't wait to steal it. You're not just a writer. You're a director."

"Oh, that means so much, Vera." Ivy smiled.

"So get going!"

Director. Vera thought of me as a director. I do have a good sense of visual storytelling. Most people think screenwriting is just writing what the characters say. It's so much more. Good screenwriting has minimal dialogue and tells the story with pictures.

Ivy went home to look at old photos for research. Not just any photos. The ones practically hermetically sealed in a shoebox under her childhood bed. The box read *IVY & NICK CHRISTMAS MEMORIES*. They had started going Christmas shopping when they were thirteen. It was their tradition. They wouldn't buy any presents for anyone until they could go together. The older they got, the more presents they bought, and their holiday bounty was harder to carry. But it was such fun.

They both shared the love of giving. For her Girl Scout Gold Award, Ivy created a toy drive that still continued with the local Girl Scouts chapter. After all the shopping, she and Nick would always visit Santa Claus. Ivy was lost in her memories when she heard a voice: *You really have to move on already.* She felt the voice had come from behind her. It did. It was her sister Carol.

"How long have you been there?"

"Long enough. This is not healthy."

"It's not what you think, Carol. I have to adjust a few scenes for the movie." Carol didn't believe her. She just started writing in her notebook. "Nick and I have talked. He's moving on. I'm moving on."

"Did he say the thing about moving on, or did you?"

"He did," Ivy admitted. Carol nodded. "Well, I was moving on. But then I came back here. Now I don't know what I'm doing. What's the opposite of moving on?"

"You're the writer."

"Stuck. Okay, I'm stuck. But when this movie is done, I will be unstuck, and I'll move on back to Los Angeles." Even Ivy wasn't sure she believed what she was saying. Carol left. Ivy dug deeper into the box. She found the inspiration she was looking for. A picture of her and Nick Christmas shopping on Main Street. It was hard to say what came faster: the words or the tears. Ivy finished the rewrite two hours later. *Done,* she said to herself. *Done* was the email heading. "Done," she said to the picture of her and Nick.

The next morning, it was all hands on deck at the closed down mall. The extras poured in. Denise had flooded social media with a casting call. *Come to the old mall for Christmas shopping. The movie needs you!* Wyck used one long row of storefronts. He and his crew put fake snow on the floor. Lampposts wrapped with garland were in front of some stores. Christmas lights lined each store window. Even Ivy's mom and dad got into it. Linda brought over boxes of Christmas decorations from her Christmas shop in town. They set up their store facade in one of the vacant windows. All the little Ilsas and Ricks were there. Ivy saw them as a ten-year-old Ivy and Nick, a middle school Ivy and Nick, and a young teenage Ivy and Nick, and Amari and Griffin as the present-day Ilsa and Rick, aka Ivy and Nick.

Amari was chatting with some extras. It took a moment for Ivy to realize the extras she was chatting with were Ivy's childhood friends, Kathy and Lauren. They started giggling. What were her friends telling Amari? Ivy couldn't go over there. She was working. Vera addressed the actors and crew and the extras. "We're going to do it in one long shot. First Ilsa and Rick go into one store, they come out older with different presents. The extras are going to wipe the frame so they keep going into stores and they come out in different looking outfits, depending on the year. Might take a while. If we have time, we'll do Rick at the jewelry store."

Everyone applauded. Ivy was confused. Rick at the jewelry store? "That's not in the script."

Vera told her, "We added it. It was Amari's idea. She thought it would be more impactful if the audience knew Rick was thinking about asking Ilsa to marry him before he dies in the snowmobile accident with the ring in his pocket."

"Okay," Ivy said, processing this news. "I'll start writing it."

"No worries. Amari already did it. Not bad. Small scene. All visual," Vera said. Ivy blanched. *Since when do the actors start writing the script?* But Vera was too busy to notice her horrified reaction.

Vera yelled "Action!" The shooting began. Ivy wanted to scream "Cut!" on the whole affair. Amari was not just hanging with Nick; she was now rewriting the script. Ivy hated herself for tearing up when Rick looked in the jewelry story for an engagement ring.

Lunch was at the food court where J. B., the super chef, made high class, off-the-chart mall food. Thin crust pizza, deep fried chicken, and gourmet sausage dogs. J. B. cooked, and Nick's mother Frannie was there cooking alongside him.

When J. B. called her for a second date, Frannie was thrilled. This time he'd remembered to tell her that having lunch with him meant that she'd also be helping him to cook lunch on the mall set.

Frannie noticed Ivy seemed sad and asked her if she was feeling all right. She lied and told Nick's mom that she was just very busy. But Ivy did wonder what Frannie was doing on the set.

Ivy sat down with her old friends, Kathy and Lauren. She thanked them for coming and being extras in the movie. They let Ivy know Amari had invited them to a sleepover at the Belhurst. Ivy smiled, not wanting to ruin her friends' fun. People loved meeting celebrities. Why should her friends be any different?

Ivy found Amari. "I like the scene you wrote."

"Thank you. I had the idea the other day when I was with Nicky," Amari revealed.

Nicky? Ivy couldn't believe he was allowing himself to be called Nicky! "It's a good add," Ivy had to admit. "So, I hear you're having the girls over for a sleepover."

"I told you I like to immerse myself into a character. There are things you're hiding that aren't in the script. What is your secret, Ivy?"

"I don't have a secret."

"Everyone has a secret. Once I find out what yours is, I'll let you know." Amari grinned as she went back to the set.

The shooting went perfectly, just as Ivy had imagined it. Drew was thrilled with her, as was Vera. Ivy had saved the day. But why was there a sad minor-key film score playing in her head? She watched Amari and Ivy's friends head out. Ivy was leaving when she noticed that one of the extras, who had come to the set in his own Santa suit, was taking pictures with the cast and crew who were into the idea that it was actually Christmas-time. Santa saw Ivy.

"What does our own Ivy Green want for Christmas?" he bellowed out. "Another foreign copy of *Pride and Prejudice*?" How did Santa know that?

Ivy joined the line to meet with Santa. It was Mr. Fowler! He used to own Fowler's Books, her favorite bookstore growing up. It had closed years ago. "Hello, Mr. Fowler," she said.

"You mean hello, Santa!" he bellowed. Ivy nodded. "So, what does our famous screenwriter who brought all this movie magic to our town want for Christmas?"

The truth was Ivy didn't know what she wanted anymore.

CHAPTER 16

A SUMPTUOUS BREAKFAST BUFFET WAS laid out for the cast and crew. The homemade blueberry muffins were calling to Ivy. So were the chocolate chip scones. She included oatmeal and fruit to add fiber. Ivy took her breakfast plate and looked over at the tables that were set up for the first meal. She always felt uncomfortable eating with the crew, as if she was a poser and didn't belong there. But Griffin beckoned her over. He was sipping black coffee.

"Come sit with me. Let me just look at those luscious baked goods. That's as close as I'm going to get to them. At least until we're done with the love scene," he said as he pinched the nonexistent fat on his stomach.

"J. B. is really outdoing himself with craft services. How are you?"

"Exhausted."

Ivy looked at Griffin. He did look tired. Dark circles were under his eyes. "Well, we're halfway through the shoot as of today," she said for no real reason. She still felt awkward around Griffin. He was a big movie star, and she was, well, just a first-time screenwriter. "So the movie is halfway over."

"Yeah. I don't know if I'm going to make it through. Last night, some Griffineers climbed into my bedroom."

"Again?" Ivy wondered. It seemed like this kept happening to Griffin.

"I had to call the manager to get them out. I can't even find peace in my own hotel room."

Ivy looked around. She couldn't believe that Griffin was confiding in her. "Maybe you should talk to Drew about it."

"He did," Drew said as he approached their table. If Ivy was expecting a morning kiss from him, she didn't show it. "And before they climbed into your room, they climbed into another room. You were in 424. They climbed into 242."

"No one said they were smart," Griffin cracked.

"An innocent guest's room," Drew said as he joined them at the table. He had just finished talking with the manager at the Belhurst. The guests were all complaining.

Things were getting more difficult for Griffin. And Ivy knew it. "I have an idea." Drew and Griffin turned to her. She suddenly felt very nervous. What if they thought her idea was ridiculous?

"Yeah?" Griffin said.

"Well, it sounds crazy, but why don't you move over to my mom and dad's house? No one would ever dream that you'd be staying there."

"That's true," Griffin said as he pondered the idea.

"I'm sure my parents would love it. You'd sleep in my bedroom, and I'll double up with my sister for the remainder of the shoot."

"Or you could move over to the Belhurst and stay with me." Drew winked.

Ivy shook her head. "We already discussed that. I don't want to give the wrong idea to the crew."

"Like the crew doesn't already know," Drew said, shaking his head.

"I know they know, but I don't want them to *know* know," Ivy insisted.

"Oh, honey, we *know* know," Griffin said, smiling at her.

"Or maybe you just don't want your ex-boyfriend to *know* know," Drew said.

"That's taboo for a public conversation," Griffin said, causing them to stop their bickering. He turned to Ivy. "You sure you want to move out of your bedroom?"

"It's fine. It's more important that you get a good night's sleep. Nick shouldn't look sleepy during the love scenes."

"You mean Rick."

"That's what I said," Ivy stated, thinking out loud. Drew got up and went over to sit with Vera who was going over the shot list.

"You said Nick," Griffin insisted.

"Oh, fuck."

"What is going on with you, girl? Maybe we can have a slumber sesh tonight. You can complete the four quadrants. Drew, Nick, Rick, and poor little Griffin." He laughed. So did Ivy. He was good at cutting the tension. She needed that these days.

And so that night, Ivy went with Griffin as he packed up his things at the Belhurst. Then he left his room but without his suitcase. Griffin went down to the bar. There he made himself extremely visible. He took selfies with everyone. The Griffineers spread the word that he was at the bar. It got crowded. But Griffin kept smiling. Taking more photos. Meanwhile, Ivy took his suitcase and left the hotel. Nobody noticed her as everyone was too busy crowding around Griffin.

"Time to get some shut-eye. These baby blues are exhausted," Griffin told his adoring fans.

The hotel manager escorted the remaining fans out of the hotel. Once they'd all left, Griffin put on his coat and baseball cap and stepped quietly out of the hotel service entrance and into the parking lot where Ivy waited in her rental car.

"You ready?" Ivy asked.

Griffin nodded and slumped down in the seat. But it was already dark outside and there was no one watching them. She drove toward her house. The whole thing was surreal to her. She'd never ever dreamed that a famous actor would be sleeping over at her house, much less in her bedroom For the first time in a while, she smiled to herself.

At the house, Mitch and Linda welcomed Griffin with open arms. They'd never had a celebrity in their home, and they were ecstatic. Linda handed Griffin a bowl of freshly picked blueberries. She'd read that actors preferred healthy snacks. He munched happily on the berries and started to relax. The family guided Griffin upstairs to Ivy's bedroom. He noticed the pink bedspread and pillows. The dance trophies. The stuffed animals. The princess wallpaper border.

"Sorry about all the pink," Ivy said apologetically.

"That's okay—I love pink." Griffin smiled. Then he collapsed on the bed. Exhausted. Linda and Mitch kept talking until they realized that Griffin was fast asleep. In his clothes. Linda placed a blanket on top of him. The family turned out the light and tiptoed from the room.

Across the hall in Carol's bedroom, Ivy was sharing a queen-size bed with her sister. They hadn't shared a room since they were kids. Carol had moved home during Covid. She'd never moved back out. She was saving money while she went to graduate school. Plus, it was so comfortable. Ivy struggled to find the right position. Her legs flailed about.

"Stop kicking me," Carol said.

"Oh, sorry. Just trying to get comfortable." Ivy turned over, her hands accidentally hitting her sister. "Sorry."

"I really don't understand why you didn't just stay with Drew for the rest of the shoot."

"At the Belhurst?"

"If that's where he's staying, then yes."

"You know how I feel about the Belhurst. It's where I lost my virginity."

"I honestly don't think Drew will mind. Guys don't care who you slept with before. As long as you're sleeping with them."

"I know that. Drew and I are fine. It's just that, for me and Nick, the Belhurst was our place for that special night."

"Which isn't in the script, by the way."

"Some parts of my life should be private."

"Good night." Then Carol turned over and went to sleep.

———————

The next morning Griffin woke up and felt refreshed. He hadn't slept so well since he was a baby. He bounced downstairs. Linda was grinding fresh coffee and Mitch was making omelets. Carol was reading the local paper and Ivy was looking over the filming schedule for the day. They all looked up when Griffin practically skipped into the kitchen singing, "Good Morning" from *Singing in the Rain*, improvising some of the lyrics.

"*Good morning, good morning! I slept the whole night through. Good morning, good morning to you!* Wow. I love this. Do you have breakfast like this every morning?" he asked.

"Actually, yes. We do," Linda said with a smile.

"They do," Ivy added without looking up.

"I'm like Little Orphan Annie. I think I'm going to like it here."

"Amari sure does," Carol said, looking up from the local morning paper. "They did an interview with her."

Ivy grabbed the paper. Hollywood In Geneva. It was by that Rory girl. It had a picture of Amari posing at the coffee shop, showing how she loved the town, loved the movie, and loved working with the local extras. How she was so glad she met Drew, Vera, and Griffin. And...

"She doesn't mention the script."

"You mean," Carol suggested, "she doesn't mention you."

"Don't take it personally, Ivy," Griffin said. "A lot of stars are like that. It's always me, me, me."

Carol *tsk-tsked*. "You see—acquired situational narcissism."

Ivy rolled her eyes. But Carol pressed on. She turned to Griffin. "Do you feel that everything revolves around you?" she asked with great seriousness.

"When I'm starring in a movie—yes."

"What about when you're not acting?"

"Then I'm just a movie star."

"So, no matter what, you're always a star."

"My parents always told me I was special."

"Yup. Acquired situational narcissism," Carol repeated.

"What is this situational narcissism?" Mitch asked, confused.

Carol looked at her dad. "Acquired situational narcissists are people who at one time behaved reasonably and diplomatically but developed an egocentric complex as the result of gaining a measure of accomplishment, fame, wealth, or other forms of external success."

Griffin just smiled. Mitch and Linda nodded.

"I'm off. Don't want to be late for my internship where they're not even paying me," Carol said bitterly. She grabbed a travel mug of coffee and ran out the door.

"Sorry about that, Griffin," Ivy said to him apologetically. She felt as if she was always having to apologize for her sister.

"No worries. It's not the first time I've heard it. I'm just happy that I'm not needed on set today. It's my day off. Nothing can get me down today."

"Do you want us to show you around town?" Mitch asked hopefully.

Griffin shuddered. "And get noticed? No. I'd rather just stay here."

"Great! I could use some help icing the Christmas cookies and hanging the Christmas stockings," Linda said.

"They're going to be filming at our house soon," Mitch said proudly.

Griffin's eyes lit up. "I'd love to help."

Later, the house was transformed into a little Santa's workshop. Griffin helped Linda to create the icing in different colors. Then he painstakingly decorated Christmas tree cookies and gingerbread cookies and made them look like works of art. Linda was impressed.

After a short nap, Griffin helped Linda to make stockings for "Ilsa" and "Rick." Griffin proudly hung up his "Rick" stocking, and Linda stuffed it with newspapers to fill it out. Linda and Griffin wrapped empty boxes to make them look like gifts.

"Mom, you know the art department can do all this," Ivy said as she looked up from her laptop.

"That's okay. I told Wyck I'd be happy to help out. I do own a Christmas shop."

After they finished, Griffin slumped in a chair, exhausted. But Linda was still like an Energizer bunny. "Can I do your laundry? I'm throwing in a load now," she asked Griffin.

"Really? That would be great."

Meanwhile, Ivy had been rewriting a few scenes for Vera. She closed her laptop.

It was 5:00 p.m., and Ivy was ready for a drink. So was Griffin. She opened up a bottle of rosé and poured two generous glasses. She handed one to him.

"Thank you. I must say, I like my new digs. Quite a lot." He smiled.

"I'm glad it's working out."

"I've been meaning to ask you—and just for my character and my personal curiosity. When was the first time you thought that you knew you and Nick were forever?"

"It's a long story."

"I've got time." Griffin laughed. "I'm not leaving this house. Can't risk giving up my hiding place."

Ivy poured herself another drink and got comfortable on the couch. "It was senior year of high school. Nick and I convinced our parents to let us go to New York City by ourselves. I wanted to see the tree and check out NYU. Nick wanted to check out

Columbia. Of course he already knew he really wanted Cornell so it was just a ruse. A way for us to get into the city. Without our parents."

"Oh, this is good. But pour me some more wine," Griffin said. "So then what happened?"

"My parents approved the trip because we'd be staying with my twenty-five-year-old cousin who they trusted. But they didn't know that my cousin practically lived with her boyfriend on the Upper East Side."

"Scandalous."

"So, my cousin threw me the keys and left. And suddenly Nick and I had complete privacy for the first time in our lives. We pretty much spent the entire day in bed." Ivy smiled at the memory.

"Oh, baby."

"It was getting dark when we realized we were starving. We stumbled outside to discover a winter wonderland. Over the course of the day, snow had been steadily falling and we'd had no idea. Christmas lights sparkled in the restaurant windows."

"Sounds magical."

"It was. We ran out onto Fifth Avenue and the roads were all white and covered with snow. We held hands walking through the empty streets to Rockefeller Center. I'll never forget that moment. Looking up at the giant lit tree while Nick was kissing me and snow was falling all around us."

"And you fell in love with Nick and with Christmas."

Ivy nodded. "And when it came time to write a script, I knew it had to be about Christmas."

"And Nick," Griffin added.

"And Nick. Our screenwriting professors were always telling us 'Write what you know.'"

"That's why the script feels so authentic. So real. What happened between you two?"

"He dumped me in front of Santa."

Griffin noticed that she teared up a bit in the telling. "That is cold. Guys can be such assholes."

Ivy opened another bottle of wine. "Wow. I can't believe I just told you that story. I haven't talked about it in years."

"We've come a long way since you nearly hit me with your car on Main Street."

She blanched. "That was so awful. Did you realize who I was?"

"Of course. Before the shoot, I Googled you. Saw your cute face at Sundance."

"Ugh. I was worried about that."

"Why? It's not like it was a bad photo."

"I was sure that you were going to drop out of the film at that moment."

"Ha-ha. I couldn't. I loved the script too much. You know I took a pay cut to do this film?"

Ivy did know. Drew had bragged about it to her. But he'd made it sound like it was because he was a great dealmaker and not because of her script. She nodded. "I'm just so happy that you agreed to star in it."

"I haven't been given such a heartfelt part in years."

"Thanks."

"Although I think we both know that I'm not really the star. It's Amari. She can be a real bitch sometimes."

Ivy was taken aback by Griffin's revelation. She'd had no idea that he felt that way. "That's not true. Well, she is a bitch. But she's not the star. You are. Why else would you have so many screaming fans following you everywhere?"

"True. The only person who seems to follow Amari around is Nick," Griffin said. He noticed Ivy had turned sad. "I'm sorry."

"It's okay. It's been over for a long time."

"Yeah, it has," he commented. Very gently he told her, "Maybe it's time to move on. With someone else. I know Drew's got a real hard-on for you."

The front door opened, and Carol walked in carrying a heavy backpack. She laughed when she saw Ivy and Griffin with the two wine bottles. "Looks like happy hour started early today," Carol said as she sat down next to them in the living room.

"It's always a party when I'm around."

She poured herself a glass and looked at Griffin carefully. "Really? Is that what people tell you?"

"I was just joking," he said defensively.

"Most jokes have an element of truth to them."

"I guess so," Griffin muttered.

"So, does that make you happy to be the life of the party? Or is it stressful to always have to be on?"

"And here we go… Time for Carol to psychoanalyze." Ivy shook her head as she got up to go to the bathroom. She left Griffin and Carol alone.

"Honestly, it's stressful," he revealed.

"Tell me about it," Carol continued.

"Sometimes I just want to be like everyone else. Invisible. With no expectations. I want to walk to the grocery store in my sweatpants with a dirty T-shirt hanging out. And I want to buy a box of Twinkies without anyone judging me."

"Uh-huh. Here, why don't you put up your feet and get comfortable," she suggested.

Griffin slipped off his flip-flops and put his feet up on the couch. He was reclining and seemed more relaxed.

"I'd like to have kids one day. But not if it means they have to live a life like mine, with no privacy. Sometimes I wonder if it's all worth it. I lost my parents because of it."

"Your parents are dead?" Carol asked.

"No. But they turned into assholes when I became a star. They might as well be dead."

"I'm sorry."

"And I wish I could go back to college. Do something important," Griffin confessed.

Carol was surprised. Griffin was not at all who she'd thought he was. She tried to reassure him. "What you don't realize is that you are doing something important. You're making people happy when they watch your movies. Cheering them up when they get depressed."

He nodded. "I never thought about it that way."

Carol slipped into the kitchen and brought out a plate of Christmas cookies. "Have a cookie. There's no judging here."

Griffin smiled. "Thanks, Carol. And thanks for the cookie too."

Ivy returned to the living room and said goodbye to Griffin and Carol.

"Where are you going?" Carol asked.

"The Belhurst."

"Someone's getting laid," Griffin said as he smiled at Ivy.

Ivy smiled. She certainly hoped so.

CHAPTER 17

THERE ARE SO MANY DIFFERENT ways to lie in bed. You can lie with your lover, lie to your lover, lie to yourself. Ivy was about to do all three. She had been determined to get Nick out of her head. By any sexual means necessary. Good thing she was in Drew's hotel room. Ivy was wearing a very sexy Santa Claus outfit.

"Not that I don't like the outfit, but isn't it a little early for Christmas?"

"I never thought it was fair that Santa came only once a year." Ivy smiled. "Let's fool around."

Drew didn't have to be asked twice. They began making out on the bed. Deeply. Passionately. Tongues swirling. Hands moving all over each other. Ivy's hand acquiring physical confirmation that Drew was up for anything.

For some unknown reason, Ivy started thinking about actors shooting love scenes. She had known that when the actor was into it—he couldn't fake it. He wore a genital guard that was basically a sock covering over the male member. It had a drawstring so it wouldn't slip off. It was easier for an actress to fake her excitement than a man. Meg Ryan in Katz Deli in *When Harry Met Sally* had taught America that. Ivy wasn't trying to fake anything. She was getting into rocking and rolling and the soft moans. Drew knew all her favorite places and was spending a lot of time visiting them. Ivy was feeling it, closing her eyes, when Nick flashed into her mind. *What the hell?* That's the guy she wanted out of her head, especially when she was getting...

"My head!" Drew said. Ivy didn't realize that her memory had jolted her physically. She had recoiled and somehow she'd kneed him in the head. Ivy quickly apologized and guided him back downtown. But the image of Nick had cooled her off. Drew sensed something was not right. "Do you like that?" he said, his voice muffled.

She did. But there was nothing. Nothing was happening. "Sorry, I'm just tense."

"How about a back rub?" Drew said, and before Ivy could answer he dived facedown on the bed. He wasn't offering a back rub, he wanted one. Ivy rolled over, straddled Drew, and started rubbing his back. It did nothing for her.

"I think I'm a little too tired," Ivy said as she stopped.

"You didn't seem tired five minutes ago."

She rolled off of Drew and laid back in the bed. She wasn't going to tell him that she was feeling excited until in the throes of passion her mind was still playing the Nick show. So she lied. "I'm worried about the movie. We still don't have a good title."

Drew got out of bed, got dressed, and went back to his laptop.

"You're working again?"

"Well, there's nothing else going on here." His phone started buzzing. "See? A work call." Then he answered, "Hey, Rory, what's up? Yes." Drew listened and laughed.

"No, not busy at all," he said.

"What the hell are you doing?" Ivy demanded.

"Ivy, this is a business call."

"But we were…"

"We were what?" Drew said as he covered his phone.

Ivy couldn't find the right words, so she threw out a bunch of them. "We were in bed… Santa… Never mind!"

Drew continued his call. Ivy grabbed her phone, clothes, and went into the bathroom. Got dressed and stayed there. She looked at herself in the mirror, folded her arms in a *Taxi Driver* manner and mumbled the iconic line: "Are you talking to me?" *I am,* Ivy thought to herself. *You'd better stop thinking about Nick.* Ivy was about to walk back and apologize to Drew when— her phone *dinged.*

It was an Insta post from Lauren. It was from the sleepover. Everyone was in matching Christmas pajamas. Including Amari. *#ChristmasInJuly #ChristmasEveEveSleepover #BFF.* Ivy was stunned. Christmas Eve Eve sleepovers were something she started with her friends when they were thirteen. They would all buy matching pajamas and watch movies. Ivy peered closely. Those were the same pajamas that she used to have. How did Amari get a pair?

DING! Another post. Another friend. Kathy. *WATCHING A MOVIE WITH A MOVIE STAR.* It was a selfie of Kathy and Amari in front of a giant screen TV frozen on an image of Amari from her movie. *DING!* Another post. The whole gang singing a Christmas song.

Ivy was about to reply when the door opened. Ivy quickly hid her phone. Drew cast a quizzical eye at her action. "What are you doing in here?"

"Nothing. I mean, I was... What do you think I was doing in here? I was going to the bathroom."

"I heard Christmas music."

Ivy lost it. Her little lies were making her feel awful. She blurted out, "If you're going to work, I'm going to work. And when I work, I play Christmas music. And for the record, I don't like the fact that you are stalking me."

"Stalking you? You left the bathroom door unlocked. And I have to use the bathroom. It's my hotel room. You wanted to stay with your parents, remember? Keep it professional?"

"Is that what you're doing with Rory?" Even Ivy wondered where that came from.

"The girl from the newspaper? She was interviewing me!"

"That's all it was?" If this were a prize fight, her strange flurry of affronts landed. Drew paused. Ivy saw the opening.

"Well, no. She asked me if I liked the town."

"And what else?"

"She asked about a rumor she heard on set."

"What rumor?"

"She promised she would keep it off the record."

Now Ivy was intrigued. She had started this line of defense so as not to admit she was thinking about Nick again, never imagining Drew was also hiding something. "Keep what off the record? Is this about Griffin?" She knew as she said it that it was a mistake.

"What's going on with Griffin?"

"Nothing. Don't deflect, Drew. What is the rumor you denied?"

"She asked if you and I were in a relationship."

That stopped Ivy. She knew she wasn't acting like herself.

But here was a moment that might reset things. "What did you tell her?"

"I told her no. I said that we were just good friends. That we had a good working relationship," Drew stated. She reacted and stormed out of the bathroom. Going right to the front door, slamming it as she heard him calling: "You said you wanted to keep it professional!"

Professional? What did that even mean? Amari wasn't very professional. Well, she could be. When she was shooting a scene, she was amazing. But off-screen, she didn't know the meaning of the word. Ivy walked home and walked in on her parents... rehearsing...with blue script pages in their hands.

"Great. You're home. We have a question for you." They quickly approached Ivy, showing her a line on the script pages. Why were her parents acting out scenes from the movie? "Can we change this line?" her dad said. "I think it's better if the neighbor says, 'Congrats on making the dean's list!' instead of 'How's college going?' It's more specific."

"Also, I read that Tom Hanks says it's better to end a line of dialogue with a period and not a question mark. He said that whenever he gets a script, he goes through all his lines and changes the question marks to periods," Linda added, proud that she knew this.

Ivy was baffled. "What, Mom? And why are you rehearsing the neighbor scene?"

"We're the neighbors. We auditioned and got the parts! We're going to be in your movie!" Mitch said.

"The director had us audition with Amari. She's really talented."

Linda held up a pretty bad selfie. The framing was way off

but the mise-en-scène was in that shot. Her mom and dad with Amari in the middle. Smiling with arms around each other. Nice family. The tea kettle that was her mind started to whistle. Ivy was that close to boiling. Her phone rang; it was Charlotte. Ivy told her parents she had to take this call upstairs. But before she left, at her dad's insistence, she approved the dialogue change.

"What's going on with you?" Charlotte asked. Ivy noted she didn't sound like an agent. She sounded like someone who really cared about her.

"I'm fine, Charlotte," Ivy said.

"Then why did your producer call me and suggest that I check in on you?"

"Drew called you? When?"

"About thirty minutes ago. He said you're acting a little weird on the set. Vera hinted at the same thing when I spoke with her. What's going on out there?"

Ivy was done lying. She trusted Charlotte so she said, "Amari who is Ilsa who is really me is trying to sleep with Nick."

"Are you talking about Rick?"

"No, Rick is Griffin. He's based on Nick."

"So Amari's sleeping with Griffin? That's normal. The costars often hook up."

"No," Ivy explained, "Griffin is playing Rick. Amari is hitting on Nick. Rick is based on Nick, and that's who Griffin is."

"Ivy, I don't think I know who I am in this conversation."

She took a breath and slowed herself down. "Amari is trying to hook up with my old boyfriend, and I don't like that. I'm going to say something to her."

"You are not," Charlotte commanded. "You are not going to tell Amari Rivers who she can and cannot fuck. If Amari wants to have a three-way with Nick, Griffin, and Rick, she is going to have a three-way with Nick, Griffin, and Rick."

"There is no Rick."

Charlotte bellowed, "And there's going to be no Ivy and no career if you get a reputation for being difficult to work with! Amari is the star of the movie. She gets to do whomever and whatever she wants."

"I think if you saw the sleepover pictures, you'd understand."

"The only thing I understand is that writers who argue live in little houses. Leave Amari alone."

Ivy didn't sleep at all that night. She forgot to set her alarm. When she woke up, there was a gaffer in her room hauling in a light. The production had arrived at her doorstep. It would take all morning to set up. Call time wasn't till the afternoon. Ivy decided to go for a run to clear her head. She ran along the Geneva Lakefront Trail. It was a beautiful, cool summer morning. The lake was shining. Ivy ran to what else: classic Christmas music.

The run was an awakening. She was going to think about the movie only. Ivy decided to grab a latte at Monaco Coffee on her way home. Monaco had a line out the door. Something was going on inside. Ivy's phone *pinged*. The question of what was happening inside the coffee shop was solved with the Insta reveal outside. It was a selfie. Of Amari. Making coffee. #CHARACTERWORK. What did that mean?

Ivy squeezed herself into the store, cutting the line. She approached Amari.

"Ivy! So great to see you."

"I need to talk to you."

"Can't right now. Orders are backed up." Ivy watched Amari performing barista duties. She was not good at it.

"Since when do you work here?"

"Since I found out you did. One of your friends told me at the sleepover that you worked here during college."

"I did," Ivy admitted, still confused.

"And the character is based on you. I told you when we started this project that I go deep into character. I want to live Ivy. I want to become Ivy."

This was crazy talk. Crazy actor talk. "I never make a latte that way." Ivy couldn't stop herself—she had to help. Monaco was always good to her. She loved their lattes, and Amari had no idea what she was doing. Ivy started making lattes. Amari studied her, watching her closely. Then, side by side, she mimicked her actions. And she finally got good at making lattes.

"Wow," Ivy said, impressed. "You learn fast."

"I'm just trying to be you. Because, you know, the character is really you. My acting coach—"

"Isn't the director the acting coach?" she asked.

"Vera's great. And I love working with her. But I learned from my acting coach that 'Amari' has the ability to transform and become what she is not. And that 'not' is you."

Ivy was already changing the grind. "Go on..."

"So I am going to do as many Ivy things as I can when we're not filming."

"Does that include Nick?" Ivy said, her head sweating.

"Kind of. Well, I thought so at first. Get a feel for what kind of lothario he was. Still is, if you ask me. Then I realized: this is a pretty nice guy. And that's when I hit on the problem in the script."

Ivy stopped making the coffees. "There's no problem in the script."

"No, there's a problem with Ilsa. With you. What's your secret, Ivy? What are you hiding away up there?"

"You sound like my sister."

"Oh," Amari said, genuinely delighted. "Your sister is a dream. The things she told me about you were so helpful."

"You don't know me at all," Ivy said, and she wondered what Carol had told her. She grabbed a coffee and headed out. Outside, Ivy took a deep meditative breath. She drank her coffee. Noticed that the cup was autographed by Amari. All around her excited people were taking pics of their Amari-autographed cups.

Call time was three in the afternoon. The first shot of the day was going to be in the backyard of Ivy's house. At magic hour. Magic hour was when the sun was setting and the natural light took on a heavenly luminescence. It was also going to be a love scene. The last kiss before Ivy/Ilsa goes off to college. The beginning of their last night together. Ivy was on her best behavior on the set. She ignored Drew and she ignored Amari. They kind of stayed away from her too. She hung out with Griffin. Nick showed up, and Ivy was surprised because she thought it was a closed set. Amari greeted him with a kiss on the lips and a wink toward Ivy. *She didn't just do that to me!* Ivy raged inside. Nick came and sat down next to her.

"What are you doing here?" she asked.

"I don't know. Amari asked me to come down and help her."

"Help her do what?"

Amari called out, "Nick! Honey-bun, come over here." *Honey-bun—Nick hates nicknames.* But Amari's little puppy bounced over.

Bruce cleared the set. Vera wanted an intimate mood. She wanted to capture the kiss when the lighting was perfect. The fewer people on the set the better. A small crew, which included Ivy, was allowed to stay. Vera asked Amari if she was ready.

"Just give me a moment to get into character." Amari launched into a full throttle make-out session with Nick—Ivy's Nick—right in front of Ivy and the crew. It kept going. It was on the monitors. Their hands were all over each other. Ivy couldn't take it anymore. She walked out of her own backyard, her own set. None of the neighbors watching outside even noticed her.

Ivy went to her house of worship: the Geneva Theater. A sign stated that it was on a classic film countdown. The old lavish theater was thirty days away from closing down for good. Each night they would screen a classic movie. Ivy got popcorn, a diet soda, and sat down about thirty minutes into Alfred Hitchcock's *Vertigo*. A movie about identity, about a descent into madness, about obsession. It wasn't a feel-good Christmas movie—but this wasn't a real Christmas, was it?

She walked back home around midnight. The crew was still filming various scenes. Ivy watched her mom and dad play the neighbors and greet Amari, playing Ilsa. Amari posed for pictures with them. The hashtag from the Insta Amari posted was the last straw. *#MYNEWFAMILY.*

"Buy you a drink?" a voice interjected. It was her sister.

They sat in her car across the street, drinking wine, watching the filming.

"Where did you go?"

"The movies," Ivy said. Her eyes were glued on Nick and Amari laughing during a break.

"Who goes to a movie when they can watch their own movie getting filmed?"

"It was *Vertigo*. Jimmy Stewart becomes obsessed with Kim

Novak. He has her dress up like the woman he loved who died. Makes her change her hair. Makes her wear the same outfits. Makes her into the same woman he was obsessed with," Ivy said, watching Amari intently. "But it turns out Kim Novak is both the dead woman and the one who is tricking Jimmy Stewart."

"I think you should have seen a comedy instead. What is going on with you, Ivy?"

She watched Amari kiss Nick, and the locals all cheered. She opened up a second bottle of wine.

"Amari is stealing my life. I'm going to get it back," Ivy stated.

CHAPTER 18

IVY WALKED TOWARD THE HIGH school where they were filming for the day. She wanted to put last night behind her. She was determined to appear upbeat and happy when she arrived on set. The sun was shining. She was wearing her favorite cute sundress, and she'd taken extra care with her hair that morning. She felt jubilant as she pushed open the front doors of the school and walked onto the set.

She saw Drew over in video village. She wanted to clear the air between them, but when she tried, he was frosty and wouldn't talk to her.

"Sorry, can't talk right now" was all he said. Then he turned away from her. She couldn't believe that he was snubbing her. But maybe she deserved it, she thought. After all, she had walked out on him. Ivy tried not to let Drew deflate her upbeat feelings. The camera department was lighting the math class scene where Ilsa invites Rick to the Sadie Hawkins Christmas Ball using a complex calculus problem set. Ivy smiled at the memory. Griffin paced nervously. Almost as if he was actually going to do a math problem.

"You okay?" Ivy asked.

"Why did you make an invite using math? I hate math," he grumbled.

"Nick and I were good at it. He solved the problem set and knew that I was inviting him."

"That makes one of us."

Ivy wandered over to where Amari was sitting. Olivia and Ella, the hair and makeup ladies, were giving her a last-minute touch-up. *She's so gorgeous,* Ivy thought. Amari was sipping a matcha latte and reading over the scene they were about to film. She looked like a beautiful porcelain doll.

"Oh, hi, Ivy," Amari said as she checked out Ivy's sundress. Ivy waited for Amari to say something like *cute dress* or *I like your outfit*, but that didn't happen. Instead, Amari returned to memorizing her script pages. Olivia curled Amari's hair with a curling iron. Ella touched up Amari's face with powder. Ivy realized that she could never compete with Amari.

Griffin watched all of it happening. He beckoned to her. "Have a seat." Ivy walked over and sat down next to him. "I'm not sure what's going on here, but if I had to guess I'd say that Amari is really getting under your skin."

"Is it that obvious?"

"It's like you're the star of your own real-life rom-com."

"How can I compete with that? She's a movie star."

"We can help," said Olivia, who seemed to be always listening closely.

"Great idea. Let's give this girl a makeover," Griffin enthused.

Ivy was whisked off to the girls' locker room, where hair and makeup was staged. She was ushered into a chair facing a mirror.

"Just 'cause you don't feel great doesn't mean you can't look great." Ella held out a foundation sponge. "Come on. Let me touch up your face." Ivy was thrilled. She had secretly always wanted to get a makeover but had always been too chicken. Even the makeup counters at the mall had been too intimidating for her.

"Not so fast. Let me wash and style her hair first," said Olivia. "Hair is always first. Then makeup."

"Fine. Is that okay, Ivy?" asked Ella. Getting a free blowout was something that Ivy would never turn down. She eagerly nodded yes. Soon she was feeling good as Olivia massaged her scalp and washed her hair. The heat of the hairdryer followed. Ivy watched as her hair became smooth and shiny. Olivia finished up and turned off the dryer. She removed the towel around Ivy's neck.

"Thank you so much," Ivy said. "My hair looks amazing."

"You're welcome."

"Now it's my turn," Ella called out.

Ivy sat down in a chair facing the mirror, and Ella started to perform her magic. Ivy closed her eyes while Ella added foundation and blush. "You have amazing cheekbones," Ella said, complimenting her.

"Totally," Olivia agreed. "Much better than Amari's."

When Ivy opened her eyes, her complexion was luminous. Like Amari's. The bags under her eyes had disappeared. "Ella, you're a magician."

Ella took out the mascara.

"Have you ever tried eyelash extensions?"

"No."

"You're about to. You've got a lot of natural eyelashes that would work well with extensions." Ivy nodded *okay* and stepped over to a reclining chair. She leaned back and closed her eyes. While Ella painstakingly applied one lash at a time, Olivia struck up a conversation with Ivy.

"We see what she's trying to do," she said.

"Who?" Ivy asked.

"Shhh. Don't move your mouth while I'm applying these lashes," Ella chided.

"You know who. Amari. She's trying to steal your man. She told me. Well, not in so many words, but she did tell me that she wanted him all for herself. That girl does not like to share. She said she always likes to have a fling during production. Makes her feel alive."

Ivy stiffened. She felt furious. Her suspicions were no longer unfounded.

"All done," Ella said.

Ivy blinked her eyes open and looked into the handheld mirror that Ella held out. And in that moment, Ivy forgot all about her annoyance with Amari because she had the most beautiful long and curvy eyelashes. They opened up her pretty blue eyes. Her hair looked lush and sexy. Ivy hated to admit it, but looking good made her feel good.

"Wow. Amazing."

"I know. I gave you the starlet lashes. Like the ones I use on Amari."

"I love them," Ivy said with more excitement than she'd mustered in some time.

Dede, the costume designer, walked over to look. "Nice work, gals." She nodded approvingly.

"Thanks. Are you busy right now, Dede?" Olivia asked.

"No. Not for another hour."

"Good. Because I think our girl here needs to complete this makeover with a new outfit."

Dede looked at Ivy's sundress and winced. "No offense, honey, but that dress is so 2010." Which it was. Ivy used to wear the sundress in high school.

"Okay. Sure. That would be great. If you're not too busy," she agreed with a big smile and followed Dede over to the wardrobe rack on wheels.

Dede handed Ivy a sexy red Christmas dress. Ivy slipped into the lacy fabric and smiled. It was short and showed off her tanned legs. "Perfect fit," Dede said. Ivy looked at herself in the mirror leaning against the wall, and she had to admit that she didn't look half bad. "Now try on these sandals." But they weren't just any sandals, they were Gucci sandals. Ivy had yearned for them at the Beverly Center's Gucci store. But at seven hundred fifty dollars, they were out of her price range. Ivy sat down on the locker room bench and buckled the sandals. She stood up and wobbled for a second before she adjusted to the height of the heels. Ivy was never one to wear heels, but this was different. She twirled in the mirror. Her smile grew even larger.

"I love it!" Ivy announced.

"My work is done," Dede said.

Olivia looked at Ivy approvingly. "You do good work, Dede."

"So do you."

"Hey, what about me?" Ella protested jokingly.

Ivy watched as Olivia elbow-bumped Ella and Dede in approval. Ever since Covid, high-fiving and handshaking had gone by the wayside.

"Just don't wear those shoes off the set," Dede reminded

her. "You can wear the dress home. Amari's not going to wear it after all."

Ivy tried not to frown when she heard the name *Amari*, but Olivia and Ella noticed.

"She's not going to wear it because it doesn't fit her. Her boobs are too small. We have to put a padded bra on her, and even that doesn't work for this dress," Dede said. Ivy relaxed. "Now go show off your beautiful self," Dede urged her.

Ivy walked out of the girls' locker room. She was tentative. Hoping not to call too much attention to herself. And praying she wouldn't trip in the Gucci heels. She went down the hall and onto the hot set. Griffin was sitting in his canvas chair while he was waiting for his scene to be lit. He was reading the real estate section in the local newspaper. He'd circled various homes that interested him. He was secretly thinking about buying a home in Geneva. A house on the lake. Maybe take some college classes at Hobart and William Smith. When Ivy approached him, he looked up. Surprised.

"Hey, beautiful," Griffin said.

Ivy blushed. "Thanks."

"Look at you, girl. Hot enough to melt an ice cube."

"Is that a thing?"

"I just made it up."

"Sounds like it." Ivy and Griffin laughed.

Drew was busy with Vera looking at the shot list, but everyone else on the crew suddenly noticed Ivy. The sound guy, the script supervisor, the lighting crew, and even the grips all complimented her. Ivy wondered if this was what it felt like to be Amari. She always looked beautiful like this.

At that moment, Amari looked over. She got out of her seat and walked over to Ivy.

"Why are you dressing like this?"

"Like what?"

"I don't know what you're thinking of doing, but don't."

"I have no idea what you're talking about." *But maybe I do,* she thought. Ivy wasn't certain, but she thought that perhaps Amari looked threatened. That's when she realized that Amari always had to be the most beautiful person in the room, and Ivy had no idea that since she'd had her makeover, she was suddenly perhaps more beautiful than Amari.

"Nice dress. They wanted me to wear it, but I didn't like it." *What a bitch,* Ivy thought. *She didn't need to be so nasty.*

Before Ivy could say something out loud that was truly mean, Vera saved her as she called Amari to the set. Amari left, but Ivy wasn't alone for long. Two cute prop guys started orbiting her like she was the star. They complimented her on the script and her outfit. They wanted to know what she was doing that night. Drew wondered what all the commotion was, and he looked up to see Ivy. He was thunderstruck. *Is that Ivy? She's gorgeous.* Drew immediately left the video village to walk over to Ivy. He couldn't take his eyes off her.

"Ivy, you look great."

"Thanks, Drew."

"I forgot to tell you before"—*Before, when you weren't talking to me,* Ivy thought—"that I'm going down to New York on Friday afternoon. I have a meeting on *Captain Midnight.*"

"Is that moving forward?" Ivy said, genuinely excited for him.

"I got some traction. Ryan Gosling is interested in playing Captain Midnight. His agent says he wants to try his hand at the superhero thing."

"Wow. That's great news."

"And the exec said they're looking for a writer to do a character polish for Ryan. I'm going to put in a plug for you." Drew smiled.

Ivy brightened. "That's so nice of you, Drew."

"We make a good team. Maybe you could stop by my hotel room to pick up the script."

"Couldn't you just email me?"

"No, Ivy. It's top secret. Every copy is watermarked. Better if you read it in my room."

Ivy suddenly felt uncomfortable. She realized that doing a rewrite might have strings attached. What if she broke up with Drew? Would he withdraw the offer? Or what if she kept dating him? Would everyone assume she got the rewrite job because she was sleeping with him? She sighed. It was too complicated.

Vera yelled out from across the way, "Has anyone seen our producer?" She knew exactly where Drew was, but she wanted him to get back to work.

"Duty calls," he said as he flashed his perfect smile. "See you later?"

"Maybe," Ivy said. She loved being in the power position for once. It wasn't a place that writers usually found themselves.

Ivy wandered over to the craft services area for a drink. Her back was to the set as she reached for a bottle of water.

"About the other day," said a deep voice. Ivy's eyes grew wide. She recognized that voice. She swiveled around.

"Nick!"

"Ivy! Sorry. I thought you were Amari. You look amazing." Nick looked caught off guard.

"Really?" Ivy smiled. She noticed that he was checking her

out. She felt tingly inside. Before either could speak the assistant director called out, "Quiet on the set."

Nick sat in a director's chair. Ivy sat in the chair next to him, making sure to cross her legs and let the high slit of the dress do its work. She kept seeing him sneaking looks at her.

"It was nice to see your mom and dad the other night. I told them they need to stop by the winery for lunch."

"Nick, you're such a good friend," Ivy said, leaning closer, putting her hand on his thigh at the edge of inappropriateness. Nick didn't seem to mind. Amari did. She could see from where she was standing for the scene.

"Hi, Nick," Amari called out. He waved but returned his focus to Ivy. Amari was frustrated. Why wasn't he paying attention to her? She tried to leave the hot set, but Vera stopped her.

"Where are you going? We're shooting the scene. Everyone back to their marks. Let's roll." The scene started.

"Betcha never thought you'd see me again," Griffin said in character. The cameras continued to roll.

"I'll always be there for you, Nick," Amari said in character. Vera called out, "*Cut!*"

"What was wrong with that?" Amari asked.

"You said Nick, not Rick," Vera told her.

"No, I didn't."

They tried filming it again. Amari kept flubbing her lines. Ivy noticed that Amari was messing up and smiled to herself. Vera called over the script supervisor to feed Amari the lines. "I hope we don't need to put this on cue cards." Vera glared at Amari. Amari glared at Ivy. Ivy only had eyes for Nick.

"I like this new look. Got a hot date or something?" Nick asked.

Ivy laughed. Did he really think she had a date? *Is he jealous?* "Just a date with hair and makeup. It's the magic of the movies."

"I never really understood that."

"Let me show you."

"A time machine?"

"There's no time machine."

Ivy took his hand and led him.

"Come on. I'll show you our twelfth-grade English classroom. Remember what happened there?"

Nick laughed. "Oh no! It might not be safe for me to go back there!"

CHAPTER 19

IVY AND NICK WALKED INTO their twelfth-grade English classroom. It was decorated for filming.

"Wow, this is our old classroom. The posters. The board. The homework looks so familiar." Nick jumped into a seat. "I think I sat here." Then he tried another chair. "No, it was here." He started looking under the desk.

"What are you looking for?" Ivy wondered.

"I scratched our names into a desk."

"You did? You vandal, you."

"I used to scratch our names into all the desks. Here. The library. The church office."

"Never knew you were such a bad boy."

Nick looked around some more. He picked up a plastic piece of coal that was sitting on the desk. "I like the way you put that coal into the script. You were so mad at me," he said.

"I'm still mad at you."

———

In their senior year, in this classroom, they had taken AP Literature together. Mrs. Gilbert, their very British English teacher, announced that they could do a holiday gift exchange, and Ivy was thrilled. When they had drawn names out of Mrs. Gilbert's elf hat, Ivy had pulled her friend Lauren's name. Nick had told Ivy he'd drawn Joey's name. They had gone shopping at the mall together, and Ivy had helped Nick to choose a CD for Joey. They settled on the new Black Keys album. On the day of the Secret Santa reveal, the class had gathered, giddy with excitement. Ivy had handed Lauren her gift and smiled as Lauren gushed over the new Taylor Swift CD. Other gifts were exchanged. An iTunes card. A box of candy. Hat and mittens. Lauren had stepped forward and given Joey a Starbucks gift card. Ivy had been confused. Wasn't Nick the secret Santa for Joey? The gifts had continued to be handed out. It had finally been Ivy's turn. She had waited with anticipation for her Secret Santa to reveal themself. Ivy had been surprised when Nick got up and walked over to her and said, "Merry Christmas. Ho ho ho." He had tricked her.

She had smiled to herself, thinking *classic Nick*. He had given her a small, wrapped gift. When she'd seen the size of the present, she'd thought it might be jewelry. Her heart had pounded with excitement. She'd hoped for a gold heart or a pearl necklace, but a simple bracelet would have been nice too. Everyone had watched as she opened it. When she'd seen what was inside the box, her face had fallen, and her smile had turned into a frown. It was coal!

———

Ivy winced at the memory.

Nick noticed that she was pouting. "Are you pouting? Come on, that was ten years ago."

"It just wasn't very nice, giving your girlfriend coal."

"I did it because you went out for ice cream with Joe Buff."

"That wasn't a date. I was just doing it to make you jealous."

"Well, it worked." Now it was Ivy's turn to laugh. Nick continued, "I kind of gave you a nice present later that night. Do you remember what that was?"

"It was a pretty gold bracelet we saw in the mall. I remember you were too embarrassed to give it to me at school."

"And that's why I gave you the coal." Nick picked up the coal and pocketed it.

"Hey. You shouldn't touch that. I think this is a hot set."

"I have no idea what that means."

"It's when the set is dressed, all the props are in place and ready for filming." Ivy was starting to sweat. Was it because the room was hot, or was Nick making her nervous?

"I thought it was because it was warm in here." It was close to ninety degrees inside, and the air conditioner was too loud to be on during filming. Ivy and Nick were both feeling the heat.

"Want to see the production office?"

"Sure."

But the moment that they arrived at the production office, Ivy regretted it because printed on a giant whiteboard was proof of Nick's fictional demise. It seemed to scream out at them. Or at least it did to Ivy. On the board was a list of scenes that were left to be filmed. Number thirteen was *Rick's death*.

Ivy stepped in front of the board, trying to hide it. She was having such a nice time with Nick and didn't want him to remember how she'd killed him off in the script. But her feet were hurting. The Gucci sandal straps were digging into her heels, and she really needed to sit down. She couldn't bear the pain anymore and finally took a seat. She noticed that Nick was no longer looking at the board anyway. She breathed a sigh of relief, but she shouldn't have because he was engrossed in the storyboards, the rudimentary drawings that showed the various camera shots for each scene. Nick was seeing the storyboard for the scene marked *RICK DIES*.

"I still can't believe you killed me off in the movie. I thought rom-coms were supposed to end happily."

"It's not a rom-com. It's a romance. Characters can die in a romance."

"That never made sense to me. Seems like you're cheating the audience to kill someone after they've met the love of their life," Nick commented.

"Losing someone makes people feel the love more profoundly. It's better to have loved and lost than never to have loved at all."

"You don't really believe that, do you?"

"I do."

"What if the love of their life does something awful to them?" Nick asked.

"Sometimes good people do mean things. There's usually a motivation."

"That makes me feel better to hear you say that." Nick smiled. "Because I—I…" Nick stopped. His mind flashed *Red alert!* He didn't want to relive the past.

"You know this movie is only loosely based on us, right? When I killed off the character that is"—using air quotes—"*loosely* based on you, I did it to create more drama. I didn't want the script to get labeled as cute or cheesy, which is what can happen with a rom-com."

"And maybe you were also a little bit mad at me?"

Ivy paused for a moment before she finally admitted, "Maybe." She smiled at Nick.

"I guess I don't blame you. But crashing my snowmobile into the ice? That's just cold. Literally." But Nick didn't look mad. "Besides, I don't even own a snowmobile."

"Like I said, loosely based on us." Ivy smiled. "Come on, let's go to the gym. Check out the winter ball."

"But I'm so underdressed."

"Oh, you're fine!"

As they walked through the hallway, Ivy's hand accidentally brushed against Nick's fingers. She wanted to take his hand and hold it. As if they were actually going to the winter ball together. In the hallway there was a table with a pile of unwrapped gifts. Handmade signs on large craft paper were painted with the words *TOYS FOR TOTS. DONATE HERE.* Nick stopped in front of them. "I remember when you organized a toy fair like this. We all had to bring an unwrapped toy in order to gain entrance to the winter ball."

"It was part of my Girl Scout Gold Award. I wanted to help the families who couldn't afford gifts."

Nick smiled. He gestured to this pile of gifts. "So is this real or fake?"

"The toys are real. The drive is fake. But I'm sure the production office will donate them to a hospital when the filming is done."

"You're such a good person, Ivy."

"Don't give me so much credit. I'm sure I only did it for the award."

"Nah. There were too many other times when you did things for no reason except to be kind. Like gathering everyone to sing

Christmas carols at the senior center or shoveling snow for shut-ins or organizing a free nighttime babysitting event so young parents could go on a date without their kids." Ivy smiled at the memories. In truth, she'd forgotten about all those things that she'd done in high school. "You really are something, you know that? You didn't deserve what I did to you."

Ivy looked away, trying to hide her feelings. But she said softly, "Thanks." She pushed open the gym doors to reveal a sparkly winter wonderland. Large white paper snowflakes shimmered from the ceiling. Ivy switched on the disco ball, and lights began to swirl around the room. A table was set up for a punch bowl and cookies.

Nick strolled over to the punch bowl and looked inside. No liquid.

Ivy pretended to scoop out a glass of punch for him. "Some punch for you, young man?" She said this in her best English accent, and they both cracked up. Mrs. Gilbert had been a permanent fixture at all their dances as she always claimed to enjoy being a chaperone. She'd also kept a close eye on the punchbowl.

"Remember when I snuck in that rum and added it to the punch?" Nick's eyes twinkled. Ivy nodded. She'd heard the story about a million times, but for once she didn't mind hearing it again. She smiled at Nick and encouraged him to continue. "I got the idea from *The Godfather*. When Michael hides his gun in the bathroom of the restaurant. Remember your dad made us watch that? Your dad is so awesome."

"We were so freaked out about the horse head in the bed." Ivy laughed.

"After soccer practice, I went to the bathroom and hid the

vodka up above the ceiling tiles. During the dance I went and got it and slipped it into my suit jacket. I passed it to Steven, and he poured it into the bowl while I distracted Mrs. Gilbert."

"You were such a flirt. Mrs. Gilbert always did have a crush on you."

"Really?" Nick played dumb.

Ivy playfully slapped him on the arm. "You knew."

They both laughed. The mood was light again.

"That dress really does look amazing on you." Nick smiled. Ivy blushed. She wondered if he was checking her out. "I'm really not bringing my A-game here." He laughed as he pointed to his jeans and T-shirt. "But I'm going to change that," Nick said as he strolled over to a wardrobe rack at the edge of the gym. A variety of men's sports jackets hung on the rack, ready for the extras who would show up for the scene later.

Ivy smiled as she watched Nick try on a gold sparkly jacket. "What about this?" He began singing the Elvis Christmas classic "Blue Christmas." Ivy watched as Nick crooned to her. He took off the gold jacket.

Ivy just laughed. "You're right—too Elvis."

Then Nick tried on a red jacket. "I like this."

"Ho, ho, ho!" Ivy chuckled, and Nick rubbed his belly. Although she noticed that his six-pack could never become a belly. She tried not to check out his physique. But he did look hot.

"Right. Too much Santa." Nick took off the red jacket and rummaged through the other jackets until he paused at a black velvet one. He put it on and posed for Ivy.

"Perfect," Ivy purred. *Did I really just purr?* Ivy told herself to get it together. "You look great."

"Thanks." Nick was swiping through his phone. Searching for something. Then he smiled. And moments later, Mariah Carey's "All I Want for Christmas" blasted from Nick's phone. Ivy's eyes lit up. She remembered watching *Love Actually* with Nick every Christmas, and the song had been the centerpiece of the movie. She loved that song.

She twirled around in the sexy red Christmas dress.

Nick held out his hand. "Can I have this dance?"

Ivy giggled. *Really? Is this actually happening?* "Of course."

"Your dress is amazing," Nick said for the second time. "Feels like we're actually at the dance." He twirled her and dipped her. Ivy was giddy. They continued to dance. They matched each other's steps perfectly. Ivy's smile could have been seen from space, it was that big. Nick was beaming too. She sang along with the chorus. He continued to smile as she sang to him. As the song ended, they were both out of breath.

"Let's see what else I have." Nick scrolled through his music. "Yes. I remember you liked this one."

"Oh, let me see."

"Wait for it." Nick laughed and turned away with his phone. "Where Are You Christmas?" from *How the Grinch Stole Christmas* emanated from Nick's phone. It was a slow song. Contemplative.

Nick put his arms around her.

Ivy laughed. "Are we really slow dancing?"

Nick laughed too. "This is nice. You know I'm really happy that your script is getting made into a movie."

"I guess I should give you some credit. If you hadn't cheated and broken up with me, I never would have written the script."

Nick's smile faded quickly. He wondered, *Should I tell her the truth?* "I'm sorry, Ivy. But I'm happy that all your dreams are coming true."

Ivy wasn't sure if *all* her dreams were coming true or not. But she decided to keep that to herself. "It's been nice to be back home. Your mom seems great."

"Yeah. I guess I have you to thank for that. If your movie wasn't filming here, she never would have met J. B."

"I love that."

"He's the first guy that she's fallen for since my dad died."

"Really sorry I wasn't here for his funeral. But I didn't know about it until a month later."

"It happened kind of suddenly. He always liked you, Ivy. Was really mad when we broke up." Nick cursed himself for bringing up bad memories.

"I liked your dad. He would have been so proud of you. Of all you've accomplished."

"Even the Poison Ivy wine?"

Ivy laughed. "Even that."

"So you're not mad about me calling the wine after you?"

"Truth? I'm honored."

Nick leaned closer. Ivy found herself learning toward him.

She looked up at him, and their faces almost touched. Ivy wondered if they were going to kiss.

"Cut!" Vera called out. Ivy and Nick turned to see Vera. They hadn't realized that Vera had tiptoed into the gym and had witnessed most of their dialogue. Ivy and Nick instinctively dropped their arms awkwardly.

Vera walked over to them. "The characters can't kiss until the end of the movie. Just before Rick dies. But I like some of the new dialogue. Especially the part about the dad being proud of him. I want you to put it in the script, Ivy."

Ivy looked at Vera, dumbfounded. Was Vera that obtuse about what was really happening in the gym at that moment?

"That's it. I was just checking out the winter ball decorations. Looks great. The toy drive is cute too. And I'm happy that you've taken this time to rework that scene. I knew it was a good idea to have you on set. I was right." With that flourish, Vera swirled out of the gym.

Ivy and Nick pulled away from each other, both realizing it was a mistake.

"I should get back to the set," Ivy said.

"I need to get back to the winery. It was nice catching up with you, Ivy," Nick said and returned the black velvet jacket to the rack before walking out the door.

Ivy walked over to the disco ball and turned it off, then switched the lights back on. Suddenly the winter ball no longer looked so magical. Ivy realized that the moment had been fake after all. Not real. The magic of the movies could quickly fade away.

CHAPTER 20

WHAT THE HECK, I ALMOST kissed Ivy, Nick thought as he drove along Route 27. It was all he thought about that night in his restless sleep. If that director hadn't interrupted them, who knew what might have happened. Would Ivy have responded? Would Vera tell Amari? How did he feel about Amari? Nick was confused. He didn't know what to think! The one thing that Nick wasn't was a deep thinker. Yes, he cared about the world and important issues like equality and the virus—but when it came to making decisions, Nick would go with his gut and act quickly.

He ran track in high school, clocked an impressive 4.5 in a forty-yard dash. His coach had told him he had what was called "scholarship" speed and he could go to any college he wanted. Nick didn't even give it a second thought—he wasn't going away from the winery. That was his life. He had gone to Cornell to learn about wine, modernize the winemaking process, and run the family business one day. But when it came to Ivy, he kind of did run away. He had loved her, which made the breakup so hard. But he had put that all behind him, taken over the winery, and prospered with his Poison Ivy wine. His mother was one of his biggest critics, not just of the breakup but of the name choice. She loved Ivy. Everyone loved Ivy. Did Nick still love Ivy? He had to talk to someone. And since his mother was always offering advice about his love life, as in *You don't have a love life, you haven't been on a date in years*, it was time to have the talk with his mom.

Nick pulled up to his childhood home. The tire swing was still in front where he had pushed his baby sister, Denise; where he'd tried to swing Ivy, and she got motion sickness.

He was surprised to find the front door was locked. His mom's car was in the driveway. She never locked the house. Especially when she was home. Nick was startled when he opened the back door and saw a man's backside. Naked. Jutting halfway out of an apron. Standing in the kitchen and holding a knife.

"What the hell are you doing here?" Nick said as he charged the man. Nick grabbed the intruder's right hand that was holding the knife.

The naked-except-for-an-apron man screamed, "No!"

The knife fell from his hand as Nick tackled him. The two men slammed into the kitchen table which was covered with flour. It flew into the air. Both men coughed.

Nick's mom ran into the kitchen, in a man's dress shirt, yelling, "Nick, stop. It's J. B. The caterer from the movie." Nick stopped, wiping the flour off his face. J. B. stood up, adjusting his apron for maximum coverage, and kissed Nick on both cheeks.

"Nick, so nice to meet you. Your mother spent half the night talking about you."

Nick looked at this mother. "Half the night...what did she spend the other half doing?"

"Making croissants. Are you hungry?" Frannie asked, trying to deflect. She seemed slightly unnerved and a bit embarrassed.

Nick observed that J. B. seemed to have no problem with any aspect of this awkward situation. As J. B. hand-whipped his batter he said, "We made beautiful, passionate love."

"And croissants," his mom added, covering. "We made croissants also."

"I'm so happy to hear that, Mom. It is so good to know you still know how to make croissants," Nick said, not really thinking.

"Yes, have one," J. B. said. Nick was staring at them both, gap-jawed, when J. B. inserted what was arguably the greatest croissant Nick had ever had into his mouth. "Good, no?"

"Nothing about any of this is good."

"Nick, outside with me, now," his mother ordered.

"Yes, you two talk. But take some coffee with you." J. B. poured Nick and Frannie some coffee. *Damn, it's good,* Nick said to himself as he sipped.

Moments later, Nick and Frannie sat in the backyard. In silence. Nick admired his mother's gardening. His dad never liked the garden. He liked to keep a field of grass in case a baseball game broke out. It never did. He was always too busy working. After his dad's death, Frannie picked up some gardening magazines, some tools, and some plants. Before too long, the backyard was a botanical oasis. She had done the same thing at the winery, framing the outdoor area with flowers.

"The garden looks great."

"I know. Your father would have hated it," Frannie said. They both laughed. Nick sipped his coffee. He already knew he was going to get a second cup.

"I'm sorry you found out this way," she offered.

"Yeah, I didn't expect to see a naked ass in the kitchen making croissants."

"I didn't expect you to come over. You always wake up and go straight to the winery."

"Do you want to tell me what is going on with you and J. B.?"

"No. I'm your mother. I am not going to talk about my sex life."

"Sex life," Nick repeated, albeit unwillingly. His mother had a sex life. He didn't even have a sex life these days. "I don't even have a sex life!"

"And whose fault is that?" Frannie said.

"And don't you mean love life?"

"Right now, it is my sex life. If it becomes serious and becomes a love life, I'll let you know. J. B. and I hooked up. Had a booty call. Whatever you want to call it. Been a while. Your father passed away three years ago."

Nick understood. His mother looked happy. Frannie always looked happy. But this was different. Now she was glowing.

He made his decision about J. B. "Well, if his breakfast is as good as this coffee, you have my permission to marry him," Nick said. Frannie laughed.

"What's going on, Nicholas? Why did you come over?"

"I need your advice...about love...about..." The words faltered. Nick couldn't bring himself to say her name. Frannie understood who he was talking about. She had wanted to talk to him about Ivy so many times since the "breakup." Nick had always refused. Sometimes politely and sometimes telling Frannie to stay out of his business. He couldn't even say her name.

So Frannie did. "Ivy," she stated. Finally glad Nick was willing to talk about her.

"How did you know?"

"It's always been Ivy, Nick. We both know that." He nodded. Waited. "When your father died, I knew I would never find someone like him again. He was jolly. Loved a great song. Wrote these great birthday cards. What we had was magical. I know I am never going to find that with anyone else in this world again."

"So J. B.?"

"It would be a different kind of love. Good, but different. What your father and I had was so special. But this is about you, Nick. You made the decision to break up with Ivy. I can't go back and be with the love of my life, but you can. If that's what your heart wants."

Clang. J. B. in his apron was calling from the doorway, banging on a pot. "The French toast—or as we say, the *pain perdu*—is ready."

"Breakfast?" Frannie asked Nick.

"Does he have pants on under that apron?"

"J. B., are you wearing pants?" Frannie called out playfully. He lifted his apron, revealing that he was wearing khaki shorts.

Breakfast broke all the taste barriers. Nick had never known a *pain perdu* this good, and with each bite he wanted to go to Paris. J. B. appreciated it. He joined Nick and Frannie at the table. With the apron removed, Nick noted J. B. had slipped on a Poison Ivy T-shirt.

"Great shirt," Nick said, a bit happy to see free advertisement but not happy to see Ivy's face across from him.

"Yes, I didn't have any clothes to sleep in. And I was cold in the middle of the night. Your mother gave me this shirt to keep me warm."

"Okay," Nick said, "you two are sweeter than the maple syrup."

"Maybe this is love," J. B. said. "Who knows?"

Nick caught his mother's smile. She deserved to be happy, Nick knew. And the more he got to know J. B. the happier he was for her.

"So, Nick," J. B. continued, pointing at the image of Ivy on the Poison Ivy T-shirt, "why does this Ivy vex you?"

"You couldn't have given him a different shirt?" Nick asked his mom.

"Nick, forget the shirt," J. B. said. "I can take the shirt off, and she is gone. But you cannot take your heart off. Do you still love this Poison Ivy? Or do you love the actress playing Ivy? You are in love with two women, but they are the same. If this was Paris, this would not be a problem."

"Why is that?" Frannie asked.

"In Paris, you keep them both."

"Nick's not in Paris, and neither are you, mister," Frannie warmly warned. "Any more advice for Nick?"

"Eat."

What the hey, Ivy thought as she walked to the Belhurst Castle, *I almost kissed Nick.* She had not slept all night. It was Friday. Call time on the set was 10:00 a.m. If Vera hadn't interrupted them, who knew what might have happened. *Would Nick have responded? Would Vera tell Amari?* How did she feel about Nick? Ivy was confused. She didn't know what to think! The one thing that Ivy wasn't was decisive. She would take hours/days/weeks to make a decision. Ivy knew she didn't have hours/days/weeks—she had five days. That was when production would wrap and she would fly back to LA. Meetings and offers were waiting.

In film school, Ivy had had a hard time coming up with story ideas. She had writer's block, and everything she wrote was a copy of a copy. Her professor kept pushing her to write what she knew, what she felt. What she knew best was her love for Nick and the loss of love she felt after the breakup. All the other scripts she wrote weren't real. *Do I have only one story in me?* she fretted. They say there are eight million people in New York City, eight million stories. And there are eight million people in LA but only one story. Had she written anything good since *When Joseph Met Mary?* Was Geneva her hometown muse?

Does home mean Nick? Does Nick mean home? Where does Drew fit into all of this? She would talk to Drew. That's why she was going to the Belhurst Castle, hoping she could catch him before he left for New York City for his *Captain Midnight* meetings. Drew would be gone for the weekend, and she hoped to finally talk about something real with him. Except Drew wasn't there. She had missed him by five minutes. She knew she should have driven there.

Ivy walked away, defeated. On her way back home, she stopped at Monaco. On the glass front door, there was a newspaper article about Amari working at the coffee shop. Ivy recognized her own arm in the accompanying photo. Inside, there were now autographed pictures from Amari thanking everyone.

Ivy got her latte and sat in her favorite spot in the corner. She remembered this was the place where she'd worked on her film school application. Ivy checked her email. There was a message from Drew: MARKETING PEOPLE ARE DEMANDING A NEW TITLE. ASAP. LET ME KNOW WHAT YOU HAVE. SEE YOU MONDAY. Ivy opened up the notes app on her phone and began typing down new titles for the movie. By the time she had finished the latte, she had come up with some pretty bad titles. *The Christmas Creep! Christmas Sucks! Christmas Mistake!* All it did was cause her to think about Nick. She had to talk to someone.

Ivy walked home. When she opened the front door she heard *bang! Kaboom!* She followed the sounds to find her dad playing video games with Griffin. Her dad wasn't the surprise. He had convinced his school that they needed to teach a class on "video game narratives." It was Griffin. He was really settling in, bonding with her family. The Griffineers had not found him. Ivy smiled at the alt-version of Nick. But that wasn't fair to Griffin, Ivy thought. He was his own person, someone who had gone through a lot in his life. So it was not surprising when Griffin said: "You look like you need someone to talk to." Ivy loved that Griffin understood what she needed. They went upstairs to her pink bedroom.

Ivy and Griffin sat on her bed. They both recognized their relationship as brother/sister. There was never an inkling of any attraction. And there never would be. All they knew was that both would become good friends.

"So, let's get to it." Griffin started it. "Is it going to be Team Drew or Team Nick? I will have you know, Ivy, that your little love triangle has split everyone on the set into two factions." He jumped off the bed and went into a warrior pose and proclaimed, "On one side we have Team Drew, the super stud from Malibu, powerful, great dresser, sweats success, but can we trust him? He's from LA." Griffin now struck a mountain pose. Standing strong. "And on the other side, Team Nick, the winemaker, the hometown honey, captain of his own boat, the original Joseph, and still rocking his high school football bod."

"Nick ran track."

"The fastest man in Geneva, the winemaker with a broken heart and a bottle of Poison Ivy. Is Amari playing Nick to get into character? Or is Nick conning Amari to make you jealous and win you back?"

"This is what people are talking about on the set? No wonder no one talks to me."

"Will Ivy wind up with Team Nick or Team Drew? Find out tonight at Eddie O'Brien's."

Ivy looked confused. "What does Eddie O'Brien's have to do with this?"

"It's where the cast and crew hang out each night. We kind of took it over."

"You hang out? What about the Griffineers?"

Griffin smiled. "The Teamsters are running security. I buy them dinner."

"It used to be a dive."

"It's authentic."

Ivy thought back to what Griffin had said. "Why tonight? Why will we find out tonight at Eddie O'Brien's?"

He looked her in the eyes.

"Because Nick will be there with Amari. And Drew's out of town. I should also tell you there's a betting pool going on."

Ivy was shocked. "People are betting on my love life?"

"Olivia and Ella from hair and makeup set it up."

"How much is it up to?"

"About two grand."

"Two thousand dollars?"

"And there's all these side bets. When will you decide? Where will you decide? Public or private declaration. Olivia and Ella are really good with numbers."

"What if I pick neither?"

Griffin checked his phone. Signaled to wait as he scrutinized the digital spreadsheet on his phone. "That's the long shot now. About five hundred to one."

Ivy was taken aback and embarrassed and upset with herself for not being more professional. She still needed advice. "Who are you betting on, Griffin?"

He was quiet again. Then softly: "I'm betting on love, Ivy. I always will bet on love. I had someone I loved and I let them get away. Broke up with them to protect them. I always regretted it. We are similar in so many ways, Ivy. So, I am betting on you and Nick."

"Can I ask you why?"

"Because," Griffin whispered sincerely, "if you have a second chance at love, then maybe I do too."

CHAPTER 21

THE CREW WAS IN A party mood. The locals were not. Tensions were mounting on the line to get into Eddie O'Brien's. For the most part, the town of Geneva was very happy that the movie had come to town. Business had been good for the local shops in the last three weeks. Geneva was receiving some great regional news coverage showcasing Seneca Lake, and there was a rumor circulating that one of the "Hollywood people" was thinking about buying and restoring the movie theater.

But some locals, specifically a group that usually gathered every Saturday night at Eddie O'Brien's, were very upset when they discovered their favorite local bar closed for a private event. Christmas music was blasting from inside. *How could Eddie O'Brien do this to us?* the locals grumbled. Eddie had gotten into the Christmas mood and decorated the bar with red-and-green lights and even brought out the Christmas Karaoke. When pressed by Rory, the news reporter of the local paper, Eddie answered simply: "The Hollywood people spend a lot more money than my usual clientele."

Still, Nick, who was selling more wine than ever before, was surprised to see the size of the crowd trying to get into Eddie's. There was even a doorman in front holding a clipboard. It was one of the production assistants.

Nick walked to the front of the line. The fact that there was a line to get into Eddie's defied all logic. It was Eddie's. The local mainstay. Pretty much a dump. It had lots of charm but was still a packed dive bar bursting at the seams with Hollywood people. The truth was the Hollywood people were mostly New Yorkers from downstate, which the locals disliked just as much. Nick talked to the guy working the door. He held up a list. A list? To get into Eddie's?

"Hey, Hollywood, get us in," someone yelled. An onslaught of rude remarks was shouted about Nick and Amari. More pictures of "Nickmari" had gone viral. Nickmari? It sounded to him like something to send back at a seafood restaurant.

"Hey, Mystery Man," a jerk from high school called out, "I saw you on one of those gossip shows. They called you Amari's boy toy." More laughter. Nick didn't smile. The doorman found his name, and Nick walked into the crowded tavern. He was Amari's plus one.

It was good to be back in a crowded bar, Nick thought. The pandemic had crushed a lot of businesses, and Geneva was just beginning to come back. The movie helped a lot with the economic month-long boom. Nick was even shipping more wine than the previous two years combined. As much as he hated to admit it, Hollywood had helped to revitalize the town. While Nick was happy about this, the *boy toy* remark was still gnawing at him. When he found Kenny and his sister, Denise, at the end of the bar, he was still thinking about it. *Boy toy. Boy toy? How could I be a boy toy?* Amari hadn't even taken Nick out of the box yet.

"What's up?" Kenny said.

"Some idiots from high school called me Amari's boy toy."

"Well, aren't you?" Denise asked. Nick smirked. She smiled, explaining, "You have been spending a lot of time with her lately."

"I have not," he protested.

"*Nickmari* would say different." Denise swiped on her phone, which was now very close to Nick's face, finding the trending *#Nickmari*, and showing pics from Amari's social media. She swiped through them quickly but with enough time for Nick to soak them in. There were shots of Amari and Nick on the boat, Amari and Nick having drinks on the pier, Amari and Nick getting a spa day...

"You hate spas," Kenny said. "I tried to get you to go, and you always say no."

"Yeah, it's easier to go with her." Nick smiled. "What can I say, Amari is someone I feel very comfortable around. She makes me laugh. I feel like I've known her my whole life."

Kenny and Denise looked at each other. Did Nick not see it?

"Amari is Ivy," Kenny said.

"No, Amari is Amari. Ivy isn't an actress."

"Amari is playing Ivy in the movie. Actors are like that," Denise said. "They become the character. You're falling for Amari because she is playing Ivy."

Nick thought about it. Was that what was happening? He searched for the answer in his beer. It wasn't there.

Denise consoled her visibly shaken brother. "Don't worry, Nick. This happened all the time with you and Ivy. And maybe in the script she wrote, you had this amazing love affair. But in real life, you were kids. You and Ivy always broke up, and you always got back together. You went through the ups and downs, breaking up before prom and then being named king and queen. Agreeing that you could date other people when you were both at college, but neither of you ever did."

"She's with this Drew guy. The film producer. She got the life she wanted," Nick said.

"What really happened at the Grove, Nick?" Denise asked.

Kenny opened his mouth to say something, when Nick shot him a look. Kenny stopped immediately. Denise tucked that away as odd and did not ask any more because that was when the texts arrived almost at the same time on Nick's phone with a double ding. One text from Amari. One text from Ivy. The same message: MEET ME AT EDDIE O'BRIEN'S. "Maybe you're in love with both of them?" Kenny said, paying for the next round of beer.

"Either way," Denise said, "Ivy and Amari will both be gone in five days. The movie wraps on Friday. There's a wrap party and people say goodbye." *Five days?* Nick thought, *Only five days to figure it out.*

———

"You have five days to figure this out, Ivy." She and Griffin were in the backseat of a car being driven to Eddie O'Brien's.

"Movies always have a ticking clock," Ivy said. "But usually in act three. This isn't act three. This is something different…late in act two…the Dark Night of the Soul…the all is lost moment. I'm doomed."

"Your life is not a movie, Ivy. You're going to go in there and have an honest conversation with Nick," Griffin told her.

As they approached Eddie O'Brien's, the driver slowed down.

"There's quite a crowd in front. I see some Griffineers trying to get in. What should I do, sir?"

"Sir? You don't have to call him sir, Dad. You're not a limo driver."

"Driving around this much talent, I feel like one," Mitch said proudly.

"Use the alley behind the theater. We'll go in the back way," Ivy said. Mitch listened and drove. They were soon at the back door of Eddie's. Ivy was reluctant to get out. "*High Noon*," she remarked without much bravado.

"If you're going to keep making movie references, then make sure I am the new best friend. And as your new best friend, I want you to text Nick, right now, that you will meet him at your old favorite booth."

"How did you know we had a favorite booth?" Ivy wondered.

"I read a lot of *Archie* comics. You're so Betty. Amari is Veronica. Archie could never decide. Now text him." Ivy did. And they were off. "Let's go," Griffin said as they walked in through the back. He tipped the Teamsters smoking by the door and waved to J. B. and Frannie in the kitchen, who had found a quiet spot to talk. Frannie admired how great Ivy looked, smiled, and gave her the thumbs-up. Maybe Frannie was rooting for them. Griffin and Ivy walked into Eddie's. The crowd parted. Ivy felt like a princess arriving at the ball.

The always-watching Olivia and Ella whispered to Griffin, "Are you and Ivy together?"

"We got a great brother-sister thing going on," he said with a wink.

"Ivy, you look great," Olivia said.

"Thanks to the two of you."

"Stunning dress," Olivia said. "I'm glad you picked that one."

"Amari had been eyeing it," Ella said.

"If you want to know what is going on on a movie set, always talk to the hair and makeup people," Griffin said. "So what's the intel?"

Olivia leaned in. "No Amari sighting, but Nick just grabbed that corner booth. Paid the sound guy a hundred bucks for it."

Ivy smiled. Nick did that, she thought as Griffin pushed her in Nick's direction. "You go to Nick. Olivia, Ella, and I are going to be watching as we drink some Christmas cosmos."

Ivy disappeared into the crowd. Griffin went to the bar. Rory pounced on Olivia and Ella. "So, ladies, what was all that about?"

"Go away," Olivia said. "We don't talk to the press."

Rory retreated. Ella commented, "I don't like that one. Gossiping. Making money on other people's lives."

Lane, the location guy, walked up to them, money in hand. "What's the pool up to?" he asked.

Ella checked a small notebook. "About twenty-one hundred dollars."

"I wanna put a hundred on our writer sealing the deal with Nick tonight here at Eddie's." Olivia took the money as Ella marked the entry.

"Of all the gin joints in all the world, you walk into mine," Ivy said, standing across from Nick.

"I got us our old booth. And isn't that from *Casablanca*?"

"Very good, Nick. I'm impressed." Ivy slid into the same side of the booth as him. It was a tight, intimate arrangement.

"There's more room on the other side," Nick suggested.

"I think with what we need to say to each other, we should be as close as possible, like on our first real date when you said—"

"There you are!" Amari called out. Before Ivy could blink, Amari had settled in the booth across from Nick, leaning in with her low-cut shirt. "So great that the three of us can get together like this."

Nick didn't know what the hell was going on. Ivy squeezed his thigh, while at the same time Amari (shoe off) rubbed his leg with her foot. The small talk about the movie started. Ivy and Amari talked about everything except Nick. Until Amari said, "Next week, we will film the breakup scene. Honestly, Ivy, I do not understand how you could ever let a guy like Nick walk out of your life."

"I didn't," Ivy said as she looked at Nick. "He dumped me. And you already know that."

"Three cosmos, barkeep," Griffin ordered. The barkeep was none other than Bruce Danton, the assistant director. "Bruce!" Griffin called out, "very happy to see you."

"Hey, Griffin. Nice to see you," Bruce said as he shook a cocktail. "I saw the bartender was backed up, so I jumped in. Bartending got me through film school." Bruce went off to make another drink. Griffin totally forgot about the cosmos. And Ivy. And Nick. And Amari as he grabbed an apron and started to help out behind the bar.

Meanwhile over in their favorite booth, Nick shifted in the corner. But he knew that he was trapped. Amari was in embarrassment mode, revealing, "When we hung out in LA, Ivy, you never mentioned you had left this stud muffin back here." Ivy didn't know what to say, so she didn't. "I mean, wow. Look at those muscles."

Nick was totally uneasy, looking for an escape. "How about I go grab us some drinks?"

"Great idea, Nicky," Amari said, adding in her coy voice, "You know what I like. Get us our favorite."

Nick left. Ivy and Amari stared at each other. Ivy offered, "You two have a favorite drink?"

"Nick and I have a lot of favorite things," Amari replied.

Ivy wasn't buying it.

"I don't believe you."

"It's true."

"We'll see." A waiter was passing. Ivy stopped him. "Give us a bottle of Jack. And ten shot glasses." The waiter rushed off. Ivy looked across at Amari. "How about a little truth or dare? Upstate New York style. Tell the truth, or take a shot."

―――――――――

"Film is always like a family to me. I did TV for a while. Never liked it," Bruce told Griffin. "I like film better. It's like a family coming together. TV production is so impersonal. People work. Go home. Very nine to five."

"I feel the same way, Bruce."

"But then the film family breaks up. And you may never see these people again. It's sad. Where are you going when this one ends?"

"Who knows," Griffin said. "Where are you going?"

They were interrupted by Nick's arrival at the crowded bar as he announced, "I need a drink." Bruce offered him a cosmo. Nick waved it off. "Give me a shot of Jack Daniel's."

Bruce smiled. "Your girlfriends just took the last bottle."

Girlfriends? Huh? What? Nick's attention snapped back to the booth where he could see Ivy and Amari talking and knocking back shots. What were they doing?

Bruce stepped in. "I gotta stop this before it gets out of control."

Ivy and Amari were three shots into the truth or dare game, and no one had told the truth. Amari downed a shot. "Truth or dare. You wrote this script so you could bring closure to your life."

Ivy took a shot. Even though that might have been the truth. She would rather drink a shot than reveal that to Amari.

It was Ivy's turn: "You are falling for Nick." Amari didn't answer. She opted for the shot. They were both getting a little drunk.

Bruce arrived at the table. "Sorry to interrupt, but I thought it would be great if Amari could maybe sing a song for the bar."

Ivy slurred, "What a great idea!" She stood up in the booth. "Hey, everyone, good news! Our great Amari has offered so generously to pick up the bar tab!"

The crowd roared. Amari stumbled up, climbed up on the table and waved. "My pleasure." She took a bow and almost fell off the table.

"And she's going to sing a song! A Christmas song!" More cheers.

Amari leaned in to Ivy and whispered angrily, "What the fuck are you doing? I don't know any Christmas songs."

"It's Karaoke. Do what you always do. Just read the lines. And try not to change the words."

"Then you're doing it with me," Amari said, pulling Ivy along with her onto the small stage in the corner of the bar. Over at the booth, Nick kept thinking: *What the hell! What the hell!* when suddenly the now-drunk Ivy pulled him on stage.

"How about our favorite, Nick?" Ivy smiled. She pressed a button, and the Beach Boys' iconic "Little Saint Nick" began to play. Someone tossed a Santa hat onstage, which found its way onto Nick's head.

Amari started it off, following the words, but the more she sang the more Ivy realized—Amari couldn't hit the notes. Ivy had heard about performers using devices to keep pitch. But now Amari was exposed—and off-key. She danced seductively around Nick. Wiggling and twerking. *Who twerks during a Christmas song?*

Ivy jumped into the second verse, and she crushed it. All those years in the church choir had paid off. The crowd cheered as Ivy wrapped Nick's arms around her. Amari then started a sing-along as she jumped into the crowd and body-surfed her way across the room, winning over the crowd. The song ended. Amari returned to the stage. She glared and winked at Ivy. Amari had won the first round.

Two more shots were handed to them. Amari was thinking she had survived and raised Nick's hand in triumph when a new song started. The memorable opening chords to Leonard Cohen's "Hallelujah." The bar crowd was enraptured. Ivy took the mic and sang it like an angel. Her voice was perfect. Amari took the second verse, did an okay job; they both broke into the chorus together. Amari masked her lack of talent under the music and Ivy's voice. Amari closed her eyes, acting as if the spirit was moving her. The music suddenly cut out. Ivy stopped singing. Amari did not. Her voice broke, missed the high C. The applause turned into confused stares as the crew heard the real Amari sing.

Bruce jumped in. "All right, let's hear it for our star and our screenwriter!" The crowd cheered.

Amari glared at Ivy. A death glare. "You embarrassed me. You did that on purpose."

Ivy wasn't going to back down, even with the crowd now watching. "Oh, really. You think I set you up, got you drunk, conned you into Christmas Karaoke, and made the music stop to expose your sorry-ass voice?"

"You are the writer."

"I am," Ivy said proudly, toasting Amari with a shot. "And I think your scene is over."

Amari stormed off the stage.

Rory jumped up, microphone in hand, wanting to talk to Ivy, but Griffin got in her way. "Not now, Rory."

Nick sprang into action. He took Ivy's hand. "Where are we going, Nick?" she said into the mic. Nick took it away from her.

"I'm getting you out of here."

He took Ivy out the back door. Ivy was emotionally exhausted and quite inebriated. She slowly walked with him. Nick knew there wasn't time. He had to get Ivy away from anyone with a video camera. Nick picked her up in his arms and carried her to his truck. He placed her in the passenger seat and buckled her in. Ivy's fingers stroked Nick's hair.

"Why did I do, Nick. Why did I do?" she slurred.

"It's going to be okay," Nick said, looking into her eyes,

trying to comfort her. "Relax. Breathe. You're just a hot mess right now."

Ivy smiled in her drunken haze. "You think I'm hot? You still think I'm hot!" That was the last thing she remembered as she fell asleep.

CHAPTER 22

SUNLIGHT STREAMED IN BETWEEN THE small opening in the curtains, finding Ivy and waking her from her deep sleep. Her eyes scanned a barren bedroom. She had no idea where she was. Lying in bed, she could feel the approach of an incoming hangover. What happened last night? The last thing she remembered was sitting in the booth with her doppelganger—Amari. After that, nothing.

Ivy looked around the room. Her clothes were in a pile on the floor. Her overactive movie imagination pitched an idea that she had been kidnapped. Like a scene from the Stephen King movie and book of the same name, *Misery*. She felt like misery. And was betting she looked like it too.

Ivy stumbled to a small bathroom that was in the process of being built. There was a sink, a toilet, and a shower, but no cabinets. Ivy knew she shouldn't, but she did: She looked in the shaving mirror attached to the sink, and did not like what she saw. Her makeup was smeared as if she'd been in a prize fight. Her hair was something out of *Young Frankenstein*. The shirt she wore was a clue to where she might be. Ivy was wearing the hated Poison Ivy T-shirt. Was she at the Shepherd Winery?

"What the hell did I do?" Ivy muttered. She looked for her phone in the bedroom. It was nowhere to be found. The curtains by the french doors parted with the summer breeze. Ivy stepped outside onto a deck, the sun doing a Dracula number on her. Ivy squinted. Her eyes adjusted to the bright sunlight as the view came into focus. She was looking at the breathtaking Seneca Lake in all its summer glory.

I'm in a lake house? she thought. *Who has a lake house?* Now she was a little nervous. Rather than call out a hello to see if anyone else was in the house, Ivy skulked her way back inside and walked out of the bedroom, slowly opening the door to the living area. She had indeed seen too many movies. The living area was unfurnished. But it was grand. A-frame ceiling. All wood everywhere. This was a large area, with nothing in it. There were tools and ladders. This was a work in progress.

Ivy's eyes darted to a table made from a large 4x8 plywood placed on five wine barrels. She should have registered the wine barrels as a clue, but her eyes and nose immediately found… "Coffee!" Ivy said to no one there. It was on the table. There were two cups that each said *Monaco*. There was also pastry. And a note. *STAY AS LONG AS YOU NEED—NICK.* This was Nick's place? Did he live here? How? It was still being built. The coffee worked like a restorative elixir.

She realized she'd spent the night with Nick. *But did anything happen?* She remembered the party. She remembered Amari. She remembered something about the Christmas Karaoke. She sipped the coffee. Looked around. The walls were bare. But there was one framed piece of art on the far wall. Ivy recognized it. It was a sketch. And her foggy mind went all clear as she remembered…

Ivy and Nick sitting on the lakeshore. They were eighteen. It was their last night before they each went off to college. The sun was setting over Seneca Lake. The summer breeze was cooling. Nick had sketched a house on the back of a pizza box from Two Trees. Ivy thought he was drawing a new wine bottle label, and Nick had laughed. He said his dad would never let him create a new label. He was old school. He liked things the way they were. Nick had been a dreamer. He wanted to see his family do more with their winery. Enter competitions. Create new wines. And Nick also dreamed about building a castle for Ivy on Seneca Lake. Ivy remembered their conversation: "I don't want a castle. On the other hand, a nice lake house." She looked at his drawing. "With a walkout basement that goes to a dock. Maybe a home gym and a home movie theater. We can cozy up in the winter and watch the Christmas classics."

"And the Buffalo Bills games," Nick said as he continued adding to the sketch of their dream home.

Ivy had looked at the sketch, imagining her life in it. "Maybe you can build me a study. A place where I can write. Maybe on the top floor. Looking out over the lake. With one of those spiral staircases to get up there."

Ivy looked up. Adrenaline cured her hangover. He had built it. He'd built their lake house. She went downstairs to the walkout basement. There was an exercise bike. Some free weights. At the other end, a large farm door. She opened it to see a small home theater. The walls were not covered with movie posters, but with pictures and pennants for the Buffalo Bills.

Ivy explored the rest of the house, including the circular staircase. She struggled up it, dizzy from the turns, like a scene right out of Hitchcock's *Vertigo*, which she had seen the other night. *Everything is not a movie*, she told herself. The study was waiting at the top of the stairs for her. There were built-in bookshelves, large windows, and more inspiring views of the lake. Nick had built it. He'd built the dream they had talked about when they were eighteen. There was an outdoor terrace. Ivy stood against the railing, leaning toward the water. She'd always loved the Finger Lakes. She took in a strong breath of summer air and that was when she noticed that she was in dire need of a shower.

The water soothed her. She was feeling much better. Maybe last night wasn't that bad. Here, isolated in the lake house, away from her phone, she had no idea. Her plan was to shower, get dressed, and start walking home. She stepped out of the shower, but there was no towel. She searched in all the cabinets, but they were as bare as she was. She walked back into the bedroom. Removed the pillowcase from the pillow and started drying herself when—

"I brought you some more coffee," Nick said as he walked into the room, seeing a naked Ivy.

"Nick!" She quickly tried to cover up with the pillowcase. It wasn't working.

"I'm sorry. I figured you were still asleep. I'll get you a towel. By the way, you look good. Have you been working out?"

"Out!" Ivy shouted, but not angrily. He had seen her naked many times before. No big deal. But now it was. Because it was now. Nick tossed a towel at her. Ivy let go of the pillowcase and missed the towel.

Fifteen minutes later, Ivy was sipping her second cup of coffee as she got into Nick's truck. Each of them was a little awkward around each other. "I love the house, Nick," she said. It was small talk but sincere small talk.

"Thanks. I got tired of living at home. Dad left me some

money. I bought the land. And each week I do a little work on it with some buddies. Should have it done in a few months."

"It's really nice to see it. It was everything you talked about."

"Everything we talked about." Ivy could feel the regret. Like Streisand and Redford in *The Way We Were*, remembering the title song of that movie. "I'm glad you got a chance to see the place. I'm putting it up for sale at the end of the summer."

"Why?" Ivy asked. She wasn't just curious. She wanted an explanation. The lake house was beautiful.

"I'm going to find a place closer to town. It gets a little lonely out here by myself." Neither said anything else.

———

Nick pulled into the driveway of the Green household as he had done so many times before. Since the breakup, he'd always felt funny around her family. Like he had done something wrong.

"You okay?"

"Yeah. Time to go back to reality. Last night…"

"Nothing happened, Ivy. You got a little out of control, and I figured it was better if I brought you to my place."

"How bad was it?"

"Montalbano pool party bad." Nick smiled. They both remembered the party in high school that got way out of control. "Everyone was pretty toasted last night. I'm sure no one remembers anything."

Ivy knew that wasn't true. She lingered for a moment. "Thank you for taking care of me." Nick smiled. Nodded. Then Ivy stepped out of the truck. He pulled away. She walked like Cersei Lannister in *Game of Thrones* toward the door. *Shame. Shame.*

Inside the house, her parents said hello as if everything was normal. No one said anything else to her. She found Griffin in the living room, playing video games.

"And there she is. Our new star."

"How bad was it?"

"Sometimes bad is good. All subjective. About ten thousand people thought it was the greatest thing ever seen. Rumor is *Entertainment Tonight* bought the video."

"Video? What video? I haven't seen anything," Ivy replied. "I lost my phone."

Griffin reached over to the coffee table. "You left this at the bar when you decided to go supernova."

Ivy turned on her phone. There were over one hundred texts that started popping up: CALL ME. WHAT THE HECK. YOU ROCK IT. CRAZY. Another CALL ME from Drew. A WTF from Vera. WHERE ARE YOU? from Drew. WE NEED TO TALK, NOW. And many more.

"This is not good," Ivy said. Griffin continued playing his video game. The conversation was punctuated with booms from the racing game.

"No, it's not."

"Can you put down the game, Griffin?"

"In a sec, going for my high score," he added, into his *Mario* race.

"What happened?"

Griffin was *en fuego* as the gamers said. Locked in. "You went one on one with Christmas Karaoke, upstaged Amari, sang a lot better than she ever will, and then she had to watch as Nick—the object of both your desires—carried you away to God knows where."

Ivy was agape. Watching the game as Griffin crashed and burned. "You should look at the video."

She found the video. There she was on stage, out-singing Amari, outing Amari's singing voice as fake.

"This is really much worse than the Montalbano pool party."

Ivy had a plan. She would ignore all texts. She would be the first person on the set the next morning, find Amari, and apologize. From there the dominoes would fall—Drew, then Vera. She should have let Amari win the Karaoke. Not Nick. He was too good for her, and she had a suspicion Amari was manipulating him. But this wasn't about Nick. It was about making sure the "you'll never work in this town again" Hollywood threat did not come for her.

"Hallelujah! Hallelujah!" The gaffers sang as Ivy walked into the high school gym, being rigged for the day's filming. The crew was slowly filing in. No sign of Vera. No sign of Drew. No sign of Amari. Ivy found the three Ivys being fitted for the final scenes which would be filmed in five days. Ivy decided to play it normal, as if the Christmas Karaoke was no big deal. It was just girls having fun. She greeted the three Ivys. "Good morning, girls."

"We're not supposed to talk to you," the youngest Ivy sniped.

"Who told you that?" They did not respond. Olivia and Ella showed up on the set; they also ignored Ivy.

"Olivia? Ella? Hi, how are you?" No response. "Have you seen Amari?"

"We're not supposed to talk to you either," Ella finally said.

Ivy went and found some coffee. Drew and Vera would be here soon. The scene was coming to life. The set looked amazing. She was supposed to be happy. On top of the world. But here she was worried and scared. She wondered if she had ruined her career. More crew passed her. Laughing. Singing more "Hallelujah"!

"Cut it out with the singing!" Vera snapped. Ivy rushed to her.

"Vera, do you have a minute?" she asked.

Vera glared. "I've got a movie to make, Ivy. And you are really trying to screw it up. Amari is in her trailer and won't come out until you are gone."

"Let me talk to her…please…"

"Nothing you can say is going to fix this. I don't have time to settle this Christmas Karaoke drama between you, Amari, and your old boyfriend."

"Five minutes. I can do a lot of groveling in five minutes," Ivy pleaded.

"Not happening. You're banned from the set. I need Amari more than I need you right now."

"But I'm the writer!"

Vera chuckled. "Like I said, I don't need you here upsetting my actress. Go."

Ivy was crushed. Banned from the set of the movie she wrote. She was emotionally drained. She'd thought she felt at her worst waking up with a hangover yesterday, but this was ten times worse. She felt sick to her stomach, trying to catch her breath.

"Are you going to throw up?" It was Drew. Ivy went to greet him with a hug. He turned away.

"Drew, can you help me?"

"You didn't need my help this weekend, did you?"

"I need it now. I messed up."

"Where were you, Ivy? I called and texted you all day yesterday, and you ghosted me."

Ivy had purposely ignored Drew because, as she said, "I was in no condition to talk."

"Because you were with him," Drew stated. "Rick."

"You mean Nick," Ivy foolishly corrected.

"You know who I mean! I saw the video. I saw him carrying you away in his arms. I would kick his ass, but I am going to be professional, unlike you."

First of all, Ivy thought, *there is no way Drew could kick Nick's ass.* She decided not to say anything about that, steering the conversation to "I thought all publicity was good publicity."

"Grow up, Ivy. You were supposed to be a professional."

"It was Karaoke. At a bar. It was fun." Ivy was desperate. Trying to find any footing she could.

"Fun? Fun? Vera and I had to fly back to deal with this. We spent the day calming Amari down enough to finish filming the movie. You insulted her. You embarrassed me and the movie. The *Captain Midnight* people thought this was amateur hour when we had to leave the meeting to go back and deal with the crazy writer and the lead actress."

"Just let me talk with Amari," Ivy beseeched Drew.

"No, Ivy, my loyalty is to the movie. Nothing else. Now leave. Or do you need me to call your old boyfriend and have him come and carry you away?"

Ivy had never seen Drew this angry. She lowered her head, gathered her things, and walked off the set of her own movie. She was crushed. Shame! Shame! Shame! Filling her mind as she walked home, went to her bedroom, locked the door, and sobbed. Her phone rang around 11:00 a.m. She thought maybe they'd changed their minds. It was Charlotte.

"What the hell did you do?" Charlotte roared.

"I'm so sorry."

"I got reporters calling me. Your video is everywhere. Amari's people are calling for your head. The next job you had lined up just pulled out. This is really bad."

"It just got a little out of hand."

"A little out of hand? Fuck me. You were at the gates of Oz, and you pissed off Dorothy."

Ivy was having trouble following the metaphor. But she knew her career was in trouble. She tried to explain that maybe she still had feelings for her boyfriend, and Amari flirting with Nick and trying to seduce him made her jealous. "This is what this is all about, an old boyfriend?" her agent asked.

Ivy felt a smidgen of empathy from Charlotte. "Maybe…"

"I told you, Ivy, if Amari wants to go reverse cowgirl on your old boyfriend with you filming the conjugal connection, you will film it and not say a word. Do you understand me?"

She sobbed a yes. "Is there any way I can fix this?"

"Maybe. Deep down Amari is an actress. So, you need to do what they love most: kiss her ass."

"I can do that," Ivy said.

"I mean really kiss her ass. Get your lips up to the stinky part and beg for forgiveness."

"I got it," she said. "I might approach the kissing ass part in a different manner, but I'll get it done."

CHAPTER 23

IVY WAS DETERMINED TO MAKE her peace with Amari. She had a three-pronged battle plan. First on her list was showering Amari with presents. The next morning, she went to her mom's Christmas shop to put together a gift basket for Amari. She included some of her holiday favorites: a snow globe, a nutcracker, a mini Christmas tree, a box of local chocolates, and peppermint hot cocoa. She had the basket delivered to the set, but Amari ghosted her gift, not that Ivy expected anything else. She knew that it was going to take a lot of convincing to get back on Amari's good side. The cellophane-wrapped goodies were only a start.

Griffin reached out via text to tell her that Amari liked the snow globe and that she'd smiled at the nutcracker ornament. Ivy felt suddenly hopeful. Griffin neglected to mention that once Amari saw that the peace offering was from Ivy, she wanted nothing to do with it and gave it to the production designer.

At lunchtime, Vera showed Amari and Griffin the dailies from the morning. Vera was really pleased with their performances. She especially praised Amari's acting. Called it award-winning.

Amari actually smiled for the first time that day. Griffin texted all of this in confidence to Ivy. He kept telling her that *he was on her side.* And he was. Ivy was starting to feel like the sister he'd never had. "Family sticks together," he'd told Ivy. When Amari tried to badmouth Ivy, Griffin just ignored her.

The second item on Ivy's battle plan was gifting the crew with baked goodies. She figured that if she could win over Drew, Vera, Bruce, and everyone else, she'd be closer to making peace with Amari. Ivy spent the day rolling out dough, making cookies that looked like each member of the crew. Her mom helped her. Together they put them each in individual boxes. Ivy wrote separate notes to each crew member, finishing each missive with an *I'm so sorry. Love, Ivy.* For Vera and Drew's cookies, she wrote a longer note: *I'm so sorry. I promise that will never happen again. Your kindness and support have meant the world to me. I hope you'll find it in your heart to forgive me.* Ivy's dad offered to deliver the cookies to the filming location, just in case they were serious about keeping Ivy off the set. It happened to be mid-afternoon, and the crew was experiencing a blood sugar drop. J. B. was nowhere in sight with fresh food. Everyone was tired of the prepackaged snacks. So when Mitch arrived on set with a little pink bakery box for every crew member, they all gathered around him like chickens. Eager for what he had to offer. They didn't care that it was from Ivy. In truth, they had no ax to grind with her. They were more concerned about the betting pool.

Even Drew smiled a little when he opened up his box. He saw that Ivy had given him big muscles in the icing on his cookie. But when he read the note, his smile faded. He wasn't ready to forgive her. At least not yet. Vera was too busy to even look at her cookie. But if she had, she would have seen that Ivy had given her a cute button nose and a clipboard. Ivy had taken extra care with Vera's cookie. Mitch told Ivy that the crew loved the cookies. He didn't reveal that Drew had ripped up the note. Or that Vera hadn't said anything.

The third item in Ivy's battle plan list was what she thought was her ace in the hole. She was going to write Amari a new scene. She'd give her some memorable dialogue along the lines of *You had me at hello* from *Jerry Maguire* or *Kiss me. Kiss me as if it were the last time* from *Casablanca*. The new scene was going to come right before the Rick character died. Ivy figured that if she wrote an amazing scene, Vera and Drew would sign off on it.

She opened her laptop and sat in her old bedroom, prepared to write. Nothing was coming to her. She couldn't really be having writer's block, she thought. That had never happened to her. Ivy didn't know what to do so she opened up Instagram and began scrolling. She stopped on Amari's latest post. It was a close-up of Nick on his boat. *Gosh, he's handsome.* Ivy closed Instagram. She knew what she had to do. Ivy put in her earbuds and searched for the Christmas song that most reminded her of Nick. Soon she was humming along to "Tinsel and Lights" by Train. It was the song that reminded her of the magical weekend she'd spent with Nick in New York City.

Before Ivy knew it, she was *tap-tap-tapping* away on her laptop, no longer blocked. Ivy crafted a magical scene where Rick and Ilsa camped out by the lake in the snow just before Christmas. Rick built a fire to keep them warm. They snuggled together in sleeping bags. Ivy realized that the scene was suddenly becoming too personal as she slipped up a few times and typed in *Nick* instead of *Rick*.

Meanwhile, on the other side of town, over at the Shepherd Winery, Nick was in a quandary. Ivy had gotten into his head when she'd emerged from the shower naked. Now he couldn't stop thinking about her. He also couldn't stop wiping down the bar. Over and over, he rubbed the cloth on the long gleaming piece of wood. Frannie and J. B. walked into the winery. J. B. carried bags from the Farmers' Market for Frannie. Nick noticed that his mom looked different. Her face was bright and happy. She'd taken care with her hair. And J. B. was grinning ear to ear. His shirt was misbuttoned. Nick wondered, *Did they just have sex?* He shook his head, trying to squash that image and bring back the one of naked Ivy. But substituting a naked image of your ex-girlfriend for your mother wasn't a good idea.

"If you wipe that bar down any more, the veneer is going to rub off," Frannie joked.

"Huh?" Nick murmured. He'd been lost in thought.

"What's going on with you?" his mother asked.

"Nothing. Nothing's going on with me."

"You look hungry," J. B. commented.

"I'm not hungry," he snapped.

"Maybe not hungry, but hangry," Frannie said to J. B.

"I'm not hungry and I'm not hangry."

Frannie walked over behind the bar and opened up a bottle of cab franc. "Do you want to try some of the riesling I've been telling you about?" she asked J. B.

"Of course."

"It's three in the afternoon," Nick protested.

"And in Paris, it's eight o'clock. I think we can have a glass."

"Don't you need to be on set, J. B.?" he groused.

"Dinner is not until eight. I went to the Farmers' Market with your mother to get groceries. I found the big zucchini she wanted. I want to enjoy the moment with my love."

His love? Nick wondered what was going on. He noticed his mother had removed the wedding ring that she'd worn for years. Was this really happening? Was she actually getting serious with this guy? What happened to just hooking up?

Frannie took out three glasses and poured the wine. She handed one to Nick. "Tell us your troubles, Nick. And be honest."

Before he knew it, Nick revealed all that had happened to him in the past few days. Hanging around with Amari, and the overnight with Ivy. They emptied the bottle of wine and opened another. His mother tried to be helpful. "Did you talk to Ivy, like I suggested?" and "How do you feel about Amari? Is it serious?" None of her comments were helpful. Then J. B. looked him in the eye.

"Love isn't convenient. You can't plan it. It can't be analyzed. Trust your gut. Stop being *une chochotte* and just go talk to her."

"To Ivy? Or to Amari?"

Now it was J. B.'s turn to look confused. "Uh, I don't know."

Frannie chimed in. "Start by talking to Amari."

"Okay." Nick got up to leave.

"Make sure she's done filming," J. B. suggested.

Nick quickly texted Amari. YOU DONE FOR THE DAY? In a few seconds, he saw the bubbles on his phone. Then Amari's text appeared. **YUP. YOU?**

He froze. This was it. He needed to tell her he wanted to talk. Frannie noticed his indecision and grabbed his phone. She quickly texted back. YES. LET'S MEET UP.

"Mom!" But Nick was secretly glad as he'd been unable to initiate a meet-up with Amari. He watched as a new text appeared. **COME TO THE BELHURST CASTLE. WE CAN GET ROOM SERVICE.**

Frannie and J. B. read the text. "What are you waiting for?" J. B. asked. "Never leave a woman waiting."

"He's supposed to break up with her. Not sleep with her."

"Can't he do both? She's very hot."

"Oh, so you think she's hot?" Frannie teased.

"Not as hot as you, my love." J. B. leaned in for a kiss. She wrapped her arms around J. B. and kissed him deeply. Nick knew it was time to get out of there. Fast.

Nick went to get his car keys and stopped. He knew he'd had too much to drink. He grabbed his bike instead and quickly rode the two miles to the Belhurst Castle. Nick dumped his bike behind a bush, not worried about having it stolen. Geneva was a safe town, and nobody was going to find it. Besides, he had bigger things to worry about.

As he walked toward the entrance, he practiced what he was going to say: *So I'm not sure where this is all going.* That didn't sound right. He needed to put it in her court. *Where do you think this is going?* He had to figure out how he felt about them as a couple. They hadn't slept together yet, but he knew it was coming. She wanted to, and he thought he did too. Nick stepped into the hotel and realized that he didn't know what room number Amari was in. He quickly texted her and waited for her answer. Nothing. He paced around the lobby and waited a few minutes for her response. Still nothing. Amari was taking a shower in anticipation of his arrival. Her phone was in the living room of her suite, far from the bathroom. She dried off her body and spritzed on some perfume. Applied a fresh coat of lipstick even though she hoped it would be quickly wiped off by Nick.

Down in the lobby, Nick was getting antsy. He saw Drew enter the hotel. The two men nodded to each other warily. Nick noticed that Drew looked tired. Drew noticed that Nick looked anxious.

"Hey," said Drew.

"Hey," replied Nick.

Drew stopped in front of Nick. Expecting him to say more. "What are you doing here?"

"Uh, looking for Amari. Do you know her room number?"

"She likes to be incognito in this hotel."

"Ah, she's expecting me."

Drew raised his eyebrows. "Oh. In that case, she's in room 414."

"Thanks."

"Is it okay if we stop by the winery tomorrow? The art department needs to start decorating for the filming in two days," Drew said as he took off his jealous boyfriend hat and put on his producer hat.

"Uh, sure. Yeah. No problem." Nick turned to leave.

"Wait."

He stopped. *Is this guy ever going to stop bugging me?*

Drew smiled at him. "Have fun. With Amari. Make her happy."

Nick nodded. *Is he telling me to have sex with Amari?* He stepped into the open elevator. No sooner had the elevator doors closed when Ivy walked into the lobby of the Belhurst. She was carrying the pages of the new scene she'd written for Amari. Ivy immediately noticed Drew at the front desk, arguing with the receptionist about the bill. Drew wanted a deeper discount than the hotel was giving him. Ivy admired his ability to save money, but at that moment, he was the last person she wanted to see. She thought Drew would be furious that she was attempting to talk to Amari. But Ivy was in a quandary as she needed to find out Amari's room number and that meant she had to talk with the receptionist. She also couldn't let Drew see her, so she was going to have to wait it out. Ivy stealthily snuck over behind a couch. She crouched on the floor and felt ridiculous. Was she really doing this?

"I see your feet," Drew said. Ivy looked around. Was he talking to her? "Yes, Ivy, I'm talking to you," he said as if he read her mind.

She stood up and shook out her legs that had cramped from crouching. "Oh, hi, Drew."

"Ivy."

It was an awkward moment. Ivy waited for Drew to say something. To do anything. But he just stood there, staring at her. "How did filming go today?" she asked, finally breaking the silence.

"Fine. We got ahead of schedule, so we wrapped early. Everyone was still a little hung over." Ivy smiled to herself. So she hadn't been the only one. But it wasn't the time to gloat. "I can guess why you're here. She's in room 414," Drew continued.

"Amari?"

"Who else?" Now it was Drew's turn to smile to himself. He hoped that Ivy would soon run into not just Amari but also Nick. "If you want to see her, you'd better hurry. Before she goes out for the night." Ivy nodded and hurried over to the elevator.

Meanwhile, outside room 414, a nervous Nick knocked on the door. His palms were sweating. His heart was racing. Amari opened the door for him dressed in a sexy black lace negligee. Nick stared at her and forgot what he meant to say.

"I didn't order room service," Amari teased. Nick had not expected this. He was confused. She pulled him inside her room.

Ivy stepped out of the elevator on the fourth floor, new script pages in her hand. She walked slowly toward Amari's door, practicing what she'd say: *I'm eternally grateful that you chose to be in my movie. You are so perfect. Too perfect.* Ivy remembered that she needed to gain Amari's forgiveness. *I got carried away with Karaoke. You sounded amazing that night.* Which wasn't true. *Just read these pages. I hope you can forgive me.*

Ivy arrived at room 414. She knocked lightly on the door. Amari's voice called out, "Who is it?"

"It's Ivy."

"Ivy Green?"

"Yes. I have something for you."

She heard another voice from inside the room. A muffled voice. A man's muffled voice.

Inside Amari's room, Nick was horrified. He didn't want to face Ivy at that moment. Not when he was alone with Amari in *that* outfit. He sprinted toward the bathroom, closed the door.

Amari opened the door. Ivy saw her half-dressed in luxe black lace lingerie.

Ivy's jaw dropped. Amari smiled, or was it a sneer? "What do *you* want? I'm kind of about to get busy."

"I just...I just wanted to tell you how sorry I am about what happened at Karaoke."

"Oh, I'm over it. Hey, Nick? Could you run the shower for us?" Ivy was caught off guard. Nick? She'd thought she'd recognized his voice. *What's Nick doing in Amari's room?* "Anything else you needed to tell me?"

Ivy fumbled. She suddenly remembered the script pages in

her hand. "Uh, yeah. I wrote you a new scene. I think it's awards worthy. For you, I mean." She handed Amari the script pages.

"Thanks. But as I said, I'm kind of busy." Amari called out to Nick again. "Oh, Nick! Make sure the water is hot enough. I'll join you in a minute." Ivy could also hear the shower running. Water pounded. Then Amari turned to Ivy, "Don't you hate it when the water is lukewarm? Especially when there are two people in the shower. These walk-in showers are actually really nice. Larger than what I've had in other hotels. Lots of things are larger here in Geneva." Amari grinned at her.

"I don't believe you. I don't think he's really here." Ivy stomped past Amari to the bathroom door. She opened the unlocked door just a little—Nick, on the other side, pushed it closed, hard, in her face. But not before she saw a glimpse of his hair.

"Oww," Ivy yelled.

Instinctively, Nick said: "Sorry." He quickly shut up.

Ivy lost it. He didn't love Amari. At least she didn't think he did. She was suddenly furious with Amari and totally forgot about trying to get her forgiveness. "You two deserve each other. He's only having a fling with you because you're playing me."

"Works for me. I'm the one getting laid."

Ivy's eyes flashed with anger. Furious with Amari. She snatched the script pages from Amari's hands. Amari pulled them back. Soon they were tussling over the script which was being ripped apart. Ivy let go. She walked out and slammed the door.

Amari entered the bathroom, ready to seduce Nick. She removed her lingerie. The shower was running. She called out to Nick, "Just so you know, arguments make me really horny!"

Meanwhile, Ivy stomped through the hallways. She didn't want to wait for the elevator, so she ran down the stairs, two steps at a time. She wanted more than anything to get out of that hotel. Far away from Nick and his dick.

In the lobby, Drew finally settled with the receptionist. He was proud of his negotiating skills. He'd saved another three thousand for the movie. Now he could pay Amari's bar tab for when she bought drinks for the entire crew at Eddie O'Brien's on Christmas Karaoke night.

Ivy burst out from the stairwell next to the elevator. She looked furious and barely noticed him. But it was enough to make Drew smile. He figured he would let her sweat it out for another night. He would forgive her in the morning. He was good at forgiving. Makeup sex was his favorite thing.

Ivy ran out of the hotel, infuriated.

CHAPTER 24

"AMARI IS FUCKING MY OLD boyfriend," Ivy said to Griffin, who fresh from the shower was wearing Ivy's bathrobe. In her bedroom. In her old house.

"Is that my bathrobe?" Ivy wondered.

"Sorry. I forgot to steal one from the hotel before I left," Griffin said, his head in a suitcase of clothes looking for something to wear. He called out, "Mom, have you seen my Hobart T-shirt?"

Ivy was surprised that Griffin was calling Linda *Mom* and even more surprised when her mother answered with: "It's downstairs drying, honey."

"Did you just call my mom—*Mom*?"

"It was her idea," Griffin explained. He found his tightest jeans and slipped them on under the robe. This was the first time that Ivy had noticed that he looked nothing like Nick, but when she watched dailies, he was transformed. The camera loved him. She had always heard that stars become stars when the cameras start rolling. Griffin tousled his hair. "Let's get back to your favorite subject: Amari."

"Amari is not my favorite subject."

"She's all you talk about, Ivy."

He was right. She did talk about Amari a lot. But only because she was stealing her life.

Griffin continued, "I don't believe Amari is having sex with Nick. She might be flirting with him, to get into character and everything. But I don't see her with Nick. Long term."

"Then why was she all dressed to seduce at the hotel, with Nick hiding in the shower?" Ivy had explained what had happened.

"How do you know it was Nick if you didn't see him?"

"I saw the top of his head. And I heard him!"

"Why do you care what he does, Ivy? You and Nick are not a couple." He hit her with the truth. She and Nick were not a couple. They used to be. The movie business had pulled them apart, but the making of this Christmas movie, which was about them, about how Joseph met Mary—Damn! She needed a new title—had brought them closer together again.

All she could say was, "I don't know anymore, Griffin. We used to be. Then we weren't. And now I don't know what we are. And Drew, poor Drew…"

"Do you know why actors hate playing Hamlet?" Griffin asked. He waited. Ivy wasn't answering. "It's because he's too wishy-washy. Dead girlfriend. Slutty mom. Hamlet can't kill someone. To be or not to be. Make a choice, dude."

"You think I'm Hamlet?"

"To Nick or not to Nick. Isn't that the question?"

Ivy sat at the edge of the bed. Looked up at pictures of herself from all the high school plays. At one of her and Nick at the prom that peeked out behind other pictures. She stared at it. "Before I was with Drew, it was Nick. It was always Nick. And then he dumped me. I was alone. I didn't want to date. I stayed home and I wrote. I think I had to kill my demons by writing *When Joseph Met Mary*. It was my therapy script. It got me through the breakup."

"And you killed Nick in it."

"I did. I gave it to my agent. She sent it to a few places, and no one was interested. Five years in and I had nothing to show. That's when I started looking for Nick on social media."

"You stalker, you."

Ivy offered a soft smile. "I found pictures on the Shepherd Winery website. They never had a website, and now they do. And Nick is all over it. I was thinking about calling him when Drew called me about that script. And that was that."

Griffin was confused. "I thought you met Drew before he bought your script."

"We met at a party in Sundance. He had heard about the script from my agent. Within a week, I had two offers: one to option the script and one to date Drew."

"Did you like Drew before he green-lit your movie?"

"You sound like my sister."

"I have been spending a lot of time with her. She interviewed me for her thesis paper. Then she interviewed me again. What started off as a paper is now a book proposal about me. About my crazy life. It's been very therapeutic."

A T-shirt was tossed into the room by Ivy's smiling dad. "Here's your shirt, G-man. The car keys are by the door. I gassed it up for you." Ivy wasn't sure her dad had noticed her.

"You're going on a date, G-Man?" she asked.

"Just meeting a friend at the local theater. I think they're showing *Scrooged*. The one with Bill Murray."

"I forgot about that," Ivy said, excited. "But it's not *Scrooged*, it's *Scrooge*. It's British. From the1950s. Totally bombed in the U.S. Supposed to be really creepy, like a *Christmas Carol* horror movie." Ivy's shoulders slumped. "It's nice you have someone to go with. Have a good time."

Griffin wanted to be out the door. But he could not leave Ivy alone. Not in her current crisis. He knew he had to ask, hoping she would say no.

"Do you want to tag along?"

"I don't want to be the third wheel."

"It's not a date. Just two friends hanging out at the movies."

She perked up. "Great. I need something to cheer me up."

———

Bruce was not smiling when he got into the backseat behind Ivy who was sitting in front with Griffin. He returned her "Hi, Bruce" with a smile. Griffin explained that she needed cheering up.

"Why? You should be thrilled, Ivy. Your movie wraps in four days. One more day shooting in the winery. Three nights in the church. And we're done!"

They parked. They went inside the old movie theater. It was more of a palace. The owner was in his last few weeks of operation. Like all movie theaters, he had struggled during the pandemic. He just couldn't keep it running and was going to sell it to a local brewery, which promised to keep some of the majestic old movie house decor.

"I'm going to get some popcorn. You two get the seats," Ivy told Griffin and Bruce as they walked in to get seats, wanting to give them a little more time together. Maybe they could figure out if they were on a date.

Ivy realized she had never answered Griffin's question: Did

she fall for Drew before he told her he was going to produce her movie, or did it happen after? Or at the same time? The popcorn line was long. Many members of the crew were there. They smiled and softly said hello—but no one was talking to her. She waited alone.

———————

Griffin and Bruce both loved to sit in the center about ten rows back from the screen. Griffin kept his hat pulled down, sunglasses on, obscuring his identity from the half-full theater.

"This place is beautiful," Bruce marveled, snapping photos.

"It's going out of business in a few weeks. It's for sale. I hope you don't mind that Ivy tagged along. She's going through a tough time."

"I don't mind. Ivy's the reason we're all here. She doesn't write that script, we are on different shows," Bruce said and added, "We never meet."

"Never is a long time." Griffin smiled. "Where are you headed next?"

"Got an offer to do a big war romance in Spain," Bruce told him. "What about you?"

"I think I need to take a break. I might stay here for a while."

"Really?"

"I know, but Ivy's parents have made me feel at home."

"Well, you can always visit me in Spain."

"I might do that." Griffin smiled. Was he flirting with Bruce? Was the rock-solid, damn-good-looking assistant director flirting with him? *Do I like dudes?* Griffin wondered.

———————

Ivy got her jumbo popcorn and candy. She saw Vera walking into the theater with a cup of coffee. Ivy practically flung herself at Vera, popcorn flying out.

"Vera!" she yelled.

"Hi, Ivy," Vera said, maneuvering around her into the theater to find a seat.

"We're sitting over here, if you want to join us. Me, Griffin, and Bruce."

"I need to sit in the front row. I like to see the film grain."

"Vera, I just want to say—"

Vera cut her off. Excited. "Can you believe this place is showing *Scrooge*?"

"I know. I heard about it in film school but could never find it. I heard it's really dark."

Vera smiled and said: "Ivy, I can't help you. This is all on Amari. Did you get her to forgive you?"

"I made it worse."

"You know, Ivy, maybe you should consider directing. You can throw a fit, and everyone is scared of you. If you throw a fit when you're a writer, they send you away."

She nodded. Vera sat down. Ivy returned to her seat. *Scrooge* began to play. It was a darker version. The ghosts seemed real. The movie looked and felt gloomy. It was nearing the end, the Ghost of Christmas Future showing Scrooge his miserable future, when Ivy's phone started ringing.

"Turn that off," Bruce snapped. A lot of people shushed. Ivy could not find her phone. She fumbled in her jacket pocket, running up the aisle and seeing the name on the caller ID: DREW.

Ivy picked it up as she entered the lobby. "Drew?"

He was direct. "Where are you?"

"At the movies. Vera is here."

"We need to talk. Can you come to Belhurst? It's important."

"Can we meet someplace else?" she asked, wanting to stay far away from the place where Nick still might be.

"Fine," Drew snapped. "Where do you want to meet?"

"How about the pier at Seneca Lake? You can walk there from the hotel."

"See you in ten minutes," he said and clicked off. Ivy was going to go back to tell her companions she was leaving when the crowd started walking out. The movie was over. Ivy stood to the side. Griffin and Bruce walked out, laughing.

"How was the ending?" she asked.

"Great. The whole movie was great. Dark. All from a bad piece of meat," Bruce said.

"Makes me glad I'm a vegetarian. We're going to grab some dinner, do you want to join us?" Griffin asked.

"I can't. Drew called me."

"The Ghost of Christmas Present or Future?" Bruce wondered.

Ivy looked confused. Griffin explained, "I told him everything. I figured everyone already knew about everything anyway."

She forged on. "He says he needs to talk to me right away. Thanks for letting me tag along." Ivy hugged them both and started her walk down Main Street to the pier.

Griffin and Bruce were deciding where to eat when someone snapped their picture. It was Rory, the reporter. She looked very happy with herself.

"You two make a great couple. Anything you want to tell your fans?" she said, as if she was Hedda Hopper 2.0.

Griffin stalled for a heartbeat. Bruce answered simply, "We're partners."

"Partners?" Rory questioned, pushing her phone, with the voice recording app running, closer to them. By now a crowd had formed. The locals and some Griffineers noticed it was Griffin.

"Yes. Griffin and I are partners. We're going to buy the movie theater together and restore it to its former glory."

"That's right. We're business partners. So, take down the For Sale sign. You are looking at the new owners!" The crowd went crazy. Cheering. Griffin and Bruce held their hands high. Triumphantly!

By the pier, Ivy could not hear the cheers. It was a quiet moonlit summer night. She could see the Christmas lights shining from Main Street. A Christmas tree had been set up near the pier for a caroling scene. The town asked if they could keep it up until the movie wrapped. People loved a Christmas tree. Any time of year. There was a portable packing crate that was collecting toy donations for a Christmas toy drive in July. Ivy gazed at the tree, making a Christmas wish, standing on the edge of the pier the way George Bailey stood on the bridge in the classic *It's A Wonderful Life.*

Ivy heard Drew talking on his phone as he walked up the pier. He waved at Ivy. (Good sign.) As he got closer said, "What a great location. This is the perfect place for a murder." (Bad sign.) Drew clicked off his cell phone. "How did it go at the hotel?" he asked.

"Not great. Amari is still angry."

"Anything else happen there?" Drew asked, wanting to know if she had run into Nick.

"I don't think I'll be writing any Amari Rivers movies in the future."

"*Captain Midnight* is green-lit."

"Oh, that's great. Congratulations."

"Yeah, I'm pretty excited. It's a franchise. Game changer for me. Not that I don't like smaller, smarter pictures."

"But the bigger, dumber ones pay more. Right?"

"I wouldn't be such a snob about it. They want to hire you for the rewrite. It shoots in two months, so they want to start now. I called your agent. It's a weekly to start—one for the week."

$100,000 for a week. Ivy had heard about the weekly. These were usually when the script was in trouble, production was on the horizon, and someone had to come in and try to fix the movie script very quickly. It never worked. But the check always cleared. Ivy kept her emotions contained.

"What do we do about us?"

"We got the condo." Ivy had totally forgotten they had made an offer on a condo in Downtown LA. "We have until Saturday to sign the lease."

"You still want to live with me?"

He didn't answer at first. "I could ask you the same thing."

"Nick is with Amari. That's over. If we don't move in together, do I still get the *Captain Midnight* weekly?"

"Yes. But personally, I think we still have a chance."

Ivy smiled. "Thanks, Drew."

He took a deep breath. "I never smelled air so good. I can see why you like this place. I need your answer by Friday."

"On the condo or *Captain Midnight*?"

"Both." Drew walked away.

CHAPTER 25

DREW WASN'T THE ONLY ONE who was figuring out his next job. Most of the crew were also searching for their future film gigs, including J. B. As a caterer with a great reputation, J. B. usually had his pick of film shoots. He liked to combine his love of travel with paid employment, so he usually chose the more unique or exotic places. Or he chose home. Not his U.S. address but his familial home in Provence, where he'd been born and raised.

J. B. was lying in bed next to Frannie. It was close to midnight, and he was on the phone with a French producer that he'd known for years. He nodded as he listened. "*Oui. Ça semble bien. À bientôt. Bonne nuit.*" Then he hung up the phone and turned to Frannie. "Looks like I'm going to the South of France. My old friend is filming a comedy there for Netflix."

"Lucky you."

"Why don't you come with me?" Frannie didn't say anything, but her mind was swirling. J. B. interrupted her thoughts. "Come on, run away and join the circus."

"It's not too soon?" She wondered to herself if they were in love.

"I have a cottage in Provence."

"Provence?"

Frannie quickly Googled it. She read aloud: "This sun-drenched countryside bursts with charm and historic attractions, including enchanting medieval hilltop towns and ancient Roman ruins. Small farms, fields of lavender, and colorful open-air markets add to the rustic appeal." She put down her phone. "It sounds magical, J. B."

"Yes. And it would be more magical if you were there with me."

"But the winery?"

"Nick can handle it."

"The restaurant?"

"That's what your staff is for. You've created the recipes. I've seen your sous chef. He's good."

"That's not a sous chef. That's a kid I hired for the summer."

"Time to let him fly."

Frannie thought about it some more. She'd never really left Upstate New York. She'd grown up in Syracuse, gone to Cornell, settled in Geneva. She and her husband had always planned to travel once the winery was on stable footing, but when that was about to become a reality, he had gotten sick.

J. B. took her hand and looked into her eyes. "*Viens avec moi, s'il te plaît.*"

She melted. She couldn't resist him when he spoke French. "That means please come with me," he said.

"I know. I remember that from high school French."

"Good. Then I am sure you will remember this too. *Je t'aime.*" And J. B. leaned in to kiss Frannie.

She whispered back, "I love you too." *Is this really happening?* It was the first time that they'd said *I love you* to each other.

Frannie hadn't said those words to anyone but her husband, and that had been over three years ago. Saying *I love you* to J. B. was a moment that Frannie knew she'd never forget. It also made her feel young again, and she liked that.

———————

The next morning at Shepherd Winery, Nick unlocked the door for the crew. Large equipment trucks were in the parking lot. Gaffers and grips unloaded the lighting and dolly equipment. Nick walked into the adjacent family restaurant to grab a cup of coffee. His mother was already in the kitchen, prepping for the day's meals. Frannie turned to Nick. "*Bonjour*, Nick. *Un café?*"

Nick was confused. "Huh?"

"Oh, I'm practicing my French. I'm going to go on location with J. B."

"You're what?"

"Going on location is how the film people say they're going to go film a movie in a different place."

"Oh."

"J. B. has invited me to go to France with him. He's working on a new French comedy there."

"What about the winery?"

"You can handle it, Nick. Besides, one day soon I'm going to give it all to you. Relinquish my co-ownership. It was always meant to be yours." Nick was stunned. He'd never thought this would happen so soon. He figured he'd have to wait until he was at least fifty before his mom handed over her share to him.

Frannie resumed her work and began humming and singing Albert De Paname's catchy French song "Si t'as été à Tahiti." As Nick stacked wine bottles, he realized that his life was changing, and it was all because of Ivy. He reasoned that if Ivy and her movie hadn't come to Geneva for filming, his mother never would have met J. B. Then she'd never talk about leaving. Almost overnight, his mom had changed her life.

Nick hated change. It was always difficult for him, which was also why he'd never wanted to move to Los Angeles. He let the rest of the crew in, and they started working their magic. They'd be filming at the winery for the entire day. Art was going to imitate life.

Amari strode into the winery. Nick went over to her. "Amari…"

"Can't talk, Nicky. Workday. Not even sure why you're here."

"It's my winery. About last night…"

"Memorable. Definitely wasn't what I was expecting."

"Sorry, I got a little crazy."

Amari chuckled. "You sure did. Why don't you help me read my lines?" She handed him the scene pages.

"Which scene is this?" Nick asked.

"Last scene with Rick and Ilsa. You go off and die tomorrow."

"Ouch."

"Hey, I didn't write it. Your girlfriend did."

"Oh yeah, she did," Nick said.

Amari noticed that he didn't say "ex-girlfriend." This confused her.

Nick was surprisingly good at running the lines. When it came time for his character to choke up and get teary-eyed, he did. Amari was impressed with his acting. But Nick knew that he wasn't actually acting. His tears were real tears. He felt like a mess. Nick learned that they would use stock footage for the snowmobile death scene, and back in LA they'd film a green screen to show a close-up of a stunt double playing Griffin falling off the snowmobile while fake snow was flying around him.

———————

Back at Ivy's parents' house, Ivy was having a heart to heart with her dad. She wasn't sure if she should take the rewrite job on *Captain Midnight*. She laid out the pros and cons. The pros were: lots of money, the movie might get made, she might get another credit, and she'd be back in LA.

Her dad listened patiently. Nodding. "And the cons?"

There really weren't any. "Well, I'd be rewriting someone else's work. Or fixing someone else's mistakes. And I'd have to work with Drew again, which isn't necessarily a con. I just don't know where we stand. He can be controlling. But then again, so can any producer." He nodded again. He really was a good listener. "So, what do you think? Do I take the *Captain Midnight* job?"

Mitch looked at Ivy thoughtfully. "Well, it's not always about the money." Now it was her turn to nod. "And you've just wrapped up your first original script which you liked writing. You got to write your own material and not fix someone else's."

"That's a good point."

"Also, you just paid off your student loans with this movie. So you're not in debt anymore." Mitch paused.

"So?"

"I wouldn't rush to take the *Captain Midnight* rewrite. Unless you're crazy about the script. You're building a brand, Ivy. Making a name for yourself. Rewriting someone else's words isn't going to help you."

"Wow. I never thought about it that way."

"Well, you should. You've come a long way in the past five years. It's been a struggle but now you're in the big leagues. I'd hate to see you take a step backward."

"Thanks, Dad." She was truly surprised by his advice. She'd been sure that he'd say to take the money, take the rewrite job. Ivy hugged her dad. "Love you, Dad."

"Love you too, Ivy."

She said goodbye to her dad and stopped in the kitchen to grab a banana. Carol was sitting at the kitchen table, typing busily on her computer. "Is that your paper about acquired situational narcissism?" Ivy asked.

"No. I tossed that idea. This is so much better." Ivy leaned closer to read the words on her sister's computer. Carol snapped her laptop closed. "Hey!"

"Sorry. What are you writing? A tell-all book about me?"

"Ha-ha. Now look who's getting acquired situational narcissism."

"I was just kidding."

"Okay, good. Actually, I'm going to write a book about Griffin and the trauma he faced with his parents. He's totally on board with the idea. Thinks it could help other child actors with problematic parents."

"That's a real thing. Sounds interesting," Ivy said.

"Griffin sent my article to his agent. She thought it was a book proposal or could be."

"That's cool."

"Then the book department at his agency got excited and they sent it to publishers, and now five places want to buy it. Griffin told me there's going to be a bidding war. What's a bidding war?" Carol wondered.

Ivy was shocked. "It means people like your writing. And more than a few companies want to pay to be in business with you. So, this is more than just your thesis?"

"Yes. And it's a bonus to get a real book published. This will not only help me get my doctorate but also jumpstart my professional life as an expert in childhood traumas."

"Wow. I haven't seen you this excited in a long time," Ivy said. "Congratulations, baby sister."

"I know we haven't been that close, but I have to thank you. This all happened because of you. If your movie wasn't filming in Geneva, I never would have met Griffin, I'd never be writing this book." Carol hugged her. "So, what do I wear to these meetings?"

"I'll help you, sis." Ivy headed out.

She knew that Nick would be on the set that day since they were filming at his winery. It was going to be the perfect opportunity to show him that he meant nothing to her. She hadn't actually seen him since the morning that she'd woken up in his house, after the Karaoke party. Since then, she'd heard him in Amari's hotel room. If he wanted to have sex with Amari, then she wasn't going to let that bother her, or at least that was what she told herself. When and if Ivy could find him, she intended to show Nick that she was moving on and didn't need him anymore. That was her plan from day one. Who cared if this was day twenty-eight!

But Ivy's confidence evaporated the moment she left her house. She couldn't believe that she was still not allowed on the set. It was so embarrassing to her. In fact, she had been too proud to tell her family. They had no idea that she'd been banned. They assumed she was on her way to the production when she left the house. She was on the way to Shepherd Winery to watch the production. But she knew that she'd have to hang outside by the equipment trucks.

Ivy parked far away. She tried sneaking in past the camera trucks to look into the winery window.

"Hey, Ivy," a voice called out. It was Max, the lead gaffer, securing the lights. Ivy thought she was busted. But Max and the rest of the crew had loved the cookies she had sent over. They thought it was unfair that Amari had banned Ivy. The gaffers and grips didn't mind if Ivy hung around the outdoor equipment area. In fact, they seemed to like having her around. Seasoned and professional, they had collectively worked on over a hundred movies. They liked to kid her about this being her first movie. They also shared food with her since they knew she wasn't allowed around the craft services table. As long as Amari didn't see her, it wasn't a problem.

The guys pretended not to notice her sad face. They knew that they were filming at her ex-boyfriend's vineyard on that day. Max set up a folding chair for her and handed her a muffin. Pete, another gaffer, had recently become a bird-watcher. He handed his new binoculars to Ivy when she was seated comfortably and eating her muffin. "What are these for?" Ivy asked.

"Bird-watching. I'm a new aficionado."

"That's cool."

"Did you know that over three hundred species of birds have been recorded here? Bald eagles, ospreys, black terns, great blue herons, American and least bitterns."

"I didn't know that."

"I just bought these binoculars so I can spot them. I found this place called Montezuma National Wildlife Refuge ten minutes from here. I'm going to check it out after we wrap. Maybe spend a few extra days."

"Pete, we need you on the set," Max called over to him. "Sorry, Ivy."

"Sure. Here, Ivy. Take a look. See if you can find a bald eagle. Upstate is such a great place to bird-watch." Pete handed Ivy the binoculars and walked toward the winery. Ivy lifted them to her face, but instead of looking into the trees for birds, she used them to look into the winery, through the windows, where the filming was taking place.

Ivy noticed Nick at the bar. Amari was flirting with him. *Of course.* Ivy watched from afar as he reached up to the top shelf above the bar and took down a dusty bottle of wine. He turned the label, and she was able to read it: *Poison Ivy.* Ivy frowned. Nick tilted the bottle and shook out a small object into his palm. Ivy squinted to see what it was. Adjusted the binoculars. Amari tapped Nick on the arm playfully. He laughed as he opened up his palm. Ivy suddenly realized it was a ring! It sparkled and momentarily blinded her.

Nick lifted up the ring. She noticed that Amari leaned over and smiled. He grinned back at her. He put the shiny object in her hand. Ivy sharpened the focus of the binoculars to look closer. She frowned. *Is that an engagement ring?*

CHAPTER 26

IVY WATCHED IN HORROR AS Amari put the diamond ring onto her left hand. Ivy's eyes grew wide. *How could that be happening already? They barely know each other.* Every promise that she had made to herself about not caring about Nick flew out the window. Ivy was angry. Jealous. Sad. Pissed off. She stared through the binoculars as Amari threw her head back and laughed her twinkly laugh, the one Ivy knew she used when she was truly flirting. Ivy wanted to rush into the winery, but she couldn't. She wasn't allowed. Ivy watched as Amari waved her hand in the air, showing off the engagement ring—just like they did on the finale of *The Bachelor.*

This can't be happening! Engaged! So it's true. Nick is in love with Amari. Ivy put down the binoculars. She looked devastated.

Pete patted her on the arm. Ivy jumped with a start. She didn't realize that Pete was standing next to her. He'd returned to the truck to pick up a bounce board. "Did you see anything?"

"I saw a vulture!"

"That's okay. You don't usually see the bald eagle on your first try. You're just learning."

"No. That's not it."

"Just relax. All good things come to those who wait. Better to be patient. Don't give up too quickly." Ivy wondered if he was talking about birds or about something else. She watched as Pete carried the bounce board back to the indoor set.

Drew walked outside for a cigarette. He'd been trying to quit. In fact, he had. But the stress of the movie shoot had made him want to smoke again. He walked over to the grip truck to get a light. "Ivy?" Drew was surprised to see her there.

"Sorry. I know I'm not supposed to be here."

"Hey, I don't care where you are. That's Amari's problem. But you know she's on set right now. So I wouldn't go into the winery." Ivy nodded. She knew exactly where Amari was, and she was trying not to explode. She was furious with Nick. How could he propose to Amari when he'd only known her for a month? "You okay?" Drew asked. "You don't seem like yourself."

"I just have a lot on my mind," Ivy said.

"At least you don't have to worry about your next gig. You're going to do a great job on *Captain Midnight*."

"Oh. Right." At that moment, she noticed that Nick walked out of the winery and into the vineyard. Ivy felt stuck between wanting to run after him and having to deal with Drew.

"You want to do it, right?" Drew asked.

Ivy breathed in deeply. She felt caught. She had made her mind up. But she couldn't tell him. Not yet. She needed to get back on her movie set first. "I think so. But first I need to check with my agent."

"Actually, you don't. I talked to Charlotte Adams last night about the *Captain Midnight* rewrite, and she was thrilled. But she sounded surprised. Said you hadn't told her yet."

Now Ivy really felt trapped. "It's on my to-do list."

"Well, move it to the top of the list."

"Drew!" Bruce called out from the open door. "We need you on the set!"

He stubbed out his cigarette. Ivy felt like she'd been saved by the proverbial bell. "Talk later," Drew said to her and rushed back inside the winery.

Ivy lifted up the binoculars again. She focused back on the winery. Nick was gone. The Poison Ivy bottle was back in place. Ivy looked toward the vineyard to search for Nick. She was determined to find out what was happening.

Ivy scanned the foliage and stopped. Bingo. She had spotted Nick. Ivy put down the binoculars and walked toward the lake. The water was shimmering. It was a gorgeous sunny day. She marched toward Nick, anger building. He seemed to be lost in thought as he paced through the vineyard, looking for signs of ripening. As the end of July was almost upon them, Nick knew that the mid-August harvest would soon be happening.

"Nick!"

He looked up. Startled. He was taken aback to see her. "Ivy!"

"Hi. I've been trying to find you."

"Here I am."

"I can see that." Ivy was suddenly losing her nerve.

"Surprised to see you at the winery. Amari told me she kicked you off the set."

"You know that Amari doesn't really like you. She's just been fake-liking you. It started when we needed to convince you to let us use the Shepherd Winery location."

"My mom was the one who convinced me. Not Amari."

"Why so defensive? You sound like you want to be with her.

At least you did when you went to her hotel room and took a shower with her."

"You're kidding, Ivy. That makes me want to laugh."

"Are you laughing because the sex was bad or because I said something funny?"

"You think I'd jump into bed with someone I just met? It took us a long time to get into bed!"

"I haven't heard from you since you dropped me off at my parents' house two days ago."

"I was trying to figure some things out," Nick said. "And one of them was how I felt about Amari."

"I guess you figured out that you were in love with her."

"Why are you saying that?" he asked.

"I saw what you were doing just now in the bar. I saw you propose."

"Me?"

"You gave Amari that diamond ring," Ivy said. Nick laughed again. She was getting tired of him laughing. "Sure, it's funny to you. But not to me."

"You sound jealous."

"Well, I'm not."

"Doesn't sound that way."

"Why did you give the ring to Amari?"

"Because she asked me if I'd ever proposed to you. I took the ring down, and she got all excited and wanted to try it on."

Ivy was stunned. This wasn't what she'd expected. She didn't know what to say.

"So you didn't buy the ring for Amari?"

"No. I bought it for you. Five years ago." His reveal hung in the air.

Ivy was shocked.

"You had that ring for five years?"

"Yeah."

"Why?"

"I was going to ask you to marry me."

"What? When?"

"The night we broke up."

"You said you had met someone else."

"I lied."

"Why the hell did you lie?"

"I lied because I loved you."

"That sounds like such bullshit, Nick."

"It's not. If I'd proposed and you said yes, you would have followed me back to Geneva. Your movie career would never have happened. I knew I couldn't move to LA. I knew you would give everything up for me. I didn't want to get in the way of your dreams. So I made up a story so you could never look back."

It took Ivy a moment—which felt like forever—to process this. Nick had lied? He hadn't cheated on her?

"You never gave me a chance."

"No. But I made it easier for us."

"Easier? By not asking me? I don't think that crying my eyes out for weeks on end was easier."

Nick struggled for his next thought. He looked at Ivy earnestly. "Please don't take this the wrong way, but you were always indecisive. It was hard for you to make decisions. So I made the decision for you."

"What? So, you took away my agency!" Ivy yelled at him. Now she was furious.

"Your agency?"

"You took away my chance to make a decision on my own."
Nick nodded his head sadly.

She continued to rant, "Wow. In some ways that was worse
than breaking up with me. And I wish that you'd actually cheated
on me with someone else. Anything else would have been better
than feeling you had to make the decision for me."

"Ivy, I'm sorry."

"I'm sorry too, Nick. For you."

"I would never do that today."

"No. You wouldn't. Because you're not going to have that
opportunity." Ivy turned on her heel and walked out of the
vineyard. Away from Nick for what she thought would be forever.

He was astounded. *What just happened?*

———————

Back in Shepherd Winery, the crew was lighting for the next shot.
Vera wanted more wine bottles in the shot, and so did the production designer. Nick was nowhere to be found. Bruce offered to go
to the basement to bring more up. Griffin jumped up from his
seat to help out. They practically ran into the basement just so
that they could be together. Vera and Drew were too immersed in
the scene prep to notice.

In the basement, Bruce and Griffin stood close to each other.
"This reminds me of *Notorious*, when Cary Grant went into the
grotto," Bruce said.

"I love that movie," Griffin gushed.

"Me too. Top ten for me."

"Number five for me."

"That must be why I'm crushing on you," Bruce stated.

"I like that. I just hope you're not going to poison me with the wines like Claude Rains did with Ingrid Bergman."

"I only want to poison you with this..." He leaned in to Griffin for a brief stolen kiss.

Griffin was surprised. He had never been kissed by a man before. This was all new to him, but he liked it. It was different but the same. At the end of the lips was affection.

"I had no idea you were so romantic." Griffin smiled. He leaned in and kissed Bruce back. Lingering longer. It was a magical stolen kiss that would have kept going if not for Drew's voice calling down for them. They both pulled away quickly.

"Now what were we looking for down here?" Bruce asked playfully.

"Oh, I've already found it," Griffin said with a flirtatious smile. They reached for each other and kissed passionately again.

"Bruce! We need the wine bottles. Quit fooling around down there!" Drew screamed from up above. Griffin and Bruce again pulled away from each other.

"Do you think they know?" Griffin wondered.

"No. That's what Drew always says when he thinks his crew is wasting time. I'll just tell him that I was looking for a 1989 bottle or something like that. He thinks that anything from 1989 is a great vintage. That's the year he was born," Bruce said.

"Actually, I wouldn't care if everyone knew," Griffin blurted out, surprising even himself.

"But everyone thinks you're straight."

"I am straight. Well, I was until five minutes ago. Do you mind if I kiss you again? I think it would be helpful." They kissed again.

"And?" Bruce prompted.

"I need to talk to Carol."

"Who's Carol?"

"Ivy's sister. She's helping me to become my true self. I think I just need one more kiss."

"Allow me."

And before they could lean in for another stolen kiss, they heard footsteps and pulled away.

Ivy jumped into her car and drove home. Heartbroken. She was tired of lying. She rushed into her family home and into the kitchen, where she told her parents the truth. That she'd been banned from her own movie set. Carol ran down the stairs, eager not to miss out.

"What happened?"

"Amari is being a total bitch and won't let her on the set," Linda said. "I don't know why I allowed her to call me her movie mom."

"She's no daughter of mine," Mitch added.

Carol rolled her eyes. "Guys, she was never your daughter."

Then Ivy blurted out that she'd broken up with Nick.

"Honey, I didn't know you were back together," Linda said.

"We kinda were for about eight hours," Ivy admitted. "Two minutes of magic. The rest was sleeping through a hangover. But it was magical."

"And then what happened?" Carol asked.

"And then it ended. Again."

"How do you feel now?"

"Just numb."

Carol listened intently. Then she grabbed a piece of paper and wrote something down.

Ivy turned to her sister. "Why are you taking notes?"

"In case I need to use this for a paper. This is too good to forget."

Linda poured a cup of hot cocoa with mini marshmallows for Ivy.

"Why are you giving me hot chocolate? It's July. It's ninety degrees outside," Ivy said as she sipped the delicious warm drink.

"Because it always used to make you feel better."

Linda was right. The hot cocoa was already improving Ivy's mood.

"Is there anything we can do for you?" Mitch asked. He was always trying to be helpful.

"Just be with me. I love you guys so much."

"Family hug," Mitch said. He, Linda, and Carol all leaned in to give Ivy a big hug, and for the first time all day, Ivy felt a little bit better.

CHAPTER 27

NICK CAUGHT FRANNIE AND J. B. in the middle of doing it, right in front of all the neighbors. He heard them doing it before seeing them. He wished he hadn't. This image would set him back years. He watched them *grunt*, *pound*, *sigh* when they were done sticking—

A FOR SALE sign in the lawn in front of Nick's childhood home. "Stop! Stop!" he cried. The last few days had been rough, and this was not making it better. "Why are you selling the house?"

"Your mother and I are going to trip the light fantastic in Paris and all over the world."

"Who are you really, J. B.? Sure, you make good pancakes—"

"Crepes."

"You give me the crepes, Frenchie. What's your scam? To steal the house and leave my mother brokenhearted and alone?"

"Stop, Nick," Frannie snapped.

"You're selling the house to travel the world with the cook from the movie. I thought you were just going on location with him. You never said anything about moving."

"It's time for me to move on with my life, Nick. And J. B. is an excellent chef, not only a cook. He's got dreams of opening a restaurant one day."

"He's got dreams. He should have been dreaming in his twenties. Not at his age. He's setting you up, Mom, been doing it the whole time. That's been his plan all along."

Frannie hadn't seen Nick this way in a while, not since he had come home from LA after breaking up with Ivy. From that moment, he was quieter, hiding in his work. "You mean to say J. B.'s plan was to get me to sell my house? How does that happen? I guess it starts when Ivy writes a script, they make it into a movie, J. B. gets the movie job, seduces me, and makes me sell my house."

"You're right, Mom, if she doesn't write that script, none of this happens. It is all Ivy's fault."

"You're the one who broke up with her."

"And now she's dumped me," Nick said as he turned and walked into the house.

Frannie sighed. "He is my moody child."

"He will not visit us much, will he?" J. B. whispered.

"No. Nick hates to fly. His whole world is the winery and this town. Excuse me a minute." Frannie walked inside the house to find Nick taking photos of every room.

As she followed him, he said, "I'm taking pictures so I always remember what my childhood home looks like."

"Why are you acting like you are twelve? You're not moving. I am."

"You took away my agency." Nick slumped into his dad's favorite chair. The fake leather was worn, but the wired remote still worked. It was one of those chairs that could be adjusted to go all the way back and also to go all the way forward. Nick could always talk to his dad about anything. This was the first time he was talking to his mom about something emotionally relevant since his dad passed. He gazed, teary-eyed, at a framed photo of a young Nick and his dad in their beloved New York Mets hats.

"Why didn't you ask me, Mom? Why didn't you give me a choice in this?"

"I didn't have to. It's not your house, Nick."

"All my memories are in this house."

"All my memories are in my head. And I'm going to take them with me wherever I go."

"And you're going to be making new memories with J. B."

"There is nothing wrong with new memories," Frannie said. Nick looked away, staring into space. Something else was bothering him, and she knew that something was named Ivy. Frannie knew Nick didn't love her directness. He was just like his father. "It's not good to live in the past."

"Where else can I live?"

Frannie had no idea what he meant by that. Nick got up and started walking around the room, taking in every framed family photograph.

"The lake house you've been building."

"I don't want to live in the lake house."

"Then why did you build it!" She regretted raising her voice, but he was so stubborn. Like his father.

Nick was calm. "You don't get it, Mom."

"No, you don't get it, son. You might know a lot about the winery and wines, but you don't know crap about love. I have a lot of life left to live. I never thought I would fall in love again, but I did." Frannie sat down across from her wedding photo with

Nick's dad. "Since your father died, it took me a while to even change the message on the answering machine. Yes, I kept the answering machine message for three years so I could hear his voice. I guess I got lucky this year."

"How so?"

"That answering machine finally broke. I realized when I stopped hearing his voice on the machine every day that I was incredibly lonely." Frannie took a breath, composing her emotions. She looked right at Nick. "That's when the Christmas miracle happened."

"What miracle?"

"Ivy and her movie came to town. And J. B. came with it. And I fell in love. And I feel good about it."

"The movie is not a Christmas miracle, Mom. It's not even Christmas! It's July!"

"You call it what you want. All I know is that this movie—whatever the hell its name is—this movie coming to town, which I know is based on you and Ivy, is one of the best things that ever happened in my life, and I think maybe it could be the best thing that happened to your life too."

Nick did not want to hear any of that. He stopped talking and headed right out that door, colliding with J. B. on the front porch, who had been listening to every word. Nick pushed through the door, knocking him against the porch railing. Nick stopped. Breathing heavily. J. B. had no idea what would happen next. Nick took two steps toward J. B., raised his arms, and hugged the Frenchman. Close to tears, he told J. B., "You'd better take good care of my mom, or I will D-Day your ass."

J. B. nodded yes; he was well aware of the historical reference. He did not know how to respond and simply said, "My country-men and I thank you." Nick left. He headed back to the winery.

Nick sat at the winery. He had finished a bottle of Poison Ivy when Denise and Kenny joined him. Frannie had called Denise, worried about him. Instead of drinking alone with his thoughts, Nick was finally sharing his emotions about Ivy with the help of another bottle of Poison Ivy.

"I can't believe what happened."

"What happened, Nick?" Denise had to lean close to him as he spoke softly, his head down.

"You can tell us anything," Kenny offered.

"Oh yeah, so you can put it in the local paper, Kenny. In big headlines: NICK STILL LOVES IVY."

"I really don't think I would print that," Kenny said, logically.

Denise was excited. "Is that true, Nick? Do you still love Ivy?"

"Who told you that?" Nick was drunk. Denise knew there were two sides of him when he'd had a little too much. Sad Nick and sadder Nick. He was well past *sadder*.

"What happened, Nick? With Ivy."

"A Christmas miracle happened," he said in a Frannie-like voice. "Ivy wrote this movie and brought it here to film. And now we're all going to live in France!"

"I told you," Denise said to Kenny. "He still loves her."

"Why are we all moving to France?" Kenny asked.

Denise shushed him and asked Nick to keep talking.

"I can't believe I let myself fall back in love with her."

"You got back together?"

"For three minutes. Then she dumped me. Did you know Mom is selling the house?" Nick looked at Denise. "She's selling your room too."

"Yes, I know, Nick, it's part of the house. I have my own house now with Kenny."

"Mom said I have to go live in the lake house."

"I love that lake house," Kenny said.

"I don't. I don't want to live there… I don't want to live there without her. I don't want to live there without Ivy."

"Sometimes you have to move on, Nick," Denise said.

"Can I live with you?" he asked. She didn't answer. "I can live in the small guest room."

"You can't, Nick. There's something we should tell you," Kenny said.

"No, Kenny, we shouldn't tell him yet."

"Tell me what?" Nick said.

"You're going to be an uncle," Kenny answered excitedly.

"I'm having a baby!" Denise beamed.

Nick lit up. Forgetting about his worries. "Congratulations!" He realized that everyone else in his family was moving on. It made him feel sad to be so stuck.

Denise noticed he was sad again. "You look tired, Nick. A good night's sleep will help. Here…" She took out a bottle of Ambien and handed Nick a tablet. Kenny helped him to the back office, where he put Nick on the couch so he could sleep.

———

The fog rolled in just after midnight. He heard a door open and someone calling "Hello?" Nick sat up, as foggy as the night. He stumbled out of the office and into the tasting room.

A stranger was at the bar. He saw Nick.

"Hey, sorry to wake you. I didn't mean to get here so late," the stranger said. He was about five-ten. In his late sixties. Wearing a New York Mets hat.

"Dad?" Nick said. He stumbled forward and hugged the

man before the stranger had a chance to respond. "I'm so happy to see you again."

The stranger, who looked like Nick's dad, said, "The place looks amazing. It's been a few years."

"Do you like it, Dad?"

"It looks great, son."

Nick was now bouncing off the wall. Showing his dad everything he'd done to rebuild the winery.

"I'm proud of you, son."

"Remember I told you how I wanted to do it when I was, like, eleven? And I took a saw to the old tasting bar."

"Yes…"

"And you didn't get mad. You said, Nick, I believe in your dream, son. Now, please put down the power saw."

His dad was worried about him. "Nick, you said you wanted to talk."

"Yeah. You're really the only person I could talk to about these things."

"What things?"

Nick held up a half-finished bottle of Poison Ivy. His dad took it from him, poured himself a drink.

"This is really good."

"Wine of the year, Dad."

"You named it after Ivy."

"Ivy kills me tomorrow. The last scene."

"That's just a movie, Nick. Shouldn't you be thinking about living?"

"Mom said the same thing."

"Always listen to your mom."

"I think Mom likes Ivy more than me."

"You know that's not true, Nick," his dad said. "She just remembers how much happier you were with her."

"I think I blew it. Twice."

"Remember that time we went to Cooperstown?"

Nick smiled. "The Baseball Hall of Fame!"

"What do you know about baseball?"

"Steroids keep players out of the Hall of Fame."

"What else?"

"Pete Rose should never have bet on baseball."

"What else, Nick? What's the core lesson of the game? Three strikes, you're out."

"What about it?"

"You said you blew it twice. You have another swing."

"So did Beltrán in game seven," Nick said. Baseball was the universal language of most fathers and sons.

"You're right. He didn't swing. Why?"

"Because he sucked," Nick said, spoken like a true New York Mets fan.

"He was too scared."

"So you're saying I should take another shot at Ivy?"

His dad said yes. Nick high-fived him. His dad helped him back to his office and said good night.

"What's it like, Dad?" Nick said groggily.

"What's what like?"

"Dying."

"It's easy if you don't take any regrets with you. If you take regrets with you, you'll never get a good sleep."

Nick had a good sleep. His eyes closed as he was looking at his father. He would wake eight hours later as the winery was opening. He stumbled out of his office. It was Kenny checking on him.

"Hey, how are you feeling?"

"Good. Better. What did I drink last night?"

"Denise slipped you an Ambien."

"That explains the dream I had."

"What dream?"

"I heard a noise. I woke up. I walked out here, and there—" Nick stopped. At the end of the bar, where he had hugged his father, there was a New York Mets cap. "Where did this hat come from?" he asked.

"It was here when I walked in. I thought it was yours."

"It's not."

"Whose is it?"

"I think it was my dad's."

Kenny was worried. "Stay here, I'm going to make you some coffee." But when he returned with the pot—Nick was gone.

CHAPTER 28

GRIFFIN, BRUCE, AND CAROL SAT riveted, listening to Ivy's tale of the breakup. Nick's lie was the missing scene that no one knew existed. The waitress at Eddie O'Brien's was also riveted, but she really just wanted Ivy to finish her order.

"I always thought he dumped me for someone else. There is no 'someone else.' And to say he dumped me because he loved me? Ha! The nerve of him." Ivy started mimicking Nick. "You're not very good at making decisions, Ivy, so I made one for you. For us." She finally took note of the waitress standing there. "I'm sorry. What did you ask me?"

"If you want french fries."

"Enough fries for me. Cancel the whatever that goes with fries. I'm going back to LA in a few days. I've got to look good. I'll take the sushi."

"We don't have sushi. We have diablo fish tacos. They're really spicy."

"I'll have the diablo fish tacos. And a fat-washed mezcal," Ivy added. The waitress had no idea what she was talking about.

"She's from LA. Just give her a Prison City Pale Ale," Carol said. The waitress was glad to go.

They all looked at Ivy and said at the same time: "A fat-washed mezcal?"

"What? I ordered one when Drew took me to the Soho House, or maybe it was the Chateau."

Carol leaned in. "That is your problem right there, Ivy. Your ass is in Upstate New York, but you're seeing it through your la-la land glasses. You're not in sushi-and-sake land. You're in beer-and-burger land."

Ivy looked at Bruce and Griffin, who were already plotting an escape. She had sat down five minutes ago and ruined the gathering. "I'm sorry," she said. "Everything that comes out of my mouth these days is *me me me*. I am so selfish. You must be sick of me."

"You mean *me me me*," Griffin joked. They all laughed. Including Ivy. It felt good to laugh. "We should be celebrating, Ivy. You got your first movie made. You didn't just get something out of it, everyone else did too."

"I got a book advance," Carol said. "Thanks to you. And Griffin."

"I got to tell my side of my story. Thanks to you," Griffin said. He looked over at Bruce. It was his turn. "What did you get, Bruce?"

"I don't know yet. The night is young," he said coyly. Griffin blushed. Carol went for her notepad. The beer arrived.

Ivy held it up and toasted.

"To my family, my film family, and to my friends. And most importantly to *me me me*!" Ivy said, smiling.

They all *me me me*'d back. She smiled. Laughed. "I'm busting out of this love triangle and making a straight line back to LA." She then devoured the diablo fish tacos. She didn't know that whatever was in them would lead to one of the strangest nights of her life but they did.

Back at home, Carol was saying good night to Ivy. "I know you always loved math. But you really covered it up with a love triangle and your *straight line* back to LA. You learned a lot from Amari. You're a good little actress. You fooled everyone at dinner, except yourself."

"I was tired of ruining people's good time. I wanted to laugh and stop thinking about everything," Ivy admitted.

"And now?" Carol wondered.

"I'm thinking about it more. I got a love triangle dinging in my head," she said.

"Nice pivot. Geometric metaphor to a musical one." Carol laughed.

"What am I going to do, Carol? Tomorrow is the last day of the shoot. And I'm still not allowed back."

"Why do you have this urge to be on the set anyway? Isn't your job all done?"

"Yes, it is, but I like watching it all come to life." Ivy looked sad. "Tomorrow, Nick dies."

"You mean Rick," Carol corrected.

"Rick, yeah. Nick's already dead to me. I can't believe I let him ruin this. He ruined Christmas for me. He's all I think about as soon as they start playing Christmas music on the radio. After he dumped me in LA, I put all my anger into this Christmas script. It was cheaper than therapy. I thought about how people go from the happiest time of the year to the worst time of the year. Do you remember the song "Have Yourself a Merry Little Christmas"? It's not a happy song."

"Sure it is."

"No, Frank Sinatra changed the lyrics. He thought the Judy Garland version was too sad. *Have yourself a merry little Christmas. It may be your last. Next year we may all be living in the past.*"

"Wow. That's appropriate. Not just for you. But the whole world."

"Isn't it? *From now on, we'll have to muddle through somehow. So have yourself a merry little Christmas now.* I guess I'll muddle through this Christmas in July. I'm sorry if I sound whiny."

"I'm your sister. I'm always here for you. You don't sound whiny. You sound confused. There's a lot going on here, Ivy. I can see how it's messing with your head. Do you want my advice?"

"No one really wants advice, do they?"

"No. But you're getting it anyway. Stop thinking about it for a second. It's consumed you since you got here. You need a brainwash."

"I do," Ivy agreed, "want to wash that man right outta my head."

"Not a movie brainwash. A real brainwash. Researchers at BU found that during sleep, the fluid present in the brain and spinal cord—called the cerebrospinal fluid—washes in and out, like waves, helping the brain get rid of accumulated metabolic trash."

"I have a lot of trash I need to get rid of."

Carol smiled. "You need to let your brain complete the wash cycle. After a good night's sleep, you can think about it more clearly."

Ivy took her sister's advice. She went to sleep trying to

remember the meditation tricks she'd learned. They didn't work. Not at all. After tossing and turning, Ivy fell into a deep, deep sleep...

...only to be awakened in a dream by the young Ivy, who looked just like the young actress she met earlier. "Wake up, Ivy," young her said. She opened her eyes to see her room decorated for Christmas.

"What's going on? Why is this room decorated for Christmas? It's July."

"It's Christmas Eve," young Ivy said.

"It's July. We're filming the Christmas movie. I'm dreaming about the set."

"This isn't a dream. It is Christmas." Young Ivy waved her arm, and the sheets flew off the bed, floated in the air. Swirling. Filling the room with snow. Young Ivy held out her hand. "Follow me."

Ivy took her young guide's hand and walked into a swirling snow cyclone. She never remembered a dream feeling so cold.

"Where are we going? You're not going all *A Christmas Carol* on me, are you?"

"You're the one who ate the diablo fish tacos, not me."

They stepped out of the snow. They were in a church. Ivy looked around. She saw her mom and dad. She yelled hello.

Young Ivy raised an eyebrow. "Really? And you call yourself a writer. You know they can't hear you."

"Of course they can hear me. They're right there. Mom! Dad!" No answer. "Great, a *Christmas Carol* trope."

"You know them better than me."

"So, what do I do now?"

Young Ivy smiled. "You watch me playing you meeting Nick for the first time."

Ivy watched Young Ivy walk to the young eight-year-old boy. Suddenly Vera was there, floating on a camera dolly filming the whole thing.

Ivy watched as Young Nick and Young Ivy "met cute" when they were in the church pageant. She watched as a younger Frannie dragged Young Nick to the church rehearsal because Denise wanted to be in the pageant. At age eight, Nick was too young to stay home by himself. So off he'd gone to the rehearsal, planning on sitting in the back with his Game Boy, but the universe had other plans for him. When he arrived at the church, he looked around and saw that there were mostly only girls there. He was also the oldest boy there. The choir director pulled him aside.

"Hi, Nick. So happy you decided to join us."

"Uh, yeah," Young Nick grunted. He focused on *Donkey Kong*.

"I was hoping that you would play Joseph. We could really use you." The choir director was practically pleading.

"Um..." Young Nick looked away, not wanting to disappoint the choir director but knowing that he was going to because there was no way that he was going to participate in the church pageant. That was for girls. He felt that way until he looked up at the front of the church and he saw the cutest eight-year-old girl that he'd ever seen. She was standing next to the cradle holding a doll baby that he realized was supposed to be the baby Jesus. He wondered who the girl was, as he'd never seen her before. The choir director noticed Young Nick's gaze.

"That's Ivy Green. She's new in town. She's playing Mary." The choir director realized that Young Nick was smitten, and she added, "So come on now, Joseph. Let's start the rehearsal."

Young Nick felt like a lamb being brought to slaughter as he obediently followed the choir director to the front of the church. He stopped in front of Ivy, who quickly introduced herself.

"Hi, I'm Ivy. I just moved here. My dad got a tenure-track job at Hobart and William Smith."

Young Ivy was the most talkative girl that Young Nick had ever met. He felt shy around her.

"Hi, I'm Nick."

"Nice to meet you, Nick." Young Ivy grinned at him. Her smile lit up her entire face.

Off to the side, watching the scene play out, Ivy noticed how Young Nick melted when Young Ivy smiled. She noticed how he looked when she was around.

"Are you playing Joseph?" Young Ivy asked.

The choir director looked at him hopefully. "Uh, yeah," Young Nick blurted out. "I'm Joseph."

"Good, then why don't you hold baby Jesus," Young Ivy said as she thrust the doll baby into his arms.

Young Nick was dumbfounded. If he had been told that he was going to be stuck holding a girl's doll baby at the front of the church, he would never have believed it. But there he was, holding a doll. And there she was, the cutest girl he'd ever seen. Even her name was cute: *Ivy*.

They are so cute, Ivy said to herself as she watched it all play out.

"It is cute," Young Ivy said, shocking her. What was she doing by her side? Another young Ivy who now looked like she did was on the set. But this one was a little older.

"That's me. I'm twelve."

"You're thirteen. You and Nick hit puberty." The thirteen-year-old Nick was now holding thirteen-year-old Ivy's hand as they got dressed in their robes for the pageant.

"I'm holding his hand. In church! I'm thirteen," Ivy said.

"Not for long." The snow swirled. The scene changed. She was now looking at sixteen-year-old Ivy and sixteen-year-old Nick, who were dressed in their robes of Mary and Joseph again.

"When we have a kid," sixteen-year-old Ivy teased, "it better not be an immaculate conception."

The Young Ivy said, "He really gets all wacky around you. I can see why. You're a tease."

"I'm sixteen!"

"Not anymore." The snow swirled. Ivy dreamed she was floating in the snow. The Young Ivy brought her to the train station. Ivy walked out of the snow, hopped onboard.

Young Ivy was sitting next to her on the train. No one else was on it. They were moving. "I hope I remember all this when I wake up. Where are we going?"

"Destination: Christmas Present—I mean Christmas in July." Ivy looked out the window. Snow was swirling. It was too hard to see. But then the train stopped, and the snow parted like a curtain. They were now in the Shepherd Winery. Ivy watched as she saw Nick for the first time in five years, the first time since they had broken up.

"I didn't stare at him like that."

"Yes, you did."

The snow swirled—now Ivy was watching the night of the forlorn Christmas Karaoke. Nick was carrying her away, to the lake house. She was watching him put her to bed, cover her and kiss her on the head.

"He kissed me. I don't remember him kissing me."

"That's because you were wasted. I'm amazed you remember anything from that night," Young Ivy said.

"Promise me when you get to my age, don't drink too much."

The snow swirled. Ivy couldn't see past it. But she could hear the opening of the Beach Boys song "Little Saint Nick," otherwise known as the Christmas disaster song. The snow stopped enough for her to see a door. She opened it to see her Christmas future. A Christmas party was going on in a lavish home high in the Hollywood Hills.

"Hey, Ivy," some guy yelled. He looked like Griffin, an older Griffin. He was wearing glasses. "You can see Santa from this view."

"Is that Griffin?" Ivy asked.

"It is. You always hired him. He's been in every one of your movies," said Young Ivy.

"How many movies did I write?" wondered Ivy.

"Credited or uncredited?" asked Young Ivy.

"Credited," she answered.

"Three."

"Really? That's it?" Ivy gasped. She'd expected so much more from herself.

"Enough with the credits. The show's running long," Young Ivy said.

"So, this place is mine," she said as she grabbed a Christmas cosmo from a passing waiter. "I guess I made it."

"You did. You're one of those highly paid script doctors. You're very rich. You fix everyone else's script problems. Never your own."

"All my dreams came true," Ivy said, not loving this dream.

"Well, not all of them," young Ivy said. The real Ivy wasn't listening. She had spotted the future Ivy being the life of the party, the center of attention.

She stepped in and found an older version of herself. "Is that me?"

"Yeah, you kept yourself in great shape."

Ivy went up to herself and looked closely at the future Ivy's forehead. "I had Botox!"

"That's not all the work you had done." Suddenly, some old white guy with a full gray beard appeared. His nickname was the Silver Turtle. He leaned up and kissed Ivy, flush on the mouth. Something that was totally gross.

"Why am I kissing Grandpa?" Ivy asked.

"That's not Grandpa. That's Eric. The Silver Turtle. Rich media guy. He's your third husband."

"My third husband? I've been married twice? To whom? Drew?"

"That was strike one. Strike two was a Spanish financier named Alfonso. You lived in Madrid for a year."

"And now I'm married to Grandpa? What happened to Nick?"

Suddenly the snow appeared. When it stopped, they were outside the famous TCL Chinese Theatre. Spotlights were spraying in the night. She saw all the people from the party, all the people from her childhood, and all the people from now—filing into the theater.

She walked in and smiled. "Everyone I know is here." Ivy stopped herself. Eyes scanning the backs of heads. She did not see who she was looking for. "Nick—where's Nick?"

Young Ivy shushed her, popcorn in hand. "The movie is about to start."

Ivy sat down. Took some of the dream popcorn, which she couldn't seem to eat. The movie started. It was a funeral. She recognized the scene. It was the one that had not been shot yet. It was Nick's funeral.

"Ivy, where's Nick?"

"You killed him, Ivy."

"Where is he?"

"It doesn't matter. You got everything you wanted. Except for the thing that mattered the most."

"What happened to Nick?" Ivy exclaimed. Everyone in the theater was now shushing her. *Shush. Shush. Shush.*

"Nick died. In the snowmobile accident. Just like you wrote it. Just like they filmed it for *The Christmas Couple*."

"*The Christmas Couple*. What's that?"

"The title of your movie."

"I like that. I should write it down."

"You'll remember. See…" Young Ivy indicated the scene playing on the screen. It was Ivy's scene—the funeral scene she'd written out of anger. "You killed Nick in your story, and he died the same way a few months later. In a snowmobile accident. It's art imitating life. You could never forgive yourself for putting that thought out into the universe. You killed him."

"I killed Nick. This is all my fault. This is no dream. This is really happening!"

Young Ivy snickered, "How very *Rosemary's Baby* of you."

"WAKE UP! IVY, WAKE UP!" a voice started shouting. It was Carol.

Ivy came out of her deep sleep. She was shaken. But in her own bedroom.

"I heard you from the other room. You were shouting, 'No, Nick. No.'"

"I'm okay."

"Good," Carol said. "Next time don't have a Christmas cosmo without me."

For a moment, Ivy was confused. But then she saw it—the Christmas cosmo that she'd been drinking when visiting her future. The martini glass was there. The drink was cold. Ivy sat up. Looked at her sister with fierce determination.

"I have to rewrite the ending."

"Of the movie?" Carol asked.

"Of my life!"

CHAPTER 29

OVER AT THE BELHURST CASTLE, Amari was having an epiphany. On that morning, she'd gotten a text from her agent. Apparently, the studio was very happy with the dailies, especially with Amari's acting. Her agent made the point that she had been given an ideal role for where she was in her career. *When Joseph Met Mary* was a game changer in her rise to stardom.

As Amari thought about how she'd loved the part that Ivy had written for her, she had one of those light-bulb moments. She finally realized that if it hadn't been for Ivy, she never would have been given the script with the perfect part. She suddenly felt horrible about how she'd treated Ivy, especially that she'd kicked her off the set. All because of her own insecurity about her voice. Who really cared if she could sing? She was an A-list actress. While she was getting dressed, she'd discovered the matching "soul sister" bracelet that she had given herself and Ivy. It was at the bottom of her suitcase. She'd meant to wear it, but she'd gotten into the fight with Ivy. Amari was applying her mascara when she started to tear up. *How could I have behaved so badly?*

Across town at the Green house, Linda was making French

toast for the whole family. Mitch was frying up turkey bacon, and Griffin and Carol were sitting around the table drinking coffee, acting like siblings. Griffin looked right at home as if it was his real home. Ivy rushed down the stairs. She was telling them about her crazy *A Christmas Carol* dream when the doorbell rang. Carol peered out the window to see Amari on the porch. Alone.

"It's the evil witch," she said.

"Uh oh. I'm going to peace out. I don't need her to see me here," Griffin said as he got up and ran up the back staircase. Carol mouthed the word "chicken" to him.

"I'll let her in," Mitch said as he went to the door. He opened it to see Amari, beautiful as always and yet looking like she'd had humble pie for breakfast.

"Hi. Is Ivy here?"

"We're all eating breakfast. Why don't you come inside?" Everyone looked up as Amari entered the kitchen. Ivy glared at her.

"Hi," Amari said shyly. "Ivy, can we talk?"

"Sure," Ivy said. But she said it in a way that indicated she was angry.

"I mean somewhere privately."

"Whatever you have to say to me can be said in front of my family."

Amari actually looked nervous. She could tell that Ivy's family no longer loved her unconditionally. "It's about Nick."

"Please. I don't have time for this. He doesn't love you."

"I know that."

Ivy looked surprised. "You do?"

"I knew I never had a chance with Nick. I was only trying to get into character. I was acting."

"You did an awfully good job at it," Carol said.

"And for the record, I hope you know that I'm not really your mother," Linda added.

"I know. It was all play-acting. But for me it also became real. I'm sorry for hurting you guys. And I'm sorry I banned you from the set, Ivy. It had nothing to do with Nick. I was just so jealous of your voice."

"Ivy does have a beautiful voice," Mitch noted.

Ivy looked irritated. "Let's see if I'm getting this right. You banned me from the set of the movie for which I wrote the script. And without said script there never would have been a movie, and all because you were jealous of my voice at a small-town Karaoke bar?"

"Yes."

"How fragile are you?"

"It's not my best quality," Amari said as she broke into tears. "I never meant to hurt you. I really liked you so much. I wanted us to be like sisters."

"She already has a sister," Carol quickly said.

"Amari, I don't have time for this. I have other things I need to do right now," Ivy said.

"Nick never loved me. It was always you. It was all he talked about. All the time."

"Even in the hotel room?"

"I think you should know what happened in the hotel room."

"Amari, I don't care what happened. It doesn't matter to me."

"It should. Nick was the first guy who ever jumped out of a window to get away from me."

"What?"

"After you left, I was able to unlock the bathroom door. Nick was gone. The window was open."

"He climbed out?"

"That's how much Nick loves you. He'd rather climb out a two-story window than be with me. I thought you should know that. I'm so sorry. Please forgive me. And come back to the set," Amari said tearfully.

And in that moment, Ivy had her own light-bulb moment as she realized that without Amari, her film might not have been green-lit. Her words would have languished on the page without the wattage of a star like Amari.

Ivy got up from the table and gave Amari a big hug. "Thank you," she said. "I'm so happy we can be friends again."

As they were hugging, Griffin skulked back into the room. "Looks safe to come out," he joked. Everyone laughed. Amari looked over at him and smiled.

"So this is where you've been hiding out," she teased.

"Best place in the world. I love this family. And these breakfasts!"

"French toast coming up!" Linda said enthusiastically.

Everyone rushed to their seats.

"Take a seat, Amari," Ivy said with a smile.

"Don't you have to get to the set for your call time?" Mitch asked.

"Not till ten a.m.," Amari answered.

"You don't want to miss this French toast," Griffin told her.

Amari joined the Green family and Griffin, and they ate breakfast like one big happy family. When Amari suggested that they go to the set together, Ivy agreed. But first she needed to see Nick. But when they got to the lake house, he was gone. They noticed that his boat slip was empty.

"Looks like he took *True Love* out," Amari said.

True Love! Ivy thought. He bought a boat and called it *True Love*. She hadn't known he'd named it *True Love*. There was one summer where the Geneva Theater showed classic movies each Sunday night. Ivy dragged Nick to all of them. Nick had surprisingly liked *The Philadelphia Story*. It was one of Ivy's top five. The name of the boat in that movie was *True Love*. In the movie, Katharine Hepburn and Cary Grant hated each other but wound up back together, married at the end. She told all of this to Amari.

"True love. You two were meant to be," Amari said.

"I hope so. First, I have to rewrite this ending. So Nick isn't killed."

"You mean Rick."

"I think we both know that this story is completely autobiographical."

"Yup. I think everybody knows that. Especially Drew."

"He's starting to get it," Ivy agreed.

"Come on, let's go to the set together."

There was a sense of excitement and a sense of relief, a feeling of exhilaration and a feeling of exhaustion at the church that July 31st morning, the final day of filming. Conversation filled the air, not just about what they had to do on that day but of small talk of where they might go next. A family—one that was formed from the shared love of making movies—was going to be splitting apart once Vera called "That's a wrap."

There would be the celebratory wrap party immediately after at none other than Eddie O'Brien's. But for a lot of crew members, this would be goodbye. They wanted to head to their homes and lives and families and rest a little before their next jobs.

Vera displayed an outward confidence but kept an inner motive. This was her second movie. Drew, who had grown up in the business, assured her that the footage so far had been terrific. But Vera was very self-critical. She was worried that she was trading art for an audience. It was tough enough to be a female director in Hollywood. Even tougher when she became distracted by the off-screen drama. She'd even put fifty dollars in the Nick/Drew betting pool, but no one knew who she bet on. That started a second betting pool. Who was Vera's pick?

Vera, Drew, Bruce, and the cinematographer huddled, going over the schedule for the last day, the number of scenes and shots they had to get. Bruce had scheduled the production way in advance. Today should be an easy day. Four scenes. One location. Three Christmas carols and the funeral of Rick. Bruce had suggested an early call—"We want to get the church mourners here when they're tired." Then they would shoot the funeral, break for lunch, and then film three Christmas pageant nativity scenes with each different Ivy. It did seem like an easy day, and that was what worried Vera.

"What are you doing here?" Drew snarled.

Ivy was walking right toward him. She was surprised by his confrontational tone but not the least bit concerned by it.

"We need to talk."

Vera rolled her eyes. "Oh God, enough with the on-set romance. I have a movie to finish."

"That's what this is about. The movie. I need to talk to both of you."

"Technically, you are banned from the set," Drew said. To

Ivy, Drew did not sound like a professional. He sounded like a jealous ex-boyfriend. Which was fine with her. But just before she was going to explain that, Amari weighed in as she strutted over, timing her entrance perfectly. Ivy marveled; even in real life she was always the movie star.

"Not anymore. I banned her, so I can unban her. This is Ivy's movie. She saw it before anyone else did. Give her a shot. And remember, I could get the both of you kicked off this movie in a heartbeat." Amari hugged Ivy, and everyone's mouths dropped open.

"There's one day left," Vera scoffed.

Amari glared. Vera stopped. All eyes were on Ivy.

"I need to rewrite the ending of the movie," she stated.

"The funeral scene?" Drew questioned.

"Yes, I want to rewrite it. Without the funeral."

Vera listened as Drew clarified. "Without the funeral. But Nick dies."

"Not anymore. And the character's name is Rick."

"Rick lives? So whose funeral is it?" Drew asked.

"No one's, Drew. No one dies."

"No one dies in the funeral scene? Why do we have a funeral?"

"We don't. People don't want to spend ninety minutes hoping our couple stays in love. There are forces ripping them apart. They are stronger than that. Love is stronger. It's a Christmas movie. Their love is resurrected!"

"Isn't that Easter?" Drew sniped. Vera shushed him.

"We want them to be together. We need them to be together. What do we get by killing Rick at the end? Sad reactions. Disappointment. Low score on Rotten Tomatoes." Ivy stopped for a moment. Everyone was riveted. Ivy continued, "So this is the ending: Ilsa thinks it's all over. But something tells her to come back. That's when she learns Rick was in an accident. We keep all that. But instead of going to the hospital for the death scene, which we already shot, Ilsa comes here. To the church. On Christmas Eve. To watch the nativity scene play out without them. Hoping. Praying."

"What happens next? Let me see the pages," Vera said.

"I don't have them yet. But they're in my head. And I do know that the Christmas couple deserves a happy ending."

"The Christmas couple? What the hell is that?" Drew was very good at the snarky tone. Ivy was finding it all very annoying.

"That's the new title for the movie. The K-25 romance. They meet at Christmas, fall in love at Christmas, get back together at Christmas."

Vera smiled. "I like it. I like happy endings."

Drew protested, "I thought you wanted authenticity."

Ivy thought about this. "Whoever said love wasn't authentic? It's the most real thing there is. But maybe we've all become too broken by so many things that we forget all about love. And maybe with our little movie and our happy ending, we can help people remember that true love can last forever."

"Bruce, write that down," Vera said. "It's good." He scribbled down what Ivy had said.

"I don't believe in happy endings," Drew said. "My father was married five times."

"This is not about you, Drew," Vera stated.

"It's not? I am the producer."

Ivy was alarmed. Drew could kill it right now. Rick/Nick would die. Real Nick would never forgive her. This was the only way she could prove to him that she loved him more than anything else. She was about to go to the mattresses (a line from *The Godfather* which meant going to war against your enemy) when—Vera jumped in and jolted Drew.

"Put your dick in your back pocket. You stopped acting like a producer once Ivy fell back in love with Nick." It was out there now. No more subtext. No more veiled lies. Drew was looking down. When he raised his chin, Ivy could see his poker face. Impossible to read.

"I did. I fell back in love with Nick. I don't know if I ever fell out of love with him," Ivy revealed.

"That's good," Vera said. "Bruce, write that down too."

"Got it," he said, reading as he wrote: *I don't know if I ever fell out of love with him.*

"But we're all set up for the funeral. She doesn't have any pages. This is the last day of shooting. You can't just change things, Ivy. There is no money to shoot another day." With each sentence Drew knew he was losing his argument. "Fine. But we are scheduled to wrap at eight tonight. One second past eight o'clock and I pull the plug on this fuckin' movie!" His voice echoed in the church. Crew members and local extras stared at him.

"Drew, we are in a church, for God's sake. What is wrong with you?" Vera scolded.

Drew said nothing. He prided himself on being professional. He was deeply embarrassed. He looked up at Ivy with sad eyes. "I'll help you get the ending you want, Ivy," Drew said quietly.

"Thank you, Drew. For everything."

Bruce quickly steered the discussion back in the right direction. "We can do this. Most of the extras are here. We just need to get the three Ivies here. We flip the funeral with the three Christmas pageants. And shoot the new ending later in the day."

"Are you okay with that, Drew?" Vera asked. He nodded. She looked sternly at Ivy. "Start writing. Make it great."

"Thank you," Ivy said.

CHAPTER 30

IVY RUSHED TO FIND A place to write. All the church preschool classrooms were being used by the production. Props. Lights. Wardrobe. The library was being used for extras. The downstairs auditorium was where craft services were set up. The church secretary saw Ivy rushing around and gave her sanctuary in the pastor's office. Ivy opened up her tablet with a keyboard. Opened the script file. She deleted the funeral scene in one quick flourish and started writing, hoping that by writing the happy ending in her movie that it would bring her a happy ending in her life. She felt momentarily blocked and realized she wanted to talk to Nick first. She called him. There was no answer. She texted him: PLEASE COME TO THE CHURCH.

———————

Thunder rumbled in the distance. Nick sat on his boat, *True Love*, watching the waves getting a little stronger. Other boats were heading back to the docks, but Nick wanted to stay a little longer. He'd decided he would take *True Love* out for a quick ride. Figure out what he needed to do and head back in. He had spent the morning processing everything. His mom's moving.

Amari. Ivy's reaction to Nick's reveal about what really happened that day of their breakup. And the visit from his ghost dad. *Could that have been my dad?*

When Nick told Kenny about it, Kenny suggested that maybe it was one of the actors who was playing his dad. Either way, his dad had the best advice as always. You get three strikes. Nick had two strikes against him. But he did have one left. He had to take one more swing at romance. One more shot at Ivy. This was true love. Nick smiled. He pressed the ignition button. Nothing happened.

True Love was dead on the water.

Back at the church, under the watchful eyes of a painting of no less than Jesus Christ, Ivy typed away. Crafting a new scene that started with the end of the Christmas nativity. In Ivy's new ending, parents, grandparents, and parishioners all got up to leave. Ilsa stayed behind, just taking it in. Across from her, on the other side of the sanctuary, was Rick. They saw each other. They found their way back to each other. Ivy paused and looked at the pages. She read them out loud to herself.

ILSA
You're here.

RICK
Where else would I be?
It's Christmas.

Isla and Rick run toward each other, serpentining around pews, and finally kiss in the empty church.

Ivy was pleased. She printed it out and walked downstairs. They were filming the church pageant. Her parents and sister were in the second pew. Vera had positioned them to be featured extras. Ivy watched from a video village monitor. The child actors playing Young Ivy and Young Nick were smiling at each other. Were they already crushing on each other? *God, I hope not.* Ivy's romance with Nick was tough enough.

Vera yelled, "Cut!"

Bruce yelled, "Moving on to the next setup!"

Ivy gave Vera the pages. "I think you're going to love them."

She read them. Smiled. And ripped them up. Vera yelled to Bruce, "Let's cue the middle Ivy."

"What's wrong with the scene?" Ivy asked, hoping for some directorial direction.

"I'm not feeling the love. Go work on it some more."

Ivy left dejectedly.

Back on Nick's boat, the rain was intensifying. The storm was getting closer. The waves were white-capping. Nick could not get the boat started. He looked in all directions. There was no one in sight. There was no phone reception to be had. Day was turning into night. It was a quick- moving thunderstorm. The small boat rocked more. Maybe he could ride the storm out on *True Love*.

Back at the church, Ivy wrote another version of the scene. Same setup. Crowded church service. Christmas Eve. This time she would have the grown up Ilsa and Rick perform the nativity play. Rick would read the lines about putting the baby in the manger, because there was no room for them in the inn. "There's always room for you at my inn any day," Isla would say, and the Christmas Couple would come back together.

Ivy brought the new scene down to the set. They were filming the second nativity scene with the middle school Ilsa and Rick. Ivy smiled.

Vera called, "Cut!" Bruce announced it was lunchtime. Vera saw Ivy, walked over to her. "You're running out of time." Ivy handed her the new pages. She scanned them quickly. "What are you writing, Christmas porn dialogue?" Vera ripped up the pages. "Try again."

Ivy worked through lunch. Thirty minutes later, she brought down another version of the scene. *Rip!* Vera didn't like those pages either. "We don't need Amari monologuing. We still need a big emotional ending. There are no stakes."

Vera hustled back to the set. *Stakes,* Ivy thought. *I could raise the stakes. I could give this a life-or-death moment.* Loud thunder echoed in the church. Suddenly everyone's phone went off. It was an emergency alert from the National Weather Service.

Nick saw the lightning flash in the not so far distance. He knew this was becoming too much to handle. He was about three hundred yards from shore. He tightened his life jacket, went to the front of the boat. He was going to try a flare gun, when it happened—one of the rarest things that could happen—but it happened.

KA-BOOM!

A bolt of lightning struck the radio antenna. The motor exploded, along with the back of the boat. The force of the explosion flung Nick into the lake, away from the fiery debris.

The warning from the National Weather Service was about the passing storm. There would be flash flooding, chance of lightning, potential power outages.

"Big storm," Vera noted, looking over the shot list as she swallowed her lunch. "Ivy, we might have to go with the funeral scene. I have to give this movie an ending."

"I'm trying…"

"Lunch is nearly over. Try harder, or Nick is dead."

Nick's arms were flailing. Grasping. He had been thrown into the water. He forced his way above the waves, which were now peaking at about ten to twelve feet. Nick had never experienced anything close to this. *True Love* was burning in the water. What was left of it. Nick realized he might die. All he could think about was Ivy and how much he'd always loved her and how she made his world so much brighter. And how grateful he should have been to have her in his heart.

Ivy was now writing on the set when the power cut out. The church was plunged into darkness. Bruce took charge—"Everyone stay where you are, find a place to sit down. We'll get the generator going. But it might take a while."

She kept writing by the light from her tablet.

Nick had surfed a few times in his life. He realized he needed to ride above the waves, no matter where they took him. It was too hard to swim to shore. The water was hitting him in his face. He was swallowing and spitting out half of Seneca Lake. He tried again to swim to shore, but he was going nowhere. The rain was blinding. Nick was struggling, barely staying afloat.

It was an hour since the power outage. Nick still had not texted Ivy back. By flashlight, the set decorators were staging the funeral scene. The casket was rolled in. Extras entered, wearing funeral clothing. Then—in the muted church, Ivy heard a shriek of terror. She recognized the voice saying, "Please, God, no!" It was Frannie. Something was terribly wrong. Ivy rushed up; her tablet fell to the ground. The screen shattered.

"Frannie, what's wrong?" she said. J. B. was consoling her.

Frannie had tears in her eyes. "It's Nick."

"What happened? What happened?"

"I don't know. He took his boat out this morning. Someone said they saw it was hit by lightning. And it exploded."

Ivy gasped. "And Nick?"

Frannie couldn't answer. J. B. looked at Ivy and said, "We don't know."

Ivy took Frannie in her arms. Frightened. Scared. Trapped by the storm outside, all they could do was hold on.

The word spread throughout the church. Ivy was not worrying about the script anymore, just Nick. As was everyone there, especially the extras filling the pews. The three Ivys started to sing "Silent Night" in the middle of this dark day. Slowly, everyone joined in. The extras, the crew, the cast.

Ivy was crying. She had killed Nick in the movie. This was all her fault.

Vera rushed over to Ivy. "I heard what happened. Don't give up hope, Ivy. Nothing's been confirmed."

"Thank you, Vera."

She was surrounded by her friends. Griffin. Bruce. Amari. Vera. All giving her words of encouragement. They hugged like a family. A film family.

Griffin said, "Film production is like getting a family. We'll get through this."

They sat in the pews, holding hands.

The power came back on thirty minutes later.

"Vera…" It was Drew. Ivy knew what he was going to say, what he had to say: "We have to shoot the funeral scene."

"I can't be here for this," Ivy said. She walked over to gather her shattered tablet which had fallen at the feet of a statue of Jesus. Ivy looked up at the statue. His story was one of resurrection. Lots of old stories and myths had moments of resurrection. She said a prayer for Nick.

Ivy was going to go to the police station with Frannie and J. B. and find out more. As she waited for Frannie, they heard Bruce shout out: "Quiet on the set!"

She couldn't watch. She looked away. Closed her eyes. Said another prayer. Then she heard a voice calling, "Ivy! Ivy!"

There was a quick yell of "Action!" by Vera. The funeral scene was starting. Ivy heard the voice again: Nick's voice. She turned. And there was Nick. Soaked. Bruised. Walking into the middle of the shot, standing on the set by the casket screaming.

"IVY!"

"NICK!" Ivy yelled, racing toward the set. Nick was here. He was alive. And he was holding a piece of wood. Ivy didn't care about that. "You're alive!"

"I was on the lake. Then there was this flash of lightning. The boat blew up! The next thing I knew I was in the water. I thought I was going to die. You know what they say: your whole life flashes before you when you're about to die. That's not true. Or maybe it is. Because the only thing I saw was you, Ivy. You're the only life I want. And look what saved me, Ivy. This piece of wood." Everyone listened to Nick. Riveted.

Nick flipped it over. The words *TRUE LOVE* clear for everyone to see. He held it high in the air like John Cusack in *Say Anything*.

"*True Love* saved my life. *I love you*, Ivy!" Nick shouted.

"I love you too. I've always loved you."

Ivy hugged him. They were both crying. He was in pain but happy. "I love you! I love you! I love you!"

Vera looked at Bruce. "Tell me we're still rolling."

Bruce nodded. "Getting all of it. Looks like you got your ending."

Frannie returned from the back to see Nick, alive, kissing Ivy. She screamed for joy and rushed to join them. Griffin and Amari joined in.

"He's alive," Ivy said. "And he loves me."

"*Cut!*" Vera yelled. Everyone laughed. She approached Ivy. "I'm glad you got your happy ending, but now we have to film ours."

"But I didn't write anything."

"Just write what happened. Bruce has all the notes you need. This whole movie has been autobiographical so why should the ending be any different? I'm glad it's a happy one."

Ivy picked up her busted tablet. It still worked. She sat on the set, Nick at her side, and punched out the ending.

A little later, Nick and Ivy, holding hands, watched the last scene of *The Christmas Couple* being filmed. It opened with Ilsa in the church. She had gotten word about Rick and the snowmobile accident. A storm had cut off the power. Everyone was in the church, praying that Rick hadn't died. Hoping for a miracle. The storm ended. Sunlight streamed through the stained-glass windows. Griffin rushed in and used most of what Nick said: *"I thought I was going to die. You know what they say: when you think you're going to die, your whole life flashes before your eyes. And the only thing I saw was you, Ilsa. You're the only life I want."*

Vera smiled. She said, "Cut! And that's a wrap!"

Ivy cheered. She hugged Nick. Her first movie had finished filming. The love of her life was in love with her. It was real love. True love. She looked up: snowflakes were falling inside the church. Everyone was laughing. Hugging. Griffin hugged Bruce, knowing he was the one who'd set the snow machines on the balcony.

As the snow drifted down inside the church, it felt to Ivy that she was living a dream.

"It looks so real." Nick smiled.

"It is real. We're real."

"It's magical," he said.

"Who said magic can't be real."

Under the falling snow, inside the church where they first met, the Christmas couple, Ivy and Nick, smiled and kissed.

"Merry Christmas, Ivy."

"Merry Christmas, Nick."

CHAPTER 31

THE WRAP PARTY WAS AT Shepherd Winery. The place was filled with love and laughter. Ivy and Nick arrived a little late as they had spent a few hours catching up. When they walked into the winery everyone cheered with full glasses of Poison Ivy.

Amari toasted them: "To the Christmas couple."

Ivy and Nick smiled at each other, loving their new nickname, loving each other even more.

"I'm so happy it worked out for you two," Amari said, hugging them both.

Ivy noted, "You're wearing the friendship bracelet. So am I!" They squealed and hugged. "Amari?"

"What is it, Ivy?"

"You said you knew my secret. What is it?"

"That you never stopped loving Nick."

Ivy nodded. She was right. Nick came over. Amari pinched him on the butt. "Sorry, I couldn't help myself." She still loved teasing Nick, and Ivy didn't care. She laughed. She loved seeing Nick get embarrassed so easily.

Frannie saw them and rushed over. She hugged Ivy. "You've made me so happy. I missed you so much, Ivy."

"So did I, Frannie."

"What? I don't get a hug?" Nick asked playfully.

"Of course you do," J. B. said, hugging him and kissing him on both cheeks.

Not to be left out of the family reunion, Ivy's parents hugged Nick and Frannie. Linda wanted to go out to lunch with Frannie next week.

"As much as I would love to catch up," Frannie said, "I'm moving to France tomorrow with J. B." J. B. was brought into the circle, meeting Ivy's parents. Frannie pulled Nick to the side. "Nick, you're not going to believe this, but I sold the house."

"Already?"

"Cash offer."

"From whom?"

"From us!" Griffin yelled, coming over with Bruce. "We bought it."

"And the movie theater too!" Bruce added.

Griffin and Bruce filled everyone in on their plans. Geneva would become their hideaway. The place was so down to earth. As they talked with Ivy, Nick excused himself. He saw someone he recognized standing in the corner. It was his dad!

"Mom," Nick whispered to Frannie. "Do you see that guy?"

"That's Trevor."

"Trevor?"

"One of the extras."

"Doesn't he look like Dad to you?"

"A little."

Nick walked up to Trevor, who smiled awkwardly. "Hi

there." Nick reached behind the bar and pulled out the New York Mets hat. "I think you left this here."

"Thanks, I was looking for that. Do you remember me?"

"I think so."

"You were pretty out of it when I showed up that night. I thought everyone was hanging out here, but I arrived too late. I walked in and you started calling me Dad."

"I was in a bad place."

"I sensed that."

"You called me son. You listened to my problems. You gave me advice. Good advice."

"I'm a father. I have a son about your age. I told you what I thought you needed to hear."

"Thanks, Dad." Nick smiled. He and Trevor had an awkward "dad hug." Nick walked back to Ivy.

"What was that about?"

"Just catching up with an old friend."

Ivy let it go at that. "Did you see that?" She indicated Carol and Amari in a deep conversation. "I bet my sister is going to write about Amari next."

"There they are. My favorite Christmas couple." Drew's voice arrived a second before he did. He was all smiles. "Congrats, Ivy. The studio loves the new ending." Ivy was thrilled. Drew turned to Nick. "I guess we have you to thank for that. Congratulations." He shook Nick's hand. "I'm very happy for you both." Drew wandered off to make the rounds but wound up spending a lot of time with Rory, the reporter.

Denise and Kenny came over to talk with Ivy and Nick. Ivy offered Denise a drink. She refused. Ivy shrieked.

"What are you shrieking about?" Denise wondered.

"You're pregnant!"

"Nick, I told you I wanted to tell her."

"I didn't."

Ivy had figured it out on her own. She had shared many drinks with Denise in her life. If Denise wasn't drinking it could only mean one thing. A baby. She gave Denise a celebratory hug. Ivy noticed Vera across the room by the food table. She excused herself and walked over to Vera.

"Ivy!"

"Vera, I just wanted to say thank you for everything. Especially for dealing with me," she gushed.

"It was fun. Always authentic," Vera admitted.

"Good luck on *Captain Midnight*. It's kind of cool. You're going from our little movie to a blockbuster," Ivy said.

"I know why you turned it down. But for me, I figured it was a good career move," Vera explained.

"It is," she agreed. "And it helps all the other women directors out there."

"Which you're going to be one day," Vera said as she hugged Ivy.

At that moment, Olivia and Ella told everyone to settle down. They were going to announce the winner of the Team Nick/Team Drew betting pool. The winner was Vera! She had bet a trifecta: last scene, last day of shooting, and Nick.

"What can I say? I like a happy ending. Especially one where I net four grand!" Vera grinned.

Ivy found Nick. People were taking pictures of them. Selfies. Group photos.

"I feel like I'm at a wedding," she said.

"Not yet." Nick smiled and jumped up on the bar. He

clanged a metal spoon on the Governor's Cup. The dinging of the cup got everyone's attention. "Hi, thanks, there's something I need to say." Everyone got quiet. Even Ivy wondered what he was about to do. "I need someone up here with me. Ivy..." She took his hand. Nick pulled her onto the bar. "Everyone here kind of knows the story of me and Ivy." Cheers. "Without her, I never would have come up with our Poison Ivy wine."

"And without him, I wouldn't have written this movie."

"Where she killed me!" Everyone laughed.

"I'm going to have a long time living that one down."

"Yes, you are. Because I plan on spending a long time with you." Nick dropped to one knee. Grabbed the bottle of Poison Ivy. Turned it over and out fell the engagement ring. "Ivy, I should have given this to you years ago." He pulled out a slip of paper. "I'm not a writer like you, Ivy, so bear with me."

"Nick, my answer is yes."

"I didn't say anything. I wrote this all out."

"It's much better when it's visual."

"Just kiss her, Nick!" Kenny yelled.

"I never even asked her if she would marry me."

"Here's my answer, Nick. Yes, I'll marry you."

They kissed. Everyone screamed. Cheered. Cried. People hugged them. There were family pictures.

"So where are you going to live?" Denise asked.

The answer was obvious: the lake house. Ivy would spend the next year writing from the lake house. With a few trips to LA. And one trip to visit Frannie and J. B. in France.

The next Christmas—the real Christmas in December—*The Christmas Couple* had a benefit screening at the newly renovated Geneva Theater. Drew was there with Rory, who was now working with him. The Geneva Theater was packed as the celebrities returned. The movie had come out well. People loved it. And not just the locals who saw themselves up on the silver screen. The Rotten Tomatoes Tomatometer was in the high 80s and the audience score was even higher.

A few weeks later, Ivy and Nick found themselves back in LA. Nick was in a tux, which made him look even more handsome. They were attending the People's Choice Awards. Ivy won. Poison Ivy was served at the table and was as popular as the real-life Christmas couple.

After the People's Choice Awards party, Ivy had the driver take them to the Grove. The fake snow was still falling. They came back to where it all started or ended. There were posters in front of the movie theater for *The Christmas Couple*. Ivy took it all in, savoring the feeling that everything had turned out so well. Smiled. Turned back to Nick. Kissed him.

"Let's go home." They headed out, deciding to go to the airport to catch the red-eye back to New York, but then—just as it had once before—Ivy's phone started to *buzz, ring, ding* at the Grove.

"It's my agent," Ivy said. She seemed nervous.

"Take it. Don't worry, Ivy. We're fine. I'm not going to run off."

Ivy answered. She listened. Nodded. It took about twenty seconds. She hung up.

"So?" Nick asked.

"I guess the buzz on the movie is good."

"That's great."

"Really good. They want to do a sequel!"

Nick laughed. Happy for her. He pulled Ivy into his arms. Letting her know how much he loved her. As the fake snow fell and the music played and the fountains danced to a Christmas tune, the Christmas couple danced at the Grove.

ACKNOWLEDGMENTS

We've been incredibly fortunate to work closely with our dynamic duo: our agent, Haley Heidemann and our editor, Deb Werksman.

To Haley, we're forever in your debt for believing we could write and sell a novel before we ever thought it was possible. You're our rock. We're so grateful for all you do. We're also thankful for many others at WME who guided us on the way including Sabrina Taitz, Pat Polite, Tracy Fisher, Mel Berger, Alicia Everett, Rivka Bergman, and Ty Anania.

To Deb, we've loved every moment of working with you, from your smart editorial comments to the seafood tower at Port Jeff. At Sourcebooks, we've also benefited from the wisdom and experience of Susie Benton, Mandi Andrejka, Jocelyn Travis, Rachel Gilmer, and Jessica Smith.

Many thanks to Paula Hart and Melissa Joan Hart for getting us into the Christmas movie game. We've had so much fun working with you. To David Breckman, our dear friend, who introduced us to Paula because he thought we should be writing Christmas movies.

Thanks to Chris Conners, our assistant, who tirelessly proofed our early manuscript.

Thanks to Imani Gary, a favorite former student, who encouraged us to write a novel.

To our wonderful son-in-law, Eric, so happy you're part of the family. And finally to our brilliant and beautiful daughters, Sabrina and Ava, who are always patient with us and never seem to tire of our crazy ideas. Our best productions will always be the two of you.

ABOUT THE AUTHORS

Juliet Giglio and Keith Giglio are a husband–wife screenwriting duo who met cute in an elevator while attending NYU Grad Film school. Their produced films include most recently *Reba McEntire's Christmas in Tune*, *Dear Christmas*, *A Very Nutty Christmas*, and *Christmas Reservations*. Other credits include Disney's *Tarzan*, *Pizza My Heart*, *Return to Halloweentown*, *Joshua*, and *A Cinderella Story*. Juliet and Keith are both professors who teach screenwriting at SUNY Oswego and Syracuse University, respectively. They divide their time between Syracuse and Sag Harbor. This is their first novel. To learn more, visit jkgiglio.com.

MOOSE SPRINGS, ALASKA

Welcome to Moose Springs, Alaska, a small town with a big heart, and the only world-class resort where black bears hang out to look at *you*.

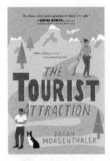

The Tourist Attraction

There's a line carved into the dirt between the tiny town of Moose Springs, Alaska, and the luxury resort up the mountain. Until tourist Zoey Caldwell came to town, Graham Barnett knew better than to cross it. But when Graham and Zoey's worlds collide, not even the neighborhood moose can hold them back...

Mistletoe and Mr. Right

She's Rick Harding's dream girl. Unfortunately, socialite Lana Montgomery has angered locals with her good intentions. When a rare (and spiteful) white moose starts destroying the holiday decorations every night, Lana, Rick, and all of Moose Springs must work together to save Christmas, the town...and each other.

Enjoy the View

Hollywood starlet River Lane is struggling to remake herself as a documentary filmmaker. When mountaineer and staunch Moose Springs local Easton Lockett takes River and her film crew into the wild...what could possibly go wrong?

"A unique voice and a grumptastic hero! I'm sold."

—Sarina Bowen, *USA Today* bestselling author

For more info about Sourcebooks's books and authors, visit:

sourcebooks.com

HAPPY SINGLES DAY

**A funny and fresh romance by author
Ann Marie Walker is something to celebrate!**

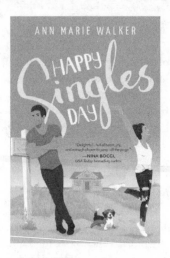

As a certified professional organizer, everything in Paige Parker's world is as it should be. Perfect apartment, perfect office, perfect life. And now, the perfect vacation planned to celebrate Singles Day at an adorable B and B.

As the owner of a now-dormant bed-and-breakfast, Lucas Croft's life is simple and quiet. It's only him and his five-year-old daughter, which is just the way he likes it. But when Paige books a room that Lucas' well-intentioned sister listed without his knowledge, their two worlds collide. If they can survive the week together, they just might discover exactly what they've both been missing.

**"A positively delightful romance full of heart, joy,
and enough charm to jump off of the page."**

—Nina Bocci, *USA Today* bestselling author

For more info about Sourcebooks's books and authors, visit:

sourcebooks.com

LUCKY LEAP DAY

A whirlwind trip to Ireland is supposed to end with a suitcase full of wool sweaters and souvenir pint glasses—not a husband you only just met!

After one too many whiskeys, fledgling screenwriter Cara Kennedy takes a page out of someone else's script when she gets caught up in the Irish tradition of women proposing on Leap Day. She wakes the next morning with a hot guy in her bed and a tin foil ring on her finger. Her flight is in four hours, and she has the most important meeting of her career in exactly two days—nothing she can do except take her new husband (and his adorable dog) back to LA with her and try to untangle the mess she's made...

"A fun and flirty read that I couldn't put down— the perfect feel-good rom-com."

—Sarah Morgenthaler for *Happy Singles Day*

For more info about Sourcebooks's books and authors, visit:

sourcebooks.com

SUMMER BY THE RIVER

**Don't miss this heartfelt romantic women's fiction by
bestselling contemporary romance author Debbie Burns!**

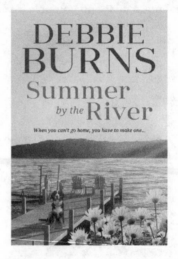

Making a fresh start in a new part of the country is challenging, but fate and good
fortune lead young single mother Josie Waterhill and her six-year-old daughter
to a cozy Midwestern town right on the river. There, Josie can raise Zoe away
from the violence of the life she once knew and make a new home in the historic
teahouse where they've been invited to stay. When a neighbor's interest in Josie
inadvertently stirs up trouble, she thinks she might never outrun it. But her new
community is more than willing to show Josie how to let go of her painful past
and create a glorious future.

**"A warm cuddly tale... This heartstring-tugger is certain to win
fans who are yearning for a wholesome summertime read."**

—*Publishers Weekly,* Starred Review, for *A New Leash on Love*

LIKE CATS AND DOGS

**All was purrfect at the Whitman Street Cat Café,
until the new neighbor moved in...**

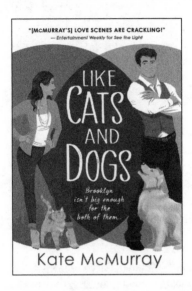

Things are getting ruff in this Brooklyn neighborhood when new veterinarian Caleb Fitch moves in next door to the Whitman Street Cat Café and gets on the wrong side of café owner Lauren Harlow. Lauren has a few things to teach the new vet on the block, and rescuing kittens is only the start...

**"Readers craving both sensual heat and snappy
humor will find this to be literary catnip."**

—Booklist

For more info about Sourcebooks's books and authors, visit:

sourcebooks.com

I HATE YOU MORE

"Romance that blends heat, humor and heart" (*Booklist*), from author Lucy Gilmore. She'll show him who's best in show...

Ruby Taylor gave up pageant life the day she turned eighteen and figured she'd never look back. But when an old friend begs her to show her beloved golden retriever at the upcoming West Coast Canine Classic, Ruby reluctantly straps on her heels and gets to work.

If only she knew exactly what the adorably lazy lump of a dog was getting her into.

"Romance that blends heat, humor, and heart."

—Booklist

"As appealing as a puppy."

—Publishers Weekly, Starred Review, for *Puppy Christmas*

For more info about Sourcebooks's books and authors, visit:

sourcebooks.com

THE UNPLANNED LIFE
OF JOSIE HALE

Hilarious, heartwarming fiction from Stephanie Eding that reminds us it's always a good idea to expect the unexpected...

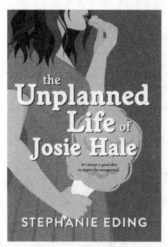

When Josie discovers that she's unexpectedly pregnant with her ex-husband's baby (darn that last attempt to save their marriage), she seeks comfort in deep-fried food at the county fair. There she runs into her two old friends, Ben and Kevin. While sharing their own disappointments with adult life, they devise a plan to move in together and turn their lives around. Soon Ben and Kevin make it their mission to prepare for Josie's baby. Maybe together they can discover the true meaning of family and second chances in life...

For more info about Sourcebooks's books and authors, visit:

sourcebooks.com

WITH NEIGHBORS LIKE THIS

**Uplifting, feel-good fiction from *USA Today*
bestselling author Tracy Goodwin**

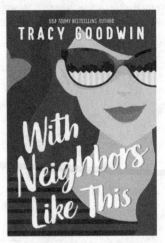

When divorced mom of two Amelia Marsh relocates to a northern suburb of Houston, all she wants is a bit of normalcy for her children. The last thing she needs is to be the center of community gossip. But that's what happens when Amelia clashes with the HOA representative over her children's garden gnome. HOA President Kyle Sanders could be a good friend—and something more—if Amelia wasn't gearing up for battle with the HOA in her determination to make her house a home and her neighborhood a community...

"Tracy Goodwin delivers every time!"

—Sophie Jordan, *New York Times* bestselling author

For more info about Sourcebooks's books and authors, visit:
sourcebooks.com